Fierce Loyalty

The Five Kingdoms Book V

by

Toby Neighbors

Fierce Loyalty

Edition 2

Published by Mythic Adventure Publishing
Post Falls, Idaho

Books by Toby Neighbors:

The Five Kingdoms

Wizard Rising
Magic Awakening
Hidden Fire
Crying Havoc
Fierce Loyalty
Evil Tide
Wizard Falling

The Lorik Trilogy

Lorik
Lorik The Protector
Lorik The Defender

The Avondale Series

Avondale
Draggah
Balestone
Arcanius

Other Books

Zompocalypse
Third Prince
Royal Destiny
The New World
The Other Side

Dedication

This book is for the people who have shown unwavering support of my dreams:

To all my Facebook fans,
I love interacting with you online, thanks for all the encouragement,

To my sisters, Lorie Mortenson & Linda Bradley,
for reading my books and always being there for me,

And most importantly, to Camille, the love of my life and my best friend,
You always knew I could do it, but I couldn't do it without you

"I saw a star fallen from heaven to the earth. To him was given the key to the bottomless pit. And he opened the bottomless pit, and smoke arose out of the pit like the smoke of a great furnace. So the sun and the air were darkened because of the smoke of the pit. Then out of the smoke locusts came upon the earth. And to them was given power... The shape of the locusts was like horses prepared for battle. On their heads were crowns of something like gold, and their faces were like the faces of men. They had hair like women's hair, and their teeth were like lions' teeth. And they had breastplates like breastplates of iron, and the sound of their wings was like the sound of chariots with many horses running into battle. They had tails like scorpions, and there were stings in their tails... And they had as king over them the angel of the bottomless pit, whose name in Hebrew is Abaddon [destruction], but in Greek he has the name Apollyon [destroyer]."

Apokalupsis

Chapter 9

Chapter 1

The sky was growing dark. Thick clouds rolled angrily up from the south, and Zollin slumped in his saddle as sheets of cold rain fell. He was tired—both physically and emotionally—from the long ride. It seemed like he couldn't remember when life had been leisurely. He thought back to when he was a boy growing up in Tranaugh Shire. He'd hated going to essentials school, hated being an apprentice with his father, and hated the daily chores that he was forced to do, but looking back he saw that life had been relatively easy.

"What's on your mind?" Mansel asked, having to raise his voice over the noise of the falling rain.

"Just thinking of home," Zollin said.

"Seems like a lifetime ago to me," Mansel said. "It's hard to believe we haven't even been gone a year."

"I know," Zollin said. "It's hard to remember a time when we weren't constantly on the move and constantly in danger."

"We're not in danger now," Mansel said. "For the first time, it's our enemies who are on the run."

"I know what you're saying is true, but it feels wrong somehow," Zollin replied. "It feels like something terrible is about to happen."

"Ah, that's just because of the weather. The days are getting shorter."

"It's not the weather," Zollin said. "Even though I don't think those clouds are normal."

"You think the Torr is behind it?"

"I can't say," Zollin said. "But something is changing, and it doesn't feel like it's a change for the better."

"I'm sorry," Mansel said, his face bowed low in shame. "I killed Kelvich. I almost killed Quinn. You have every right to feel bad."

"I miss Kelvich," Zollin said. "What happened was tragic, but I'm as much to blame as you are. He told me something was wrong, but I was too self-absorbed to see it. If I had listened, perhaps things would have turned out differently."

"Well, I'm the one who killed him."

"You were bewitched," Zollin argued.

"That may be true, but it doesn't help me sleep at night."

"I don't blame you," Zollin said. "You shouldn't blame yourself."

"Can't help it," Mansel said. "I was in love with the idea of being a great warrior, but in the end I was just a killer. This isn't the life for me, Zollin. I'm going to help you as long as you need me, but then I'm going to disappear."

"Disappear where?" Zollin asked.

"To a quiet life on the coast. I met someone," Mansel explained. "I promised her I'd come back. Even when I was under the witch's spell I could see her in my mind."

"What's her name?"

"Nycoll," Mansel said. "She has a little cottage on the coast in Falxis. Her husband was a fisherman, but he was lost at sea. When I ran into trouble on my way to Osla, she nursed me back to health. There's just something about her—I can't really describe it. All I know is that's home, not Tranaugh Shire. Not flitting about from town to town looking for adventure. When this is all over, that's where I'm going."

"You really think Quinn is happy in Felson?" Zollin asked.

"I guess," Mansel said. "He's your father, you should know better than anyone."

"There's a lot about him I don't know," Zollin admitted. "I'm glad he's found someone who makes him happy, but it seems odd to be on the road without him."

"And what about Brianna?" Mansel said. "How are you doing with that?"

"I don't know," Zollin said. "And that's the hardest part. I don't know what happened to her. I don't know if she's alive or dead. I don't know if I'll ever know, and it's like a wound that won't heal. If I knew she was dead, perhaps I could move on emotionally, but it's so hard to even think that she might be dead. When I settle things with the Torr and deal with the witch at Lodenhime, I'm going to search for her. I can't rest until I know for sure."

They rode in silence after that. The rain soaked through their clothes and made them miserable. Zollin felt especially bad for Eustice. The tongue-less servant who had been cast aside by

Offendorl, the Master of the Torr. Poor Eustice couldn't even complain about how cold and miserable he felt.

"We need to find some shelter," Zollin said to Mansel. "We'll all be sick if we stay out in this weather."

"There should be a settlement or farm close by," Mansel said. "I can't believe how cold this rain is. I mean, I know autumn is upon us, but this feels more like winter weather."

"I know," Zollin agreed. "Like I said, it's unnatural."

They rode another half hour, their mounts plodding through mud, the wind finding every gap in their sodden clothing. Finally, they came to an abandoned farmhouse. The farmhouse had no roof, but there was a small barn that still had half a roof. They led their horses into the barn, but were surprised to find that they weren't alone.

"This is our place," said a surly looking man huddled in the corner. "Go find someplace else."

"There's room for all of us," Zollin said cheerfully, even though he felt anything but cheerful. "I can start a fire and we have food."

"There's no dry wood to burn," the man said, standing up and drawing a rusty knife from behind his back. "If you want to keep breathing, I suggest you find another place."

The man had three companions. They were all soaked from being out in the rain and looked menacing. They had weapons too, although they were crude instruments. One had a club, and the other two had ancient looking knives. Zollin had a knife in his belt, but no other weapons. Mansel, on the other hand, was fully armed. He had a long sword, a dagger, a round shield, and armor—although he wasn't wearing the armor at the moment.

"We don't want trouble," Zollin said. "We won't bother you, but we're not leaving."

"It's your funeral," the surly man said.

Zollin concentrated for moment, sending his magic out silently. It heated the handle of the man's weapon. In the past, using his magic would have sent a warm, wind-like sensation blowing through Zollin. But he had constructed a magical barrier around the reservoir of power that existed inside him. Now he could sense his magic, but it did not affect him physically—at least not to the extent that it had in the past, when working magic would leave him drained as if he'd been exerting all his physical strength.

"Ahhhh!" shouted the surly man, dropping his knife. His companions looked over at their friend in surprise. "What the devil?"

"Not the devil," Zollin said. "A wizard. Now, if you'd be kind enough to put your weapons away, I promise you'll not be harmed or molested in any way. We just want a dry spot to ride out the storm."

Then Zollin let his power kindle a fire in front of the men. It was nothing more than a dancing flame on the ground, which was hard-packed dirt. There was no wood, not even old straw, but the flame was bright and hot.

"Well?" Zollin said impatiently. "We're waiting."

"Put 'em away, lads," said the surly man.

"Thank you," Zollin said as he swung down from his horse. "My name is Zollin. This is Mansel and Eustice."

Eustice took the horses to what used to be a stall. He unsaddled the mounts and cleaned their hooves. Mansel used his sword to break up some of the wood from the far end of the barn and made two piles—one for the group of men already occupying the old barn, and one for himself and his friends.

Zollin gave the other men some of their food. It was mostly dry rations, but there was some fruit, bread, and cheese in their saddlebags too. Then he used his magic to pull the water out of the rotting wood. He could have set it ablaze wet, but he didn't want to fill their small shelter with smoke. Once the wood was dry it kindled quickly and crackled merrily. The men all stripped down and hung their clothes by the fire to dry. Zollin and Mansel had dry clothes in their saddlebags, but Eustice and the other men were forced to huddle near the flames until their clothes were dry.

They drank water and ate, mostly in silence. The rain pounded on the ancient wooden shingles, but while there were a few leaks, the old roof kept them dry through the night. Zollin tried to sleep, but his mind was filled with the horrors of what he'd seen—men slain on the battlefield, the horrifying black dragon spewing flames, and worst of all, carrying Brianna away.

The next day was dim, with thick clouds filling the sky and threatening more rain, but Zollin and his companions pressed on. They rode through short-lived showers, pushing their horses to carry them as far and as fast as the animals could. Everywhere around them they saw signs of the invading army. Farms were burned, villages abandoned, and crops trampled. The path was churned to mud by hundreds of feet, trudging south. The armies from Osla and Falxis had been defeated at Orrock, and now they traveled home. King Felix had accepted their surrender and allowed them to return to their kingdoms. Only Zollin, Mansel, and Eustice followed them.

"How far ahead is the old wizard?" Mansel asked when the rain finally let up a little.

"Too far to catch him on the road," Zollin said. "I don't expect to find him until we reach the tower of the Torr in the Grand City."

"And when we get there, what do you plan to do?"

"I'm not sure," Zollin said. "But he can't be allowed to lead armies to invade Yelsia. And I don't want him hunting me down anymore either."

"So you'll offer him terms of surrender?"

"I suppose," Zollin said.

"And if he refuses?"

"I'll let you kill him," Zollin said.

"No thank you," Mansel replied. "I've seen what you wizards can do. I'll guard your back though."

Eustice waved his hands to get their attention. He'd become rather skilled in communicating by gesture. He pointed ahead at the trail where a group of four men were sitting under a tree. They all had armor and weapons, which was a dead giveaway that they were soldiers. What wasn't plainly obvious was why they weren't marching ahead with the armies from Falxis or Osla.

"What are they doing?" Mansel asked quietly.

"I don't know," Zollin said. "Eustice, fall back behind us."

"You think it's a trap?" Mansel asked.

"Possibly. I'd rather err on the side of caution at this point. I can handle these four—you keep an eye out in case there's more of them."

They rode forward, staying on the trail and not slowing as they approached the soldiers.

The men had gotten to their feet, and when they realized that Zollin didn't plan to stop they spread out across the narrow road.

"Hold there," said one of the soldiers, a big man with a long sword. "We need to commandeer those horses."

"I don't think so," said Zollin.

"Under the king's law, we have the right to commandeer your mounts," the big soldier continued. "We'll leave them at the coast."

"I understand," Zollin said with a smirk. His grief over Brianna left him with a short temper, and the truth was, he was spoiling for a fight. "Unfortunately, your king is running back to the coast with his tail between his legs."

The soldier's eyes narrowed.

"You think because some crackpot wizard got lucky enough to scare the king into surrender that it will somehow save you from our blades?" the soldier threatened. "Get off the horses now, and we'll spare your lives."

"Crackpot wizard, eh?" Zollin said with a smirk. "And what would you say if I told you I was that wizard?"

"Get off your horses now!" shouted the soldier. "I've had enough of your lip, boy. One more word from you and I'll cut your tongue out and feed it to you."

"Oh, really," Zollin said, smiling. "That I would truly like to see."

"Now!" ordered the soldier.

The four men moved forward instantly. They had almost drawn their weapons when they ran headlong into the invisible wall that Zollin had magically erected in front of them. The impact knocked them back, but Zollin wasn't finished.

"You were warned," he said quietly.

Then he raised a hand and sent crackling, blue energy at the big soldier who had threatened him. His magic was churning like a blacksmith's billows, but Zollin managed to keep his anger from killing the soldier. Holding back the power of his spell was difficult, but he knew it was imperative that he control the magic or the magic would take control of him. The energy hit the soldier squarely in the chest, as if Zollin had tossed a lightning bolt. The power knocked the soldier backward, sending him flying through the air to land in a crumpled heap, his armor blackened from the attack.

"Now," Zollin said, leaning forward and crossing his arms on the saddle horn as he looked at the other soldiers, who suddenly seemed very frightened. "You're not wanted here. You have no authority in Yelsia. And if you do anything other than make for the coast as fast as you can, I'll see to it that you're all hanged."

Just then a shout sounded from behind them. Zollin turned in his saddle and saw three more soldiers rushing forward, but Mansel was already in motion. He kicked his horse into a tight spin and charged at the rushing men. The soldiers spread in opposite directions to avoid Mansel, two men turning to the left and one to the right. He focused on the two men who were now on the left side of the road, guiding his horse toward the nearest of the two. Mansel's sword wasn't a true cavalry sword. Most warriors fighting from horseback either used a curved saber or a long sword, but Mansel's weapon was more of a bastard sword, longer than a short sword but shorter than a broadsword. It could easily be wielded with one hand, and Mansel had no trouble knocking the soldier's own weapon aside and landing a glancing blow on the soldier's skullcap. A longer sword might have reached the soldier's neck, but Mansel's strike knocked the man unconscious.

Zollin immediately let his magic flow out around him. It felt like he was unblocking a dam as the magic rushed out. It was hot and powerful as it charged through his self-constructed containment field. He could feel the soldiers around him as they struggled to regroup. The two men attacking from the rear were still rushing toward Zollin and Eustice, while the three soldiers in front of them scrambled back to their feet.

Zollin lifted the two men behind him into the air with a simple levitation spell, and send them flying toward two of their comrades who were in front of him. It was growing harder and harder not to simply kill them. Zollin couldn't remember feeling the urge to destroy so strongly since he'd learned to insulate his magic, but now his anger and grief were flooding into his power, churning it like river rapids and pulling him toward a place of darkness he knew he didn't want to go.

He clamped down on the magic, forcing his mind to concentrate on his own hands, which were balled into fists and crackling with so much magical energy that his reins had crumbled into ashes where he'd been holding them.

Fortunately, the soldiers were now scrambling away, pulling their comrades off the road as quickly as possible. As soon as Zollin regained control of himself he leaned down and snatched the shortened reins, then urged his horse into a gallop. His magic was still churning, but the wind whipping through his hair and the need maintain his mount using the muscles in his legs, stomach, and back helped to soothe his emotions. He could hear Eustice right behind him. Although the mute servant was no horseman, his mount followed Zollin's and Eustice managed to hang on to the saddle horn.

Mansel was further back, riding easily while ensuring that no one else came at them from the rear. Once the horses had run for a while, Zollin reined his mount in and climbed out of the saddle. He stretched his tired muscles as he waited for Mansel to catch up.

"I want to walk for a while," he said.

Zollin didn't wait for a reply, but turned and led his horse down the muddy path. Thunder rumbled across the sky and soon rain was falling in fat drops that pelted Zollin and his companions. Mansel and Eustice gave Zollin space, leading their own horses through the mud several paces behind.

Zollin didn't like the fact that he had almost lost control, but he knew that he had every reason to struggle. He felt more alone than ever before in his life. Brianna was gone and it wasn't likely that he would ever find out what happened to her. She had changed before his very eyes, from a young woman to a powerful, magical being that he didn't fully understand. She had been given a gemstone by dwarves that had somehow unlocked a part of Brianna no one knew existed. She looked the same, but her ability to control fire was dumbfounding, even to Zollin. And then, when the dragon was finally at their mercy, she had healed the beast. There was nothing Zollin could do to stop her, and when the dragon was well enough, it had taken her and fled.

Zollin had given chase, but as had happened so often in the last year, events around him drew him away from his purpose. The armies from Osla and Falxis, led by the master of the Torr, had invaded Yelsia. As much as he had wanted to track down the dragon and find Brianna, he couldn't turn his back on an invasion. And then, the dragon had appeared—alone—spewing fire onto the walls of Orrock. Zollin had managed to drive the beast away, but his hopes of finding Brianna were shattered. He couldn't imagine that she had survived, even though he wanted desperately to believe that she had. Still, it was obvious that Brianna had a connection to the dragon, and he had hoped that she might somehow manage to survive. But seeing the dragon doing

Offendorl's bidding in the war crushed that hope. If the dragon was now serving the master of the Torr, Zollin was almost certain that his love was dead.

Added to his grief for Brianna was the fact that Kelvich was gone too. Mansel had killed Zollin's mentor while under the spell of the witch in Lodenhime. It was almost too much to think about—his mind kept rejecting the facts. He hadn't seen Kelvich's body, and while Mansel had confessed to the murder, it still didn't seem possible. Zollin didn't blame Mansel for the crime, but he had to admit that he saw the young warrior differently. So much had changed about Mansel—he was quieter, less volatile somehow —but Zollin missed the days when they had laughed and talked together, when the future seemed bright and hopeful despite the fact that they were being chased by wizards and armies.

Their friendship had not been easy at the start. Mansel had been his father's second apprentice, and the young warrior's obvious talent with his hands made Zollin's ineptitude at his father's trade all the more obvious. Zollin had spent years jealously despising Mansel, but when they had been forced to flee their small village, Mansel had refused to be left behind. He had proven himself a faithful friend and talented fighter, but that didn't mean that Mansel didn't have his own problems. His drinking had landed him in trouble more than once, and his friendship with Brianna had sparked new fires of jealously in Zollin's heart. Now, his friend and fellow adventurer seemed just as dark and moody as Zollin, and although he was glad that Mansel didn't try to cheer him up, there were times when he longed for happier times.

They walked until dark and by chance came upon a small village with an inn. They took rooms and enjoyed a hot meal. They were soaked and cold, so the innkeeper prepared mulled wine. Eustice had trouble being served, so Zollin allowed him to see to their clothes and turned in early for the night.

Mansel drank by the fire long after Zollin had gone to bed. His dreams were often haunted by images of things he'd done under the spell of Gwendolyn, the witch. His guilt for those murderous actions plagued him, and not even strong wine could dull the pain. He longed to be back in the small cottage by the sea. He felt that if anyone could ease his pain, it would be Nycoll, the widow who had nursed him back to health. She was a quiet woman, one who had dealt with her own share of pain and loss. Mansel knew he couldn't turn his back on Zollin, not when he had so much to make up for, but his heart was with Nycoll, far away. He knew that he would not be happy until he was with her again.

The next morning dawned brighter than the days before. The sky was still cloudy, but the sun was making a valiant effort to break through. Zollin found his clothes dried and laid out for him when he woke up. He dressed and went downstairs, where Eustice was waiting. The mute servant had already eaten and, after seeing that Zollin was being cared for, went to ready their horses.

Mansel came into the common room halfway through Zollin's breakfast. "You hungry?" Zollin asked.

"No," Mansel said darkly. His eyes were bloodshot and skin seemed pale.

"You sick?" Zollin asked.

Mansel nodded but didn't elaborate. He refused breakfast, but drank a little ale and took a sack of provisions from the innkeeper's wife. They set out soon after and rode hard all through the day, even opting to walk their horses late into the night.

Though they traveled at a brutal pace, it took them a week to reach the coastal town of Lorye. They had no more trouble on the road, but they were exhausted just the same. It was evening when they arrived, and Eustice saw to their horses while Mansel and Zollin booked passage on a ship traveling south.

They bought supplies in the market and then settled onto the ship for the night. It was a big vessel, with three masts and more sailors than the population of many of the small towns they had passed through. They had to settle for one cabin for the three of them. The cabin had two bunks and one hammock, along with a small table and three stools. Even in port, the ship, which lay at anchor a short boat ride from the shore, rocked and swayed so that Mansel was soon seasick. Zollin used his magic to isolate the cause of his own queasiness and was surprised to find that there was fluid in tiny canals deep inside his ears that seemed to be causing his distress. He used magic to calm the movement of fluid and immediately felt better.

He was about to help Mansel, who was already much more ill than either Zollin or Eustice, but he hesitated. For a brief moment the thought of letting Mansel suffer seemed appropriate. His friend had murdered Kelvich, after all, and had tried to kill Zollin's father. In fact, Mansel would have succeeded if Zollin hadn't found his father and been able to heal him using magic.

Then Zollin shook the hesitation away. He hadn't fully forgiven Mansel, but he also understood that Mansel wasn't himself when he had committed the heinous crimes, and keeping his friend sick wouldn't make their journey any more enjoyable.

He let his magic flow into Mansel without saying anything. The motion of the fluid in Mansel's inner ear was almost violent. Zollin concentrated on settling the fluid down. It took several minutes, but in time Mansel appeared to feel better. He went immediately to his bunk and went to sleep.

"It doesn't seem that sea travel suits our friend," Zollin said to Eustice, who was swaying in the hammock.

Eustice nodded. The former servant of the Torr was almost like a child in his energy and enthusiasm to help Zollin. He had a perpetual smile on his face and was always quick to help. He accepted the hammock immediately, even though Zollin had proposed that they take turns sleeping on the swaying canvass.

"Are you feeling ill?" Zollin asked.

Eustice waved his hand as if to say, "Not really."

"You're stronger than I am then," Zollin said. "I was afraid I was going to lose my lunch before long."

Eustice smiled and pointed at their rations, which were stored in a sea chest. He made the gesture that Zollin had come to recognize to mean cooking.

"No, I don't think I want much tonight. Just some bread and olive oil. Maybe a little wine to help me sleep."

Eustice nodded and Zollin stepped out of the cabin and took a walk around the deck. The ship was loaded with cargo, and most of the sailors were spending their last few hours on shore. There were only a few men on watch. One officer stood near the big, round wheel that was used to steer the ship. A few moved around in the ropes that stretched from the ship rails to the towering masts. Zollin could see the sails neatly bundled and tied to the crossbeams of the masts. He leaned against the ship rail and looked into the water. The sun had set and the water was dark below him. Lights from the city reflected on the surface, but Zollin occasionally saw the darkness that indicated deep water.

He let his magic flow into the water. He had learned through the winter in Kelvich's small cabin how to let his magic touch the world around him. He would go out at night to hunt, standing still in almost complete darkness and learning to see with his magic, which was often much more sensitive than his eyes alone.

The magic plunged beneath the surface of the water and began to drift down. At first, Zollin was just curious how deep the water was, but he was soon fascinated with the amount of life he found in the watery depths. There were sedate creatures fixed to the hull of the ship. Schools of fish swam together with speed and agility that would have made flocks of birds envious. The sandy seafloor was not too far below the surface—Zollin guessed a tall tree's leafy peak would rise above the waves. There were larger creatures too, some moving slowly, innocently, while others were obviously hunting.

Zollin didn't disturb the sea life. He stood, silent and still, leaning against the ship's railing, completely absorbed by the world under the waves. Then, suddenly, the fish swam away, leaving the waters around the ship empty except for the waving flora and the tiny sea creatures that merely floated through the water, too small to be seen. Zollin was puzzling over the strange turn of events when an old and evil presence came over the young wizard. He felt the cold relish of death, almost as if he could smell the sickly sweet odor of rotting flesh. Zollin suddenly felt very cold, and fear began to run a jagged claw down his spine. Goosebumps rose on his arms and the hair on the back of his neck stood out.

Then Zollin felt the monster enter his magic. It was a large creature, swimming with powerful but precise movements. Its body was long and thick, as long as the massive ship Zollin was standing on. From the long, tube-like body came over a dozen tentacles. To Zollin they seemed like giant snakes, each moving independently. On the massive body were two large, black eyes, and in the middle of the sprouting tentacles a large maw with thick pincers instead of teeth.

"Captain!" Zollin shouted, running along the dark deck. "Captain!"

"What is it?" said the officer on watch. "The captain is in his cabin and doesn't wish to be disturbed."

"Some kind of sea creature," Zollin said. "It's huge. It's swimming toward the ship right now."

"I believe you've heard one too many stories, sir," said the officer. "There's no creature in the ocean that would bother this ship."

Just then there was blow to the side of the ship that echoed through the hull and reverberated up onto the deck.

"What was that?" Zollin asked.

The officer didn't respond. He stood silent, almost frozen with fear, unsure what to make of the sound. Suddenly a huge tentacle shot up out of the water. It was too dark to make out the writhing appendage, but seawater cascaded off of it, splashing back down into the ocean. Zollin watched as the sailor's eyes opened wide in terror, and then the tentacle smashed down onto the deck with a crash. The ship rail splintered and the other sailors began to shout in fear. The entire ship rocked under the blow before six more tentacles rose up out of the water.

Chapter 2

"Mansel!" Zollin shouted, throwing up a quick magical shield above him and the ship's officer.

The tentacles fell hard on the ship, like massive trees falling in the forest. The wooden railing on the seaward side of the ship was destroyed and the smaller mast near the front of the ship was snapped in two. Several of the crossbeams were also broken so that the deck of the ship became a jumble of splintered wood, ripped canvas sails, and rope. Several of the sailors on watch had been injured, but even though one of the tentacles had fallen on them, Zollin and the officer were unharmed.

Zollin felt his magic shooting through him as he struggled to hold up the massive limb. It rolled clumsily and Zollin guessed that its massive weight out of the water made it difficult to control. He pushed the frightened officer back toward the raised platform where the captain's cabin was located.

"Move!" Zollin screamed. "Get away from that thing."

The door to the captain's cabin burst open and a short man with a long, thick beard and an equally thick belly came storming out.

"What in the name of Neptune is going on out ..." His voice trailed off as he saw the tentacles that had smashed into the ship rise back up in the air.

"Take cover!" Zollin shouted, pushing the captain and his officer back into the cabin just as the tentacle dropped again, this time splintering the deck.

He turned and unleashed a gout of molten energy that struck the tentacle in a sizzling, steaming spray. The tentacle swung away from Zollin and wrapped around the ship's mast. Zollin didn't wait for instructions. He ran forward and began blasting the tentacles with bolts of white-hot magical energy. His power was roaring like a fire inside him, but his mind was reeling. The sea creature was even larger than the black dragon he'd fought, and although most of its body was in the water, the monster's tentacles were like separate enemies, each one a grave menace.

There was a loud crack, like the pop of a lightning strike, as the mast broke. Zollin was attacking the beast, but even more tentacles were rising up out of the water.

"What the hell is that?" Mansel shouted as he ran up beside Zollin.

"Sea monster," Zollin said matter-of-factly.

"What should I do?" the young warrior asked.

"Beats me," Zollin shouted. "I think our best bet is to get out of here."

"You mean swim for it?" Mansel asked in an incredulous voice.

"No way," Zollin said. "Get Eustice and I'll try to levitate you back to shore."

"That's a long way, Zollin."

"I know it, but would you rather stay here?"

Mansel only hesitated for a second, then ran toward their small cabin. He came back pulling Eustice along. The mute servant was so scared he was shaking. Zollin didn't wait—his magic felt like an inferno and he didn't want to exhaust himself before he got his friends to safety. He raised a hand and sent them flying back over the water. It took all his concentration to avoid the tentacles and keep his friends in the air, but finally they were over the docks and he lowered them slowly to the ground. Then the exertion hit him all at once. His legs felt weak and his stomach queasy. He was reminded of how he'd felt as a boy trying to hold a heavy piece of wood for his father, sometimes for several minutes. When he'd finally been able to let go, his body had ached at the effort and his muscles felt stiff and clumsy. He staggered back to the landward side rail and sagged against it.

Then a new tentacle smashed into the far side of the ship, rocking the entire vessel, and before he knew what was happening, it tossed Zollin overboard. He hit the water with barely any air in his lungs. He instinctively clawed his way to the surface and gasped for air. The water was cold and his body felt weak, but more than anything he felt completely exposed in the water, and on the verge of panic. His magic was raging, fed by his emotions into a furnace of heat and power. He was just about to levitate himself out of the water when he felt something wrap around his ankle. He had time for one quick breath, then was jerked down into the black depths.

His mind was in full panic now, but his magic was flowing. Even though his eyes were closed and there wasn't enough light for him to see if they had been open, he was completely aware of his surroundings. He sensed the sea monster eating one of the unlucky sailors who had been knocked into the water before Zollin. He could also sense the creature's beastly delight. The monster was feeding not just on the sailor—which it had devoured in its huge, beak-like maw—but on the chaos all around its huge tubular body. There were smaller tentacles in the water, which moved faster and with more agility. One of these wrapped around Zollin's waist and began pulling him toward the creature's mouth.

Zollin didn't give his actions much thought—he simply let his magic go. With a snap that was heard even out of the water, Zollin broke one of the creature's thick mandibles. The monster writhed in pain, its tentacles lashing the water, but it didn't know where the attack was coming from.

Zollin's lungs began to burn and he turned his attention to the tentacles holding him. He let his magic flow through his body and into the beast's tentacle, causing the powerful, snake-like appendage to heat up instantly. Zollin burned the sea monster's tentacles until they let go of him. He began to swim toward the surface and the air he needed so badly, but the sea monster was aware of him now and three more tentacles swung like giant clubs through the water toward him. Zollin threw up a hasty shield between him and the tentacles, but the force of the blow sent him plowing through the water and almost pushed all the air from his lungs.

His body was aching for oxygen and he used his magic to propel himself up out of the water, like a fish jumping. He gasped for air, but then was sent crashing back into the water when a tentacle dropped down on him. He shielded himself from harm, but it took a long moment to get around the massive appendage and back to the surface.

The ship was beginning to break apart nearby, the wood snapping and popping under the weight of the tentacles. Zollin heard the desperate cries of the sailors, but there was nothing he could do to help them. He was dizzy and weak, struggling just to keep his own head above the water. He felt more tentacles moving toward him, and this time he took a massive breath before allowing himself to be pulled under the water. He tried his best to stay calm, even though the tentacles were squeezing him so tight that he could barely hold his breath, and the pressure of the water as he was pulled deeper made him feel like he was going to be crushed to death.

He pushed back against the water pressure with his magic, and as he drew near to the monster's beak-like mouth he cast off the tentacles holding him. Then he let his magic flow into the beast, ripping and tearing at the soft flesh inside the creature. He drew his legs up and wrapped his arms around them, conserving his body's energy as his magic did the work.

The sea monster whipped and twisted in the water. It flailed its tentacles, but Zollin was a small target. He surrounded himself with a bubble shield that both held back the crushing weight of the water and kept him from being hurt by the thrashing tentacles. He was hit several times, but the beast only succeeded in pushing him through the water. Zollin stayed focused on the magic that was now inside the creature. It was the same technique he'd used so many times to heal—only now he used it to wound. He burned organs, tore blood vessels, and shredded tissue. It was surprisingly easy, and although he knew in that moment it was necessary, it also scared him. The ability to kill was so easy, he thought. He wasn't finished hurting the creature before he needed more air. He turned his attention toward rising to the surface and felt the sea monster flee. It moved quickly and gracefully through the water, excreting a dark fluid in its wake. Zollin didn't bother to investigate. He lifted himself out of the water and began levitating to shore.

His head was spinning and his body shivering when he lowered himself onto the quay. Every part of his body ached and he could hear people shouting all around him. Then rough hands were grabbing and lifting him.

"Get your hands off of him," Mansel shouted. "Let him go or I'll gut you like a fish and feed you to that monster."

"He's a sorcerer," someone shouted with a thick accent.

"He called up the kraken," another voice said.

"Burn him; it's the only way to kill a sorcerer."

Zollin knew he should be doing something, but he was so tired he could barely keep his eyes open. He'd had to let his magical containment field down, and his magic had tasked his physical strength to its limits.

"Zollin," Mansel yelled again, his voice closer.

"Here," Zollin said.

"Don't let him talk," some shouted. "He'll curse us all."

"Get your filthy hands off!" Mansel shouted as he and Eustice finally made their way through the crowd.

"You can't have him," some in the crowd screamed.

"We found him and we'll deal with him ourselves," someone else cried.

Zollin heard the zing of Mansel drawing his sword. People began to scream and run, but the rough hands that were holding Zollin—one on his shoulder, the other wrapped around his throat—tightened.

"Who do you think you are?" said a voice near Zollin's ear. "This man's a sorcerer and we'll do what we want with him."

"Over my dead body," Mansel said in a low, menacing voice.

"If that's the way you want it," the voice said. "Get him lads."

Two men darted toward Mansel, but a low, arcing swipe of his blade caused them to leap back just as quickly. Then Mansel kicked out to his side, hitting one of the men on the edge of the group in the chest. The blow sounded like a sharp strike on a large drum. Then the man went flying into the water.

"Hey!" another shouted, but Mansel was in constant motion now, driving the men back with his blade and striking like a viper with fists and feet.

The sword tip ripped through one man's shoulder and Mansel kicked a third man in the crotch so hard it lifted him off his feet.

"I swear I'll kill you all if you don't let him go," Mansel screamed.

"Let 'em go, Dorn, afore som'un gets hurt," said one of the sailors with a thick accent. Zollin felt the man's hands loosen somewhat, and the young wizard opened his eyes.

"I need a drink," he said.

Mansel laughed. "I'll bet you do," he said. "Something besides seawater, from the looks of you."

"Can we go now?" Zollin asked.

Mansel took Zollin by the arm and led him away from the group of sailors, who stood cursing him under their breath. Eustice hurried over and took hold of Zollin's other arm. They half carried him away from the harbor.

"I don't think we're going to get another ship here," Mansel said as they hurried along.

There were people shouting and running all around them. Cries about the sea monster echoed all around them. People were weeping and cursing. Sailors had run from the taverns and brothels to see what had happened. The ship Zollin had booked passage on was destroyed.

Mansel led them from the harbor and deeper into town. He was looking for the kind of inn that didn't cater to sailors, and when he found one he went straight in.

"Try not to seem too hurt, Zollin," he whispered. "I don't want any more crazed mobs calling for your blood."

"Me either," Zollin said, swaying lightly on his feet.

They went inside the inn and Zollin stayed by the door with Eustice while Mansel talked to the innkeeper. They were escorted up a flight a stairs and shown into a small room.

"Why's he all wet?" the innkeeper asked.

"He got mobbed by some sailors and knocked off the quay. That's why he's so shaky," Mansel lied. "I need to get him warmed up and dry."

"Well, I can dry his clothes near the fire," the man said, not quite sure he believed Mansel.

"That would be grand. And if you can send up some wine, we'll be paying with gold."

"And food," Zollin said, trying not to slur his words. "Something hot."

"I feed all my guests," the innkeeper said.

"Great. Give us a few moments and we'll have him out of these wet clothes for you then," Mansel said.

"I'd like to see the gold," the innkeeper said.

"Here, take it," Mansel said, holding out a golden coin with a crown embossed on it. "And get us that wine. And don't skimp, either—we want several bottles of your best."

The innkeeper put the coin between his teeth and bit down to test how soft the gold was. Then he looked up, pleased.

"I'll get it right up here," he said happily. "And the best food in Lorye too."

"Excellent," Mansel said.

He closed the door behind the innkeeper and turned back to Eustice.

"Let's get him out of these clothes," he said.

They stripped the cold, wet clothes off of Zollin and then wrapped him in a blanket and sat him on the bed. A serving girl knocked timidly on the door. When Mansel opened it, she handed him three goblets and a bottle of wine.

"Master Orrin said there was wet clothes," she said.

Eustice handed them to her, along with Zollin's boots.

"Get those dried quickly and there's a silver mark in it for you," Mansel said.

"Yes, my lord," she said. "Right away."

She hurried out, and Eustice handed Zollin a goblet of wine. He drank it greedily, letting the wine warm his insides and spread a feeling of strength through his arms and legs. After a few moments, Zollin had drunk three goblets of wine and the innkeeper returned with their supper. It was a thick stew with hearty loaves of golden-crusted bread. Zollin ate two bowls then fell asleep.

"Did you sell the horses?" Mansel asked Eustice.

The mute servant shook his head.

"Good. I want to ride out of here before dawn. Do you think you can fetch them without drawing too much attention?"

Eustice nodded enthusiastically and hurried out.

"He's a useful one to have around," Mansel said to Zollin, even though the young wizard was asleep. "I'll keep watch, why don't I," he said as he paced back and forth through the room. "So far this little adventure seems right on course—according to our luck, anyway."

Chapter 3

It had taken all Offendorl's strength to fight back the seasickness. He was alone on a trade ship sailing south. He had booked passage on a ship sailing to Brimington Bay that included sharing the shipboard rations. Unfortunately, the sailors seemed to exist on bland gruel and stale biscuits that were more often than not crawling with weevils.

He had been carried from Orrock to the southern coast of Yelsia by Bartoom, but the dragon was not gentle. The trip and Offendorl's wounds almost had been enough to stop his ancient heart, but a fortune find of Zipple Weed had given him the boost in stamina he needed to rejuvenate his body. He would live, but the magic and battle with Zollin had weakened the master of the Torr. Normally his servants would have nursed him back to health, but he had abandoned the last of his tongue-less eunuchs after the battle when he had called Bartoom to carry him away. The dragon was a vile creature, in Offendorl's estimation, but it had served a purpose. The trip to the coast, which would have taken over a week on horseback, was traversed in just one day by the dragon, but the beast was neither gentle nor caring. It did as it was bid because Offendorl had learned its name and inscribed it on a golden crown, giving him full control of the dragon.

He could have been back in his tower high above the Grand City by now if only he could have suffered the dragon's harsh treatment, but he had sent the beast away to the Walheta Mountains between Yelsia and Falxis, preferring to travel home by sea. But that had not been a great solution either. The ship was dank and smelly. Offendorl's cabin was little more than a closet with a bunk and had no access to fresh air. For over a week the elder wizard lay in a state of semi-consciousness, too sick to move and too weak to work the magic he needed to regain his strength.

A normal person's body would heal naturally, but Offendorl was over 400 years old. His body was kept alive through magic, and even though Offendorl was an incredibly powerful wizard, it had been over a century since he had participated in a magical battle. He had over-extended his resources and now he was caught with barely enough strength to stay alive and no one to help nurse him back to health. The only good news had been the strong winds that were pushing the small trading vessel south. They had made excellent time over the last week, completing over half of their journey.

The captain of the ship had prepared a canvas seat for Offendorl on the deck, and he was determined to make his way to that chair. He had only brought a bottle of wine and the golden crown—which he carried in a burlap sack—to his cabin. The wine was long gone, wasted because his stomach refused to keep it down. The crown was hidden beneath his bunk in the tiny cabin, but he doubted that anyone suspected the ancient wizard of possessing treasure. He left it behind and staggered out of his room. He needed spirits and food to regain his strength and he was determined to get more than the sorry fare the sailors had been giving him.

His first challenge was to climb the stairs that led from his cabin onto the deck of the ship. There was no handrail to lean against, and Offendorl was forced to crawl up the steps. He was queasy and out of breath by the time he reached the top, but he forced himself to keep moving. He didn't want to appear weak.

The sunshine felt glorious and the fresh sea air invigorated him a little. It was enough to keep the elder wizard moving. He saw the canvas chair under an awning not far from the helm of the ship. The captain was standing near the ship's wheel, his long, blue sea coat immaculate. Offendorl tried to steady his gait but the ship was plunging through the gentle swells like a galloping horse.

"Ah, you are getting your sea legs, I think," said the captain.

"Yes," Offendorl croaked, falling into the canvas chair. His voice sounded terrible, the result of a combination of vomiting for several days and lack of use.

"I was afraid you would miss our glorious journey, my friend," said the captain, approaching from his position by the helm. "We have been blessed with good winds, yes?"

Offendorl nodded. "I need better food and spirits. I cannot continue on the gruel and tepid water your men bring me."

"I was under the impression that you were seasick," the captain explained. "Rich food would be wasted on you, no?"

"No, I need food and drink to regain my strength."

"Well, I will have food prepared, my friend." Then, turning to one of the sailors, he said, "Hines, bring our guest a ration of grog."

"Aye Captain," the sailor said, hurrying away.

"What is grog?" Offendorl croaked.

"It is the fiery spirit of the sea, my friend," the captain explained. "Maybe not as refined as what you are used to, but it is strong enough to cure or kill, if you take my meaning."

"Fine, it will do," Offendorl said, not relishing the idea of grog, but satisfied that he had made an improvement in his health and care on board the ship.

"I am wondering who it is you are running from," the captain asked. "A man of your age and wealth should be surrounded by luxury, yes?"

"I'm not running," Offendorl said. "I'm returning home."

"As you say, my friend, but not many men who book their passage with gold carry no change of clothes, or goods of any kind. It is strange, no? You are obviously a man of importance. It is, as you say, curious."

"Curiosity is dangerous," Offendorl said. "Better to keep your mind occupied with matters of the sea."

"I see," the captain said, frowning. "Ah, here is your grog. It is best to drink it slowly. I would hate to see you fall ill again, my friend."

There was nothing friendly in the captain's look as he peered down in disgust at Offendorl. The elder wizard could read the young sea captain's mind. He knew that he was an easy target.

He had paid for passage on the ship with gold. The captain intended to find out if there was more, then throw the old man overboard. Offendorl had expected as much. In fact, he was surprised that the wily sailor hadn't robbed him sooner, but now that he was out of his cabin, Offendorl expected that the tiny space had been thoroughly searched. The captain would know about the golden crown. It wouldn't hurt Offendorl to lose it—he could easily make another once his strength had returned—but the sailors would almost certainly try to kill him while they were at sea. He knew he had to be on his guard and that meant he needed as much strength as possible.

The cup he held was a simple tin cup, almost full of a clear liquid. Offendorl knew that most sailing ships carried strong spirits on board, both for health reasons and because they simply couldn't stock enough ale or wine to satisfy their sailors. Grog, as the captain had called it, was probably a mixture of spirits from different ports, all mingled together in shipboard oak barrels. He took a sip and had to fight the urge to spit the liquor out. It was very strong, almost so astringent he couldn't swallow, but he forced himself to drink it. The grog burned its way down his throat and into his completely empty stomach.

Offendorl was used to drinking wine throughout the day, so alcohol in general didn't affect his faculties greatly, but he was certain there was enough grog in his cup to get him very drunk. He guessed that was what the captain expected. Fortunately for the elder wizard, the grog strengthened his magical prowess almost immediately. He felt the burn in his stomach spread through his body like lapping waves of a warm ocean. He took another sip and grimaced, but swallowed the spirit down.

"And food?" he asked.

"Oh, yes, your supper is coming, my friend," the captain said.

Offendorl had drunk half his cup of grog when the food arrived. The elder wizard was glad for the food, having decided that he had reached his limit of the strong liquor. He felt stronger, but also warm and relaxed. The motion of the ship, which had been an aggravation up until then, seemed completely natural. The food was roasted fowl with stewed vegetables and more of the ship's stale biscuits.

After eating, Offendorl felt considerably better. The sun was setting low and the first stars were twinkling overhead. The captain had kept a sharp watch on the elder wizard all through the meal. Offendorl knew he would be expected to finish the grog and in an inebriated state give the sailors no fight when they came to toss him overboard.

He lifted a hand in the air and discretely tossed the grog overboard while sending to the captain a magical impression of himself drinking the liquor down quickly. For the first time since Offendorl sat in the canvas chair, which was a simple piece of furniture made with a wooden frame, the captain smiled.

Offendorl closed his eyes let his magic flow through him. The hot wind of magic was as familiar to the wizard as his own hands. He could feel the captain and the sailors nearby, although he was extremely careful not to let his magical senses touch the water below them. He couldn't read the minds of the men on board, but he could sense the malice in their hearts. It wouldn't be long before they sprang into action, and Offendorl guessed he had just enough strength to fend off their attack. The master of the Torr despised weakness, but there was nothing more he could do. His body needed time to adjust and regain his former strength.

He opened his eyes and slowly rose from the canvas chair.

"I think I'll call it a night, Captain," he said.

"I hope you rest well, my friend," said the sailor.

Offendorl kept his magical senses tuned to the men around him, and so he felt the two brutish sailors approaching from behind. He whirled around, moving much faster than anyone on board the ship could have guessed his ancient form could move. Both men had clubs, and with a wave of his hand Offendorl levitated the blunt weapons out of their hands, jerking the clubs high in the air. The sailors looked shocked, almost paralyzed with surprise at what had just occurred.

"Take him," shouted the captain. "Throw him overboard!"

The two sailors started to move, but Offendorl clapped his hands and two waves of magical force slammed the big sailors' heads together with so much force that the men dropped to the deck, completely unconscious.

Offendorl looked toward the captain, who was standing with his mouth open in surprise, as another sailor ran toward the elder wizard from the side. Offendorl waited until the last minute and then with a flourish sent the sailor flying through the air and over the railing of the ship. The sailor's scream of panic was quickly cut off when he splashed into the water.

"Man overboard!" came shouts from all over the ship.

"Put that man in chains!" screamed the captain as he pointed at Offendorl.

Several men came running to do their captain's bidding, but the master of the Torr stopped them in their tracks.

"Enough!" he shouted, letting his magical power enhance his voice so that it was supernaturally loud and deep. Everyone on the ship froze.

"I am Offendorl, Master of the Torr and Wizard of the Five Kingdoms," he thundered on. "I shall reduce any man who lays a finger on me to ashes and send this ship to the bottom of the sea."

He was bluffing of course. They were several miles from the coast, too far for Offendorl to levitate himself in his weakened condition. He wouldn't sink the ship, but he didn't want the sailors to know that.

Several of the sailors bowed; others cringed in fear. The sailor lost overboard was forgotten. The captain was terrified, but he came forward meekly.

"I am sorry," he said.

"Not as sorry as you will be if you try to harm me again, is that clear?"

"Yes, of course."

"You shall bring me food and wine at first light, do you understand?"

"I shall bring it from my own stores."

"And if my possessions are missing from my cabin they shall be returned promptly."

"Yes, I will see that it is done, my friend."

"So be it," Offendorl said in a menacing tone. "And get me to Brimington with all haste."

"We shall fly every stitch of sail, my friend, day and night."

Offendorl spun on his heel, his head held high as he walked across the deck toward the dark stairwell that led to his room. A sailor hurried forward with a lamp. Offendorl took it and walked down the stairs. He was sweating when he reached the bottom, his hands trembling slightly, but he had done what needed to be done, and no one had seen how weak he actually was. He stumbled into the room and collapsed on the bed. He would need to stay on his guard, he knew, but for now all he could think of was sleep.

Chapter 4

It took Zollin nearly an hour to rebuild his internal defenses. The concept was easy to envision, but containing his magic was difficult. It was like trying to channel a raging river into a small tube, but once he got his power under control, it seemed to increase exponentially.

Mansel had roused Zollin before dawn and Eustice was ready with their horses and fresh supplies. They rode in silence, Zollin working to contain his magic while Mansel and Eustice battled just to stay awake. They rode along the coastline, which angled northeast. The next towns of size were the Twin Cities, each located on the points of two peninsulas that arched out into the sea, curving toward one another. The land created a sheltered harbor that was perfect for ships to take refuge in, and the cities were situated on the points of the peninsulas so that you could see from one city into the other.

As dawn broke, Zollin spoke up.

"What's our plan?" he asked.

"Not sure," Mansel said. "I would prefer to ride down to Osla, but that's probably not a good idea. It would take months."

"It's safe from sea monsters though, isn't it?" Zollin joked.

"You going to tell me what that was?"

"How should I know? The captain called it a kraken—you ever heard of that before?"

Eustice shook his head.

"No, can't say that I have," Mansel said after some thought. "It was a nasty piece of work though. Destroyed that trading ship and killed everyone on board except us."

"It's a good thing most of the crew were still on land then," Zollin said. "It was by far the biggest living creature I've ever seen."

"Bigger than the dragon?"

"Yes, considerably bigger. I fought it, but I don't think I caused any lasting harm."

"You drove it off though," Mansel said, trying to be cheerful.

"Some would say I woke it up," Zollin said. "Just like the dragon, and those forest dryads we ran into in Peddingar."

Mansel didn't respond. He wasn't sure how to say something that wouldn't be taken the wrong way. He wanted to encourage Zollin, but the fact was, since he had become a wizard there were a lot of crazy things happening that couldn't be explained. Mansel had never believed in dragons or wizards, but now he was convinced that anything was possible.

"So we ride," Mansel said. "Hopefully we can get ahead of the rumors. Perhaps we book passage separately, at least you and me. Eustice can stay with you. That way people who are looking for the three of us won't be suspicious."

"Won't they be suspicious when we ride into town together?" Zollin asked.

"I was thinking about that," Mansel said. "Perhaps you could charter a boat. There are plenty of fishermen along the coast. You and Eustice sail up the coast, and I'll ride. We can book passage on the same ship, but separately. That way, we won't rouse suspicion."

"That's fine by me, although I'm not anxious to get back on the water."

"Surely you drove that beast off for a while. By the time it's ready to attack ships again, hopefully we'll be halfway to Osla."

"Alright, that works for me. What about you, Eustice?"

The mute servant nodded enthusiastically.

An hour later they came to a small village and Zollin traded his horse and Eustice's for passage to the Twin Cities. The boat they found was small and smelled of fish, but it seemed sturdy. The owner of the boat promised to have them in the big harbor by dawn the next morning. Zollin hoped that Mansel would be able to ride through the night.

On the boat, Zollin once again had to tap into his magical power to stop himself from being seasick. The big ship had been constantly moving, but the smaller fishing boat was almost like being adrift in the sea. It rose and fell in a clumsy but steady trek up the coast. Eustice tried to sleep, but waves were large enough that the small vessel sent water flying as it splashed into each breaker. They were soon soaked and shivering, but the fisherman didn't seem to notice.

They ate soggy bread and smoked fish. Everything tasted strongly of salt, but despite their thirst they were forced to ration their supply of water. Zollin had a jug of wine, but it did nothing to slake his thirst. Their night was miserable, wet, and cold, but when the sun finally dawned they could see the Twin Cities.

It was mid-morning by the time they docked the small boat and made their way to an inn where they could sit by the fire and enjoy a hot meal. Zollin sent Eustice with silver for dry clothes. He couldn't help but think of Brianna whenever he thought about tailors. Her father had been a skilled tailor, and Brianna was talented as well. It made his heart ache to think of her. Her memory was becoming cloudy in his mind, which only made him even more angry. He didn't want to forget what she looked like, but he couldn't help it. He remembered her raven black hair, high cheekbones, and full lips, but he couldn't remember exactly how her eyes had looked. She was becoming more shadow than memory, they way people often look in dreams. He could remember her form, but not her substance.

Zollin went out in search of a ship on which they could book passage. He tried not to worry about Mansel. The big warrior could take care of himself, and he seemed to have a compulsion to see Zollin safe. It was probably born out of guilt, and as much as Zollin regretted Mansel's crimes, he didn't want his friend to suffer under the weight of actions he was not responsible for. It took nearly the rest of the day to find a ship willing to take on passengers. Rumors had reached the Twin Cities of the kraken attack, and they had grown stranger with each mile. He heard that the invading army had sunken the ship. He heard about hideous sea creatures that were nothing like the huge creature that actually attacked them. He even heard about an army of mermen rising up out of the water in a unified attack. But no matter how the story had grown, the one common denominator was the story of the three men who drew the beast and sabotaged the ship. They had become famous, the sole survivors of the heinous attack. Now, most of the ships were unwilling to take on passengers.

When Zollin finally found the Northern Star, he paid for their passage with silver. There were rumors that the three men in Lorye had paid with gold, and Zollin didn't want to do anything that might make the sailors think that he was the wizard who had fought the kraken.

When Zollin returned to the inn, he found Eustice waiting for him with new clothes. The mute servant had managed to buy new breeches, several shirts, and even new boots for them both.

"I'm not sure how you do it, Eustice," Zollin said. "I mean, how do you haggle when you can't talk?"

The mute servant only waved a hand of dismissal at Zollin.

"You did an excellent job," he said. Eustice beamed under the praise. "I don't know how you knew what size boots to get me, but these are a perfect fit. And very comfortable too."

They went together to get food. They bought several bottles of wine and a keg of ale, along with fruit, eggs, cheese, and three dozen loaves of bread. They paid a man with a pushcart a few bronze coins to haul their load to the boat. Then, they waited in separate inns as the sun set, hoping to catch sight of Mansel. Zollin wasn't sure how the warrior would know which ship to book passage on—in fact, he wasn't even sure if Mansel hadn't suggested that they split up just so he could get as far away from Zollin as possible. Zollin wouldn't have blamed his friend for that. It seemed like death followed Zollin as closely as his own shadow. He had taken great strides not to kill anyone since the battle at Orrock. The last thing he wanted now as more blood on his hands. He knew he would have to defeat Offendorl and the witch at Lodenhime, but just thinking about how easily he'd been able to inflict damage on the kraken made him feel ashamed. It was the realization that at any moment he could do the same thing to anyone around him. He could stop a man's heart, eviscerate organs, or collapse lungs with hardly a thought. It was like holding a tiny baby bird in your hands, knowing that with only the tiniest effort you could end that life. The realization weighed heavily on Zollin.

He drank cider and watched the sailors and merchants moving around on the quay. Boats loaded with cargo were rowed to the docks and unloaded. Carts full of merchandise rumbled over the cobblestone streets. Zollin couldn't help but think of Todrek as he sipped his drink. It was cool and tart, reminding Zollin of his old friend and how they had spent the day together at the harvest festival in Tranaugh Shire. It had been a good day, at least until Brianna's father had announced Todrek's betrothal. Zollin had not been jealous of his friend, only envious of Todrek's good fortune. He had been planning to leave their village, and Todrek's betrothal had solidified that decision. He had only stayed into the winter because his best friend had asked Zollin to stand with him at the marriage ceremony.

So much had changed that day, Zollin thought. Looking back, it was as if that day had set everything that came since into motion. Still, sitting comfortably, watching the hustle and bustle of the harbor in the last light of the day, Zollin couldn't help but think of how much Todrek would have enjoyed being there with him. The smell of the ocean was sharp, mingling with the smell of roasting meat and freshly baked bread. It was a moment of peace and happiness, a rarity in Zollin's world.

It was late before Zollin caught sight of Eustice. He hurried over and gestured for Zollin to follow him. They passed a sullen looking inn that overlooked the harbor and Eustice gestured at it. Zollin guessed that Eustice had seen Mansel go inside.

"We need to let him know what we've done," Zollin said. "But I don't want us to be seen with him. Perhaps I could send him a message."

Eustice nodded as Zollin looked around. A young boy was sweeping outside the inn. Zollin approached him.

"Can you carry a message for me?" he asked, holding up a silver mark.

"Aye," the boy said, mesmerized by the silver.

"There's a man in your inn here, a big man with a sword. He's wearing a leather vest and goes by the name of Mansel. You think you could find him and give him a message?"

"Aye, that I could, sir."

"Good," Zollin said. "Tell him, 'The Northern Star.'"

"And…" the boy said.

"That's it, just 'The Northern Star.' And let him know it sails with the tide tomorrow. What time will that be?"

"Just before noon day," the boy said.

"Good, that'll give him time enough to square things. Repeat the message."

"The Northern Star sails with the morning tide."

"Good enough," Zollin said, flipping the boy the coin. "Wait a few minutes, then go find him. Alright?"

"Aye, sir," the boy said.

"Let's go," Zollin said to Eustice.

They turned and went in search of a boat that would take them to their ship. A few coppers paid their fare, and the boat ride was smooth. Unlike the open waters of the coast, the harbor was calm and the skiff glided over the water. They had to climb a rope ladder up the side of the ship and were met by one of the sailors. The Northern Star wasn't as big as the ship that had been destroyed by the kraken, but it had a long corridor of rooms just under the main deck. Zollin and Eustice shared a room with two bunks, a sturdy table with canvas chairs, and even a small porthole with shutters. Their belongings and food had already been neatly stored away in the sea chests at the foot of each bunk.

"Nothing left now but to wait, I guess," Zollin said.

Eustice nodded and began preparing food for their evening meal. Zollin was tempted to go up on deck and explore a little, perhaps even let his magic down into the sea again. But he didn't want to take the chance that he had actually attracted the kraken.

And he knew he would be worried until Mansel was safely on board the ship with them.

They ate a light meal of bread and fruit with a little cheese and wine. They were tired from their travels so sleep came easily, and at dawn they awoke to the cries of the sailors. An officer was seeing that everything was ready for the ship to set sail with the tide. He barked and shouted, and the sailors answered in kind. Zollin was still sleepy, but it was impossible to rest with all the noise around him.

"I think I'll take a walk on the deck," Zollin said.

He stepped out of their room and was met by a woman in a long cloak. She glared at him for a moment, until he stepped to the side, then swept past him and entered a much larger set of rooms at the end of the corridor.

"That's Lady Roleena," said a sailor who had just come down the stairs from the deck. He was carrying a large chest on his shoulder. "I'd steer clear, if you take my meaning. She's got a razor sharp tongue, she has."

"Thanks for the advice," Zollin said.

He turned and headed back up to the main deck. There were people everywhere—mostly sailors, but some were passengers overseeing their belongs as they were hoisted up from the ships below. Zollin went out to an empty spot along the ship rail and looked out over the water. He wasn't surprised that the ship was filling up. It had been the only ship still taking passengers when he had searched, but he was afraid that Mansel might be too late to get on board.

He was hungry and tired, but too nervous to eat. He watched the ships and the myriad boats moving between them. Some of the boats were large, with over a dozen men working the oars, while others were simple wooden platforms, hardly wider than their passengers, being expertly rowed around the harbor by a single sailor.

Zollin had almost lost hope for his friend when he saw the big warrior in a crowded boat of surly looking men. Zollin thought the men looked hungover and sick. Mansel would have blended in well if not for his size. When the boat came gliding up beside the Northern Star, an officer started barking orders.

"Henson, get those men aboard. I want them berthed down between decks. Have their gear stowed and each man assigned to his duty, then report back to me."

"Aye, sir," the sailor on the boat shouted back, knuckling his forehead. "Alright, you dandies, you heard the man. Get your gear and get aboard. This isn't a pleasure cruise."

Zollin watched in surprise as Mansel jumped up and grabbed a rope that hung from the side of the ship. He climbed hand over hand to get on board. He had his belongs in a simple sack that was the size of his sword. The sack was slung across his back on a leather strap, and when he got on board he hurried with the other sailors down into the bowels of the ship.

The deck was busy and most of the passengers had retired down to their cabins, but Zollin waited by the ship rail. He wanted to see what his friend had gotten himself into. It was a brilliant plan. If he couldn't book passage on the ship, he had gotten hired as one of the many hands that worked the ship. Mansel had never been the kind of person to shy away from hard labor, but Zollin had to wonder if his friend knew what he was in for.

It only took a few minutes before Mansel came jogging back up on deck. The sailor who had rowed them across the harbor pointed to a short, leathery skinned sailor not far from where Zollin was watching. Mansel hurried over to the man and presented himself.

"Carpenter's helper Mansel, reporting for duty," the warrior said.

The sailor looked him up and down for a minute, his eyes mere slits in the bright morning sunlight.

"So you think you want to be a sailor, eh? I think maybe you wooed the wrong woman and now you're looking for a quick way out of town."

Mansel shifted on his feet but didn't say anything.

"Well, you're certainly a big lad. Have you got any skills?"

"I was apprenticed to a carpenter for three years," Mansel said, darting a glance at Zollin. "I've never worked on a ship, but I learn fast and work hard."

"You'll have to," the sailor said. "My name's Ern, and we're the only carpenters on board at the moment. You'll have plenty to keep you busy. Get started by stowing all those supplies below." Ern pointed to a pallet full of freshly milled wood. There were stacks of thick planking as well as oak staves and iron hoops for making barrels."

"You want these…" Mansel obviously wasn't sure where the supplies went.

"Down in the workshop," Ern growled. "And make sure they're stored away neat. I don't want to find my shop littered with broken wood once we're underway."

Zollin decided he'd seen enough. Mansel was on board and they would soon be sailing south. The ship would make several stops, but its ultimate destination was Brimington Bay, the closest point to the Grand City in Osla. Zollin descended the steps that led to his cabin and found Eustice resting leisurely inside.

"He made it," Zollin told his companion. "He had to come on board as one of the hands."

Eustice made a gesture.

"There wasn't enough space on board for more passengers, at least I think that's why. The ship is full of people."

They ate some fruit and then headed on deck as the anchored was lifted and the sails unfurled. Zollin had never sailed on a ship. His first experience at sea had been on the little fishing boat, and it had not been an enjoyable journey. He was amazed at the sheer number of men it took to sail the ship.

The Northern Star was a simple vessel, with two large masts. It had three decks. One was elevated over the others and was only as long as the last third of the ship. The ship's captain called all his passengers up onto the elevated platform as they headed out to sea.

"You'll find no better crew anywhere," he explained, "so there's nothing to worry about. We've got favorable winds and should make good time. I'll ask that you remain in your cabins or here, on the command deck. I don't want anyone wandering the main deck—it can be dangerous. Supper's at six bells. If you need anything, Lieutenant Yagger will see to your needs," he said, gesturing at the man who had been shouting orders all morning. "Any questions? No?" the captain continued. "We'll be leaving the harbor soon. If you are prone to seasickness, I suggest keeping a bucket in your cabin."

Everyone filed back into their rooms. Zollin noticed that the haughty woman he'd seen in the passageway wasn't present for the speech by the captain. He found that curious, but not entirely surprising. She was a beautiful woman, in Zollin's opinion, although just admitting that made him feel ashamed. The people he loved most in the world had died with him, and it felt as if guilt was his constant companion. Not that he had any reason to feel guilty—the woman was certainly not interested in him. It was the way his mind worked though, puzzling out problems and imagining what might happen.

He stood on the command deck, well behind the captain, who stood next to the helmsman giving quiet orders to his lieutenant, who then barked out the orders to the men working the main deck or climbing through the rigging like spiders. Zollin looked for Mansel but he was nowhere to be seen. Neither was the ship's carpenter, Ern.

The Northern Star sailed smoothly through the harbor with just one large sail unfurled. There was strong wind at their back and they made good time through the narrow pass between the

Twin Cities. Once they reached the open water, the motion of the ship became much more pronounced. Zollin felt his stomach trembling and his head began to hurt, so he let his magic soothe the pressure in his inner ear. Then he let his magic flow through the ship. It was a small space that was teeming with life. There were sailors in the galley, carefully preparing meals, some for the captain and his officers, others for the crew, and still others for the passengers. There were men sleeping in hammocks slung so closely together they lay shoulder to shoulder. There were men in the rigging and along ropes near the crossbeams where the sails were tied. Zollin watched as the lieutenant shouted for more sails to be released. Some of the sailors untied the carefully bunched canvas. As it fell from the crossbeams, unfolding as it went, other sailors caught the ropes and carefully tied the bottom sides of the sails with long ropes. The canvas whipped and popped as the sails filled with wind, and soon there were three sails on each mast, each one bulging full of wind and pushing the ship faster and faster through the gentle swells.

Zollin also found men working below decks. Some were checking the cargo, others doing routine maintenance. Zollin discovered Mansel, already feeling very sick. He wasn't the only sailor made ill by the ship's rocking motion, and many of the passengers were too, but Zollin was only interested in his friend. If Mansel had to work, Zollin didn't want him feeling sick too. He used his magic to help his friend adjust. It took several minutes. The magic was warm, like standing next to a fire on a cold day. It felt good to exercise his power. It was tempting to let the magic fall into the water, but he was still afraid he might attract another magical creature like the kraken.

Once Zollin had helped Mansel, he returned to his cabin. There was nothing more to do but wait, as difficult as that seemed. He found Eustice asleep in his bunk and decided to follow the mute servant's example. As he lay down, he couldn't help but think of Brianna. His heart ached at the thought of her. He couldn't believe that she was gone. He missed her so badly he would have given anything to see her, even for just one more moment. He wanted to tell her so many things and to hold her in his arms one last time, to savor the way she made him feel and the smell of her skin. He fell asleep and dreamed of Brianna.

Chapter 5

Brianna stirred slowly. She was surrounded by warm, sleek bodies. Sun was shining into the mouth of cave, but it didn't reach to the recesses where Brianna was resting. She had slept for days after her work. The desire to create had been so strong it had held her in a feverish state for days without rest. Now, after leaving the dark cavern she had carved deep under the mountain, she was content to rest and watch her dragons fly.

They had needed time in the sun, time to hunt and feed, but most of all, time to adapt to their world. Many had chosen a life of solitude over the last several days, bidding her and the dragons that remained with her goodbye. It was hard to watch them go. Brianna wanted to keep them close to her and protect them, but she was not their mother. She had given them life, but they were dragons and, although she was dragon-kind, she could not protect them or insist on their loyalty. She didn't feel betrayed by those that left her—in fact, she was happy for them in a way. Her desire had been to bring dragons into the world, to share their strength and wisdom with others. It was a task she had been part of, but they would have to complete it.

She had flown with them, racing high into the sky where the air was thin and cold. She loved letting flames cover her body in the icy wind, to feel the freedom of flight and to see the world from high above. She could not fly like her dragons, but she was at home in the air. Her bones had grown light and she could flip and turn, catch thermal updrafts and glide for miles and miles. Her dragons would carry her up into the air where she would leap away and fly down on her own, circling and looping with the dragons before landing softly. The dragons brought her food, and during their short time together their personalities had begun to shine.

Five dragons had chosen to stay with Brianna. Selix was her firstborn and the biggest of all the dragons she had made. Selix had bright golden scales and a broad back with small bony plates that ran from just behind its head all the way down to the end of the tail. Brianna often rode on Selix's back, perched lightly between the massive, leathery wings and holding onto the plates.

Tig and Torc were the smallest. Their scales were dark blue and they had short tails that were forked on the end. They were much faster than the other dragons, often flying far ahead and scouting out game when the pride went out to hunt.

Ferno was green and, although smaller than Selix, the most ferocious dragon of the pride. Ferno's body was thick with muscles. There were short spikes on its tail, as well as two long, spiral horns on its head. Ferno was very protective of the pride, and especially of Brianna.

Gyia was purple with a long, thin body and two sets of wings that gave it the most maneuverability of any of the dragons in flight. Gyia had a long, tapering head and seemed to be the most reserved of the group.

Brianna loved each of the dragons and thought of them as her brothers and sisters more than her children, even though the dragons were neither male nor female. The pride had bonded, and even though they understood that Brianna wasn't a dragon, she was the leader. She loved being with the dragons, loved the freedom of flight and the ferocious playfulness of the dragons with one another, but now that her urge to create was sated, she longed to return south and find Zollin. She wasn't exactly sure how long she had been in the heart of the mountains, but now that the other dragons were gone and she had regained her strength, she knew it was time to move on.

Communicating with her pride was much more intuitive than talking, although the dragons were capable of human speech. The dragons used mental images to communicate with each other, and with Brianna more often than not. Brianna was teaching them to speak, often voicing her thoughts out loud so that the dragons grew more familiar with language.

"It is time for me to go," she told the pride late one evening as the sun set and their cave grew dark.

She kindled a dancing flame and sent it up toward the roof of the cave so that it cast a soft, warm light all around. The dragons were watching her with bright, inquisitive eyes that were very different from Bartoom's. Brianna had spent many days with the black dragon. It had angry, distrustful eyes, although it had come to trust Brianna. Time spent among men and wizards greedy for power who had forced Bartoom to do their bidding by harnessing the power of gold had made the beast angry and cynical. Her pride had not yet felt the sting of disappointment, and for that matter, neither had Brianna, but she understood that there were people in the world who would not trust her or the pride. They would see only fear and danger when they saw her dragons. Even though she longed to see Zollin, to hold him and tell him all the wonderful things she had discovered, she knew that she had to be careful to protect the pride.

In her mind she saw pictures of the hunt, and of dragons playing games high in the air over the mountain peaks.

"No," she said, imagining the forest and cities in the south. "I need to go in search of my friend." She thought of Zollin and sent the mental image to the pride. "He is my partner, my soul mate. It is a human trait, a need I have, and I will not force you to come with me. Humans may fear you, or even try to harm you."

Ferno growled menacingly.

"But you must not harm them. We must learn to live in harmony with man," she said, imagining the dragons being warmly greeted by humans.

She received another image of Selix flying among the clouds with Brianna on its back. One by one the other dragons joined the image. Brianna knew they were all seeing it, all sharing their desire to stay together.

"I will do my best to keep us safe," she said. "But we must be cautious."

The dragons growled and settled in around Brianna. She let the dancing flame go out. Her vision had improved the longer she had stayed with the dragons and she could see quite well at night. She lay facing the cave opening, staring at the stars that shone in the distance as the dragons slept around her. She wondered where

Zollin was. She regretted that she had not been able to tell him what she was doing, but at the time she had left with Bartoom, she hadn't known herself. So much had changed. She had followed Zollin from Tranaugh Shire when the Torr had come to take him away. She had stayed with him for nearly a year, even though she often felt more like a hindrance than a help. Zollin had power that was both amazing and frightening. He could do so much it made Brianna feel small and weak.

And then everything had changed. Hammert the dwarf had given her a ruby, and the magical gem had kindled something deep inside Brianna. No one had known the ruby's power, and perhaps, Brianna wondered, it was her own power that connected with the gemstone. Zollin often talked about objects having magical powers, but she now understood that there was powerful magic in many of the minerals found deep in the earth. When she had delved deep into the mountain, her molten fire melting through rock, she had sensed the power of the minerals she had passed, most specifically gold. It drew her dragon nature like a magnet. If given free reign, gold could mesmerize her, and she guessed any other dragon as well.

Gold had also played a pivotal role in creating her dragons. She had molded each dragon from the earth, shaping the beasts with fire, with her hands, and with her mind, but each of the dragons she had created started with gold. It was part of the dragons, lending them a magical power that was both potent and mysterious.

She thought about how Zollin had tempted Bartoom with gold, luring the dragon into a trap set by Zollin and the Felson legion. Then she realized that Felson was the perfect place to begin her search for Zollin. The city was big enough to have news from all over the kingdom, and there were people there that Zollin knew and cared about. She decided then, watching the stars twinkle in the autumn sky, that she would leave in the morning.

The next day dawned bright and Brianna's first order of business was to feed her pride. She had lost her clothes when she'd used fire on her body—the clothes, obviously not impervious to flame like she was, had simply burned away. But she had saved the skins of many of the animals her pride brought to her as food. She had worked carefully to make clothes for herself, although she knew that she couldn't wear them when she flew high above the clouds where the air was so cold it could freeze her breath. So she had fashioned a satchel of sorts and stored the makeshift clothes there. Gyia could carry the satchel, but first her pride needed to hunt, and so did Brianna.

"Go, hunt and eat well," she told them. "We have a long journey ahead of us."

The dragons took to the air, all except Ferno, who stayed at the entrance to the cave, watching for any signs of danger. Brianna slipped back down the long shaft that led to the cavern in the heart of the mountain. At first the tunnel was pitch-black, but Brianna let blue flames erupt from her skin as she slowed her descent. Flying for Brianna was a dance of the body and the mind. She could do many things simply by thinking them, but she used her body to help shape the flight path she wanted. She extended her arms and let her fingers glide over the sides of the tunnel as she fell. The shaft was straight and the tunnel walls smooth to the touch. She had let her fire burn hotter than molten rock when she made her way down the shaft. The heat she produced was so intense it had melted the stone beneath her feet. She had slipped down into the molten rock, diving deeper and deeper until she found the place she needed, far from the eyes of the world, deeper even than the dwarf kingdoms. And along the way she had found veins of gold. She could sense the precious metal as she drew close to it and she slowed her descent even more.

When she reached the gold vein she spread her legs, letting her feet settle onto the smooth tunnel walls and locking her legs in place so that the pressure of her weight, light though it was, held her in place. The gold vein was rich. She had used many such veins in making her dragons, but this gold would be useful to help her get the supplies she needed to walk among the villages of men again. The gold looked like lightning streaking across the night sky.

She put her hands on the tunnel wall and funneled her heat into the stone. It only took a few moments for the gold to begin to melt and seep out of the stone. It ran down the wall of the tunnel in a golden stream. Brianna moved one hand to cup the molten metal. It pooled into her hand and began to cool. It was heavy and hot, although the heat did not bother Brianna. Still, she needed it to solidify so that she could carry it to a village and trade it for clothes and supplies.

She relaxed her legs and began to fall again. This time she held her arms against her body and pointed her toes until she was speeding through the tunnel at the highest speed possible. When she shot out of the tunnel into the cavern she looped around and used her own momentum to shoot back up. She couldn't explain how she flew, in fact she didn't understand it herself, and didn't bother trying. She couldn't launch herself off the ground, but she had often stood on Selix's tail and been launched into the air. Once she was off the ground, she could do almost anything, and the freedom of flying was more intoxicating than any drink.

She flew back up into the cave and landed gracefully on her feet. Then she put the gold on the cold, stone floor. It was soft, like bread dough, and she mashed it flat with her hands and then tore small pieces off, rounding them with her fingers into little golden nuggets. There was enough gold that she had a baker's dozen of small, pebble sized nuggets.

Then she got an image in her mind of the other dragons returning and she gathered her satchel, stashing the gold inside.

"I'm ready," she said, thinking of flying with the pride.

Ferno roared, then leapt off the lip of the cave, wings flapping hard as it soared up into the air. Brianna ran and jumped out of the cave, diving first downward and then looping back up high into the air. She glanced down at the cave and bid it a wistful goodbye. Then she settled onto Selix's back as the pride turned south and began to fly away.

Chapter 6

Life aboard the Northern Star took Mansel some getting used to. There were strange duty rotations, constant work, poor food, and claustrophobic conditions. Mansel's back ached from constantly stooping over to make his way through the between-decks area, which was where the crew ate, slept, and, in Mansel's case, did most of his work.

Mansel had made barrels with Quinn in the past, but with the space limitations and the need to be extra careful with fire on board the ship, he struggled with the task. Ern kept Mansel busy and life merged into a routine of eating, sleeping, and working. Mansel wasn't sure that Zollin had helped him, but he had only started getting seasick when he suddenly felt much better. Still, sleeping in a hammock in the crowded between-decks was difficult and certainly didn't help his back. Fatigue was also a big problem for Mansel. He felt like there were bells ringing to wake him up almost as soon as he closed his eyes. The only bright spot in the misery of his days was his daily ration of rum. The liquor was strong and helped him relax, although it wasn't enough to get him drunk.

Mansel occasionally saw Zollin on the command deck, but the big warrior was only allowed on the main deck when something needed to be repaired. They were almost a week into the journey when Ern sent him up to the passenger deck.

"There's some sort of problem in one of the passenger cabins," Ern said. "How the hell they smash up wooden furniture is a mystery to me. I don't have the patience to deal with sprogs."

The insult wasn't lost on Mansel. He knew a "sprog" was an untrained person at sea, which was exactly what he was. Still, Mansel had an idea who needed a little carpentry work and didn't complain.

"Aye," he said sarcastically.

Ern just waved Mansel away. The big carpenter's helper picked up his bag of tools and arranged the strap over his shoulder. He left Ern in the workshop and headed for the stairway that would take him up to the main deck. The passenger deck did not run the entire length of the ship and could only be accessed from the main deck. Mansel guessed that either the passengers didn't want to rub shoulders with the crew or the officers didn't want the crew to get any ideas about visiting the passengers in secret. Either way, he would have to get permission from the officer of the watch to go onto the passenger deck.

"And just where do you think you're going, toad?"

Mansel sighed. Toad was the nickname some of the crew had given him. He had been content to keep to himself, but in the close quarters of the "'tween" decks, that had been impossible. He had been polite to the other sailors, but a new recruit was always a target and Mansel's size made him an easy one. He was constantly bumping his head or accidentally stumbling into someone.

"He's going up on deck," said one of a group of sailors who had taken it upon themselves to torment Mansel.

"I've work to do," he said simply, but they stepped in front of him, blocking his path to the stairs that led up to the main deck.

"Toads aren't allowed on the main deck, Sprog, or didn't you know that?"

"I'm working," Mansel said again. "Ern sent me."

"Sure he did," said the vocal sailor in the group. He had a scar across one check, and the other sailors called him Slice. "I see you've got your tools there. Are you enjoying your pleasure cruise while the rest of us do all the work?"

"I am working," Mansel said, making the monumental effort it took to keep his temper in check with the group of bullying sailors.

"Sure you are, Toad. Just hopping about, and smashing everything you touch. I guess it's good that you're a carpenter, eh. You can fix things."

The other sailors laughed but Mansel wasn't sure what was so funny. "Let me pass," he said.

"It will cost you your ration of rum," Slice said.

"No," Mansel immediately replied.

"Oh, he's a brave one, he is," Slice said.

"Foolhardy," one of the other sailors said.

"Show 'em who's the big man 'tween decks, Slice," said another.

"I know you're new," said Slice, "so you may not have the lay of the land, so to speak. We all have different duties on deck, but down here there's just two kinds of sailors. There's them that do what I tell 'em, and there's them that don't. That second group is small and they don't generally live too long, if you take my meaning."

"Is that a threat?" Mansel said, his hand slowly dipping into his tool back and taking hold of his mallet.

"You take it however you want, but you best decide what you're gonna do, Toady. I want that rum today or things are going to get very uncomfortable for you."

Slice stepped out of Mansel's way and the big warrior eyed him fiercely for a moment, then stalked past. He was surprised that the smaller man was so confident he could best Mansel in a fight. Normally, people gave him deference because of his size, but on the ship his muscular frame had only caused him problems. He longed for a horse and the open road. He was tired of the cramped quarters, the constant work, and the awful stench of the lower decks.

He climbed the stairs to the main deck, stretching his back and breathing the clean sea air deep into this lungs. He had to squint in the bright sunlight, but made his way straight to the officer on watch.

"Permission to go on the passenger deck, sir?" he said.

"Ah, you're the carpenter?"

"Aye sir," Mansel said, trying to remember the correct way to speak to a superior on board ship. The discipline of sea life he could endure, but the sailors had their own ways of doing everything. His plan had been to blend in, lay low until they reached Osla and then slip away with Zollin and Eustice.

Unfortunately, blending in hadn't exactly happened yet. "My name's Mansel, sir."

"Very good, Mansel. I'll escort you down," the officer said. "Bollen, you have the watch."

"Aye, aye, sir, I have the watch," said the sailor at the helm.

"Do your work as quickly as possible," the officer instructed as he led Mansel down onto the passenger deck. "Don't speak unless spoken to, and if you have any questions, come back to me. Is that understood?"

"Aye," Mansel said.

"Good, here we are."

The officer knocked on the door and Zollin opened it. He ignored Mansel completely, doing his best to give no sign that he knew the bigger man.

"This man will fix your problem," the officer said. "If you have any complaints, please find me."

"I will, Lieutenant, thank you," Zollin said.

The officer spun on his heel and walked briskly back up to the main deck. Zollin stood aside and let Mansel into the cabin. The table was smashed, as were both of the canvas chairs.

"How did you explain that?" Mansel asked.

Zollin waved at Eustice, who was sporting a black eye and grinning.

"We had a bit too much to drink and had a disagreement, didn't we Eustice?" Zollin said. Eustice nodded and they all tried not to laugh.

"So how's life as a sailor?" Zollin asked.

"I hate it," Mansel said as he slumped onto the bed. "I'm too big to move around 'tween decks. I have to stay bent over almost the whole time."

"Couldn't you get on as a passenger?"

"No, you picked the most popular ship in the kingdom."

"It was the only ship still taking passengers."

"Well, at least it won't last too long. My real problem is getting along with the locals. They all seem to think I'm not cut out for life at sea. I'm beginning to believe them."

"Well, try not to cause trouble. What can we do to help?"

"Nothing that I know of," Mansel said. "I'm trying to keep a low profile, but it's getting harder. I may have to crack a few heads before we get to Osla."

"Be careful," Zollin warned. "I'm trying to lay low as well. The last thing I want is to attract another monster."

"Tell me about it. This is the first time I've been allowed above deck in days without Ern. He's worse than your father. I don't want to be down in the workshop if something happens to the ship. There's no way I could get on deck fast enough not to drown."

"Are you getting enough food?"

"Not really," Mansel admitted.

"Okay, Eustice, fix Mansel something to eat. I'll repair the furniture."

"Wait, you can't use magic. It has to look like I patched it up. I'll need to go down and get some wood."

"Can you spare a moment to eat?"

"Yes," he said enthusiastically.

Eustice gathered food from their stores. The bread wasn't fresh, but it wasn't crawling with weevils, and they still had some fruit and cheese. They gave Mansel a small sack full of dried meat, which he stashed in his satchel. They had wine and ale, but he forced himself to drink water, since he had no way to hide the smell of alcohol on his breath.

Once he'd finished eating, he shuffled out of the small cabin and returned to the workshop. Ern was busy making another barrel. Mansel understood the desire to have fresh casks, since the water he usually drank tasted like it had been drawn from a stagnant pond. The water barrels had to be moved to shore and refilled at every port they stopped in. The constant wear and tear often resulted in barrels that weren't watertight, and it didn't take much seawater to ruin a barrel and its contents.

"What's the problem?" Ern asked.

"The damn fools got into a drunken fight and smashed up the furniture," Mansel explained.

"The captain should make them do without it," Ern said bitterly. "If that happened 'tween decks, we'd get the cattails for certain."

"What's the cattails?" Mansel asked.

"You don't want to know, boy. You just keep your nose clean and do you duty."

"Aye," Mansel said as he secretly stashed the food Zollin had given him among the supplies he was gathering. He felt a pang of guilt at hiding the food, but he knew that if he told Ern, the old sailor would just take it from him and perhaps even report him to the captain. The last thing Mansel needed was to be kicked off the ship before they reached Osla.

He was thinking about the last time he'd been at sea, with Quinn. They'd been forced to stop along the way for repairs and Mansel had gone ashore, gotten drunk, and missed returning to the ship. Quinn had left him in the middle of Falxis. The memory was still bitter in his mouth, but he would never have met Nycoll if it hadn't happened. Getting back to Nycoll was what Mansel wanted more than anything in the world, but he had to help Zollin. After all the terrible things he'd done under the witch's spell, he felt compelled to repay his friend somehow. And the truth was, he had to make sure Gwendolyn the witch was stopped. He remembered the small army of men willing to kill and even die for her. She couldn't be allowed to spread her foul sorcery across the kingdoms, he thought. Then, when that was done, he would return to Nycoll.

"Toady," came a sing-song voice from behind Mansel.

He turned toward the voice just as something slammed into his stomach, forcing all the breath from his lungs in a whoosh. He dropped to his knees and gasped for breath.

"Look, he's kneeling before you, Slice," said a rat-faced sailor with rotting teeth and one eye that was turned out at an unnatural angle.

"Of course he is," said the sailor with the scar. "They all do, sooner or later. How's it feel, Toad? Aren't you more at home on your knees? Maybe you miss the mud. We could help with that."

Mansel was still struggling to get his breathing under control when Slice swung a small wooden club at his head. Mansel dodged the blow instinctively.

"Ah, you want to play, eh? That's good Toady, very good indeed," said Slice.

He feigned one direction and then swung the club in the other. It caught Mansel on the shoulder. Pain exploded across the young warrior's neck, shoulder, and arm. He slumped back, but Slice moved in close and kicked Mansel hard in the ribs. Mansel fell over onto his side, sharp pain stabbing through him with each breath now. He felt shaky and weak, but he was angry too. He pulled the mallet out of the satchel of tools that still hung around his head and shoulder.

"Look, he's still got a little fight left in him," said the rat-faced sailor.

Several sailors stood with the rat-faced man, away from the fight. Slice's gang, who seemed never to be working, were the bullies between decks. Fighting on board was forbidden, Mansel knew, but he wasn't going to lie down and take a beating if he could help it.

"That mallet won't help you, Toad," said Slice.

"Leave me alone," Mansel warned.

"Or what? You can't stop us. You going to run to the captain and rat us out? If you do, you'll never make it off this ship alive. No, I think you're going to take your knocks like a man. But first we'll send you someplace you're more at home. Get him, boys."

The other sailors rushed forward. Mansel tried to rise up and swing the mallet, but he was too weak. Slice caught the mallet on his club and then the hammer was snatched roughly from Mansel's hand. They picked him up by the arms and legs. He started to struggle, but the pain in his side and shoulder was devastating. The sailors carried him a short way and then Slice pulled open a trap door. The sailors slung Mansel into the darkness below.

Fear made his stomach feel as if it were going to jump out of his throat, but the drop wasn't that far and it ended quickly. The Northern Star was made up of three decks. There was the main deck, and immediately below that was the passenger deck, which also housed the officer's quarters. The lowest deck was the cargo deck, but there was a small space between the cargo deck and the passenger deck, and the crew called the cramped area the "'tween decks." From the 'tween decks was a shaft that allowed crew members to access the lowest part of the ship—the space below the cargo deck, which the sailors called the bilge.

The smell hit Mansel just before he landed in the thick, wet sewage. The passengers and officers used chamber pots in the cabins, which could be emptied out of their small windows and washed with seawater. The crew used a privy, which was designed to empty out of the ship, but a portion of the sewage inevitably found it's way down to the bilge. Seawater also found its way in, no matter how well made the ship or how thick the pitch was applied to the seams of the hull. The bilge was a nasty place that had to be pumped out regularly, and the foulest job aboard the ship was working the bilge.

The area was as dark as a cave and Mansel landed with a splash. Seawater was free standing above the sludge that was thick like mud and had settled onto the hull. Rats were tolerated on board the ship because they ate the waste that ended up in the bilge. Mansel could hear the vermin scurrying around the bilge, reacting to his crash.

It took a few moments for the shock of what had happened to pass. Then pain swept over Mansel. His shoulder ached terribly and the muscles in his neck and back were spasming from the pain. He knew that at least two ribs had been broken, perhaps more. His entire left side was awash in pain. He knew he had to get out of the filth of the bilge, but he had no idea how he could possibly climb the ladder that lined the shaft.

He rolled onto his knees, using his right arm to lift his body out of the sewage. He moved slowly, despite the overwhelming urge to get out of the darkness as quickly as possible. Mansel didn't fear rats normally, but knowing they were around him now, in the darkness where he couldn't see them, made him feel weak and exposed. His mind, struggling with the shock of pain and fear, had trouble focusing on the task at hand. The water in the bilge rose and fell in motion with the ship.

Mansel had been thankful for the food his friends had given him, but now it came back up violently. After several moments of retching that was made unbearably painful because of his broken ribs, he passed out. He fell onto his side at a time when the water was low, but it only took a moment before the small wave rushed back toward Mansel, dousing him in the filthy water and rousing him.

He coughed and sputtered as the filthy water filled his nose and ears. He screamed as he pulled himself back to his knees. He could see bright specks of light dancing at the edges of his vision. He knew he had to get out of the bilge. Somehow he had to get back to Zollin. He knew his friend could end the pain and restore his health so that he could deal with the band of bullies between decks, but the obstacles between him and Zollin seemed insurmountable.

He crawled forward slowly, hoping to find the ladder that led back up to the 'tween decks. There was no light and Mansel was completely disoriented from his fall. He did know the ladder should have been close, but he didn't know in which direction to look. It took him almost half an hour of slow searching before he found it. To Mansel, that half hour seemed like a lifetime. The pain was almost completely debilitating, but once he reached the rough-hewn ladder, he felt much better. He sat on his knees, which were aching from the rough floor of the ship, and tried to calm himself down.

"You're going to be okay," he told himself out loud. It was a silly sentiment, he knew, but during his search for the ladder he had felt reasonably sure that he would die in the bilge. His next task was to stand. Even though he couldn't see, he still felt like the ship was spinning in circles around him. He held tightly to the ladder with his good hand and pulled himself slowly to his feet.

His muscles were screaming for relief and the thought of closing his eyes was so tempting he had to shake his head to fight it off. Unfortunately, shaking his head sent sharp stabbing pain through his neck and shoulder.

"Use it," he told himself. "Use the pain to keep yourself focused."

He slowly raised one foot, groaning with the effort. It was natural to raise his left leg since his right arm was pulling upward, but his ribs couldn't take the pressure. Instead, he lifted his right leg and, after finding the lowest rung, pulled himself up. It was painful and difficult, but he knew he couldn't stop. If he did, he would fall again and risked hurting himself much worse. He climbed, the effort so demanding he couldn't remember ever working so hard. Sweat poured off him, dizziness threatened to make him sick again, but through it all he kept moving. Finally, his hand felt the heavy trapdoor above him. He gnashed his teeth as he took one more step up the ladder and then heaved with his right arm.

The trap door opened slowly. It took all of Mansel's strength just to push it up enough to stick his arm out. The dim light of the 'tween decks was the most welcome sight Mansel could remember, but pushing his way out of the trap door proved too difficult in his weakened state. He hung in the hunched over position with one arm out of the trap door for several minutes until finally another sailor saw him.

"Hold on, mate," the sailor shouted. "Hey, you louts, get over here and help me. This man's trapped in the bilge shaft."

A moment later the heavy trap door was thrown open and rough hands pulled Mansel up out of the shaft. He lay curled on the floor, panting for several minutes. The sailors around him were all murmuring, but he couldn't make out what they were saying. Finally, the sailor who'd seen him bent over and spoke quietly. "Hey mate, it wasn't Slice who threw you down there was it?"

Mansel nodded.

Without another word the other sailors all drifted away. They were afraid of Slice and his gang, Mansel knew that, but he was aghast that they would simply leave him on the floor. Mansel struggled back up onto his knees and began crawling toward the stairs that led up to the main deck. His tool satchel had been pulled off of him, and was now near the foot of the stairs, along with the extra wood he needed to repair Zollin's furniture.

It took all his strength to crawl up the stairs, but he forced himself to keep moving. Just at the top, two sailors met him.

"Oh, good god man, what happened to you?" one of the said.

Mansel didn't answer, he was too busy clenching his teeth to keep from crying out in pain.

"He smells worse than the privy," the sailor said to his companion. "Are you the carpenter's helper?"

Mansel nodded this time.

"Run and tell the lieutenant," the sailor said. "Looks like he fell down into the bilge. I'll get started cleaning him up."

One sailor hurried off and the other called for a bucket of water. Seawater was used to clean the decks regularly, and soon Mansel was doused with a bucket of cold saltwater. He gasped.

"Well, he ain't dead, is he?" said another sailor.

"What is going on here?" Zollin shouted.

Zollin had gotten worried when Mansel hadn't returned. He had gone to the lieutenant to find out what had happened, and the first officer had sent the two sailors in search of Mansel. Now, Zollin and the lieutenant were walking quickly across the main deck to find the young warrior.

"Please, sir," the lieutenant said coldly. "Let me deal with my men."

"But that man's obviously hurt," Zollin said. "I'm a healer," he added quickly. "Let me help him."

"We've a ship's surgeon on board. I assure you he'll get the best care possible."

Zollin sent a suggestion magically toward the young officer, who looked puzzled for a moment and then said, "Actually, the sick bay is rather full. I wonder if you might help him?"

Zollin nodded, ignoring the strange looks the other sailors gave their lieutenant. "Certainly. Let's get those clothes off of him. We'll get him cleaned up and then he can rest in my cabin."

"You heard him," said the lieutenant in a sharp tone to his men. "Cut those clothes off and toss them overboard. They smell like the bilge.

Mansel moaned as the sailors went to work on him. Rags were brought and seawater was poured over his head. They used knives to cut away his clothes. His boots were pulled off and cleaned. Then a stretcher was brought out, just a strip of canvas sewn around two long poles. They gently laid Mansel on the stretcher and carried him down to Zollin's cabin.

"Are you sure you want to do this?" the lieutenant asked Zollin. "It's highly irregular. I'm not sure the captain would allow it."

"Just let me see what I can do for him. If the captain objects, send him to me. Now, all of you, get out. Eustice and I will see to his needs."

"Very well," said the lieutenant. "I'll be on the command deck if you need anything."

"Thank you, but we'll be fine," Zollin said, shooing everyone out of his cabin.

Once he had the door shut, he turned to Eustice.

"Make sure no one comes in until I'm finished."

The mute servant nodded and Zollin sat down beside his friend. He let his magic flow into Mansel's body. Mansel had lost consciousness on deck, so Zollin first let his magic sweep through the entire body. Three ribs were broken and two others were cracked. There was some minor internal bleeding, and Mansel's collarbone was broken. Zollin's first job was to mend the bones. It was a simple process now that he was accustomed to doing it. It took longer to relax the muscles that were in spasm and to remove the buildup of fluids that was causing the bruising. Zollin decided he couldn't heal the bruising completely—if he did, the crew would discover his powers. Zollin wasn't ashamed of being a wizard, or afraid of the crew for that matter, but he didn't want to send the sailors into a panic of fear. Rumors of the sea monster attack had included his magic, and there was no need to deal with superstitious sailors if he could avoid it.

The internal bleeding keep Zollin busy the longest. He had to delve deep into the tissues around Mansel's ribs to find exactly what was wrong. Once he isolated the bleeding, however, he was able to repair the damage. He could feel the hot wind of his magic coursing through the containment field he had surrounded it with. Soon, everything about Mansel seemed to be okay.

"I'm done," he said, sagging back against the opposite bunk.

Eustice had a small goblet of wine ready and handed it to Zollin.

"Thanks," he said, then took a long drink. "He's going to be fine. I couldn't heal him completely without giving away—"

Wham! Wham! Wham!

"This is the captain," came an angry voice. "I'm coming in."

Eustice started to hold the door closed but Zollin waved him off. The captain stepped boldly into the small cabin. The lieutenant waited outside with two other sailors.

"Has he said anything?" the captain asked.

"No, he's resting," Zollin said. "I've inspected his injuries. There's nothing serious about his wounds. Just some minor cuts and bruises, but he was covered in filth. I'd like to watch him and make sure he doesn't get sick."

"That won't be necessary," the captain said. "I won't let the crew be a burden to our passengers."

"It's no trouble," Zollin said.

"No, it won't be. Thank you for your help..."

"Zollin, my name is Zollin Quinnson."

"Very well, Zollin," the captain said. "Alright, get him up," he said to the sailors out in the passageway.

Zollin stood back and watched as two men in threadbare clothes came into the room. One had a livid scar across his cheek and shot Zollin a baleful glance before grabbing Mansel roughly by the arms. They pulled him off the bunk and he slowly came to.

"What's going on?" he mumbled.

"You're in for it now," said the man with the scar. "The captain don't abide fighting on board his ship."

"Stow that talk, Ulber, and get him down to the surgeon."

"Captain, may I have a word with you?" Zollin asked.

"Of course," he said, waving his men away.

"I get the impression that you aren't happy with that sailor."

"Yes," the captain said, with a trying look on his face as if he were indulging an inquisitive child.

"Is there a reason? The man was obviously accosted by someone."

"No, I'm afraid that's not how he came to his injuries. He's a new member of the crew. I'll see to it that he knows his business from now on. And I'll get our carpenter up here to repair this furniture."

"I'm sorry, I don't understand. Are you saying he wasn't attacked?"

"Master Quinnson, it isn't my practice to share details of the crew with passengers, but if you must know, your patient attacked one of the other sailors with a mallet. There was a scuffle and your patient fell down the bilge shaft. It was an unfortunate break in shipboard discipline and I shall see that it is corrected immediately. Good day."

Zollin was so surprised that the captain was out of the cabin before Zollin realized it. He hurried after the man.

"Captain, I don't think you have the whole story," Zollin said, hurrying up behind the officer.

"No, I'm sure I don't. But I will very soon. Please don't continue to worry about that sailor. He's my responsibility, and I'll see to it that he's dealt with in a fashion that befits the dignity of this ship."

"I'd like to go with you if you're going to question him," Zollin said.

"Absolutely not. Now excuse me," the captain said gruffly.

Zollin started to push a magical suggestion toward the man when a voice spoke up from behind him.

"Let the captain deal with his men as he see's fit," said the icy voice. "And be so kind as to remove yourself from the passageway."

Zollin turned and found the woman he'd seen the day they'd set sail. She was tall and fine featured, but her face was pinched in a look of complete disdain. Her narrow nose was held high and there were two brutish looking armed men behind her.

"Excuse me?" Zollin said.

"Stand aside, if you please," the woman said angrily. "It seems you are always in the passageway. I wish to go on deck."

Zollin glanced back toward the captain, but he had already ascended the stairs to the main deck. Zollin turned back to Eustice, who was waiting in the doorway to their cabin.

"Come on, Eustice, this isn't over."

They hurried out of the passageway and came out on deck. The sky was dark with heavy, gray clouds hanging low overhead. In the rigging the sailors were busy taking in the sails. The captain and his lieutenant were walking quickly back up to the command deck.

"Ahem!" came the woman's voice from below them. "Once again you are blocking the way."

Zollin realized he was standing at the top of the stairwell. He took Eustice by the arm and they stepped aside. The woman walked briskly past and went straight to the command deck, followed by her bodyguards and then Zollin.

The woman ascended the stairs and then went immediately to the ship rail. Zollin watched her go and then turned to the captain.

"Sir, I must protest—"

"No, sir, you must not," said the captain angrily. "There is a storm coming, in case you hadn't noticed. We have perhaps half an hour before we're in the thick of it. I suggest you go back to your cabin, make sure your belongings are stowed away safely, and latch the shutters on your porthole."

"I'm not going to stand aside—" Zollin started, but once again he was cut off.

"You shall stand aside," shouted the captain angrily. "You will not interfere with this ship in any way. Nor shall you continue to plague me with your questions. Now go below, or I'll have you locked in chains and taken below. Is that clear?"

Zollin felt his magic raging and he wanted more than anything to set it loose on the captain, but he knew better than to push his luck. He could fight the captain and the sailors on board the ship, but he couldn't sail the vessel in calm waters, much less through a storm.

As he turned to leave the deck he wondered exactly what kind of mess Mansel had gotten himself into this time.

Chapter 7

Rain began to fall before Zollin got back to the passenger deck. He turned to look at the woman on the command deck, expecting to see her hurrying after him, but she was still by the ship rail. Her hair was expertly combed and held in place by expensive ivory combs. She wore a beautiful silk dress and dainty shoes that Zollin had only seen on the wealthiest nobles in Orrock, yet she stood with her face pointing toward the sky, a look of rapture on her face.

"What the hell is she doing?" Zollin asked.

Eustice merely shrugged his shoulders and hurried down the stairs to the passenger deck. The raindrops were fat and cold. Zollin looked up and saw that all the sails had been taken in except the smaller sails at the top of the masts. The sailors were hurrying down from the rigging as the lieutenant barked his orders. Zollin was getting soaked, but he continued to watch the activity on the ship. Any loose materials were quickly carried down to the 'tween decks areas, and trapdoors were being closed and latched.

A sailor hurried to where Zollin stood at the top of the stairs and shouted to him. "Best go below sir, this looks to be a bad 'un," the sailor cried.

Zollin glanced back at the command deck and saw the woman still at the rail. He made a quick decision then and stepped away from the stairs. "No, I want to stay out here."

"It's not safe, sir."

"I'll chance it," Zollin said, heading back toward the command deck.

The rain was falling in heavy sheets now and the wind was starting to pick up. Zollin was cold, and it was difficult to climb the stairs as the ship lurched in the heavy waves.

The captain shot Zollin a dirty look, but Zollin sent peaceful thoughts toward the officer with his magic as he circled the helm and went to the ship's rail not far from the woman. He thought she was arrogant and rude, but she was also very attractive. As much as he didn't want to be, he found himself hoping that she might be attracted to him. He didn't know what to think of that, but the storm soon made it too rough to think about anything other than survival.

Zollin held onto the rail with a tight grip and did his best to keep his balance as the ship rose and fell on the waves. It was only a few more minutes before the wind began to howl, blowing the rain so that it fell at such an odd angle that Zollin thought it was falling sideways. He was beginning to wonder what crazy thought had prompted him to stay out of his cabin when he heard the woman laughing.

It was hard to see in the rain, but Zollin held his hands up to block the rain and he could see the woman gripping the rail with one hand and laughing like a child. He'd seen similar looks from children riding a horse for the first time. It was as if she was experiencing something thrilling and wonderful, but Zollin was just cold, wet, and frightened. The sea had turned so dark it was almost black, and the water on the crests of the waves was white, highlighting the towering walls of water. The ship rose and fell so steeply that it was hard for Zollin to keep from falling over.

Like the woman, the captain and the lieutenant were standing easily, with just one hand each on the post in front of the helmsman's large wooden ship's wheel. They seemed unfazed by the wind and rain whipping into their faces. The woman's two guards were struggling as much as Zollin was. They had both hands on the railing, and one even knelt on the deck to escape the worst of the raging wind.

Zollin's magic was churning. Strong emotions seemed to stoke the magical fires that burned in him. He had been angry before, but now he was scared. The ship, which had seemed massive at first, now seemed tiny and weak before the anger of the sea. Zollin looked east for the coast, but he could just barely make out the Walheta Mountains. He thought briefly about the fact that he was leaving Yelsia for the first time in his life. The thought was both frightening and exciting, but the storm made it seem more monumental somehow.

Soon the waves towered over the ship and more often than not crashed onto the main deck. Zollin was fascinated to watch the seawater slosh across the deck and drain out of the scuppers along the ship railing. Luckily the waves normally broke over the front of the ship, and since the command deck was at the rear of the vessel, Zollin only had to worry about staying on his feet and not being rocked overboard.

The worst of the storm only lasted a few minutes, but it was a full hour before the seas calmed enough that the captain ordered his men to open up the hatches. Zollin was soaked and very cold. He hurried down to his cabin and stripped out of his wet clothes.

"That was a complete waste of time," he said, his teeth chattering.

Eustice wrapped a blanket around his shoulders and Zollin knelt down and kindled a small flame in midair, directly in front of him. He rubbed the blanket over his head to help dry his hair and then dressed in dry clothes. He could have used magic to dry his wet clothes, but then he might have to explain how the clothes got dry so quickly.

"I think that woman is insane," Zollin went on. "At least the storm is giving Mansel some time to figure things out. I hate that something happened to him. I can't imagine anyone giving him that much trouble. They must have ambushed him or something."

Eustice nodded, but didn't add much to the conversation. At first the eunuch's silence had bothered Zollin. His sense of justice couldn't stand the thought that someone had been so cruel as to cut off part of his tongue. It just reaffirmed his opinion about Offendorl and the Torr. He'd been right not to go to the Torr when they had come for him in his village almost a year ago, but resistance had cost them all so much. People had died who could have lived if he'd gone, and it seemed that everywhere Zollin went magical beings appeared, many of them viciously cruel. Still, he knew that much worse could have been done if he was under the evil wizard Offendorl's control. Eustice was living proof of that. The wizards of the Torr had no regard for non-magical people. They were just pawns to be used and cast aside, regardless of their well-being.

Zollin squatted by his magical fire again, holding his hands close to the flames. He was thinking hard about how to help Mansel. He needed to find his friend and see what they could do to get him out of the mess he had landed in.

"We have to find a way to help Mansel," Zollin said to Eustice, who nodded in agreement. "I'm not sure what the captain has in mind, but he obviously felt like Mansel did something wrong. We can't let them hurt him anymore."

Eustice was still nodding when someone knocked on the door. Zollin looked surprised and snuffed his magical fire as Eustice opened the door.

"Hello," said the woman who'd been on deck. Her hair was still wet and her clothes were dripping water onto the wooden floor. She looked at Zollin for a moment with an appraising eye and then said, "I love the storms at sea. They make me feel more alive than almost anything else. I think perhaps company would be nice. Will you join me for dinner?"

Zollin couldn't believe what he was hearing. The woman had been rude before, and now here she was asking him to dinner. He had half a mind to tell her off, but the other half was lonely. He missed Brianna so much. Her tender smile, the way she made him feel about himself, the excitement of holding her close and feeling her soft lips on his. The woman in his doorway didn't make him feel the same way, but it was similar, and he couldn't refuse it.

"Yes," was all Zollin managed to say.

"Good," the woman smiled. "Meet me in my cabin in half an hour."

She walked quickly away, leaving a trail of water behind her. Zollin stood as still as a stone, flabbergasted at what just happened. Eustice was looking at him questioningly, but Zollin had no idea what had prompted the woman's change of heart.

"I don't know," he said. "I didn't even speak to her outside. I just went up on the command deck to see what was going on. She just stood by the railing and laughed. She thought the storm was funny, I guess. I found it terrifying."

Zollin sank onto his bunk as Eustice hung the wet clothes to dry. He'd grown used to letting Eustice do most of the chores. He'd tried to get Eustice to stay in Yelsia. He'd argued that Eustice didn't have to be a servant, and even though the eunuch insisted on staying with Zollin and Mansel, Zollin had tried to keep him from doing the small labors around their camp. But then it occurred to Zollin that it was Eustice's only way to contribute. So he'd spoken to Mansel, and although they never ordered Eustice to do anything, the mute servant happily took care of them.

Guilt was plaguing Zollin. He wanted to have dinner with the woman from the storm, but he felt like he was betraying Brianna. He didn't even know if she was dead, although whenever he considered that he felt like a fool. Of course she was dead, he thought to himself. The dragon, which Zollin now thought of as

Offendorl's dragon, had almost certainly killed her. And if he'd left her in the mountains, she wouldn't have survived on her own. She had no way to hunt or protect herself. She had no gear to scale the treacherous mountain heights. And there were no reports of her anywhere in Yelsia. If she'd managed to make it to one of the villages, she would have come to Orrock, or at the very least sent word. Still there was a little part of Zollin that refused to believe she was gone, and it was furious that Zollin dared to have dinner with someone else.

It isn't romantic, he told himself, although he hoped that it would turn romantic. The woman was beautiful, and Zollin couldn't help but hope she found him attractive. He felt a little like a child seeking approval, but the thought of the woman being attracted to him was much more exciting. It made him feel strong and somehow confident, even though he was also scared of doing something that would break the tenuous connection he had formed with her.

Finally he stood up.

"Well, that's settled then. I'll go to dinner with this woman. You take a stroll on the deck and see if you can learn anything about Mansel."

Eustice nodded his head and Zollin ran his fingers through his hair. The little cabin had no mirror, and neither Zollin nor Eustice had included one in their supplies. He used his hands to make sure no part of his hair was standing out at an odd angle.

"How do I look?" he asked Eustice.

The mute servant smiled and nodded, giving him a thumbs up gesture.

"Okay," he said, "I guess I'm going to dinner."

Zollin walked down the passageway toward the double doors of the cabin where he knew the woman was staying. He could hear the moans of seasick passengers as he passed their rooms. The storm obviously had made some of them sick again. He'd seen the other passengers occasionally walking the deck, but knew some of them had been too sick to leave their cabins. The passageway seemed long and his nerves grew more jittery with every step. Guilt warred with excitement as he approached the doors. He took a deep breath before knocking firmly.

It was only a moment before the door was swung open by one of the lady's guards. He was a well built man, and well armed as well. He didn't smile or speak, but merely stepped aside. The lady's cabin was much larger than Zollin's. There were padded chairs, rugs, a long dining table and two large portholes. The lady came sweeping out of one of the side rooms. She was in a new dress with a low neckline and a billowing skirt. She wore a pearl necklace and matching earrings. Her hair was dry now, and pinned up with small, exotic looking combs. She smiled, revealing white teeth, but the gesture made her look almost menacing, like a wolf eyeing its next meal.

"We haven't been formally introduced," she said. "My name is Roleena of Shupor."

"It is nice to meet you," Zollin said, feeling more self-conscious by the minute. "I'm Zollin Quinnson."

"I hope you're hungry, Zollin," she said, taking his hand and leading him to the dining table. "A good storm always gets my appetite up. You don't get seasick, do you?"

"No," Zollin said.

"Good."

He pulled out her chair for her at the head of the long table and then took a seat beside her.

"Are you traveling somewhere in particular?" he asked, immediately feeling embarrassed by the question.

"Aren't we all, Zollin?" she said, fixing him with a piercing stare.

"I just…" He struggled to find the words. "What I meant was, where are you going?"

"Oh, that is a good question. I'm going to Brimington Bay. And you?"

"We're going to Brimington Bay too," he said.

A servant appeared with wine. It was an older man, walking slowly, his back straight and stiff. He carried a bottle of wine and two crystal goblets. He also had a white towel draped over one arm.

"This is Marcus, my personal valet," Roleena explained. "He's cooked us quite a meal this evening."

"Thank you, my lady," Marcus said in a deep voice.

He sat the bottle of wine down on the table and removed the cork with a little tool. Then he turned to Zollin and sat the cork down and waited. Zollin wasn't sure what to do. He enjoyed a glass of wine, especially after working magic. Stronger alcohol didn't appeal to him, and in fact many wines were too pungent for his taste. He felt embarrassed and yet frozen in panic at the same time.

"Would you care to inspect the cork?" Roleena asked.

"No, I'm not a connoisseur."

Roleena smiled as if Zollin had just affirmed what she already knew. Zollin had spent time with King Felix, as well as some of his nobles and the generals of his army, but none of them had taken on airs the way Roleena was doing.

"That's fine," she said. "This is a very nice red, from Ortis. I find their wine delicate, but with a complexity of flavor."

Zollin nodded, still not sure what to say. He watched as Marcus poured the wine from the bottle into a large, strangely shaped glass decanter. Then he left the room.

"Marcus enjoys the appropriate decorum. In fact, he feels that by inviting you here for dinner alone I've been too forward. I hope you don't agree," she said.

"No, of course not. I'm from a small village. I don't know much about decorum."

"Well, I sensed that perhaps you were a kindred spirit when you joined me on the command deck during the storm. Most people prefer to hide in their cabins, but I feel that a storm is one of the rare occasions that make sea travel so exquisite. Wouldn't you agree?"

"This is my first sea trip," Zollin admitted. "But I've never experienced anything like the storm. It was…" he searched for the right word. He felt like admitting that it was terrifying wouldn't be welcome. "Exhilarating," he said.

"Yes, I thought you would understand," she said, her smile seeming sincere for the first time that evening. "Would you mind to pour the wine?"

"Of course," Zollin said.

He lifted the ornate bottle and poured the wine into Roleena's goblet. Then he poured some in his own. He was surprised when Roleena tilted her goblet slightly and put her nose so far into the glass that it almost touched the wine. Then she sat back in her seat and swirled the wine before taking a sip.

"Well?" she asked. "What do you think? It's much better than the swill they serve in the inns at the Twin Cities."

Zollin took a sip, but all he could tell was that it tasted like wine. He could taste the grape flavor even though the liquid seemed to burn its way down his throat. He waited for a moment for the familiar heat to spread through his body. It mingled with the heat from his magic in a way that he could only describe as delicious.

"I think you like it," she said with a small giggle. "To be honest, I didn't think you would."

"I like wine," Zollin said. "But I admit I haven't had the chance to travel much. I haven't tried many wines. This is my first from outside Yelsia."

"Oh, no," Roleena said. "There are many things that our fellow countrymen do quite well, but winemaking isn't one of them." She smiled, sipping more wine. "What is it that takes you to Osla, Zollin? You're a healer, right?"

"Yes, but I dabble in a lot of things. This trip is just routine business," he said. "And you?"

"My mother requires silks from Osla. She won't wear anything else. I make the trip three or four times a year, depending on how often she wants new clothes."

"Oh, that's…nice of you," Zollin managed to say. The idea of buying clothes more than once a year would have made Quinn laugh out loud.

Marcus came back into the main room of the cabin carrying a large platter. It had several small birds neatly arranged with vegetables and a dark sauce. He sat the platter down and slowly walked away.

"Doves," Roleena said, "excellent."

Marcus returned with plates and served their food. He was slow and deliberate, even though the ship was rocking more than normal from the recent storm.

They ate quietly, no one speaking. Zollin was very aware of the guard near the door, and that Marcus was watching his every move from across the room. Zollin felt like he should initiate more conversation, but with so many spectators he felt it wiser to concentrate on eating. He had just finished his first dove, which was a small bird, so getting the meat off the bones without snapping them into splinters was a delicate job. He wasn't quite full, but he decided to finish eating before he did something truly embarrassing. He had just slid back his plate and wiped his mouth with the linen napkin Marcus had given him when there was a banging at the door.

The guard drew his long dagger and the other guard came running from one of the side rooms. Marcus seemed shocked but Roleena continued eating as if nothing had happened. She nibbled her food in small, quick bites.

The banging intensified and Zollin stood up. One of the guards flung open the door and Eustice appeared. He looked disheveled and as near panic as Zollin had ever seen him.

"Eustice," Zollin said loudly. "What is going on?"

Eustice pushed his way past the guards and hurried to Zollin, gesturing madly. He kept pointing up at the ceiling.

"What is it?" Zollin said. "You have to slow down. I don't understand."

Eustice was making a worried moan. He grabbed Zollin's arm and started pulling him toward the door.

"You can't leave," Roleena said so simply it was as if she was discussing the weather.

"I have to," Zollin said. "You can see something has happened."

"I'm sure," Roleena said. "But it is unimportant. You will stay, my guards will see to that."

Zollin was surprised. He couldn't imagine what was going on to get Eustice so worked up, and Roleena's response didn't make any sense at all. It was as if she had expected something like this to happen. Then it hit Zollin. He couldn't believe that he hadn't recognized that he had been set up. The captain must have asked

Roleena to keep Zollin occupied. Roleena's invitation was much too out of the blue to be coincidence. In fact, she hadn't shown any interest in Zollin whatsoever before knocking on his door. He should have seen that it was a setup from the start, but the truth was, he wanted her to like him. He wanted to think that he could attract a woman as beautiful and sophisticated as Roleena. It was what he wanted, so he hadn't questioned it. And then the awful truth of what was happening set in. Zollin couldn't guess what was going on above them on the main deck, but he was sure it had something to do with Mansel.

His friend had sacrificed so much on this trip, and here Zollin was eating and drinking, thinking only of himself.

"No, they won't stop us," Zollin said grimly. "Call them off and they won't get hurt." For the first time Roleena laughed a genuine laugh.

"I warned you," Zollin said.

He marched toward the guards, both of whom had their daggers drawn now. They watched him approach with gleeful expressions that reminded Zollin of the way cats watched a cornered mouse. He smiled in return, knowing they were underestimating him.

He waved a hand and both men were knocked off their feet by an invisible wave of magical force. He heard Roleena's laughter stop suddenly. Zollin turned to her and smiled.

"Thank you for a memorable evening," he said coldly.

She looked so pale Zollin thought she might pass out. Eustice was tugging him through the doorway. They were a few paces down the passageway when one of Roleena's guards ran headlong into the shield Zollin had erected behind him. There was a crunching sound followed by a grunt of pain as the guard fell to the rough wooden floor. Zollin didn't bother to turn.

He and Eustice hurried up on deck and were shocked to see a mass of sailors all crowded near the stairs that led up to the command deck. Zollin glanced up and saw the ship's captain staring balefully down at someone near the stairs. Zollin didn't have to look to know that it was Mansel. He was being tied to a large post while another sailor uncoiled a wicked looking strap that was cut on one end into six individual ribbon-like sections, each one weighted down with a bit of metal.

The ship's lieutenant had been watching the stairwell to the passenger deck and leaned over to whisper in the captain's ear.

Zollin began pushing his way through the mob of sailors. Just as he made it to the clearing, the captain spoke.

"This is a ship matter and is strictly off limits to all passengers," he bellowed. "Remove yourself or I'll have you removed."

"Captain," Zollin said loudly. "This man is under my care and I'll not see him harmed. Your men have already beaten him."

"Seize him," the captain shouted. "Lock him in irons and carry him below."

Three sailors came forward but Zollin's anger was causing his magic to rage. It flooded through him, appearing on his skin, snapping and popping. The energy looked like lightning and began to singe his clothes, adding smoke to the already frightening appearance. The sailors faltered and hesitated, but the man with the whip, the one with the long scar on his cheek, swung the "cat's tail," as the sailors called it. The ribbon-like ends rushed forward and were caught in an invisible grip just before they reached Zollin. He raised his hand and the whip was jerked magically from the sailor's grip.

Then Zollin focused on the ropes holding Mansel. He was still sore and bruised, but he had no major injuries and Zollin was sure he could fend for himself. Zollin caused the rope to burst apart and Mansel turned around, facing the crowd of sailors.

"Who did it?" Zollin asked.

"This one," Mansel said, pointing at the man with the scar on his cheek. "They call him Slice. He hit me from behind with a club."

"Well, teach him some manners," Zollin said.

"Gladly," Mansel agreed, rolling his arms to loosen the muscles in his shoulders.

"Belay that!" shouted the captain. "I'll have no more fighting on my ship."

"But you'll have an innocent man tied to a post and whipped bloody?" Zollin shouted back. "Did you even give Mansel a chance to explain what happened?"

"You don't give orders here," the captain growled. "I want them both in chains. Now!"

Zollin looked around at the sailors. They were afraid and none of them seemed ready to move against him, but Zollin knew it would only take one person moving forward to help them find their courage.

Zollin let his magic go, shooting crackling bolts of energy high into the evening sky. It wasn't dark yet, the sun was just halfway into the sea far to the west, but the magical energy lit up the deck just the same. Then Zollin looked back up at the captain.

"Don't be a fool," he said. "Your men nearly beat Mansel to death. It wasn't a fair fight and Mansel didn't start it, but he's sure as hell going to finish it."

The captain looked frightened and didn't speak. Zollin turned and nodded at Mansel, and the big warrior rushed forward. The sailor named Slice wasn't a coward. Zollin had expected him to run away or fall on his knees to beg for mercy, but Slice stood his ground. At the last instant, Slice drew a small knife, surprising Zollin but not Mansel.

The big warrior spun to the side just as Slice tried to stab him. Mansel grabbed the sailor's arm and twisted. The knife flew to the deck and Slice was flipped over. He landed hard on his back. Mansel was on top of him in an instant, dropping hard punches that found their way through the sailor's arms, which he was holding over his head in a feeble defense. Blood spurted from a cut under Slice's right eye. His lips split and a tooth was knocked out before finally Slice's eyes rolled back and his body stiffened as he lost consciousness.

Mansel could have kept up the beating—he was certainly angry enough, and no one was willing to even try to stop him. But instead he stood up and looked down at Slice, spitting on the wretched sailor and then looking up at Zollin.

"Does anyone else have an issue with this man?" Zollin shouted, pointing at Mansel.

Most of the sailors looked down at their feet. Zollin looked up at the captain, who was so angry he was red in the face.

"You have a good crew here, Captain," Zollin continued. "Treat them the way they deserve or next time it may be you who gets what he has coming."

Zollin turned and started back toward the passenger deck.

"And just where do you think you're going?" hissed the captain.

Zollin turned but the sailing master wasn't talking to him. Instead, he was glaring hatefully at Mansel.

"Get below deck and back to work, all of you!" shouted the captain.

Zollin was about to complain, but Mansel stopped him.

"It's okay," he said. "I signed on to work this voyage. I can do my part."

"You sure?" Zollin asked.

"Of course," Mansel said smiling. "These guys are nothing compared to your father."

Chapter 8

Gwendolyn could not remember ever being so happy. She had expected a vicious fight when she returned to the Torr. She had thought that perhaps the army she had led could somehow best her old master. Offendorl had brought her to the Torr as a young girl and had learned to control Gwendolyn's power. For over a century she had lived in isolation, trained by Offendorl alone. No other man had been allowed to enter her chambers in the tower, not even the eunuch servants. She lived with Andomina as her only companion, but from an early age Gwendolyn's sorcery robbed her sister of the ability to communicate. So Gwendolyn had grown old and then learned the spells that could make her body young again. Her mind, however, was stunted and twisted. In some ways she was like a spoiled child, and in others she was like an ancient crone.

What Gwendolyn hadn't expected was to find the tower of Torr undefended. It wasn't deserted, alchemists still labored on the lower levels, but they were of no concern to Gwendolyn. Only the wretched souls in the labyrinth of corridors and chambers under the tower were of value to the sorceress. Gwendolyn could feel them. Offendorl had hidden the warlocks from her before. Most were insane, or catatonic like Andomina, and none of them able to wield or even control their magical power. As a sorcerer, Gwendolyn could control and manipulate other magic users, especially warlocks, and she understood why Offendorl had shielded them from her. She could feel her power growing as they drew near the city.

Prince Wilam had seen to the deployment of their troops, but aside from a small battalion of reserve guards, there was no army to keep them from marching in and taking over the city.

The Grand City of Osla was by far the largest city in the Five Kingdoms. The city was old and patched together like a quilt as new developments were built and then walls extended to protect and include the growth. Gwendolyn's army was actually the military forces from Ortis and a band of merchants, sailors, and skilled workers from the city of Lodenhime in Falxis. Every man that came within sight of Gwendolyn was soon captured under her spell. They gave up all other interests and pursuits, choosing instead to give everything in a vain hope of winning her heart.

Prince Wilam was the crown prince of Yelsia who had fallen under her power when he came to Lodenhime on his way back to his own country. Since then, he'd worked tirelessly to build and develop Gwendolyn's army. When King Oveer had fallen under Gwendolyn's power, he had ordered his army, even the reserve troops used to maintain peace and guard the Wilderlands from the Norsik, to follow Gwendolyn. He had no desire to lead the army, and so Prince Wilam had taken up the role of High General, with only Gwendolyn—Queen of the Sea, as many described her—over him in command.

They had sacked the city when they found it unguarded. The reserve troop surrendered and was brought under Gwendolyn's spell. The people of the city were slaughtered. Many fled, while others were enslaved by Gwendolyn's power and set about serving her every need, including feeding her army. The women of the city were driven out or killed. Soldiers now patrolled the walls to the city and Gwendolyn was given free reign of the tower of the Torr.

She had expected the remaining servants and apprentice wizards to resist her, but they had not. Instead, they welcomed her, perhaps because of her power, but she thought it was because they were relieved to have a new master. She had seized control of the tower and moved immediately to the upper floors. Her old chamber had been one of many on the third floor of the tower, but the upper floors were wide open rooms that took up the entire space. There was no staircase in Offendorl's audience chamber, merely a hole in the ceiling above the throne-like chair that her old master had occupied when greeting visitors, be they kings or servants. No one was allowed in the upper two floors and Gwendolyn was anxious to find out why.

She had explored the lower floors, finding small libraries and ornate shrines, most of which were worth more gold than a mortal could spend in a lifetime. When the Torr had purged the Five Kingdoms of magic users they had consolidated all known magical books, along with anything else they wanted in the tower. It had given them unsurpassed power and sent the Five Kingdoms into an era of waning magic. All that had changed when Zollin defied the Torr. In less than a year everything had changed, and Gwendolyn was determined that she would never submit to anyone ever again.

She levitated through the hole into Offendorl's personal chambers. Then she raised up her sister. Andomina was tucked quietly into a richly upholstered chair while Gwendolyn explored her old master's domicile. There was a richness to the furnishings the likes of which Gwendolyn had never imagined. The floor was covered with thick rugs that depicted epic battles from long ago. There were large mirrors on one section of the wall. A large tub near a window. A huge poster bed with a thick canopy and heavy drapes. There was a row of wardrobes along another section of the curving walls. The wardrobes were custom made to fit against the walls, with large drawers at the bottom and even bigger storage spaces above the racks of clothes. Another part of the wall was taken up by a huge wine rack. The bottles were old and dusty. Beside the wine rack was a small table with golden goblets covered in bright jewels. There were also large windows, almost floor to ceiling. Osla was a hot country with rarely any respite from the high temperatures, but the tower was tall enough that a breeze blew almost constantly through the open windows, keeping Offendorl's chambers pleasantly cool.

There was another hole in the ceiling leading to the top floor. Gwendolyn rose slowly into the final room. It was just as she had hoped it would be—a simple yet magnificent library. There was a large desk near one of the two windows. The room was warmer, but it wouldn't do to have papers flapping in the wind, not when many of the books in that room were older than remembering. There was also a large table where charts or maps could be unrolled and studied. As Gwendolyn had suspected, the room was spotless, although she doubted that anyone had been allowed in this room other than Offendorl since he'd become the master of the Torr.

She walked slowly around the room, studying the books. Some were bound in leather, others had bindings of slate or even precious metals. Some books were covered in exotic animal skins, eel, mud dragon, whale, and even human skin. She felt giddy as she walked around and around the room, letting her fingers rub lightly over the ancient tomes. She had everything she needed to defeat her master, she knew that without a doubt. All she needed now was time.

***

The ship had navigated the narrow channel that led from the coast to Brimington Bay.

Offendorl was eager, but his strength was only just returning. He had spent the rest of the voyage resting and eating. The captain had kept him fed with rich food and wine that wasn't great, yet wasn't horrible either. Offendorl had walked the deck every day, trying his best to seem strong, but secretly struggling to maintain the illusion. Offendorl was anxious to get back to the Torr, to regain his true strength and then face Zollin again. So much had slipped through his fingers of late, but he felt certain he could retain everything and more if he could bring the young wizard under his control.

He was ready now to find passage back to the Grand City, and he waited, conserving his strength, at the rail of the ship as the captain oversaw the handling of the jolly boat that would row him from the deep waters of the harbor to the quay. When the boat was ready, Offendorl levitated himself into the boat from the deck of the ship. The sailors were all too happy to be rid of him. They were a superstitious lot and had done everything to see to Offendorl's comfort since he had revealed his power to them. They rowed him to shore almost in a frenzy to be rid of him, but Offendorl didn't mind. In fact, he rather enjoyed it when the mortals around him lived in a state of constant fear.

The elder wizard walked to a nearby rickshaw, which was a light cart with a covered seat pulled by a man on foot that were a common form of transportation in the larger cities of Osla, where just walking down the street could drench a man in sweat during the hottest parts of the day. Offendorl ordered the rickshaw puller to take him to the nicest inn in the city. It took nearly ten minutes, and the man pulling the rickshaw was panting from exertion by the time they arrived.

The inn was an old building, but Offendorl could tell immediately that it was opulent. He was met at the door by a tall man who offered to carry Offendorl's belongings, but the elder wizard ignored him. Unlike the inns in the north, which were focused around large fireplaces, the common room of this inn was on an elevated platform and the walls were mere panels with hinges at the top so that they could be propped open to let the breeze flow through.

Offendorl was alone in the large room and settled himself into a padded seat. He pulled one of the gold nuggets from a small purse inside his shirt and set it on the table.

A woman appeared in short order with a tall glass of blue crystal, filled with an effervescent beverage. She set the glass on the table and made the gold disappear almost like a traveling illusionist.

"I require a room and a bath," Offendorl said. "And I want to arrange transportation to the Grand City in the next few days—something comfortable."

"It will be my pleasure," the woman said, bowing slightly then hurrying away.

Offendorl sampled the beverage. It was fruity and cool, but not entirely to his liking. Still, he was glad to be off the dreadful ship. The vessel had begun to stink and the tiny cabin he occupied was about to drive him insane. He enjoyed the shady common room of the inn with its view of the surrounding city. It wasn't taller than the buildings around it, but being elevated from the street level gave Offendorl a sense of familiarity.

Soon the woman returned and led him to a large room with marble floors and long brass tubs filled with water.

"Do you prefer a cool refreshing bath, or a hot relaxing soak?" she asked.

"Give me something cool," he said. "And have these clothes washed as well."

The woman helped Offendorl undress. He had neither modesty nor sexual desire—his body was well past its ability to be moved by the presence of a woman. He climbed carefully into a tub of cool water while the woman poured in salts that dissolved and filled the bath with bubbles. She also added mint, which gave the bath a pleasant scent as well as a refreshing coolness. Then, as he sank into the bath, she walked away.

It wasn't long before the water had darkened from the dirt and grime of his travels. He moved to another tub and allowed two young serving girls to gently wash him with soaps and then pour pitchers of water over his body to wash the soap away. Then they wrapped him in a simple robe made from a light material that wicked the moisture from his body.

He was taken to a room on the third floor where he propped himself on pillows across the large feather bed and waited for his evening meal. He was tired, but he was close to the end of his journey. He felt better than he had in weeks. The bath had helped more than he had expected and he hoped with a little more time he could complete his next task. He removed the small pouch of gold nuggets. It was heavy, and hiding it from the women who had helped bathe him hadn't been easy, but with a little misdirection and magic he had accomplished it. Now he began to roll the nuggets between his palms, like a child playing with modeling clay.

He let his magic pour into the gold. His ancient body felt the pinch of too much magic. It was like pressing a blade into his stomach. The light pressure of minor magic was not painful, but as he extended his power into reshaping the gold the pressure was beginning to build. He could feel the magic taking a toll on his body, but he wasn't transmuting the gold, just reshaping it. Gold was a soft, pliable metal to begin with, so he was betting the effort wouldn't tax him greatly.

Soon he had eight pieces of pure gold, all rolled into tubes about as long as his fingers. It took more magic to meld them together, and his head spun from the effort. Luckily, a woman soon knocked softly on his door.

"Come in," he said after slipping the gold under a pillow.

She entered carrying a large tray. There was a bottle of wine, a small crystal goblet, and a large bowl of food. She sat the tray on the bed and poured the wine.

"What else can I do for you?" she said in a sultry voice.

"More food," Offendorl said through clenched teeth. He felt as though his magic was eating him alive.

"More?" she asked in surprise.

"Yes, I require more food," he said crossly. "Now go."

She hurried from the room and he watched her go before sagging back against the pillows. He knew his work was going to be difficult, but he felt old and weak. Fear crept into his mind, taunting him. He was close to death, it whispered. He had pushed himself too far and now he was dying.

He shook the morbid thoughts away and took a long drink of the wine, almost emptying his cup. The wine helped. He devoured the food, hardly tasting it. His body seemed to absorb the nutrients instantly. He felt better but his body was crying out for more. He had finished the food and almost the entire bottle of wine when the woman returned.

She had another bowl of food, but no more wine.

"I need more wine as well," he told her. "In fact, keep bringing it to me until I tell you to stop."

"As you wish," she said.

He waved her away and ate the second bowl of food, finally feeling sated and ready to try using his magic again. He pulled the long strip of gold out from under his pillow. It was thin, certainly not as heavy as the first crown he had fashioned. Still, it was big enough to do the job, and he let his magic flow into the metal, bending it into a circle. When he was finished, he sagged back once again, his heart thundering in his chest and his lungs heaving to get enough air.

It was probably the ugliest crown ever made, he thought to himself, but it was finished. He drank the last of his wine, although the dregs were bitter with sediment. Then he hid the crown and waited for the woman to bring more wine. She did, and another bowl of food as well. He drank first, letting the alcohol spread through his system. Then he ate again, this time more slowly. The bowl was some type of seafood stew. He enjoyed the rich taste of the stew this time, noting how well made the meal was. When the woman returned with a third bottle of wine and a fourth bowl of food, he told her he didn't need more.

When she left, he finished the second bottle of wine. Normally, that much wine would have left him a little drunk and very relaxed, but not now. His body trembled and felt weak, with food being the only remedy. He thought about how Zollin must be feeling. The young wizard was like a volcano of raw, unrefined power. Still, Offendorl guessed that power would come at a price. It was difficult for the elder wizard to remember how it felt to be young. He knew that in his early years his own power taxed his physical body less than now. He was old, ancient even, but still powerful. He had equated power with strength before he fought Zollin, but now he understood the difference. In his tower, surrounded by servants and boosted by the other magical users of the Torr, his power was unmatched. But his strength was no longer sufficient to wield that power fully.

He needed to do more than extend his life. He needed to find ways to rejuvenate his physical body, to strengthen it. And he needed more magical aides if he was to fight Zollin again. He needed to be able to use power outside of his own so that it didn't weaken him so greatly. Most of all, he needed to be ready. He would have to use strategy to best the young wizard, not just magical power.

He lifted the crown and gazed at it. It took very little effort to magically inscribe the name of the dragon inside the crown. Bartoom would be waiting for him. The dragon would wait high in the Walheta Mountains until Offendorl called for him or died—it was the only way the dragon could be free of the elder wizard's power. Of course, if someone else learned the dragon's name and could inscribe it on a crown of gold, they could override Offendorl's orders, but in that case the elder wizard would know it—at least he would once he set the crown on his head. He could use the crown to boost his own magical power to call out to the dragon, to see what it saw, and to control the beast.

He sat the crown on his head and closed his eyes. His magic mingled with the innate power of the gold and then reached across the miles toward the beast. It took several minutes to find

Bartoom—the dragon was flying high in the night sky, searching for food. The Walheta did not have large game like the Northern Highland Mountains. Bartoom was lucky to find a small goat or occasionally a human scratching out a living among the barren peaks.

Bartoom, Offendorl thought, pushing his will out toward the dragon with his magic. Bartoom, search for the young wizard. He is coming south, probably by sea. You must find him and destroy him, but do not endanger yourself. Frustrate his plans, and do not wander far from him. Do you understand?

Offendorl was suddenly struck by an image of Zollin and then the sea and then fire.

Good, go my pet. Do my bidding.

The elder wizard's head was spinning. He pulled the heavy crown off his head and slumped back against the pillows. He had done it, he thought. He had done what he needed to do. He could not have risked showing how weak he was to the sailors on board the ship he had taken to Brimington Bay, but here he could rest. He could do the work that had to be done without having to explain his constant need for food and wine.

He ate the last bowl of food and drank the wine greedily. Then he fell asleep, his magic still churning and his mind trying to soothe the malice it had felt from the dragon. The beast hated him, but it would obey, and that was all that mattered to Offendorl. He didn't need love or affection—just simple, unwavering obedience.

Chapter 9

Things were different on board the Northern Star. Zollin and Eustice were treated with deference by the crew—even the first officer—but not by the captain, who avoided them. Mansel had gone back to work with the crew and found a new sense of respect among the crew. Slice recovered from his beating quickly enough, but his gang was in constant turmoil. They fought amongst themselves for supremacy while their fallen leader waited patiently, biding his time and planning his revenge.

It was three days before Zollin saw the Lady Roleena again. She was still arrogant, but she gave him a little more respect. They crossed paths on the command deck, both seeking a way to cool down in the sweltering heat. It was early autumn and in Yelsia the temperatures were falling, but the Northern Star had sailed far enough south that the days were sunny and hot still. Unfortunately, the winds had waned and the sun beat down on the ship without mercy. The ship still moved, but only in fits. The sails hung limp, only fluttering occasionally, and the captain forced his crew into boats to tow the heavy ship. It was hard, difficult work.

Mansel was called into service. He rowed until his back ached and his hand bled from blisters formed by the rough oars. It was a depressing time for all involved. Zollin was eager to reach their destination. At first, sailing had been a relaxing way to travel, but it had become tedious. Now, he longed for a good horse and the open road, although he knew that the ship could carry them south much faster than riding ever could, even if they had to suffer through a few days of calm winds.

"You could do something about this wind, couldn't you?" Roleena asked, raising an eyebrow at Zollin as they passed one another.

He ignored her comment. He could have filled the sails with magical wind, but he didn't think the effort was worth an hour of travel. He wasn't even sure he could keep up the effort that long, and he refused to tax his powers. It would only leave him weak and vulnerable. They might need his power for something else, and he didn't want to waste it.

He walked to the end of the railing and was forced to turn and walk back. He couldn't help but look at Roleena—she was beautiful, after all. Despite his attempts to ignore her, she wasn't trying to hide the fact that she was staring at him. Zollin felt a little trapped on the ship—he was used to moving on quickly after a confrontation and rarely had to deal with the infamous reputation his power earned him. On the ship though, he couldn't escape it. Rumors had spread among the other passengers, while Zollin and Mansel had become somewhat of heroes to the crew. Only Mansel's superior, Ern, the ship's carpenter, treated him the same, barking orders and checking his carpentry with a critical eye. Slice and the gang of bullies avoided Mansel, but the other sailors treated him kindly and even showed him favor in the cramped world between decks.

"Silence is a tactic I'm used to," Roleena said to Zollin as they approached one another. "I doubt you have the fortitude to try my patience."

Zollin still said nothing, he just kept walking. He wasn't normally a pacer, but he thought he would go out of his mind sitting in his cabin with Eustice. He liked the mute servant, but even though they could communicate via gestures, it was still difficult not to be able to talk.

He had just reached the end of the deck and was turning around when the sails began to flap. The big canvas sails and long lines of rigging were extremely noisy in fitful wind. When combined with creaking of the ship and the shouts of the sailors, it was sometimes difficult to think straight. Everyone stopped what they were doing and watched the sails, hoping to see them fill with wind and begin propelling the boat again. Zollin actually held his breath as the canvas flapped, whipping and popping like a sheet before it was hung to dry in the sun.

A bead of sweat rolled down Zollin's forehead and he reached up to wipe it away, when suddenly the sails billowed out and the ship lurched forward. The captain began shouting orders to the crews of the boats who were cheering the return of the wind. It took nearly half an hour to get the sailors out of the ship's boats and back on board. They used the intricate systems of pulleys to hoist the heavy, wooden boats out of the water. The Northern Star was like a stallion set free—it seemed to rush headlong over the easy sea, leaving a long, frothy wake behind it.

Zollin stayed on deck, relishing the cool breeze and the sense of momentum returning to his quest. He was leaning on the railing, watching dolphins race along beside the ship, jumping and playing in the turbulent water beside the ship's hull.

"They're amazing creatures, aren't they?" Roleena said.

Zollin looked up, frowning but not wanting to be rude.

"Yes," he said sternly.

He was angry at Roleena for using her charms on him. If Eustice hadn't come to the rescue, he'd have stayed in her cabin while Mansel was beaten for a crime he didn't commit. It made Zollin's stomach turn, but no matter how angry he was or how guilty he felt, he couldn't keep his heart from racing when Roleena was close to him.

"Oh, don't be surly," she teased. "It doesn't become you."

"I'm not trying to impress you," he said.

"Nor I you. I admit, I underestimated you. I took you for a merchant, or perhaps a healer, although I thought you much too young for that. But a wizard—now that is something. I'm rarely surprised, Zollin Quinnson, if that is your real name. I've never met a wizard before. The tricks you did with my guards were impressive. I don't believe they've ever been thwarted before. It was a blow to their egos. They've been even more sulky than you."

"I don't care," Zollin said.

"Of course you don't. You have bigger fish to fry, as the saying goes. What takes you to Osla?"

"I have business there."

"Oh, rubbish," she said. "Wizards don't conduct business, but I think I know. There is someone there you are trying to catch or kill. Isn't that what wizards do? It's all shadows and mysteries in the songs and stories, but when it comes right down to it, wizards are men. And men are all the same."

"So why bother asking?"

"I rarely do," she said. "But I must admit you intrigue me, and so few people can do that."

"You have everyone figured out?"

"For the most part, yes. In fact, I'll lay odds that you are going Osla to kill someone. Am I right?"

"It's none of your concern."

"Oh, I think it is. What if you being on this ship endangers us all somehow? I heard about the sea monster in Lorye. You were the wizard it attacked, weren't you? I doubt there are two wizards in the same kingdom, after all. I mean, we've heard rumors of dragons and wizards. My brothers took men to fight with King Felix when the armies from Osla and Falxis invaded. I heard a wizard saved the kingdom. Was that you too?"

Zollin didn't answer. He wasn't sure what was worse—being responsible for the destruction of the ship at Lorye, or being the hero of Orrock. He wasn't on good terms with the king, and although some of the people in the capital had shown him deference, most didn't even know who he was. He preferred it that way—being famous seemed overwhelming. He remembered when all he wanted was to learn more about his magic. That had been such a simple time, yet full of hope for the future and excitement just the same. He had felt that way when he thought of marrying Brianna, but now those dreams were dashed. His only hope now lay in killing the master of the Torr. It was his only chance for peace, or at least the only chance he could see.

"It was you," she said. "I know it was. My brothers sent word home. They said the wizard was a young man, that he healed the king and fought off a dragon. I'm sure they were both green with envy. They dream of greatness on the battlefield, but yet here you are, fleeing Yelsia. I wonder why?"

"I'm not fleeing anything," Zollin said.

"Of course not, but then I wonder why you weren't honest about who you were."

"Going around telling people I'm a wizard is foolish."

"Perhaps, but that doesn't stop most men from bragging about their accomplishments. How did you come to be a wizard, I wonder?"

"I don't know."

"Was your father a wizard?"

"No."

"How about your mother—was she a witch?"

Zollin didn't answer. He didn't like Roleena talking about his mother. Zollin had never known her. She had died giving birth to him and it was a deep wound in his soul. Brianna was the first woman to ease the pain he felt over not knowing his mother, but she had left a wound almost as deep.

"You don't like me talking about your mother," Roleena said, as if she had just discovered something important.

"I don't like you talking at all," Zollin said.

"Oh," Roleena said, acting as if his words had hurt her feelings. "I'm sorry, Zollin. I thought we were friends. I thought you liked me."

"No," he said. "Friends don't treat each other the way you treated me."

"I thought I was perfectly civil," she said innocently. "It was the captain who betrayed you, not me."

"Really? Then why did your guards try to keep me from leaving your cabin?"

"They must have been told to do that by the captain."

"I find that hard to believe. I doubt they take orders from anyone but you."

"It all turned out okay in the end," she said soothingly. "So, why not be friends," she placed her hand on his forearm, "or more than friends?"

Zollin looked up at Roleena, a lump forming his throat. She was beautiful, but there was a danger to her beauty, like a white wolf. He knew that getting close to her was foolish and would only end in pain, but he was tempted. A very basic part of him burned with desire for her. He wanted to take her, to make love to her, to hold her tight until all the pain and regret he felt was gone. But she was not that kind of lover, he knew. He could see the trap she was setting, see the desire was not for Zollin but for his power. She wanted to use him the way a warrior used a sword, but even knowing all of that, he still wanted her. He was wavering between what he knew to be right and what he wanted. Part of him wanted to be her lover—wouldn't that privilege be enough to satisfy him, even if all she wanted was to use him?

"Dragon!" the sailor high on the mainmast shouted down. "Dragon ho!"

Zollin looked up. The sun was setting and the light was golden, almost magical, but the sailor in the crow's nest high on top of the mast was pointing and shouting.

Zollin squinted for a moment, straining to see, but it was useless. Then he sent his magic surging out and he felt the beast. It was Bartoom, the big black dragon that had been his nemesis in the Northern Highlands. The dragon had almost killed him, but Brianna had saved him. Then she had saved the dragon, and it had taken her away. Anger burned white hot in Zollin, setting his magic into a frenzy.

Zollin looked up, hoping for clouds. He needed a way to generate lightning to drive the dragon off, but the sky was completely clear. Zollin had used the friction of the tiny particles in the clouds to create lightning in Orrock, but now he wasn't sure what to do.

"Zollin!" the captain roared. "One spark could set this whole ship ablaze."

"I'll do what I can," Zollin said. "Send for Mansel."

Zollin didn't wait for the captain to reply. Instead, he levitated himself to the crow's nest. He wasn't sure he could have climbed the rigging like the sailors, but even if could have, he wouldn't have reached the lofty perch in time. He could feel the dragon swooping toward the ship now, even though the black beast was difficult to see in the twilight. Zollin gathered his magic and sent out an invisible shield.

The dragon roared just before it spewed forth fire. Zollin heard the screams and curses below him, but the voices didn't register. The flames hit his magical shield and bounced harmlessly away, but the light from the fire showed the fearsome beast. Zollin saw the malice and hatred in the beast's eyes as it swooped past, the downdraft from its wings making the sails flutter.

The dragon disappeared into the darkness again, but Zollin tracked its motion through the night sky with his magic. His containment field was holding up well and he felt strong, although he was relieved that he hadn't wasted his strength producing wind to fill the sails. Bartoom circled back toward the ship and Zollin held one hand out, palm facing the beast, ready to produce a shield to block the flames. He was pleased to discover that blocking the dragon's fiery breath only took a fraction of his power. Unlike magical fire, the dragon's breath was not a powerful force and there was no danger of the fire knocking Zollin out of the crow's nest.

With his other hand he began to conjure his own magical energy. His power often imitated lightning. Branock, the powerful Torr wizard who had kidnapped Brianna, produced fire, and Zollin could produce a molten plasma that resembled volcanic lava, but his power in its rawest essence was like bright blue lightning. It crackled and popped up and down his body in waves now, building in force as the dragon approached. Zollin also knew that if he angled his shield the fire could be deflected with much less effort than stopping a straight-on blast. He braced his feet against the wooden frame of the crow's nest and waited.

The dragon came in low, close to the water, hoping to ignite the ship's hull, but Zollin was ready. He dropped his shield down, angling it so that the fire bounced harmlessly into the water, sending clouds of steam shooting up. The dragon stayed low, but Zollin cast his magical energy at the beast like a mythical god throwing lightning bolts. The blast of power hit the dragon on the back, scattering across the hardened scales like a web of lightning, charring the dragon's skin where it hit.

The dragon roared a high-pitched scream of pain and rage that caused most of the sailors to grab their ears. Zollin whooped for joy, realizing he'd hurt the beast in at least a small way. It was the first time he'd been able to land a blow of his own against the dragon. The beast's scales were still flashing with sparks as it flew out past the ship and beat its wings to gain altitude. Zollin wasn't positive, but he had an idea. He jumped out of the crow's nest, his heart hammering even as he used his magic to guide and slow and his descent. He landed on the command deck near the captain, who had Mansel next to him. Mansel had his sword, but the weapon would do little good against the dragon.

"I have an idea," Zollin said. "Do you have spears?" he asked the captain.

"We've some harpoons."

"That should work. Get your best throwers on all four sides of the ship. I'm not sure where the beast will strike again, but this time, when I hit it with magical power, order your sailors to throw their harpoons in the exact same spot."

"But they won't be able to penetrate the dragon's scales, will they?" Mansel asked.

"They might. I think my magic weakened the scales. Its worth a try, right?"

"Absolutely," Mansel agreed. "What can I do?"

"Direct the fighting down here," Zollin said. "I need to get back up top."

"Go!" Mansel said loudly, clapping his friend on the back.

Zollin didn't wait—he jumped and used his power of levitation to propel himself back to the top of the mast. The dragon was not as close as before, but it wasn't moving away either. It had retreated into the darkness but was pacing the ship. Zollin could hear the sailors below, most with buckets of water or manning the ship's water pump to hose down any fire that might be kindled on board the vessel. Mansel was jogging around the ship, checking each sailor's position and weapons. There were a few bows and Mansel had the archers stationed on the command deck. Other sailors were sent into the rigging to act as lookouts and to be ready to cut away the sails if they caught fire.

Finally, after several long, tense moments, the dragon returned. It was higher in the sky this time and Zollin turned to face the beast. Once again he raised a shield with one hand and kindled his magical power in the other. From a distance he saw flames as the dragon exhaled, letting the bright orange fire dance back across his body. Many of the sailors screamed as the dragon approached, letting their fear give them strength as they prepared for the worst. But this time the dragon didn't breathe fire at the ship. Instead, it swerved away at the last moment, lashing out with its tail. The beast's tail hit the mast near the top, just below the crow's nest. It tore through sail and rigging alike, smashing the mast and snapping off the masthead.

Zollin had held back his own strike, surprised by the dragon's change of tactics. When the tail hit the mast, it sent Zollin flying through the air. Zollin was shocked by the blow. The top of the mast swung down, still connected to the rigging, but he was thrown clear of the ship. His preservation instincts kicked in just before he hit the water, throwing up a shield of protection around his body like a bubble. Hitting the water at speed still stunned Zollin, and his weight made him sink. He tried to swim, but his shield made that impossible. He took a deep breath and then lowered his shield. The cold ocean water was almost as much of a shock as being knocked off the ship. Zollin kicked hard for the surface and came up gasping for air. He could hear sailors on board the Northern Star shouting, "Man overboard!"

He knew he needed to get back to the ship, which was all but defenseless without him on board, but his mind seemed numb. He could hear a tiny voice in the back of his mind telling him to levitate, but all he could think of were the waves that kept slapping against him and the cold. He wanted to close his eyes and sink below the waves, but he swam instinctively, treading water and fighting to keep his head up.

"Zollin!" he heard Mansel shouting. "Zollin!"

Then the dragon roared again, shooting down toward the vessel on the opposite side of the ship from where Zollin was languishing in the water, and he knew all was lost.

Chapter 10

Adrenaline kicked in and Zollin lifted himself out of the ocean and toward the ship. He knew he was too late, but he had to try something—it was against his nature to give up. He sent his magic down into the water, letting it spread and touch thousands of fish until it finally brushed against the ocean floor. He was flying to the ship when the dragon attacked. Mansel had sent all his harpoon men to the far side of the ship and they were casting their weapons at the beast, which caused it to pull up. The harpoons hit the dragon's underbelly, but none penetrated the beast's scales.

It roared out and set the sails ablaze with its fiery breath. The canvas burned quickly, sending flaming fragments floating toward the deck as the dragon circled around for another pass. When Zollin finally lowered his soaked and shivering body to the deck, both masts were burning like torches and the crew was working feverishly to extinguish the fires on the decks. People were shouting, and a few even jumped overboard.

Zollin took a massive breath and let his magic blast forth in a kinetic wave that rocked the ship as it snapped both masts near the deck and sent the sails, rigging, and masts hurling into the water. Steam flew up in a hot jet of air where the flaming wood landed in the seawater as Zollin sagged to the rough deck planks.

Eustice appeared from nowhere with a blanket, which he wrapped around Zollin's shoulders. Then he pushed a small metal cup into Zollin's hands. The young wizard drank without thinking, not realizing how strong the grog mix of alcohol was. It burned all the way down his throat, as if he'd swallowed a live coal from a fire. He sputtered and coughed, but then he felt the alcohol spread soothing heat through his body. His eyes seemed to focus and he let Eustice help him back to his feet.

"What's the damage?" Zollin shouted to Mansel.

"I think we're okay for the moment," his friend said as he hurried over to Zollin. "We lost a few men when the dragon hit the mast, but we've got the fires under control. Is it coming back?"

"Yes," Zollin said, "and it's not alone."

The dragon was flying toward the front of the ship but angling to make a strafing pass. Zollin shrugged off the blanket and ran toward the far side of the ship, pushing out a hurried magical shield to protect the ship, but the dragon was moving too fast. He blocked part of the fiery bombardment, but another portion slipped past his defenses and boiled over the ship. The fire was so hot it ignited the wooden hull almost instantly. Zollin and the crew threw water onto the fire. Zollin used his magic, which was beginning to crack through his containment field. He could feel the heat growing painful to his body, but he sloshed ocean water against the burning ship anyway. He could kill himself if he pushed his magic too hard, but he also knew that everyone would die if the ship burned.

They had just gotten the worst of the fire extinguished when the dragon appeared again. This time the beast was approaching from the rear, swerving back and forth so that Zollin couldn't tell which side of the ship it would attack.

"I can't protect both sides of the ship," he shouted to Mansel. "Keep the crew here and I'll do what I can on the far side."

Mansel just nodded as Zollin ran for the far side of the ship. It wasn't a long distance, but the deck was littered with bits of wood, rope, and even the bodies of some of the fallen sailors. It was also soaked with water, which made the crossing treacherous. Zollin was watching where he was going and didn't see the massive tentacles that shot out of the water and snagged the dragon's tail, but everyone on board heard the roar.

Very few creatures could match Bartoom in size and strength, but the kraken was even larger. The dragon's wings flapped uselessly as the sea monster's tentacle held tight to its tail. Zollin cast a quick glance out at the dragon. It was difficult to see what was happening, but then the dragon craned its long neck down and blew a bright plume of fire down at the thick tentacle that was holding it. The sea monster recoiled from the fire, but before the dragon could escape another tentacle wrapped around its neck.

Zollin ran for the smallest of the ship's jolly boats. It wasn't much larger than a skiff, easily manned by just one person.

"Where are you going?" Mansel shouted at him.

"I've got to lead that kraken away from the ship."

"Are you insane?"

"You saw what it did in Lorye," Zollin shouted.

"Well then I'm going with you," Mansel insisted.

"No, I'll have to levitate back, and I'm not sure I can carry us both. You help get the ship moving."

"What? How am I supposed to do that?"

Zollin closed his eyes and focused on the fire inside him. He needed several moments to rebuild his personal defenses, but he didn't have time for that. He reached out with his magic and took hold of the nearest mast, which was floating in the water nearby. It took Zollin a moment to remove the rigging, and in the meantime the dragon had sunk its razor sharp teeth into the kraken's tentacle.

Zollin lifted the mast out of the water, causing fiery pain to shoot into his stomach and chest, as if he were being stabbed by red-hot pokers. Still, even with the pain causing sweat to break out all over his body and his physical strength starting to lag, he set the mast on the wooden stump sticking up from the deck of the ship. Then he used his magic to fuse the wood before he slumped into the jolly boat.

"Eustice!" Mansel bellowed.

The mute servant was almost as white as a sheet. He'd seen terrible things in the tower of the Torr. Offendorl was a cruel man who had no qualms about making people suffer, but seeing the dragon attacked by a sea monster was almost too much for the eunuch.

"I need a bottle of wine right now," Mansel snarled.

Eustice bolted away and Mansel turned to the captain of the ship, who was staring up at the mast in disbelief. Two of the three crossbeams were still in place, but the top of the mast had been snapped off. Still, it would be enough to get the ship moving.

"What are you staring at," Mansel shouted. "Get your sails up and get this ship moving, you fool, or we'll all be killed."

"What?" the captain sputtered angrily. Then he realized that Mansel was right.

"Man the braces!" he shouted. "Get new sail on that mast, men, before we're broken to bits by the kraken."

The sailors ran to their tasks, some shimmying up the mast to help with the rigging. Others disappeared below to carry up the heavy canvas replacement sails. Most ships carried extra sails and even spare masts in case of an emergency, but without Zollin's help it would have taken hours to remove the butt of the old mast and install the new one. They didn't have time for that—not if they were going to escape the kraken.

The dragon seemed to have the same idea, but after freeing itself from the second tentacle it was swatted by a third. This time the sea monster seemed less inclined to pull the beast down under the water. Instead, it focused on knocking the dragon out of the sky. The first blow stunned the dragon, but the second cracked several of its ribs. The dragon roared hatefully and turned its attention on fighting rather than fleeing the monster.

The dragon landed on the surface of the water, floating like a swan. Then it plunged its head under the surface, snapping its massive jaws at the tentacles that reached up for it. Its wings were useless in the water, but its tail moved like a sea snake and propelled the dragon out of the way of the larger tentacles that would have injured the beast. Finally, after several frantic moments, the dragon sensed a lull in the kraken's attack. It flapped its massive wings and rose straight up into the night sky.

When the dragon finally reached a height where it felt safe, it turned for the shore and flew slowly away. Zollin felt the boat he was in swing out over the water. It had been attached to a small hoist that hadn't been blown overboard by his magic. Then Mansel appeared, towering over Zollin with his sword in one hand and a bottle of wine in the other. Mansel cut the ropes holding the boat with one mighty swing of his sword and the boat fell to the water.

"Here, drink this," Mansel said, tossing Zollin the bottle of wine.

Mansel sat on the wooden bench and lay his sword beside him. Then he pulled out the boat's oars and set them into the their cradles. He leaned forward, then pulled the oars hard, straining his back and propping his feet on the bench in front of him so he could push back with his legs. The small boat rocked with the waves, but moved quickly away from the ship. Zollin pulled himself into a sitting position. He was relieved not to have to row the boat. His arms and legs were shaking and it was taking all his strength not to curl up into a ball just to deal with the pain.

He drank some of the wine, not tasting it, just hoping it would give him the strength he needed to get himself and Mansel back to the ship when the time came.

"Any particular direction you want to go?" Mansel asked.

"Out to sea," Zollin said between gulps of wine. "Take us further out to sea."

"You got it," Mansel said.

The big warrior strained against the oars. It was too dark to see what was happening to the dragon, but he could see the sailors scurrying around the ship. He wondered briefly what it would be like to die at sea. He thought of Nycoll in her little house. She was waiting for Mansel to return, but he would probably be lost at sea, just like her husband. That thought made him sad, but Mansel knew he didn't really have a choice. He couldn't let Zollin go out to face the sea monster alone. If that meant he died, then so be it.

Zollin couldn't see the dragon either, and although he wanted to reach out with his magic to see what was happening, he knew he had to reserve his strength. He had to make sure his internal defenses didn't break down completely—that would incapacitate him. The wine was helping, but he couldn't seem to get enough of it. His body burned through the alcohol and calories faster than he could consume them.

"Watch the ship," Zollin told Mansel. "If you see it getting attacked by the sea monster, tell me."

"Why? What are you going to be doing?"

"Getting ready to fight the beast," Zollin admitted.

Mansel shuddered at the thought, but kept rowing. Zollin knew he was too weak to fight off the giant sea monster, but it was attracted to his magic. That had been his fear after the attack in Lorye Harbor, and now that fear was confirmed. It had been the reason he'd shot his magic into the water. If the kraken was drawn to magic, he had hoped it would be drawn to the dragon as well. It had been a huge gamble, but there was simply no other way to drive the dragon off. Even with all his power, he could only weaken the dragon, not kill or even injure it. Brianna had been successful in wounding the beast with arrows of dwarfish steel, but he had none with him now. The harpoons might have broken through the beast's scales after he weakened the dragon's hide with his magical energy, but they had missed that chance when the dragon knocked Zollin off the crow's nest.

The ship was small in the distance after only a few minutes of rowing. Zollin hoped they were far enough from the big ship, but he couldn't be sure. He only knew that if they moved much farther away he wouldn't have the strength to levitate Mansel and himself back to the ship.

"This is far enough," Zollin said.

"Okay, what now?"

"Now we get ready to run," Zollin said.

Mansel wasn't sure what that meant, but he shipped the oars and took up his sword.

Standing in the boat wasn't easy, but he couldn't fight sitting down. Zollin was sitting on the bench in front of Mansel. He closed his eyes and let his magic flow into the water beneath the boat. He could feel the schools of fish and the current several feet below the surface. It only took a minute before the fish began to dart away, leaving the water under their small boat empty. It sent chills up Zollin's spine. He was confident he could escape the kraken, but he needed to stay until the beast arrived. He needed to lure it further out to sea, but if the boat was attacked too soon he might not be able to save Mansel. That thought scared him almost as much as the giant sea monster itself. He thought of Todrek, his old friend in Tranaugh Shire. Todrek had not wanted any part of Zollin's magic, and in the end it had been that magic that had killed him. Todrek had been struck down by a mercenary when the wizards of the Torr had come to take Zollin back to their master. Zollin had tried to save his friend, but hadn't known enough magic at the time. The thought made Zollin's stomach lurch. Tears stung his eyes. He vowed not to let the same thing happen to Mansel.

Suddenly, he felt the huge beast slide into the water beneath the boat, and there was no more time for thinking. Zollin could sense the pain the kraken felt. The dragon had burned the creature and bitten off the ends of several tentacles. Zollin waited, fighting his instinct to flee from the sea monster. The last thing he needed was for the beast to follow them back to the ship. If that happened, all was lost.

Suddenly a tentacle rose up out of the water.

"Zollin!" Mansel shouted, his voice laced with fear.

"Not yet," Zollin said.

Mansel watched as the tentacle moved closer, and then, just before it reached the little boat, he swung his sword. Cutting through the tentacle was like chopping wood. His sword cut almost halfway through the thick appendage before sticking. The tentacle jerked back into the water, almost pulling Mansel out of the boat. His heart dropped as he saw his beloved sword disappear beneath the waves.

"Okay, don't panic," Zollin said. "It'll only make my job harder."

Mansel wasn't sure what to say, but then he started rising into the air. It was only natural to panic, but Mansel just froze, every muscle in his body going rigid with fear. He'd never been afraid of heights. He'd climbed trees as a boy, and being on top of the king's castle in Orrock hadn't bothered him, but whenever Zollin levitated him it filled Mansel with dread. He felt completely out of control and weak.

Zollin ignored the fear that was pouring off Mansel like leaves from a tree in an autumn storm. He focused on holding them up, rising higher and higher, watching the little boat bobbing in the water in the darkness below them. He fully expected the kraken to attack the boat now, but when it shattered the little craft with a single blow from under the water, his heart sank a little. He raised them higher into the air, his magic so hot now it was beginning to break apart his inner defenses again. Then he sent a wave of his magic out into the water, moving further out to sea. He pushed it as far as he could, straining his mind and magic almost to the breaking point. Then he withdrew all of his power, containing it in the small bubble around himself and Mansel.

He didn't dare check to see if the kraken had taken the bait and followed the magic further out to sea. He waited for just a moment, straining his eyes in the darkness for any sign of the sea monster, but there was none. Then he turned and levitated back to the ship. He was seeing spots by the time they arrived, and when they got over the deck his control slipped and they fell the last few feet.

Zollin and Mansel lay side-by-side, both panting from exhaustion. Zollin saw the ship's white sail flutter for a moment, then fill with air. He felt the ship moving, and then he passed out.

When Zollin woke up he was in his bunk. Light was shining through the porthole and Eustice was hovering nearby. At first, Zollin didn't move. His stomach was rumbling with hunger and his muscles felt stiff. His mouth was so dry it was difficult to move his tongue. He checked his magical containment and was happy to find it still in place and working. He rolled over, stretching his aching muscles, and then sat up on the bed. Eustice hurried over with a cup of water. Zollin took it gratefully and sipped a little, letting the water swoosh around in his mouth and moisten his tongue. Then he turned up the cup and drank the rest greedily.

"Ah, that may be the best water I've ever tasted," he said. "Is there more?" Eustice poured more into the cup from a small pitcher.

"How long was I asleep?"

Eustice held his fingers close together, almost in a pinching motion. "Not long?" Eustice nodded.

"That's good. Is Mansel okay?"

Eustice nodded again.

"We're sailing again, huh? Any sign of the sea monster?"

This time Eustice shook his head to say no.

"I want to go up and see the damage for myself," Zollin said.

Eustice helped Zollin to his feet and after a moment he felt strong enough to walk. He was tired, but it felt good to stretching his muscles. He drank some more water then went out on the deck while Eustice stayed behind to fix his breakfast.

Zollin was surprised to see that the deck had been cleared of all the debris and there were two large sails up on the mast he had repaired. There were several sailors lying out in the sunshine on makeshift pallets. Most had thick globs of what appeared to be grease on their wounds. Zollin went straight to the sailor who was checking on the wounded men.

"What happened?" Zollin asked.

"Burns mostly," said the sailor, who was the ship surgeon's helper. "A few broken bones. Lady Roleena got the worst of it, and those poor souls we lost overboard. I've never seen a dragon before. We'd all be dead if it weren't for you."

"That dragon probably attacked because of me," Zollin admitted. "It's the not the first time we've run into each other. What do you mean Lady Roleena got the worst of it?"

"Shattered her leg when one of the blocks fell from the rigging. It's a shame, really. The surgeon had to amputate. Not sure if she'll make it or not."

Zollin's blood ran cold.

"Where is she?" he demanded.

"She's below, in the sick bay. The healer didn't want her moved."

"Show me," Zollin said.

"Alright," the sailor said, "this way."

He led Zollin to the stairwell opposite the entrance to the passenger deck. Zollin looked up at the command deck as they passed it, noticing the captain's unveiled look of disgust. He ignored it and followed the sailor down into the dark interior of the ship. They moved past several storerooms and finally came to a closed door that Zollin knew was the sick bay. The smell was horrid—a mixture of human waste and putrefied flesh that made Zollin want to vomit.

"She's inside," the sailor said. "The surgeon should be with her."

It was hot on the cargo deck, which was below the water line and had very little ventilation. Zollin opened the door, breathing through his mouth to avoid the horrid stench of the sick bay. The room was quiet and dim, with only a single lantern giving any light to the room. The healer was asleep on a small bunk, and on a table stained with blood lay Lady Roleena. She was naked, with only a thin sheet covering her body. Zollin approached her side, feeling sick at the sight of her. Her skin was very white and covered with a thin sheen of sweat. Her lips were almost completely blue and the stump of her left leg, which ended right above the knee, was bleeding through the bandage and staining the sheet.

Zollin let his magic flow into her and was appalled to discover her organs shutting down. The shock of the amputation had been too much for her and her mind had retreated from the pain. His first order of business was to stop the bleeding in her leg.

He knew he could re-attach the limb, although it would take a great deal of time.

"Healer!" he said sharply. "Wake up!"

The older sailor stirred and looked up.

"What?" he asked irritably. "You aren't supposed to be in here."

"What did you do with her leg?" Zollin asked.

"We threw it overboard," he said, as if it were the most obvious thing in the world.

"Damn!" Zollin said. "I could have saved her leg. Now she'll be crippled."

"She won't live, I'm afraid," the healer said. "I had to amputate, there was no other way to save her life, but she fought us every step of the way. She has a strong constitution, but I wasn't able to stop the bleeding in time, I'm afraid."

"That much is obvious," Zollin said angrily. "I need water, wine, and food. Send for Eustice—he's in my cabin but he doesn't speak. Tell him what I need. He'll see to it."

"What are you planning to do?" the healer asked.

"Save her life," Zollin said. "Now, do what I tell you."

"I don't think she needs your sorcery," he said.

"Shut up and get out," Zollin said angrily.

The ship's healer looked stern, but he did as he was told. It took nearly an hour to stop the bleeding. Zollin took his time mending the nerve endings and reforming the bone. By the time he stopped, he had mended the end of Roleena's leg so that there was no scar, and he hoped no pain. She was still unconscious, so he took some time to eat the food Eustice had prepared him. He drank some wine for its rejuvenating effects, but he mostly drank water. His body was still sore, as if he'd worked strenuously for days without rest, but his magic seemed as strong as ever.

His next task was to increase Roleena's blood supply. He didn't create blood for her—instead, he sped up her body's natural blood making process. Then he coaxed her organs back to health. There was nothing specifically wrong with them, other than a lack of oxygen from the blood loss. Finally, he gently nudged her mind. It took several moments, but finally she woke up.

"How are you feeling?" he asked her.

"I had the worst dream," she said.

"It wasn't a dream."

Her face grew stern and her eyes narrowed, but she didn't speak. Instead, she sat up on the table, holding the sheet up to cover her body.

"What did you do to me?" she asked.

"You were injured," he explained. "Your leg was shattered and the ship's healer amputated."

"No," she said simply, as if her denial could change reality.

She reached a shaking hand down and pulled back the bloody sheet. The end of her leg was smooth skin.

"You did this to me," she said, almost hissing.

"Yes, I did all I could to fix the damage. You lost a lot of blood."

He was caught completely off guard by the slap, which landed hard across his jaw, making his eyes water and his ear ring a little. He staggered a few steps, looking up in surprise and trying to dampen his anger.

"I'll kill you," she hissed. "I'll take everything you love and make you watch it die. You'll beg me to end it, but I won't. I'll make you suffer."

"You've lost your mind," Zollin said, backing away.

"I curse you." She spat the words as if they were bile. "I curse you and your descendants to the fifth generation."

"You're insane," Zollin said as he backed slowly away from her. "I helped you. You were dying."

"I'll kill you, Zollin Quinnson," she screamed as he left the sick bay, her voice echoing through the dark cargo hold of the ship. "I'll kill you and everything you love."

Her voice echoed in his mind long after he left her in the bowels of the ship.

Chapter 11

Brianna couldn't help but love the feeling of flying with her pride of dragons. They were playful and fun. She would sometimes leap from one dragon to another, flipping and gliding through the air as effortlessly as a leaf floating on a gust of wind. Selix—the biggest dragon—and Ferno had little trouble carrying Brianna. She was lighter than most humans her size anyway, but they were large, and incredibly strong creatures. Gyia could carry her for short distances. But Tig and Torc, even though they were the size of large horses, could not handle her weight. Instead, the two smaller dragons spun and frolicked through the air with her.

They had left the mountains and flown mostly at night. Brianna could see at night almost as well as she could in the daylight, but the dark skies helped hide her pride. She didn't want to frighten anyone or cause her pride to be injured by fearful humans. Their scales were hardening more and more every day, even though they were avoiding sunlight and sleeping through most of the days. Still, a well-aimed arrow or spear could penetrate their skin, which meant they were vulnerable, so she used caution despite her overwhelming desire to find Zollin again.

The second day of their journey she had left her pride and used the gold she had collected deep in the mountain to purchase clothes and food. She now had thick woolen clothes to keep her warm high in the air, and she was eating fruits and vegetables again, which she relished after weeks of eating nothing but meat.

They didn't hurry, and it took three days to reach Felson. They watched the city from high in the air. Her dragons were curious and they flooded her mind with questions. They had seen small villages on their journey, but Felson was the first community of real size. Felson was a central city in Yelsia, and although the city had no walls or keep, it did have a very tall watchtower, and an entire legion of cavalry was stationed just outside the city. There was also a ring of tents, wagons, makeshift shelters, and huts that had been erected by refugees from many of the northern villages who had been forced to flee their homes by the large black dragon Bartoom, before the mighty beast had abandoned Brianna and flown south to answer the magical call ringing in its head.

The pride found a place to hide in a thick copse of trees and brush. The dragons didn't like hiding and their curiosity was so strong that they had trouble staying behind, but Brianna insisted they stay hidden. She wasn't sure what she would find in Felson, but she was hopeful that she could find out where Zollin might be. She also wanted to start rumors of her own pride, so that when she revealed her dragons they might have a chance to show that not all dragons are monsters.

She was several miles from the city, so she left her pride well before dawn. Walking felt both good and strange. It was like she was crawling after the thrill of soaring through the air with her dragons, but stretching her muscles and feeling the strength in her legs was good as well. She got to the edge of the city an hour after sunup and it took nearly another hour to find her way back to the house of the one person she knew in Felson.

Miriam's home had not changed much, although Quinn had made a few minor repairs. He was outside, gathering his tools and supplies in a small wagon, to which Miriam was hitching a large brown mare. Brianna saw them before they spotted her approaching and she was happy to see the easy way they worked together. Quinn had become like a father to Brianna since she had fled Tranaugh Shire with him and Zollin almost a year ago. She had been surprised to learn that Miriam had strong feelings for Quinn, but she was happy to see them together now. It made her yearn even more for Zollin and for the opportunity to have a life with him.

When Quinn glanced up and saw her, he did a double take and then rushed to her, his arms open wide and a huge smile on his face.

"Brianna!" he shouted as he ran.

She felt a warm sense of love and acceptance flood over her. She couldn't help but run to Quinn, even as tears sprung up in her eyes.

"Look at you, girl," Quinn said happily. "I'm so glad to see you. You look well. I mean, even better than well."

"I am well, Quinn," Brianna said.

"Miriam, it's Brianna," Quinn called over his shoulder, and then said in a quieter voice, "We thought you were dead."

"What? Why?"

"Zollin said the dragon carried you off into the mountains. He's heartsick over your loss."

"But I'm not lost," she said as they walked back toward Miriam's house and barn.

"Well, he doesn't know that. And he's gone south. I suppose you heard about the invasion."

"Not really, just rumors. What happened?"

"An army from Osla and Falxis invaded. It's a long story, really. Why don't we go inside? It looks like you could use a good meal—you're little more than skin and bones."

They went in and Miriam fixed Brianna breakfast. She wasn't that hungry, but she ate a little of her food while Quinn talked. He explained how he and Mansel had come under the witch's spell in Lodenhime, and how the big warrior had thrown Quinn overboard in the Great Sea of Kings. Then he told how he had been rescued by a fishing boat, and raced across Baskla and Yelsia to Orrock in hopes of saving Zollin. He told her how he'd been almost killed by Mansel—who was still bewitched—and then healed by Zollin. How Mansel had come back to his senses after being grievously wounded himself, and how Zollin had learned to use lightning to fight the dragon when it attacked the city.

Brianna shivered at the thought. She had never considered that lightning might be a danger to her pride, but just the thought of flying in a storm with thunder and lightning made her tremble. Then Quinn told of Zollin's battle with Offendorl, and how they had defeated the invading army. Brianna was completely engrossed in the tale and didn't even notice when Miriam refilled the small cup of wine in her hand.

"Did Zollin kill him?"

"No, the black dragon came and took him away," Quinn said sadly. "Now Zollin has gone south to finish things with the Torr. Mansel is with him. He promised to return once the fighting was done."

"And you're content to just wait here?" Brianna said.

She remember the feeling she'd had when Zollin had given her the white alzerstone ring in the alley at Tranaugh Shire. From that point on she had lived in fear that he would leave her behind. When the wizards from the Torr attacked the village with their mercenaries, her new husband Todrek had begged her not to follow Zollin, but she couldn't stand the thought of being left behind. Todrek had come with her, only to be struck down just outside Quinn's cottage. It was a bittersweet memory. She had thought Todrek a good person, but she had not loved him. But now that feeling of being left behind rose up like a wave of nausea and she felt sick. She knew what she had to do now. If Offendorl had a dragon, she would bring her pride to protect Zollin.

"I have to go," she said, before Quinn could even answer her question.

The truth was, he was having difficulty staying put and waiting for Zollin, but he was happy with Miriam. Their love had blossomed and grown. They were planning a wedding when Zollin returned, but a part of Quinn felt like he was betraying his son. He knew there was little he could do for Zollin, but if his son was in danger, how could he sit back and do nothing?

"Where are you off to?" Miriam asked.

"I have to help Zollin."

"You can't," Miriam said. "He's hundreds of leagues away by now. He may already be in Osla. Besides, even if you were with him, what could you do?"

"I'm going," Brianna said. "Thank you so much for the meal and the information."

"Brianna?" Quinn said. "I know how you feel, but if you leave you may end up in trouble yourself, long before you ever catch up to him. Besides, how do you know you could even find him? He could be anywhere."

"I'll show you, if you don't mind a detour from the city," she said.

Quinn looked at Miriam. "I guess we could," he said.

"I'll hitch the horses to the carriage," Miriam said.

It took them an hour to ride back to the small copse of trees where Brianna had left her pride. She was tired, but excited to know that Zollin was on his way to Osla. She wasn't sure how she was going to find him, but she was sure she could.

Quinn reined in the horses when they approached the trees. He was on the bench seat with Miriam close beside him. There had been just enough room for Brianna on the far side.

"Stay here," she told them. "And keep your horses calm, they're in no danger."

"What is she on about?" Miriam asked Quinn.

"I don't know," he admitted. "But there is definitely something different about her." They watched her disappear into the shady stand of trees, then the trees rustled and she reappeared leading two small dragons. They were dark blue, with large intelligent eyes. Then another dragon appeared. This one was long and slender, moving gracefully even on the ground.

Brianna waited, watching Quinn and Miriam's reaction. They were shocked, but not terrified. In fact, Miriam, who was an animal healer, seemed almost thrilled at the small group of dragons.

"You okay?" Brianna called.

"Yes, we're all right," Miriam called.

"Speak for yourself," Quinn said under his breath.

"There are two more," Brianna said. "They're larger, but they won't hurt you, I promise." Ferno stepped out of the copse of trees. The sun glinted off his forest green scales as his powerful muscles rolled and flexed with each step. Then Selix appeared, moving to stand next to Brianna.

"I can't believe it," Miriam said. Then she laughed a long, full laugh that made the carriage shake.

Brianna knew her pride was surprised, but they all liked Miriam almost instantly. They knew she wasn't laughing at them, but was delighted to see them. They were almost as happy to see other humans as she was to see them.

"Are you sure this is safe?" Quinn called out to Brianna.

"Yes, I'm sure," she said. "This is my pride, Quinn. They chose to stay with me. You can come closer. They're very curious."

The horses were nervous and Quinn moved them farther away before setting the brake on the carriage and climbing out. He helped Miriam down and they approached the dragons together. Gyia, the slender, dark purple dragon, was the first to step forward. It lowered its narrow head and gazed deeply into Miriam's eyes.

Brianna watched as Miriam looked suddenly surprised.

"Did … Did she just speak to me?" Miriam asked.

"Yes," Brianna said. "They communicate mostly through mental images, but you can use words with them too. Vocalization is difficult for them, but they're learning," she said as she patted Selix's long neck.

"What did it say?" Quinn asked.

"She wanted to know if I'm a healer."

"How did it know that?"

"I don't know," Miriam said.

"They're very perceptive," Brianna explained. "They can't read your mind, but they often sense a person's nature. And they aren't male or female, Miriam. They don't mate or reproduce like other animals or humans."

"So where do they come from?" Quinn wanted to know.

"I gave them life," Brianna said. "So much has changed and it's difficult to explain, so just bear with me. I'm still human, still the same Brianna you've known all my life, but I'm different too. I'm one of them, now. The dwarves called me a Fire Spirit."

Brianna held out her hand and a dancing flame appeared above her empty palm.

"So you're a wizard too?" Quinn asked.

"No, not a wizard," Brianna said. "But I can create and control fire. I'm not hurt by fire. I'm like a dragon in that sense."

"So they breathe fire?" Miriam asked?

Tig and Torc threw back their heads and belched fire into the sky.

"Yes," Brianna said, laughing at the twin dragons. "They all breathe fire, and these two like to show off. Their fire, like mine, is a type of magic."

"So it isn't some sort of physical ability?" Miriam asked. "I've often wondered about that."

"No, there's nothing physical about it. They conjure fire magically."

"And they fly, I presume?" Quinn asked.

"Yes, and that's how I'll catch up with Zollin."

"You're going to let them carry you?" Quinn said skeptically. "What if they accidentally

drop you?"

"I'm going to ride the dragons, Quinn. I can fly too, in a way," she said gently. "I know it's hard to take in, but I'm still Brianna. I just have a few more skills and some new friends."

Quinn shook his head. "I thought the strangest thing I'd ever see in my life was when Zollin blasted the wizards with magic in Tranaugh Shire. I was so shocked that day that if we hadn't been running for our lives, I might have keeled over on the spot. Now, here you are with a herd of dragons."

"A pride of dragons," Brianna corrected him.

"It's a little too much for me to take in," he said. "I need a moment."

Brianna felt a little hurt. She had always known Quinn to have an open mind and to be quick with an encouraging word. She knew that some people would never accept her pride—their fear would be too much for them to control—but she had never expected that Quinn wouldn't welcome her with open arms as he had in town.

"They're my family, Quinn," she said softly. "They're not monsters."

"I believe you, Brianna," Quinn said, looking up. "If you vouch for them, that's good enough for me, you know that. I just feel…" He let the thought trail off. "I guess I'm just not very good with change. You're growing up, and I feel… Well, the truth is, I've thought of you like a daughter for a while now. Seeing you and Zollin together in Orrock brought me happiness that I'd never experienced before. I feel a little bit like I'm losing you."

"Losing me?" Brianna said, as tears rolled gently down her cheeks. "How?"

"You're growing up, that's all," Quinn said. "You don't need me as much."

"Oh, Quinn," she said, her voice choking.

She ran to him and threw her arms around his neck, letting her tears soak his shirt. The dragons moved around them then, nudging Quinn and Miriam. They saw images in their minds of Brianna with the dragons, flying through the air, covered in flames and looking so happy it made Quinn's heart ache.

"I'm happy for you," he whispered. "And I know that Zollin needs you," he added.

"And I need him," she said.

"We'll be here waiting for you both," he told her. "Do you need anything?"

"Just your blessing," she said.

"You've got it," he said loudly. "You all do."

Chapter 12

The Northern Star limped into the harbor at Lixon Bay. Lixon was one of the biggest cities in Falxis, with a well-maintained road that ran straight to Luxing City, where King Zorlan ruled his kingdom. Falxis was a large kingdom, but since the treaty of peace between the kingdoms three centuries ago, it had no enemies. It was surrounded by other kingdoms on three sides, and the long western coast was home to a vast shipping enterprise.

It had taken almost two days to sail back to the coast and into Lixon Bay from the scene of the attack. Zollin had spent that time healing the wounded sailors and helping with repairs to the ship. The Northern Star needed major refitting. While there was an emergency mast and supplies to refit the ship, there was not enough to totally repair all the damage the dragon had caused.

The ship's captain of course blamed Zollin for the whole ordeal, and had sent word that he was to leave the ship once they reached the harbor. Zollin might have argued the point, but he knew they had been lucky to survive in the open waters. It gave the dragon too much of an advantage and put too many people at risk. Zollin had spent the remainder of his time on board transmuting some lead weights into gold. He also fashioned Mansel a new sword. This time the warrior had made some specific requests. The sword was slightly longer that the previous weapon, with the lower part of the blade thicker and serrated. It was a true broadsword, made to be wielded with a two-handed grip. Zollin thought the weapon was too heavy, but Mansel made the weapon sing. He practiced with it on deck, and his speed and skill with the blade was almost frightening to behold.

As they sailed into the harbor, Zollin was surprised by the number of ships. He, Mansel, and Eustice were leaning on the rail at the bow, taking in the sights of the port and harbor.

"What's with all the ships?" Mansel asked.

"I don't know," Zollin said.

Eustice waved his hands, pointing to himself and then Mansel's sword, then making a wave-like motion and pointing north.

"What's he saying?" Mansel said.

"I'm not sure."

Eustice pointed to the ships in the harbor and then pretended to march like a solider. "Oh, you mean these are the ships that brought the army north?" Zollin asked.

Eustice nodded enthusiastically.

"Well, I guess that makes sense," said Mansel. "We made good time traveling south."

"But why are there so many ships?" Zollin asked. "There are enough in the harbor to

transport both armies."

"And that is strange because?" Mansel asked.

"Why would the troops from Osla stop in Falxis?"

"Maybe it's just to get fresh supplies."

"I don't know," Zollin said. "If you'd just been defeated, would you want to stop somewhere or get home as quickly as possible?"

Mansel thought about the question for a moment, then agreed. "Okay, so it's a bit strange. I guess we could poke around a bit and find out what's happening. But I wouldn't go bragging about who you are. I doubt there are many friendly people around here."

"Agreed," Zollin said. "Eustice and I will get horses and supplies—you get information."

"I know exactly where to go," Mansel said, smiling.

"How could you? You've never been to Lixon Bay before, have you?"

"No, but taverns are the place to get the latest gossip. Buy a few rounds and men will share their darkest secrets," Mansel said.

"I'll remember that," Zollin said. "Just don't get falling down drunk. We need to ride hard."

"Trust me," Mansel said playfully, a bit of his old sense of humor returning. "When have I ever let drink get the best of me?" Zollin didn't answer—he just shook his head.

A few minutes later they were climbing down the side of the ship on a rope ladder. The captain had made getting Zollin off his ship the first priority once they weighed anchor. Zollin looked up from the little boat that was rowing them to shore and saw Lady Roleena staring out her window at him. The ship's healer had fashioned her a set of crutches and she had been able to get around rather well with them, but she had not given up her intense hatred of Zollin.

The boat wove through the other ships in the harbor and came to the dock quickly enough. Zollin and Eustice went to find the city's stables. Falxis was known for breeding fine horses, and Zollin didn't expect to have any trouble getting good mounts. He had broken the gold into small pieces and flattened them out like coins. There was no official coinage in the Five Kingdoms, although some monarchs had stamped their likenesses onto coins. Zollin didn't bother trying to recreate an image on the coins. He had found that pure gold was enough without embellishment. He'd given Mansel the last of his silver marks to buy drinks with. A silver mark was usually more than enough to keep one man eating and drinking throughout the night at any inn, but covering the tabs of other drinkers would require more coin.

Zollin and Eustice found the stables. There were several on the outskirts of the city. They were tired and dusty by the time they made the long walk through the busy streets of Lixon Bay. They had passed the large market, but decided to wait until they had horses to carry their provisions before they did their shopping. It took Zollin an hour to inspect the horses. He bought eight horses—two for each rider and two for their provisions. With two horses for each rider, they should be able to ride all through the day and into the night without having to stop and rest their mounts very often, and certainly without having to walk them. It would still be slower than traveling by sea, but they had no other options.

Zollin took the two packhorses back to the market, while Eustice stayed with the other horses at the stable. Zollin's first priority was to get saddles for the six horses. It was expensive, but he didn't want to waste time saddling and unsaddling their horses throughout the day. With each horse ready to ride, they could stop, stretch, and then remount their fresh horse. He bought bridles and saddlebags for each horse. He was forced to go to three saddler's shops before he had enough tack for all of their mounts. He paid extra to have the gear delivered to Eustice at the stable yard.

Then he went to the market, where vendors were hawking their wares. It reminded Zollin of the harvest festival in Tranaugh Shire. There were brightly colored booths and merchants selling everything from weapons to jewelry. He bought dried fish and smoked fish, a large sack of black-crusted bread, a cask of butter, vegetables, and a cask of salted pork. Most of the rations were made for sea travel, but he packed the horses well enough. He bought blankets, large cloaks with hoods, and some wine. He was just about to leave the market when he saw a booth with a wide assortment of objects. One caught Zollin's attention—it looked like a polished stone, perhaps volcanic rock. It was strangely shaped and not set in any kind of holder. It was just laid out among some rather plain looking jewelry.

Zollin picked the piece up, examining it. It felt like it was almost vibrating in his hand, as if it gave off a sense of magical power. He looked at the merchant, who was an old man with a deeply lined face.

"What is this?" he asked.

"It's a Veppra stone," the merchant said. "They used to be valued for warding off evil, but they aren't in style much anymore."

"A Veppra stone," Zollin said, trying the word out. It made him wish Kelvich were with him. The old sorcerer would have known what it was. The ache of his mentor's death was acute at the moment and Zollin had to shake himself to keep from sinking into sadness for his old friend.

"How much do you want for it?" he asked.

"They're quite rare," the merchant said. He seemed to come to life once the haggling began. "I couldn't take less than five silver marks for it."

"Five?" Zollin asked. He wanted to laugh. He knew the stone wasn't worth more than one silver coin to most people, but the stone's magical properties made it much more valuable.

"Would you take a gold crown? It's all I've got left."

"A gold crown?" The merchant looked stunned.

Zollin flipped him the coin and walked away. He examined the stone as he made his way back through the city toward the stables. It was about the size of a large walnut, and Zollin already knew what he was going to do with it.

When he returned to the stables the sun was beginning to set. Mansel was with Eustice and they had the horses saddled and ready to leave. Zollin was tired, but he climbed into the saddle without complaint.

"Give me your sword," he told Mansel.

The big warrior handed it over without complaint. It had been fashioned from an old anchor that Mansel had found on board the Northern Star. The anchor had somehow broken almost completely in half, so the crew had stopped using it. Zollin had used his magic to transform the rusty metal into a rugged sword for his friend. He place his hand over the crosspiece where the hand guard and hilt met. He let his magic flow into the metal, softening it and then pressing out a section. Then he placed the Veppra stone into the hole and made the steel flow around it. He left a small opening about the size of a coin where the Veppra stone could be seen, but the irregular edges of the stone were covered by the steel. The sense of magical strength could now be felt in the sword, although Zollin wasn't sure what the stone really did or if Mansel would even be able to notice the power the stone gave his weapon.

"There," he said, handing the sword back to Mansel.

"What did you do?" he asked, looking at the sword's new addition.

"Just a little decoration, that's all."

"I've never known you to care about appearances," Mansel said.

"Well, the sword just needed a little something to make it complete," Zollin said. "Now what did you find out on your reconnaissance mission?"

"You mean my drinking excursion? Come on, Zollin, you can't be a famous adventurer unless you get the lingo right."

"Well?" Zollin asked, ignoring Mansel's joke.

"Okay, well, you were right. Both armies landed here. Apparently, rumor has it that King Belphan didn't survive the invasion."

"Really?" Zollin said in surprise.

"Lots of different rumors about what exactly happened, but most of them have to do with your friend from the Torr killing Belphan. But that's not the best part. Apparently all the generals from the Oslan forces died too. It seems that King Zorlan has some ambition after all. He's taken control of both armies and is claiming stewardship of the Oslan throne."

"So he wants to rule both kingdoms," Zollin said. "Offendorl breaks the treaty and already we're at each others' throats."

"So it would seem. But there's more news. I asked about the witch in Lodenhime and found out she marched south with an army of her own."

"What army?" Zollin asked.

"All of Ortis' forces. Even the reserve troops. From what I can tell, King Oveer was supposed to march north with his army and invade Yelsia, but instead he turned south with Gwendolyn and made for Osla."

"What do you think about that?"

"I don't know, Zollin. I know the witch has power over men, but I wasn't there long enough to find out her plans. She sent your father and me north the day after we arrived in Lodenhime."

"But Prince Wilam is still with her," Zollin said.

"I'm sure he is. She's probably got him wrapped around her little finger. Cutting him loose from her power won't be easy."

"No," Zollin said. "This is getting out of hand. If King Zorlan marches south, we're looking at three armies in Osla. It'll be a bloodbath."

"Not to mention leaving Ortis and Falxis vulnerable to attack."

"If King Felix finds out, he's liable to send troops south as well."

"The big question now," Mansel said, "is what we plan to do. I mean, it might be better for us to just lag behind and let them fight it out. Then we can come in and make sure the Torr isn't a threat to you anymore."

"I don't know," Zollin said. "There's so much at stake. If Gwendolyn is as powerful as you say, what's to keep her from combining all three armies and marching north again? She may be set on ruling all Five Kingdoms."

"True," agreed Mansel, "but I don't want to get caught in the middle of a war, especially one we have no stake in."

"I've got to make sure Offendorl isn't a threat to me anymore. If he killed King Belphan, then he probably means to take over Osla."

"But how can he do that without the army?"

"He would have the reserve troops, and we don't know that the returning soldiers won't join him."

"I wish we knew more," Mansel said. "I hate walking into a fight when I don't even know what side we're on."

"Me either, but it can't be helped. Luxing City is on the road to Osla—perhaps we can find out what's really going on."

"I hope you're right," Mansel said, his hand unconsciously gripping the hilt of his sword.

* * *

Offendorl was angry. Bartoom had failed once again. He'd seen the fight through the dragon's eyes. The effort had taxed the elder wizard greatly, but he knew that Zollin wouldn't give up without a fight and he was hoping the boy would be killed. It would set back Offendorl's plans, but at least it would put an end to the fighting.

The elder wizard had seen the dragon's tactics and had been sure that victory was at hand, when the kraken had risen up and attacked Bartoom. Offendorl had read stories of the infamous sea monster. He knew that the kraken was drawn to magic, but he had no idea the monster was active again. In his youth, centuries ago, wizards avoided the seas as much as possible. It was almost as if the oceans created a magical barrier few dared cross. But Zollin had managed to use the kraken to save himself from Bartoom. The boy had skills and brought a creativity to his magic that Offendorl found both frightening and exhilarating.

But now he had no choice. He'd spent a day resting, but now he had to return to his tower in the Grand City. He would have to prepare to battle Zollin again. He needed to find new strength and a way to tilt the odds in his favor. He couldn't underestimate Zollin any further—the young wizard was too strong and too determined.

He was now in a carriage that was taking him to the Grand City. It was not as comfortable as his wagon had been, but he'd lost the wagon in Yelsia when the invasion failed. Now, he was forced to use a rented carriage. It had a long padded bench and a cover to keep the infernal sun from beating down on him, but there was no stopping the dust, which was everywhere. It stuck to his skin, which was dampened by the heat. It clung to his nostrils and lips so that everything seemed to smell and taste like dirt. Offendorl was not so weak that he couldn't endure the journey, but he disliked the notion of arriving at the Torr exhausted. He despised weakness, and the thought of revealing his own to the servants and other magic-users in the tower was repugnant to him.

They had traveled from sunup until dark, then stopped at one of the many roadside inns that lined the wide road from Brimington Bay to the Grand City. Offendorl had known something was wrong by the lack of soldiers along the road. King Belphan had always kept troops on the road to deter bandits, but now they were strangely absent. He was sure the news of Belphan's death hadn't reached the Grand City before him, but he couldn't imagine what would cause the troops to be pulled from their duty on the road.

"I want wine," Offendorl told the innkeeper. "And not that watered down piss you give everyone else. I want the best you have. And food, a double portion."

"Yes, of course," the man said.

"Bring it up to me yourself. I want the latest news."

"Certainly," the innkeeper said, his hand still holding the gold coin Offendorl had given him. "My wife will show you to your rooms."

Offendorl followed the portly woman up the stairs to a stuffy suite of rooms. There was a sitting area and a large desk in the first room, and a large bed in the second. The windows were thrown open by the innkeeper's wife.

"It's a bit stuffy," she said, "but it will cool down shortly. I can have one of the maids bring up some cool water to wash with," she said with a wink and a knowing smile.

"No," Offendorl said. "The room shall suffice, now be gone, woman."

The innkeeper's wife was shocked by Offendorl's tone, but she left and Offendorl settled into a chair by the window. He would have enjoyed a bath under normal circumstances. In the tower he bathed regularly, but all he wanted at the moment was food, sleep, and to get on the road again. He despised traveling and didn't trust anyone, especially not young wenches who would almost certainly do anything for money, including slicing his throat when they were supposed to be washing him. He pushed the thoughts away and waited for the innkeeper to return.

The man was thin, with a thick mustache that seemed too large for his face. He entered the rooms carrying a large tray. There were two racks of grilled short ribs, a large bowl of fruit, and cheese. Freshly baked loaves sat cooling on the tray and there was a bottle of wine and two goblets. Offendorl knew at a glance that the innkeeper hoped to share the expensive wine with his guest, but the elder wizard had no such desires.

"Here we are, a feast fit for a king," the innkeeper said as he set about opening the bottle of wine.

"Tell me why there aren't any soldiers guarding the road," Offendorl said, tearing a rib from the rack and then biting into the tender meat.

"The queen's recalled all soldiers," the innkeeper said as he settled into a chair nearby. "Do you mind if I—"

Offendorl cut him off. "The queen? Why is she giving orders to the King's Army?"

"She's taken over," the innkeeper said. "There were a lot of people fleeing the city, but it's all settled down now."

"Why would anyone flee the Grand City?" Offendorl said.

"The queen is said to hate all women, if you believe the rumors. I don't, of course, but some do. She marched in with a big army though. They're all camped out there north of the city, and all the regular troops were recalled. I guess she's expecting King Belphan to go to war with her when he returns."

"Go to war with his own wife?" Offendorl said incredulously. He was starting to think the innkeeper was making up the outlandish tale.

"No, not King Belphan's wife—the Queen of the Sea, from Lodenhime," the innkeeper said. "They say no man can resist her. She's even moved into the tower of the Torr, if the rumors are true."

A wave of invisible magic hit the innkeeper so hard it knocked his chair over backward. Offendorl cursed and the entire inn shuttered as his magic erupted. The innkeeper looked up from the fallen chair, terrified, only to find Offendorl's eyes glowing.

"The Queen?" he bellowed. "She is no queen." He was snarling now. "She is a sorcerer, a witch. And she dares to invade my tower? Never!"

Offendorl's anger was channeled into his magic, fixing on the closest target he could find, and the innkeeper's spine started to arch against his control. The pressure was intense and soon the man was screaming.

"I will make her pay," he said. His voice was enhanced by his magic and could be heard throughout the inn.

The people who had gone running up to see what was happening suddenly stopped in their tracks. They waited down the hall, too frightened to move.

"I will make them all pay," he was shouting now.

"Please!" the innkeeper screamed. "Stop, please. You're killing me."

"I will kill everyone who bows a knee to that witch," Offendorl shouted.

There was a loud crack and the innkeeper died instantly, his back broken. His bowels released, soiling the rug the poor man had been writhing on. Offendorl slumped back into his chair, his anger spent and a wave of weakness washing over him. Then fear breathed a whisper into his ear. Was he strong enough? He was sure he could best Gwendolyn, but by now she would be linked to the other magic-users. There were other warlocks in the Torr, and Gwendolyn could tap into the power of almost any magic-user. Offendorl alone knew how to control and resist her, but he wasn't sure if he could in his weakened state. Plus, she had an entire army.

Fear began to gnaw at his resolve. He realized that word would soon reach Gwendolyn that he was here, less than a day's ride from the Torr. He was alone, weakened by his ordeal in Yelsia and the subsequent trek across the sea. If he was to defeat Gwendolyn and regain his home, he would need help and a safe place to wait until the moment was right. He didn't want to spring into action at the wrong time.

He ate his meal, ignoring the dead innkeeper, whose body was growing fouler by the minute. Once he'd eaten his fill, he cast a spell of darkness around himself and became like a living shadow. He moved slowly out into the hallway. There was no light in the hallway, and he was certain no one could see him. He slipped into a room at the far end of the hall and secured the door. Then he slept, his plan for the days ahead simmering in his mind and slowly taking shape.

Chapter 13

Brianna continued her journey, traveling only at night even though she had to fight her impulse to rush to Zollin. Quinn had said he expected his son to travel by sea from the southern coast of Yelsia all the way down to Osla. Brianna's only experience traveling by sea was with the Torr wizard Branock, who had kidnapped her and sailed from the Great Valley to Orrock. It had not been a pleasurable trip and gave Brianna no real indication of just how far ahead of her Zollin really was.

Still, there was no sense in looking for Zollin at sea. Even if they found him, they couldn't land to make contact as long as he was on board a ship. She decided instead to fly down the long Western coast. It would be easy to miss Zollin, she knew that, but if he was going south she wanted to be nearby. She would keep looking until she found him.

Her pride was growing stronger. They took turns hunting. The twin dragons Tig and Torc often scouted ahead, finding good places to hunt and isolated areas where they could take shelter and rest during the day. The dragons liked to lie in the sunshine whenever possible, their scales growing darker and harder from the sunlight.

They made good time, flying over the Rejee desert and then turning west to find the coast. They reached the Walheta Mountains in just three days. The dragons preferred the high mountain peaks of the Northern Highlands, but they all felt safer in the mountains than on the rolling hills of Yelsia. The Walheta Mountains were covered in thick evergreen forests and rugged bluffs, their jagged peaks softened by thick carpets of bright green moss. From there they could see the coast, which was much more densely populated than the open countryside they had been passing through, which was mainly farmland and large tracts of forest.

"We should rest here," Brianna said. "I feel like there is something here, something familiar."

The image of the cave where she had created the dragons flashed into her mind.

"No, Selix, not just a lair. I think there is someone here," she said, trying to place the sense of familiarity. "I know it will come to me. Go and hunt. You will be safe among the mountains."

Brianna knew that the Walheta were too rugged to be populated. Even as the sun began to rise, she didn't worry about her pride the way she would have before. If they were spotted, so be it. They didn't need to hide in forest groves or abandoned farms. No one could reach them among the high peaks of the mountains —certainly not enough people to threaten her pride. She sat alone on a high bluff, looking out to the sea. The ocean was beautiful in the dawn light, reflecting the pink and orange hues of the morning sky.

Brianna was tired, as was Selix, who had carried her most of the night and was now staying with her while the rest of the pride hunted. She sat, gazing far out to sea, letting her thoughts wander in hopes that the nagging sense of familiarity would rise to the surface. She thought of Zollin. He was never far from her mind. She wondered what he was doing. Did he miss her? Had he moved on? The questions had frightened Brianna ever since Quinn had told her that Zollin believed she had died. She honestly didn't know why Zollin would think that. If Bartoom had wanted her dead it could have killed her in the mountains. Instead, the ancient black dragon had taken her to a new lair, where it could find out more about her. She had healed the dragon's wounds and done her best to convince the dragon to stay with her, but in the end Bartoom was pulled away by someone else, someone whose voice was too alluring for the dragon to resist. Brianna guessed it was the wizard from the Torr, the same wizard Zollin had fought. She wondered how many magic-users would come for him before they could find peace.

Suddenly, she realized what was familiar. It was the sense that Bartoom was near. She had felt the same way in the mountains as the wounded black dragon had approached. She rose quickly to her feet. She wasn't sure what to expect, but she knew that sooner or later Bartoom would appear.

"Don't be afraid," she told Selix. "Another of our kind is coming. An old dragon. But he will not harm us."

The image of Brianna and Selix flying away from the mountains appeared in Brianna's mind, but she shook her head.

"No, we can't flee," Brianna said. "It is better if we stay. I need to know what has happened to Bartoom."

Brianna pictured the dragon in her mind and willed it to connect to Selix. Fire erupted from the dragon's partially opened mouth. Brianna moved back, not because she feared the fire, but because she did not want her clothes to be singed or burned. She had other clothes for warmer weather in her pack, but it was chilly high up on the mountaintop.

"We will wait," she said patiently. "We must learn from our brother. He will not harm us."

Brianna suddenly felt uncertain, and she put her hand on the side of Selix's large head.

"Do not fear," she said. "Bartoom is enslaved, but still one of us. We must help and learn, so that we can find and help Zollin."

Brianna settled in beside Selix, the dragon curling its body so that Brianna was surrounded. They watched the sea for nearly an hour before the pride returned. They brought back a small deer. Brianna cut a small section of meat out of the deer's hind leg, then Selix ate the rest. Brianna roasted the meat in her hands, relishing the heat. Then she ate the venison along with some bread and cheese from her pack, washing it down with water from her canteen while Selix went to drink from a stream the other dragons had found on their hunt.

She was inundated with images and emotions of happiness and wonder. The dragons were beginning to like the Walheta Mountains. There was game aplenty, although most of it was smaller animals rather than the large rams and elk of the Northern Highlands. And the Walheta were warmer than the mountains in the north, more alive with foliage. She knew they could stay there, make the mountains their home if she didn't have to go in search of Zollin. But she couldn't rest until she found him. She had no idea what they would do—perhaps make a home together near her pride. Or perhaps the pride would go on without her, she didn't know. It made her sad to think of the dragons leaving, but she knew they needed a life of their own, like children who have come of age. Soon, she thought, they will move on. Still, she was glad they were with her now.

She ate slowly, still watching the sea. She was just finishing her meal and fighting the urge to sleep (which all her pride but Selix had given in to), when she saw Bartoom. At first the dragon was just a speck far out to sea, even farther than her dragon eyes could see. But as she watched the shape grow, the feeling of familiarity grew as well. She knew it was the great black dragon, returning to the mountains. As it got closer, she sensed that it was injured. It flew slowly, almost favoring one side. She could sense that the dragon was exhausted, and she guessed it was so focused on rest that it had not noticed them. Her pride was stretched out on the ridge, basking in the sunlight. Only Selix was watching the big, black-skinned dragon.

"We'll wait," she said reassuringly. "Bartoom is hurt. We'll let it rest and then approach. I can heal it, and Bartoom knows that. Let's get some sleep while we can."

Brianna wrapped herself in a blanket and lay down on the soft bed of moss beside Selix. The big, golden dragon stretched a wide wing over her and they slept. Brianna dreamed of Zollin. He was flying beside her on Ferno, looking happy and free. It was a good dream and she woke with a sense of yearning that made her almost weep.

She rose and stretched, taking a drink from her canteen. The sun was beginning to set and she marveled that the day had seemed to pass in an instant. She turned, looking at the other mountains until she settled on a direction to search for Bartoom. Then she roused her pride. They set off just before twilight, gliding on the air currents and circling the mountain peaks. It was fully dark before she found Bartoom. The big black dragon was hidden in a cave, still sleeping, she sensed.

Brianna guided her pack down onto the mountainside, which was steep and covered with trees, but the dragons settled between the thick, prickly boughs and waited. They were well back from the entrance to the cave and Brianna approached alone, although it made the other dragons in her pride nervous.

"Bartoom," she called out in a gentle voice. "Where are you, old friend? Wake up and come meet my pride."

There was a low, menacing growl from the cave, like a dog warning its owner of danger.

"It is me, Brianna," she said, hesitating near the entrance to the cave. "I know you're hurt. I want to help."

"Enter," hissed a deep voice.

Brianna walked boldly into the cave. It was dark outside, but the sky was full of stars and the moon was near full. But inside the cave there was no light. Even with her enhanced vision, Brianna could not see into the recesses of Bartoom's lair. She kindled a small flame and let if float up above her head. The light was reflected by Bartoom's eyes.

"How did you come to be here?" it hissed, the dragon's forked tongue flickering as it spoke.

"I flew, with my pride," she said. "They are anxious to meet you."

"You have created more dragons," Bartoom said. He spoke slowly, his mouth and tongue working hard to form the words.

"Of course I have," she said simply. "It is what I was created to be. I am dragon-kind and humankind. You know that."

"I do, but you are not safe here. I am no longer in control."

"So the wizard has enslaved you?"

"Yesss," Bartoom said, drawing out the word as anger took hold. "I was foolish, but you are not. Why have you come?"

"To help you, and to help Zollin."

"Your wizard friend," Bartoom said, looking away. "What do you know of him?" Brianna said.

"I cannot say."

"Yes you can. Have you seen him? Is he well?"

"I have seen him. He plies the seas."

"He goes to confront your master," Brianna said. "The wizard of the Torr enslaves his own kind as well, but Zollin will stop him."

"He may," Bartoom said.

"May I help you?"

"There is no need," the dragon hissed.

"But you are hurt. I can sense it. Let me help."

Bartoom lowered his head. Brianna stepped forward, the heat in her hands growing and then slowly seeping into the black dragon. Its fractured ribs healed, and then the burns on its back.

"What happened to you?" Brianna asked, trembling now.

She had known that Bartoom was hurt, but she had not expected the dragon to be burned. Fire would not damage the great beast's scales, but something had. She wondered briefly if Bartoom had flown into a storm and been struck by lightning, but that seemed absurd. She couldn't imagine why a dragon would willingly fly into a storm. Then the thought struck her that Zollin had wounded Bartoom. She felt almost sick at the thought of it and couldn't help but push a mental image of Zollin toward Bartoom.

"Yes," the dragon hissed. "The wizard is powerful. A dragon slayer in the making."

"No," she said. "He wouldn't kill if he could help it. Why did he attack you?"

"It isn't important."

"Of course it is," Brianna said, tears stinging her eyes. She felt betrayed and frightened. She couldn't imagine Zollin killing dragons, even though that had been his intent in the Northern Highlands. He would have succeeded too, if Brianna had not healed Bartoom and helped him escape. She knew he was a good man, but he had used his powers to hurt Bartoom and the thought of him becoming a dragon slayer was repugnant to Brianna. He didn't know her kind, not yet. But she had dreamed of flying with Zollin, of welcoming him into her pride. She knew the other dragons would never do that if he was a dragon slayer.

"I was attacking the ship he was on. My master sent me to the sea to attack the wizard's ship. I had no choice."

"Did you kill him?"

"No."

"Did you destroy his ship?"

"No. But there was a sea creature that may have. That was two days ago. I have not seen the ship again."

Brianna's heart fluttered in her chest. Fear of losing Zollin was so strong it was almost tangible. She wanted to run, to leap high into the air and race to the ocean to find her love, but she knew that was foolish.

"How far away was he?"

"Almost a day's flight south," Bartoom said.

"I will go to him."

"And I will stay— "

Its voice was suddenly choked off, as if someone had taken the giant beast by the throat. Bartoom's eye's glazed for a moment, then focused on Brianna. Then Bartoom rushed forward, forcing Brianna aside and running out into the open. The dragon roared, setting the trees around its lair on fire. The other dragons of Brianna's pride roared back, then they took to the sky.

Brianna ran back out of the cave, her small flame extinguished. She looked up and saw her pride rising around Bartoom, who was flying straight up. The big black dragon feinted one way, then swung to the other, lashing out with its tail at Gyia. The smaller purple dragon swung just out of reach as Bartoom's mighty wings sent it shooting higher into the air. Tig and Torc were faster than the big black beast, but they dared not engage the larger dragon head-on. They flew up higher and higher.

Ferno was not as fast as Bartoom, but pursued the black dragon with a vengeance. Brianna's pride had been startled by Bartoom's sudden appearance from the cave and the blast of fiery breath, but they had not anticipated attack. They had flown up into the air with Bartoom out of instinct. On the ground, most dragons felt exposed and weak, but in the air they were stronger. Their huge bodies flew as nimbly as humminbirds. When Bartoom had attacked, they were shocked, frightened, and angry.

Ferno's jaws opened wide as it lunged for Bartoom's tail, but another flap of the black dragon's wings took it beyond Ferno's reach. Then Selix closed on the huge beast. They were almost the same size, Selix's golden scales reflecting the moonlight while Bartoom's black scales seemed to swallow any light that came near it. The two dragons clashed in mid-air, their tails lashing and their talons tearing. Fire lit the sky and Brianna could see the dragons as they fell, battling one another as they raced headlong toward the ground.

Selix was ferocious, but Bartoom's scales were much harder and the older dragon was taking less damage than its golden opponent. Selix felt its scales being shredded by Bartoom's talons and fought savagely to keep the black beast's massive jaws from its golden neck.

Brianna felt the communication as her pride fought. There were flashes and images racing through her mind, but she couldn't keep up. She ran and jumped off a rock that was jutting into the air, catching a thermal current and gliding upward. She wanted to be with her dragons, but she couldn't match their speed.

Selix pushed off of Bartoom just as Tig and Torc slammed into the larger dragon's side. Their talons impacted Bartoom, but their mass wasn't enough to injure the larger beast. Selix pulled away as Bartoom turned to face the new attackers, but they sped away before Bartoom could retaliate.

Then Ferno reached Bartoom. Bartoom was larger, but Ferno was thicker and just as heavy. Ferno's massive muscles tensed as it clashed with the black dragon. Bartoom roared fire, but Ferno ignored it, choosing instead to sink its razor sharp teeth into the black dragon's shoulder, ripping away flesh before letting go and looping back up. Bartoom was hurt and angry, but the voice inside its head was ordering it to kill the other dragons.

Bartoom flapped its massive wings and flew away from the other dragons, gaining altitude as it flew. Gyia was high overhead, directing the other dragons. Tig and Torc harassed Bartoom, one flying in from one direction, drawing the older dragon's attention while the other raced in from the opposite side for a hit-and-run attack.

Selix was bleeding from a dozen wounds, but flew to Brianna, who settled lightly on the golden dragon's back and began immediately healing Selix's wounds. They flew high over the mountains, where the air was very cold and it was difficult for Brianna to catch her breath in the thin air. Then they dove, hurtling at breakneck speed back toward the fight.

Ferno followed Bartoom, closing with the larger dragon when it slowed to attack the twin dragons. The green dragon's strength was enough to batter Bartoom off course. Ferno started with a massive charge, slamming into the black dragon, then following Bartoom in freefall. Brianna suddenly saw in her mind Bartoom's wings, the message clear. Ferno twisted around and tried to bite Bartoom's left wing, but missed. Then the green dragon clawed out with its massive talons, raking across the black dragon's leathery wings, ripping and shredding.

Bartoom's tail wrapped around Ferno's throat and pulled the green dragon backward, then the big black beast flapped its wings, shooting upward. The force of the bigger dragon's change of direction wrenched Ferno's neck, but the green dragon's massive muscles and Bartoom's wounded wing kept the force from breaking the green dragon's neck as Bartoom had been trying to do.

Brianna sent out images of the pride regrouping and of Bartoom escaping. She pushed her thoughts toward the other dragons and they flew to her. Selix was growling angrily.

"I know," she shouted. "But Bartoom is under the control of an evil wizard. We must follow and find this wizard to free our brother."

Ferno sent images of ripping the dragon apart, but Brianna shook her head.

"We must not kill our kind, not if we can help it."

They hung back, flying closely together. Brianna sent Tig to watch Bartoom while the others landed and rested from the fight. She checked each of the other dragons, but only Ferno was hurt. She had healed the lacerations that Selix had endured from Bartoom while they were still in the air. The cuts had not been deep and healing them was easy. Ferno, on the other hand, was worse off. The green dragon had several pulled muscles that were spasming in its neck and back, causing the dragon a great deal of pain. Healing those muscles took time.

Once she finished, Brianna took a long drink of her water and took a loaf of bread from her pack. Then she jumped in the air, flipping like an acrobat and landing softly on Selix's back.

"Okay," she said. "Let's fly!"

Chapter 14

It took Zollin three days of hard riding to reach Luxing City. The town was not all that large. The most impressive building was the castle, a massive structure with high walls and lookout towers on all four sides. The structures around the castle were small, mostly wooden buildings. The entire city seemed quiet, almost empty.

Zollin and Mansel rode into the city while Eustice took the other horses and their supplies around. Zollin didn't want to waste time in Luxing City, but he did want to find out what was happening with the army. He hoped they might be able to skirt around the army at Luxing. He had thought that King Zorlan would stay in the castle, or at least make camp for a few days. The road had been trampled by the army, and many of the small villages along their route had been picked clean of food and supplies. Some of the farms had even been burned. It made no sense to Zollin, who couldn't understand why the king would let his army raze his own people.

Unfortunately, it was obvious that the army wasn't still in Luxing. There were plenty of signs that they had been there, but the town was almost completely empty. Even from a distance Zollin could tell that. Still, they rode into the city to see what they could learn.

"It seems to me that perhaps the rumors of King Belphan's death weren't true," Zollin said.

"What makes you say that?" Mansel said.

"None of this makes sense," Zollin said. "Why wouldn't King Zorlan stay here, even for just a few days?"

"Maybe he is here," Mansel said. "He could have sent the army on ahead of him."

"But you saw the burned farms. Why would he let his army sack his own villages?"

"I don't know," Mansel said. "But to be honest, I don't know why most people do the things they do."

"So you think it's normal behavior, even for a king?"

"I don't know what's normal and what isn't. I just know that the king I met was more than a little crazy. You saved his life and his kingdom from his usurping son, yet he was ready to hand you over to the enemy. None of that makes sense to me."

"I guess you're right, I just don't understand what is driving Zorlan so hard."

"It's probably because he thinks that if he doesn't go lay claim to Osla, someone else will. The witch was marching south with the army from Ortis. At least that's the rumor. If we've heard it, surely King Zorlan has too. I doubt he'd want to sit around in his castle and let someone else beat him to the throne of Osla."

"How come kings are never content with their own kingdoms?" Zollin asked. "They're always invading some other kingdom or trying to expand into someone else's lands. It's almost predictable."

"Yet here we are, trying to figure out what is going on with another king and his army."

"We could just go home if there wasn't an evil wizard trying to hunt me down."

"Not to mention the dragon," Mansel said with a smile. "We've got to do something about that dragon."

They both laughed at the absurdity of their situation. It made no sense to think that two men and one servant could affect the outcome of kingdoms whose armies were at each others' throats—not to mention the magical creatures that seemed bent on destroying them wherever they went.

They passed several quiet homes and a few workshops. If people were inside, Zollin couldn't see or hear them. They certainly didn't reveal themselves. They rode further into the town and found several inns near the castle walls. Zollin swung off his horse and handed the reins to his friend.

"What?" Mansel asked with a grin. "You think I'm really going to sit out here and hold onto the horses?"

"I guess that was a little silly, wasn't it?" Zollin replied.

"I'd say so," Mansel agreed. "You get information. I'm getting ale."

They tied their horses to a post outside the inn and went inside. A tired looking woman stood up.

"Can I help you, gentlemen?" she asked.

"Ale," Mansel said.

"And maybe a little news?"

"There's not much news," the woman said, stepping into the kitchen and returning with two large mugs of ale. "The king didn't even stop on his mad dash to Osla. Just paused long enough to resupply and gather the reserve troops."

"It's awful quiet here in the city," Zollin prompted.

"That's because King Zorlan's got every able-bodied man in the supply train. There're tailors and blacksmiths—even leather workers. All of 'em forced into service. The gods only know what for."

"We saw some farms and small settlements burnt out," Mansel said, wiping foam from his lips with the back of his hand.

"That would be the dogs from Osla," the woman said. "They have no respect for anything other than killing and raping every innocent in the Five Kingdoms."

"Why doesn't King Zorlan stop them?"

"He isn't interested in what's behind him. He only cares about getting to Osla. From what I've heard, he thinks that King Oveer betrayed him, and King Belphan as well. We've heard rumors about the witch in Lodenhime, but I think that's just poppycock, myself. I think Oveer waited until King Belphan was well on his way to Yelsia, and then moved his forces south. It's no accident that King Belphan was killed. I imagine Falxis was next on his list, once he had control of Osla's treasury."

"That makes sense," Zollin said, although he knew the rumors about the witch in Lodenhime were true. "We thank you for the news," he said as he laid a silver coin on the table.

"And for the ale," Mansel agreed.

They stood up to leave.

"This is too much coin," the woman said. "At least stay and have some supper."

"We're in a hurry," Zollin said. "But if you have some food we can take with us, we'll pay."

"You've already paid enough," the woman said.

"Oh, I'd say that ale was worth that silver mark," Mansel said good-naturedly.

"You're too kind, both of you. But let me get you some fresh bread and smoked cheese. It's my specialty."

She hurried away and returned a moment later with a canvas sack filled with bread and cheese.

"I'm sorry there's not more. The army took most of what we have."

"This is more than enough. Thank you," Zollin said.

They rode through town and saw only one other person, a small child who looked half-starved. Zollin gave the boy a loaf of the bread the woman at the inn had given them. Then they rode out and met up with Eustice, who was waiting near a stream not far from the city. They stopped long enough to switch mounts and refill their canteens.

"I'm glad we got some ale back there," Mansel said. "I'm getting tired of drinking water all the time."

"Me too. We should have gotten something for Eustice," Zollin said.

The mute servant waved his hand as if to say it was okay, but Zollin still felt bad for the man. They rode hard, late into the night. Then made camp and slept for a few hours. Zollin and Mansel took turns standing watch, even though they didn't bother with a fire. They ate the last of the smoked fish and enjoyed the cheese they had gotten at the inn. It was soft and had a rich flavor that went well with the salty fish.

The next day they pushed on at dawn, riding hard all day, but still not catching sight of the army ahead of them. They passed several small villages, most of which were either completely wiped out or almost. There was no wine or ale to be had, and most had barely enough food left to see the inhabitants through winter. Zollin had a feeling that bad times were in store for the people in Falxis. If Zollin didn't stop Offendorl and the kings of the south, then bloodshed and hard times could devastate all five kingdoms. The way Zollin saw it, only Baskla had managed to avoid the bloodshed and senseless loss brought on by Offendorl's invasion of Yelsia.

The trail left by the armies led south and Mansel was becoming visibly nervous the farther they went.

"What's bothering you?" Zollin finally asked.

"I thought we'd have caught up with the army by now. I was hoping to get around it before they got to the coast."

"You're worried about the woman you met there?" Zollin asked.

"Nycoll," Mansel said, nodding. "She's all alone. If the army hurts her, I'll never forgive myself."

"It wouldn't be your fault, Mansel," Zollin said, knowing the words didn't make a difference even as he said them. "Even if you were there, you couldn't hold off the entire army." Mansel just looked at Zollin. He knew his friend meant well, and Mansel had no right to argue. He had killed Kelvich to keep the old man from asking too many questions when Mansel was under the witch's spell. Still, if he lost Nycoll, he didn't think he could take the loss. He pushed on, increasing their pace south. Zollin and Eustice struggled to keep up. Zollin understood his friend's motivation and did all he could to help. They rode late into the second night, and then rode through the third night. Eustice slept in the saddle as they rode on the fourth day out from Luxing City, even with the sun beating down on them and Mansel continuing his punishing pace.

When they finally caught sight of the army, it was merely a dust cloud in the distance, but it was enough to spur Mansel into an even more frantic pace. Zollin knew that even swapping mounts they couldn't keep up the grueling pace for much longer, but he didn't resist. He knew that if Brianna had been at the mercy of a marching army he wouldn't stop either. When night fell they were close enough that they could make out the marching troops. Zollin was surprised that they army didn't stop or make camp.

"What do you make of that?" Zollin asked Mansel.

"What?"

"They aren't stopping for the night. Don't most armies make camp at nightfall?"

"How should I know?" Mansel said in a surly tone.

"Maybe we should slow our pace a bit," Zollin said. "We could be running straight into a

trap."

"I'd welcome a fight at this point," Mansel said. "If you want to stop, go ahead. I'll be waiting with Nycoll for you to catch up."

"I'm not stopping," Zollin said. "You rode with me to rescue Brianna. I'm not suggesting that we don't ride as hard as possible. I just want you to have your feelers out for danger."

"You're the wizard; you do that."

Zollin frowned, but he understood his friend's dilemma. So they rode hard and finally caught up with a contingent of soldiers near midnight. It was a large group and they were making camp for the night. Most were laughing and talking. Zollin and Mansel left Eustice with the spare horses and rode forward together. They stopped for a moment just outside the light from the large fire. There were a dozen soldiers, all fully armed.

Finally Mansel rode forward into the light, causing the soldiers to rise to their feet and draw weapons.

"Who are you?" Mansel demanded.

"King's soldiers," said a tall man with thick, wavy hair. "And you?"

"We're just travelers," Zollin said, riding up beside his friend. "Actually, I'm a magician. I'll do a few tricks if you'll share your supper?"

"And who's he?" the soldier wanted to know, pointing at Mansel, who was glaring at each of the soldiers in turn.

"Oh, he's just riding guard with me. It's not very safe to travel alone these days," Zollin explained, trying to keep his tone light.

"I don't like him," said one of the other soldiers.

"Just ignore him," Zollin said. "He has a surly nature. No idea how to have fun, that one."

Zollin threw his hand up and sent a flaming ball of light shooting sparks in every direction. It sailed through the air and then disappeared like a firework.

"What do you say, fellas? You in the mood for some fun?" Zollin said, trying to imitate the traveling performers he'd seen as a child.

"No," said the soldier with thick hair. "We aren't in the mood for fun. Jens, go see if they're alone."

"Yes sir," said one of the other soldiers, running into the darkness behind them.

"There's no one back there but our servant Eustice," Zollin explained. "We'll move on if you aren't interested in a night you'll never forget. There's no need to get hostile."

"They've got horses," the soldier named Jens called.

"Bring them forward," the wavy-haired soldier shouted.

"Really, there's no need for this," Zollin said.

"Shut it and get down off those horses," the soldier demanded.

"Fine," Zollin said. "They're all yours, Mansel."

The big warrior drew his sword and spurred his horse forward. The sword that Zollin had crafted gleamed in the firelight. It was a simple weapon, with only the Veppra stone decorating it. Still, it looked like a fabled weapon from a bard's song. At first the soldiers seemed captivated by it, then it fell on the closest man, slicing through his neck and raining an arc of blood that landed sputtering in the flames.

The soldiers were shocked into action, but it was too late for the next man, who fell under Zollin's horse and was trampled. Three soldiers ran toward Zollin, but he batted them away with a wave of magic so hard they were knocked unconscious.

Mansel jumped from his horse and whirled into action. Zollin watched his friend fight with a sense of awe. Mansel was big—easily a head taller than Zollin—and his frame was so muscular it was almost bulky. Zollin rarely saw Mansel move quickly, but with a sword in his hand Mansel was all precision, grace, and speed. He moved almost too quickly to keep up with. The soldiers fell before him so easily it was almost laughable, but their screams made the spectacle all too real.

Mansel slashed the first soldier before the man could even raise his sword. The blade ripped through the thick padded doublet easily, tracing a crimson line down the man's chest and stomach from one shoulder to the opposite hip. The next soldier raised his sword, but Mansel's flashed under the upturned blade and severed the man's arm at the elbow, somehow cleaving through the joint and avoiding getting lodged in the bone.

The third soldier Mansel engaged had just enough time to swing his own weapon in a level arc that would have ripped out Mansel's throat, but the big warrior went down on one knee, letting the blade pass harmlessly over his head while in turn he rammed his own sword straight into the soldier's stomach. The soldier froze in pain and shock, but Mansel jerked the weapon free and stood up.

He was immediately set upon by two soldiers at once, but he caught both of their blades on his own, then kicked the legs out from under the closest soldier and shoved the other backwards. He drove his blade down into the chest of the fallen man, killing him instantly, then spun, jerking his sword free of the first man's body and swinging it in a low arc that cut cleanly through the second man's leg at the thigh.

Zollin was surprised to see the damage the big sword could do. He had honed it to a razor's edge, but the weight and strength of the blade made it even more deadly, strong enough to sever bone and flesh alike.

The rest of the soldiers fell back. There were four in the firelight, but the soldier sent to check on Eustice had not returned. Mansel stalked toward the last four, who threw down their weapons, all except the soldier with the wavy hair. He drew a large sword and stepped forward. Mansel feinted to the left then attacked to the right, but the soldier was ready. He brought his blade up to deflect Mansel's blow, but the impact staggered the soldier. He was a trained swordsman, but he was unprepared for Mansel's brute power. He tried to set his feet as Mansel's next blow came down—it was an overhanded arc, like a man chopping wood. The soldier raised his sword and the two blades met with a ringing clash that caused sparks, and the soldier was knocked off his feet.

"We need some of them alive," Zollin called out to his friend.

"Not this one," Mansel snarled.

The soldier was on his knees, swinging his blade at Mansel's hip, but the young warrior caught the blade with his own, then smashed the hilt of his sword into the soldier's face. Blood and teeth flew forward as the man's head snapped back. The soldier dropped his sword and fell on the ground, senseless.

"That's enough, Mansel," Zollin said, sliding down from the saddle.

"Not for the damage they've done," Mansel replied coldly. He was turning on the other soldiers, who were cowering in fear now.

"Hold it right there, or your man dies," came a voice from the darkness.

The soldier named Jens came walking back into the firelight with Eustice in front of him, a blade at the mute servant's throat.

"I'll kill him," said the soldier. "Throw down your weapons or your man dies."

Zollin concentrated on the blade the soldier had near Eustice's throat. The handle began to grow hot and Zollin watched the soldier's eyes grow round with surprise. Then he shouted and dropped the blade, shoving Eustice toward Zollin before running away. Mansel, like a dog caught up in the madness of battle, went chasing after him.

"This is turning into a real mess," Zollin said. "Are you okay?"

Eustice nodded.

"Tell me what is going on with this army," Zollin demanded of the remaining soldiers.

Before they could answer, they heard the soldier Jens screaming in pain as Mansel killed him. The soldiers all started talking at once.

"Shut up," Zollin shouted. "I can't understand all your babbling. You," he pointed to the closest soldier, "start talking."

"We're the rear guard," said the man. "We're marching on Osla."

"Aren't you from Osla?"

"Yes, but the wizard is trying to taking over."

"The wizard from the Torr, Offendorl?"

"I think that's his name," said the soldier.

"It is!" said another. "I heard someone call him that."

"And you are going to do what?" Zollin asked.

"We're taking back our kingdom," the first soldier said. "We won't just let some wizard take it from us."

"But you'll let King Zorlan?"

"He's leading the armies, but he isn't going to take the throne. King Belphan has sons."

"They're children," Zollin said. "And you're all fools. Are you the ones burning and looting the villages?"

"Not all of them," the soldier said. "There's other groups been taking what they want too."

Zollin shook his head and turned away as Mansel came back into the firelight. His friend went straight to his horse and mounted.

"You find out what you need to know?" Mansel asked.

"Yes," Zollin said. Then he turned to Eustice. "Ride along the coast until you find us, okay? We'll wait for you once we make sure Nycoll is safe."

Eustice nodded and then Zollin swung up into his own saddle.

"Let's go, there's no time to waste," he said.

Mansel looked at him appreciatively and the both whipped their horses into a gallop.

Chapter 15

Zollin and Mansel rode fast. Zollin let his magic flow out in front of them. Even though it was dark and hard to see, he could sense the contours of the terrain. They rode hard all through the night, only pausing an hour before dawn to walk the horses. They were exhausted—especially the horses—and Zollin knew they needed help to keep moving.

"We aren't far from Nycoll's cottage," Mansel said. "Maybe an hour at most."

"Let's just keep moving then," Zollin said, but as they traveled he inspected every weed and flower, looking desperately for something that might help them. He knew that some plants had rejuvenating powers. They had just remounted their horses when he spotted a small clump of brightly colored weeds.

"Wait a second," Zollin said, jumping off his horse.

His whole body ached. His stomach felt like it was tied in a knot, but his bowels felt loose, almost watery. His joints hurt and his head was a dizzy. His eyes felt like they had sand in them, and his mouth seemed to be producing a sticky, pasty muck instead of saliva. He snatched up the handful of weeds and climbed back into the saddle, ignoring the pain and his body's desperate cry for sleep. He let his horse follow Mansel's while he studied the weeds. He sensed both strength and danger in the plants. He knew he couldn't consume them, that was the first rule of woodsmanship—never eat anything you aren't sure won't kill you.

Still, he could feel a vibrant power in the small plants. It was like a spark, easy to miss if you weren't looking for it, but with the power to create something significant under the right circumstances. He let his magic flow into the weed and discovered what felt like a bubble. It was like a ripe piece of fruit, almost flowing with sweet, succulent juices. He squeezed the bubble with his magic and it burst almost instantly, filling his body with a sense of strength and energy he didn't think he'd ever felt before. It was like waking up from a long sleep, totally refreshed and energized. His stomach no longer felt sick, his joints didn't hurt. He looked up and realized he wasn't fighting his eyelids to keep them open.

"Mansel," he said, urging his horse forward. "This is amazing. Here, hold this," he said, handing one of the little weeds to his friend."

"Why?" Mansel asked, his body drooping and even his voice sounding weak.

"Just trust me."

Zollin let his magic flow into Mansel first, and then into the weed. He popped the magic bubble and watched his friend's shoulders suddenly straighten.

"What the hell did you do to me?" he asked.

"How do you feel?" Zollin said.

"Amazing. I feel like I could run all day long."

"Awesome," Zollin said. "Let me try it with the horses."

In a matter of moments the horses were galloping again, this time with a wild sense of abandon. They were like children racing through a field to see who was the fastest.

It took them almost twenty minutes to slow their pace, and then it was only because they saw smoke in the distance. They hadn't seen the army yet, which meant the group they had run into the night before were stragglers, probably falling back so that they could pillage at will. Still, the smoke in the distance was not a good sign. The continued forward at a fast pace, but were more careful.

It took several minutes to reach the source of the smoke, but when Mansel saw it he shouted a gut-wrenching cry that made Zollin's heart ache. He recognized the note of grief in his friend's voice.

"No!" Mansel shouted. "The bloody bastards," he said, his voice cracking under the strain. "Oh, no, no, no."

He slid down from the saddle and staggered forward toward the smoking ruin of Nycoll's cottage. The stone-lined well was caved in, the yard trampled. Only the great oak tree in the yard stood untouched.

"No!" Mansel cried as tears streamed down his face.

Zollin dismounted and tied their horses to the tree, and then went to his friend, who was shaking with silent sobs. He put his hand on Mansel's shoulder, unsure of what to say. The cottage had collapsed inward and the fire had been burning a long time. Very little was left but ash and charred foundation stones.

Zollin let his magic flow over the ruined house. He took his time searching for any sign of Nycoll, but there was no indication that she had died in the fire. So he let his magic flow out in a greater circle, into the tall weeds and down the hard-packed dirt path that led to the ocean. There was a wooden dock on the rocky shore, but no boat. Zollin was just about to turn his attention elsewhere when he noticed something hidden in the water. He probed further, reaching with his magic into the water, even though he was afraid of what might happen. There was a person in the water, hiding under the wooden dock.

"Mansel," Zollin said. "There's someone in the water."

He helped his friend to stand up, then they ran around the ruined cottage and down the path. Zollin could feel the hope pouring off Mansel in waves, like heat radiating from a fire.

"Is it Nycoll?" Mansel asked.

"I don't know."

"Nycoll!" he shouted. "Are you there? Nycoll?"

They reached the wooden dock and Mansel jumped into the water. There was splashing and then Zollin heard his friend crying.

"Is she okay?" Zollin called out.

"Help me, Zollin. She's tied to the piling. I can't get her loose."

Zollin let his magic flow into the dock and water. He found the rope and it burst apart. "Okay, I've got her. I've got you, Nycoll. You're going to be okay."

The water just steps from the shore was deep and Mansel struggled to pull the unconscious woman from under the deck.

Zollin lifted them both onto the dock, then let his magic pour into the woman. Her body was in shock. Even through the magic Zollin could feel that she was near freezing. She had been in the water too long. Her tongue was swollen and she was dehydrated. The rope had rubbed her skin raw where it had held her out of the water through the night.

"Is she alive, Zollin?" Mansel asked.

"Yes, I can help her. I just need a little time."

Zollin knelt on the dock beside Nycoll, letting his magic flow into her. He began to warm her body, healing the effects of hours spent in the seawater. "She needs fresh water, Mansel. Go get the canteens."

Mansel dashed away as Zollin continued to inspect every facet of Nycoll's health. She was well—she only needed time and nourishment. Mansel returned and they lifted her head and dribbled water into her mouth. After a few moments she began to come around. Her eyes fluttered open and she worked her mouth, trying to speak.

"It's okay," Mansel said, tears streaking down his face. "You're okay now."

"Mansel?" she asked, uncertain.

"Yes, it's me. You're safe now."

"They burned the cottage," she said. "They burned everything."

"I know," he said gently.

She was remembering the events slowly. Her eyes opened wider. “I hid under the dock but I couldn’t untie the ropes. I couldn’t get free.”

“I know,” Mansel said soothingly. “I know it. But you’re safe now.”

“How did you find me?”

“Zollin found you,” he said.

She glanced over at Zollin. “Your friend?” she said. “The wizard you told me about?”

“Yes,” Mansel said. “I’m sorry I wasn’t here.”

“You saved me. You came back for me.”

“I promised you I would.”

“Give her more water,” Zollin told Mansel. “Then we should move her someplace more comfortable.”

Mansel dribbled more water into her mouth. She drank it eagerly, then closed her eyes.

“Is she okay?” Mansel asked.

“She will be,” Zollin said. “She’s been through a lot.”

“Can’t you heal her?”

“I have,” Zollin said. “I’ve taken care of the physical things. She just needs rest.”

“What about the weeds, the ones you found on the road? Couldn’t those help her?”

“I think it’s best if she sleeps,” Zollin said. “We aren’t in a hurry anymore. She’ll be fine after she rests. We could all use a rest.”

“Okay,” Mansel said.

He was just getting to his feet when the trident struck. It was a heavy, brass spear with three separate points. It flew and landed solidly in Mansel's thigh, driving him to the ground, the shock and pain knocking the big warrior unconscious.

Zollin immediately raised a magical shield around himself, Nycoll, and Mansel. He scrambled back, looking for the threat, and saw almost a dozen heavily bearded men rising out of the water. They all had tridents and were staring at him balefully.

Anger erupted in Zollin and he lashed out, sending a stream of molten magical energy at the mermen, who disappeared below the surface of the water. One by one they popped up, throwing their tridents with a strength and accuracy that was hard for Zollin to believe. His magical shield held, but each blow came with such force that he was pushed backward.

He used his magic to levitate Nycoll and Mansel away from the dock. He withdrew from the water's edge and the bombardment of heavy spears ceased. He was breathing hard when he finally settled by the large oak tree where their horses were tied. Mansel was unconscious, his leg bleeding heavily. Zollin pulled the trident free and then put both his hands on his friend's leg, using pressure to slow the bleeding.

"I hate the ocean," Zollin said from between clenched teeth.

He let his magic flow out toward the shore, being careful not to touch the water. It seemed he wasn't welcome in the ocean. Luckily, there was nothing near the shore—no sign that the strange looking mermen wanted to continue the confrontation.

Zollin turned his attention back to Mansel, letting his magic flow into his friend's leg. The bone was broken and a large blood vessel severed. He repaired the damaged blood vessel first and then mended the torn flesh to stop the bleeding. Mansel's leg looked fine, but the bone was still broken. It took Zollin several minutes to locate all the tiny shards of bone and mend everything back together. When he was finished, Mansel seemed to be resting easy, so Zollin felt he could get up and prepare their shelter. But when he stood, the world seemed to spin and tilt off balance. He staggered, closing his eyes and holding tightly to the tree until the wave of dizziness passed. Then he got some food out of his pack and began to eat. All the symptoms from lack of sleep returned with a vengeance. It was all Zollin could do to lay out blankets and levitate Mansel and Nycoll onto them. The big oak gave them ample shade, and once he had everything unpacked and near to hand, he rolled himself in his cloak and fell asleep.

When he woke it was dark out. He kindled a small flame in the palm of his hands. Nycoll was looking at him and sipping water from a canteen.

"You're awake," Zollin said.

She nodded, but didn't speak. Mansel was still asleep. Zollin made a mental note that the weed he had found to give them stamina didn't take away the need to rest, it merely postponed it. Zollin was still exhausted, but he got up, started a fire nearby, and checked on the horses. He didn't expect Eustice to catch up until the next afternoon at the earliest. He was thankful the mermen hadn't continued their attack. He and Mansel would have been easy prey sound asleep only a few hundred yards from the shore, but the sea creatures didn't reappear. They seemed drawn to his magic only when it entered the water.

The horses were tired as well, not even nibbling the grass around them yet. Zollin unsaddled the horses and rubbed them down. Then he returned to the fire with more food. He didn't know about the others, but he was famished. He ate a loaf of bread and wished he had more of the smoked cheese from Luxing City, but they had eaten the last of it days before. There was dried meat and a few old vegetables, but Zollin didn't have the energy to cook anything.

"Are you hungry?" he whispered to Nycoll.

She nodded again and he handed her a loaf of bread.

"Sorry I don't have something better than stale bread."

"It's fine," she said quietly.

They ate in silence. Zollin tried not to let Nycoll's staring bother him. It wasn't even that she was looking at him—it was that she didn't seem to trust him. She watched him like someone might watch a mischievous child. After he ate, he went to sleep. He knew that it would have been wise to stand a watch, but he was just too exhausted.

The next morning he felt better. He woke up when he heard Mansel moan. Nycoll helped the big warrior get a drink of water and sit up.

"I feel like I drank an entire cask of ale," he said.

"It's just fatigue," Zollin said. "Eat something and get some more rest and you'll be fine."

"Nycoll, how are you feeling?"

"I'll be fine," she said softly. "You should eat."

"I could eat a horse," Mansel said.

The horses neighed and Zollin laughed.

"I think they heard you," he teased.

They ate and napped through the day. Eustice didn't arrive by nightfall, and Zollin didn't think the mute servant would continue traveling after dark. He let Mansel and Nycoll have some privacy while he took first watch. He walked out into the darkness away from their fire and let his eyes adjust. Then he let his magic flow out around him, but was careful not to let it go near the shoreline. The last thing he wanted was some other sea creature rising up and attacking them in the dark.

There were small creatures all around—field mice, small birds, bats, and insects. There were even a few snakes, but none were close to Zollin or his friends. The night was quiet and Zollin allowed his mind to wander as he stared out into the darkness. He thought of Brianna, his heart aching as it always did. He wished more than ever that he could have had more time with her, or maybe just seen her once more. He would tell her how much he loved her, and then just hold her for as long as he possibly could. He thought of his father and wondered if Quinn had found happiness in Felson with Miriam, the animal healer. Miriam was a strong-willed woman, compassionate but unyielding in her personal beliefs. Zollin though she would make a good match with his father, but he found it hard to imagine Quinn being romantic with a woman. His father had never shown any interest in women in all the years they had lived in Tranaugh Shire, but a lot had changed since they had fled from the small village to escape the wizards of the Torr.

Thinking of the Torr gave Zollin a strong sense of dread. He knew that a hard fight lay ahead, and even if he won there was no guarantee the fighting would stop. If King Belphan was really dead, the Five Kingdoms could be thrown into a war that could last for decades. It made Zollin almost sick to think that he was the cause. He knew intellectually that he wasn't to blame, that he hadn't made the decisions to hurt and kill others, to send armies across the Five Kingdoms, but his emotions made the case that if he had just gone with the wizards of the Torr, none of the atrocities of the past year would have happened. Then again, thinking of Eustice, who had been a servant of the Torr for years, made him sick as well. Eustice, who had been taken into Offendorl's service as a child, castrated, and then had his tongue cut out, was a living example of the Master of the Torr's cruelty. Zollin knew he could never serve someone so twisted and evil. Going to the Torr would have been a death sentence, or worse—a life of torturous enslavement.

Zollin watched the moon as it slowly moved across the sky. The days in Falxis were hot, but the nights were cool and so Zollin let his magic burn brightly, filling him with a supernatural warmth. He let the magic flow out in a sort of blanket awareness. He wasn't sure exactly how long he stayed that way, his magic burning like a bonfire, sensing everything around him in every direction simultaneously but losing himself completely in the process. He might have stayed in the blissful state of magical awareness through the night if he hadn't sensed the dark, angry presence that flew by overhead.

At first Zollin was shocked by the discovery. He let his magic flow up as well as out around him. He had felt the nocturnal avian creatures passing by overhead. Insects buzzed about, flicking from one spot to the next. Bats dove and fluttered, their wings flapping almost clumsily but drawn to any small movement. Occasionally, owls flew past or swooped down on an unsuspecting creature moving slowly through the tall grass that grew among the sandy dunes this close to the shore. But the angry beast was flying higher than the other night animals. It was large and surprisingly familiar. Bartoom, Zollin realized. He retracted his magic, feeling as if he had just come up for air after a long underwater dive. He sucked in great lungfuls of air as he hurried back to the small camp where Mansel and Nycoll waited.

"Mansel!" he shouted. "Get up, the dragon is back. Mansel!"

Zollin searched the star filled night sky, but the dragon was almost impossible to see. Bartoom's scales were jet black, blending into the space between the stars perfectly. Zollin sent his magic up again and found the big dragon circling around. Zollin held his connection with Bartoom for a moment, sensing the dragon's wounds. They were several days old and none of them severe, but the dragon had seen difficult action not long ago. Zollin wondered briefly if the kraken had hurt the dragon more than he had thought.

"What in the bloody blazes are you on about, Zollin?" Mansel demanded.

"The dragon just flew by and it's coming back."

"Where?" Mansel asked.

"There," he said, pointing in the distance although neither of them could see the dragon.

"You sure?"

"Positive," Zollin said.

"Okay, Nycoll, get out of here!" he shouted. "Stay low, but get some distance from us. This thing is deadly."

Nycoll didn't say a word—she just hurried away, disappearing into the darkness.

"What do I do?" Mansel asked.

"I'm not sure, we don't have anything to attack the dragon with," he said. Then an idea

struck. "Oh, wait. The tridents."

"The what?" Mansel said.

Zollin was already moving, running back along the path that had led from Nycoll's cottage to the sea.

"There were mermen in the ocean," Zollin shouted. "They attacked us. Don't you remember?"

"No!" Mansel shouted. "Are you insane? Mermen? Really?"

"Most of the tridents fell back into the water, but a few didn't," Zollin shouted as they reached the dock. He kindled a flame and held it high over his head. There wasn't much to see—

the grasses around the shore, which was rocky and steep, were strangely flattened.

"Oh, curse it all," Zollin said. "They must have come ashore and collected them all."

"You are losing it, Zollin," Mansel said.

"No, they were here, right here," he said in frustration.

There was a roar that made them both look up, just as a wave of fire consumed their horses and set the massive oak tree ablaze. Zollin immediately covered them in a shield of magic, but the dragon didn't press the attack. It flew harmlessly past and out to sea.

"You think it didn't see us?" Mansel asked.

"I have no idea," Zollin said. "But it's leaving the area."

"Or pretending to. And we don't have mounts or supplies. Everything but the clothes on our backs was under that tree."

"Eustice should be along tomorrow," Zollin said. "He's got the extra supplies."

"If he wasn't waylaid somewhere. We could be in serious trouble."

"Isn't there a village nearby?"

"One of the smallest I've ever seen," Mansel explained. "It's really just a few people spread along the seashore. But if the army didn't spare Nycoll's home, they probably didn't spare the village."

Zollin felt his heart sink a little. Their best chance for survival would be the ocean, but he didn't relish going back to sea.

“Make sure that dragon isn’t circling back,” Mansel said. “I’m going to find Nycoll.”

Zollin expanded his magic in the sky in a broad, arcing circle, like the top half of a bubble. He didn’t bother filling the sky with magic so that he could feel every small creature—instead, he pushed the limits of his power, expecting that something as large as the dragon would be easy to find. The big dragon, Bartoom, was gone. Zollin wasn’t sure where the beast had gone, but he didn’t linger long on the question. Instead, he focused on the two smaller dragons that were circling the burning tree.

“Mansel!” Zollin shouted. “We aren’t out of the woods yet.”

“What now?” Mansel bellowed.

“More dragons,” Zollin said loudly. “There are more dragons.”

Chapter 16

Prince Wilam stood in the great round audience room of the Torr. He was anxious. Scouts had reported that an army from Falxis was marching south and was almost to the border of Osla. Unlike King Oveer and his worthless generals, Prince Wilam felt that the best way to win Gwendolyn's affection was through performance. That meant leading the army fell to him alone. The king and his generals lazed around the audience chamber of the Torr like house cats, ignoring their duties in hopes of catching a glance of Queen Gwendolyn.

Prince Wilam had outlined a plan that included dividing the army into a small force and a large force. The larger force would go out to meet the invading army north of the Grand City. There was still time for the prince to find suitable ground to meet the enemy on so that they went to battle on their own terms. The smaller force would be held in reserve. If Prince Wilam failed to stop the invaders, the smaller group could defend the city. Gwendolyn had shown very little interest in his preparations for defending her prize. He had thought that marching to Osla and taking the richest kingdom in her name would have pleased the queen, but she was caught up in the books that Offendorl had left behind. She spent days working through the translations of ancient texts, ignoring everyone and everything else.

"Have you seen her today?" Wilam asked King Oveer, who was lounging on pillows near one of the room's many windows and drinking wine.

"Do not address me as an equal," King Oveer said, his words barely understandable through his wine thickened tongue. "Leave your message with General Vaslic. We shall pass it along to Her Highness."

"I do not leave messages with the likes of you drunkards," Wilam hissed. "You lazy fools are worth less than the wild dogs nosing through the refuse in the streets."

"You cannot insult me, Prince." King Oveer said the last word with such disdain he nearly fell off his mattress.

"I already have, King Oveer. I have taken your army," he said, then lowered his voice, "and soon I shall take your pathetic life as well."

"I will have your head for such an insult."

"Come take it, if you're man enough."

"Vaslic, Ormon, slay this spineless fool and bring me his head. I shall make a gift of it to

Her Highness."

"Still letting other people fight your battles?" Prince Wilam said coolly, his hand resting on the hilt of his sword.

"It's about time we deloused Her Lady's tower."

Prince Wilam heard the swords being drawn behind him, but he didn't turn to face the two generals who had been ordered to attack him. He stood, watching King Oveer, who slurped from his wine cup and then wiped his nasty beard with the back of his hand.

"I will feed what's left of you to the dogs in the street," King Oveer said. "Since you know them so well."

"I know Her Highness, and the queen knows me," Prince Wilam said with a smirk.

"Liar!" King Oveer shouted.

Prince Wilam spun around, drawing his sword in one fluid motion. The two drunken generals were lurching toward him, but both moved slowly, their balance ruined by too much wine. He stepped toward the closest man and swung a hard blow straight at the general's sword. Ormon couldn't hold onto his weapon, which went spinning across the floor. Prince Wilam ignored the weaponless general and faced Vaslic.

"Throw down your weapon and flee Osla," Prince Wilam said, "or I'll kill you."

"I shall not leave Her Highness," Vaslic said.

"Then die, dog!" Wilam shouted as he rushed forward.

Vaslic raised his sword in a clumsy attempt at defending himself, but Prince Wilam smashed the drunken general's knee with a savage kick. Vaslic fell to the ground, dropping his weapon and grabbing his leg. The blood lust ringing in Prince Wilam's ears, he drove his sword deep into the general's stomach. Then he wrenched his weapon free and turned on General Ormond, who had recovered his weapon but was staring wide-eyed at his slain colleague.

Prince Wilam didn't give Ormond the chance to flee. He feinted to his right, then slid to his left, slashing his sword across Ormond's shoulder. Blood arced and the general screamed, but

Wilam followed his initial attack with a thrust under his opponent's blade that split Ormond's sternum. Prince Wilam's blade stuck fast and he was forced to put one foot on the other man's chest to jerk his weapon free. Then he spun to face King Oveer, who was climbing from his pile of cushions to his feet.

"Your worthless generals are dead, oh King," Wilam said. "And your pathetic reign has come to an end."

"You dare not lay a hand on me. I'm the sovereign ruler of Ortis. I command armies who will avenge me to the fourth generation of your villainous family."

"Do not speak of the royal family of Yelsia," Wilam said in a mocking tone. "We did not plot against your kingdom and murder defenseless members of your royal court. Did you think I would not hear how you baited my high counselor and then murdered him in cold blood?"

"Because he was spying," King Oveer whined.

"And his spying was greater than your plotting against my family and my kingdom?"

"You have a wizard."

"And you had a whole tower full," Prince Wilam said as he shoved the king.

"You dare touch me?" King Oveer shrieked.

"I'll do more than touch you," Prince Wilam said. Then he stabbed at Oveer with the point of his sword, drawing blood from the king's shoulder.

"Guards!" King Oveer shouted. "Guards, to me."

"Your guards are not allowed in the tower, remember?" Wilam said, stabbing at Oveer again, this time drawing blood from the King's thigh.

"Gwendolyn!" Oveer screamed like a child calling for his mother. "Gwendolyn, help me."

Prince Wilam backhanded Oveer, sending him reeling and spitting blood. Piss stained his pants and he began to beg.

"Please don't kill me," he cried. "I'll do anything."

Wilam again shoved the king, who stumbled back almost to the open window. The tower of the Torr had large windows that opened like shutters. They ran from the ceiling almost to the floor. Wilam could only think of how the spoiled king spent day and night fawning for Gwendolyn. He was jealous of any man who might lay claim to the Queen of the Sea, but only King Oveer stood above Prince Wilam in rank. One day Wilam would be a king and Oveer's equal, but for now he was just another suitor to the woman both men were infatuated with. He kicked out hard, slamming his foot into the king's chest. Oveer stumbled back, gasping for breath until his legs hit the windowsill. Then time seemed to slow as King Oveer of Ortis struggled to regain his balance. It was a lost cause—he simply had too much momentum moving him backward, not to mention his inebriated state. His arms circled and his face became a mask of terror. Then he fell, screaming until he landed, his head smashing against the polished flagstones and split open like an overripe melon.

"Good riddance," Prince Wilam said, spitting from the window.

"What have you done?" shrieked Gwendolyn.

She was levitating down from the floor above. Her face was sternly disapproving, but all Prince Wilam could see was the woman he loved. He felt weak in the knees whenever he saw her and his heart seemed to leap whenever she spoke to him.

"I am here to bid you farewell," he said, ignoring her question in his excitement. "I will destroy King Zorlan's army and bring glory to your empire."

"Do not speak to me of glory," she said angrily. She rarely feigned interest in the men who longed for attention anymore. She had grown in power, not just from drawing on the other magic-users of the Torr, but from the knowledge she had poured into herself from Offendorl's library. She no longer cared about bringing men under her power and she despised the way they fought one another for her affection.

"Go!" she ordered. "Go play war before news spreads that you killed the king of the men you lead."

"They will not care," Prince Wilam argued, taking a step closer to Gwendolyn. He was within an arm's reach of her and her proximity made him tremble. "They serve you now, not that fat slug. Once I destroy Zorlan's army, there will be nothing keeping us from uniting the Five Kingdoms under your rule, my love."

"Do not speak to me of love," she said. "Not as you march to slaughter other men."

"I will win you an empire."

"You win me nothing. You only hasten the inevitable."

"I shall lay his crown at your feet, then nothing will stop us from being together."

"You overstep your bounds," she hissed in warning, but Prince Wilam was undeterred.

"I shall make you love me," he said. "No one can stop me now."

Anger radiated off of Gwendolyn, although she controlled her urge to bring the love-struck young prince to his knees in front of her. She had agreed to Wilam's plans if for no other reason that it would occupy her hotheaded suitor.

"Go then," she said, her magic filling the air between them until she wavered from the barely contained heat of it. "Slay them all."

"As you wish," he said, bowing and hurrying away.

Gwendolyn walked slowly to the window where King Oveer had fallen and looked down. The sight both sickened and thrilled her. Her heart was growing dark, and violence, which she had always abhorred but tolerated as necessary, was beginning to appeal to her in a whole new way. She stepped back from the window and smiled, savoring the grisly memory and letting it push her toward her goal. She had to embrace the darkness of death completely if she was to succeed, and she couldn't allow anything to stop her—least of all her useless human emotions.

* * *

Brianna was flying with Ferno when the image of the burning tree and the two men came to her. At first she wasn't sure why she was seeing it. A tree consumed by fire was unusual, but it wasn't an obvious indication of danger. Then she looked more closely at the mental image, almost like examining a memory. She saw the carcasses of the two horses and the burned track of grass that she realized came from a dragon.

Bartoom, she thought. The mighty black dragon they had been following for days had attacked…a tree? That made no sense, she thought. Then she looked at the two men. They seemed vaguely familiar, but she couldn't see them clearly enough.

She sent the hazy mental image of the two men back to Tig, who had spoken to her in the dragon way. She waited impatiently for a reply, partly because she felt that she somehow knew the two men, and partly because it was a departure from the tedium of following Bartoom. The big black dragon had seemed tireless at first, and her pride had grown weary in pursuit. Finally the bigger dragon had gone to ground, taking refuge in a large thicket of wiry bushes. They were surrounded by miles of plains and there were no other places where her own pride could rest. Brianna had stood watch while her dragons slept. Then she had gotten rest on the back of Selix.

The pride flew together unless it became necessary for one or two to hunt. Wild horses were common on the plains of Falxis. Horseflesh wasn't the first choice for dragons, but being on the move made it difficult to hunt at all and they took whatever they could find.

When the image came back to her, Brianna had to hold onto Selix to keep from falling off. Her heart beat madly and she felt like shouting. She had found Zollin at last. She couldn't wait to see him, and at the same time she felt afraid. What if his feelings for her had changed? She wasn't sure exactly how long they'd been apart, but she knew a lot had happened in that time. She wasn't the same girl. She knew exactly who she was and what she wanted now, but her heart was divided between her love for her pride and her love for Zollin. She wondered what she would do if they weren't compatible.

There wasn't much time for consideration, however, as images came back to her of Zollin and Mansel preparing for battle. She understood their need to defend themselves against unknown creatures, but it frightened her as well. She knew Zollin's power was great—she had seen him do things she never thought possible—and she was more than a little worried that he might use his power against her pride.

The dragons were fascinated by the magical power radiating from Zollin. Brianna couldn't sense it, but the dragons could, as if it were a delicious aroma from a finely cooked meal. They had questions and were insatiably curious creatures. She had to remind herself that they were really just newborns. Their instincts were incredibly strong and they were very intelligent, but so many of the things they were experiencing were brand new to them.

She pushed out a mental image of herself floating down to the burning tree alone. Immediately she was hit with several mental images from the other dragons. Some were mere emotional discharges, such as fear or just surprise, while others showed her being attacked, and some showed her surrounded by the pride.

She did her best to reassure them, but they were quickly approaching the area where Zollin and Mansel waited. She could see the light from the burning tree in the distance and she prepared herself to leap from Selix's back. She sent one last message to her pride, instructing them to circle the area but to stay high in the sky until she called them down.

Selix was almost directly over the burning tree when she leaped from the large, golden dragon's back. She flipped several times before slowing her decent. She could see Zollin and Mansel with her own eyes now. Mansel had his sword drawn and ready. Zollin was watching her with fascination, but he was also in a defensive stance. She swayed from one air current to another—most weren't strong currents, but she was so buoyant in the air now that she could use almost any movement of air to lift herself up or slow her descent down.

She landed near the tree, close enough that she knew Zollin and Mansel wouldn't be able to come because of the sheer heat. She saw Zollin's face contort for a moment, then he was running toward her, shouting her name.

Brianna's heart felt as if it would burst, and even though she was getting mental images of danger and worry from her pride, she ran to Zollin. He caught her in his embrace, swinging her around in circles for a moment before setting her down again.

"Are you real?" he asked. "Are you really alive?"

"Yes," she said. "I'm alive and well, Zollin. I'm so glad I found you."

"What are doing here?" he asked.

"I came looking for you, but we were following Bartoom."

Zollin looked confused.

"The big black dragon," she tried to explain as a look of panic crossed Zollin's face.

"You're with the dragon?" he asked. "The dragon that tried to kill me?"

"No," she said. "I'm not with Bartoom. It's a long story, I'll explain it all soon, but first I want you to meet my pride."

Zollin looked dumbfounded and Brianna felt an icy stab of fear. She knew that she had as much to explain to Zollin as she did about Zollin to her pride.

"Look, a lot has changed, but I'm still the same girl from Tranaugh Shire," she said, holding his arms and looking into his eyes. "I still love you, Zollin. I still want to be with you, to be your wife."

"I want that too," Zollin said, finally finding words.

"Okay, so let me show you what I mean," she said, sending the mental command to her pride high above.

"The dragons are coming down," Mansel said nervously. "We've got to find cover." He was pulling on Zollin's arm, but Brianna grabbed Zollin's other hand.

"No, wait," she said. "They're with me."

"The dragons are with you?" Zollin asked.

"Yes, they're my pride."

"Your pride?" he asked, incredulously.

“Yes, you know, like a pack of wolves or a pride of dragons,” she explained. Zollin and Mansel’s eyes went wide with wonder, and then the dragons touched down all around them.

Chapter 17

Zollin could hardly believe his eyes. The light from the burning tree illuminated the glistening scales of the dragons around them. His heart was racing with fear. They were beautiful, but even the smaller dragons looked ferocious, and every instinct was telling him to run, to get as far as he could from the dragons.

"This is Selix," Brianna said, walking over to the golden dragon, who lowered its head in a sort of bow. Brianna patted the golden dragon's neck.

"This is Ferno," she said, and the dark green dragon growled menacingly. "They're friends, Ferno," she said firmly. "You can trust them." A puff of smoke shot out of the big dragon's mouth, but it didn't move forward.

"You can put away your sword, Mansel," Brianna said. "I promise they won't hurt you."

He shook his head, "Sorry, force of habit I guess. It's not every day that I get this close to dragons."

"These are Tig and Torc," Brianna said, approaching the two smallest dragons. "And finally, Gyia," she said, giving the purple dragon a scratch on the top of the head.

"How did you find them?" Zollin asked.

"I didn't find them," Brianna explained. "I made them."

"Hang on," Mansel said. "You made dragons? What am I missing here?"

"My power," Brianna said, still speaking to Zollin. "You remember what the dwarves said?"

"I do," Zollin said, with awe in his voice. "They said you were a fire spirit, and that dragons were the offspring of fire spirits."

"Offspring isn't really the right word," Brianna said. "I made them using my power, but I'm not their mother. These five chose to stay with me, but we're more like siblings."

"I've got to sit down," Mansel said. "If ever I needed a drink…"

Mansel backed away from the dragons, then walked slowly into the darkness.

"I know it's a lot to take in," Brianna said. "But I'll do my best to explain it."

"I know you will, but we have time. For now, we need to check on Nycoll and get settled in for the night."

"Alright," Brianna said, a little hurt that Zollin's excitement had been replaced with uncertainty. She wasn't sure what she had hoped for from him, but his attitude wasn't making her fears any less pointed. "What would you like us to do?"

"I'm not sure," Zollin said. "We found Nycoll yesterday. She and Mansel are close, but I'll let him tell you that story later too. She's had a difficult time lately. I'm not sure how well she'll take to seeing dragons."

"We're not horrible creatures," Brianna said.

"No, but I don't think scaring her will help."

"We won't scare her."

"You won't have to," Zollin tried to explain. "Let's just give her some time, okay? I'll check on her, and then I want the whole story."

"All right," Brianna said.

It hurt Zollin to see Brianna looking so disappointed, but he was in a slight state of shock himself. He didn't know how else to respond. He was fascinated by the dragons, but in the dark, as tired as he was, he had to admit they were frightening creatures. He wanted to make sure that Mansel was okay and that Nycoll didn't need anything.

He walked away into the darkness, letting his magic flow out in search of Mansel and Nycoll. He felt a little guilty for keeping his magical shield up, but he couldn't shake the feeling that he was going to be roasted alive the second he let his guard down. All around the yard where Nycoll's cottage had once sat were small hills. The hills were formed by sand and most were covered with thick weeds. Zollin found Mansel not far away. Nycoll had fainted and Mansel was trying to wake her up.

"She's out of it," he said. "You think she's okay?"

"Yes," Zollin said. He was letting his magic probe Nycoll to ensure he hadn't missed anything physical. "She's been through a lot, but physically she's fine. She just needs rest. We all do."

"Where do you suggest we do that?" Mansel asked.

"Here's as good a place as any. I'm going back to talk to Brianna. You stay here and shout if you need me."

"All right," Mansel said. "But be careful."

"You don't trust Brianna?"

"I'm not even sure that is Brianna. Did you see the way she came down out of the sky? It was like she was a bird or something. I've never seen anything like that."

"I have," Zollin said. "She was jumping and flipping like an acrobat before the dragon took her."

"Well, what do you think of her new friends? How can we know they aren't using her to get to you?"

"I don't know," Zollin said. "I guess I've just got to trust Brianna."

"Your funeral, pal," Mansel said. "But don't say I didn't warn you when one of those beasts cooks you for its next meal."

Zollin laughed and gave Mansel's arm a reassuring squeeze before walking away. He was pretending that the dragons didn't bother him, but the truth was, he didn't like dragons. They were vicious and cruel. He wished more than ever that he had killed the big black dragon in the Highlands, but he hadn't. Brianna had convinced him not too, and now she was with a whole group of them. It made him feel sick to this stomach, but he remembered the power that Brianna had discovered in the caves of the dwarves and how she seemed to embrace that power completely. It made him feel like a hypocrite to judge Brianna after she had given up everything to support him when he revealed his own magic.

He walked back out into the clearing and found Brianna all alone.

"Where are the dragons?" he asked.

"I sent them to hunt," she said, her irritation showing. "We've been tracking Bartoom for days now and they haven't had the time to feed the way they should."

"I'm sorry," Zollin said. "I know I'm being a bit skeptical, but I thought you were dead."

"Why?" Brianna asked. "Bartoom didn't take me by force. If he wanted to kill me, why wouldn't he have done it in the valley instead of taking me away?"

"Come on, what was I supposed to think? Our plan was to kill the dragon, remember? Not heal it, and certainly not to take off with it. I was worried sick. I tried desperately to find you, but you were just gone. And then…" he let his voice trail off.

"And then what?" Brianna said.

"And then things just went from bad to worse. We lost Kelvich, and we almost lost my dad. I didn't know what had happened to you, but the way things were going I couldn't help but think you were dead. When I saw the dragon, I fought hard hoping to find a clue as to what happened to you, but he slipped past me. You know he's working for Offendorl, the master wizard of the Torr, don't you?"

"Yes, but it isn't Bartoom's fault. The wizard has found a way to enslave Bartoom. It doesn't have a choice but to obey."

"You're saying the dragon doesn't want to do bad things?"

"No, it really doesn't," Brianna said. "It didn't kill me, and it could have."

"It killed a lot of people, though—hundreds of them. It burned villages, and it even fought with Offendorl, attacking the

Orrock city walls. It even carried Offendorl away, just when I almost had him."

"I'm sorry for that," Brianna said. "And honestly, I think Bartoom is too. It's hundreds of years old and has survived countless atrocities, most of them at the hands of people. It's no wonder that it acted so viciously. Look, I'm not excusing what Bartoom did, but I have a different perspective now. I can relate to how they feel."

Zollin took Brianna's hand and they walked to the far side of the tree from where the horse carcasses were burning. The poor animals had died instantly from the dragon's fiery breath, and Zollin was a little embarrassed that his stomach was growling from the smell of the roasting horse flesh. They sat down on the grass, facing each other.

"Well, I am very happy that you are alive," he said.

"Did you miss me?" she asked.

"Of course I did. I wanted to curl up in a ball and die. If I wasn't forced to fight armies and chase down evil wizards, I probably would have."

"You could have come looking for me," she said.

"I would have," Zollin said. "I would have spent the rest of my life searching for you."

She smiled and squeezed his hand.

"My pride can help you," she said. "The dragons are powerful, Zollin. They almost killed Bartoom less than a week ago."

"I wish they would have," Zollin said.

"Bartoom is returning to the wizard that enslaved it."

"Not without taking a shot at me every chance it gets," Zollin said. "And the wizard's name is Offendorl. He's old and powerful, but I've got to stop him. He led an army to attack Yelsia and used the dragon against us."

"I know," Brianna said sadly.

"And the army that invaded Yelsia is now on its way to Osla. Rumor has it that King Belphan was killed during the battle of Orrock. And there's a witch too—have you heard about her?"

"Yes, your father mentioned something about a witch," Brianna said, fear stirring in her heart again.

"You've seen him?" Zollin asked. "Was he with Miriam?"

"Yes, they seem very happy, although he's worried about you."

Zollin nodded, happy that his father had found a place to call home.

"I think the witch is actually a sorceress, but apparently she has some sort of magical control over men," Zollin said. "She bewitched Mansel and Quinn. Mansel tried to kill Quinn twice, and he did kill Kelvich."

"What? No, Zollin, that can't be true."

"It is, but he wasn't acting on his own. That's why he's been with me. He feels like he owes me something. He met Nycoll on his way down to Osla with Quinn. They got separated and he ran into trouble. She patched him back up and now he's in love with her."

"Well," Brianna said, raising her eyebrows in disbelief. "Of all the things I've seen, that's the hardest to believe. Who would have ever thought that Mansel could fall in love?"

"Not me, but it's true. In fact, it's obvious. We've been on a mad dash to get here before the army that's marching south, but we were too late. They had already burned down her cottage. Lucky for her she hid, but even then she almost didn't make it. We were waiting here for Eustice and getting a little rest. I hope he shows up soon. We don't have any supplies left now," he said, waving at the tree.

"Who is Eustice?" Brianna asked.

"He was a servant of Offendorl's, but the coward left Eustice behind when he fled. The poor man was so grateful that we let him live that he's been following us ever since. He's a eunuch, and Offendorl cuts out their tongues too. It's horrible."

Brianna wasn't sure what to say. She had heard of eunuchs in stories from long ago. There was a time when people were enslaved, their bodies mutilated because of some insane belief that without the normal desires of men they would work harder and be more subservient. She shuddered at the thought.

"So, tell me what happened after you were carried away by the black dragon."

"Bartoom," Brianna said. "We went high into the southern range of mountains and found a cave. I stayed with Bartoom and learned as much as I could of dragons. They are really incredibly creatures. I tried to get Bartoom to stay with me, but the wizard's call was too strong to resist. After Bartoom left, I had an overwhelming urge to create more dragons."

"How?" Zollin asked. "Did the dragon…do something to you?" he asked quietly, partly ashamed for asking and partly afraid of the answer.

"What? You mean sexually? No," she said sternly. "That's not even possible. Dragons don't reproduce. They're not even male of female, Zollin. How could you ask that?"

"I don't know," Zollin said. "I'm sorry, but I don't know how else you could create dragons."

"With fire," Brianna said, letting tongues of flame dance on her palms. "I did things I didn't know I could do. It was amazing. I got so hot, Zollin, that I was literally swimming through solid rock."

"What do you mean?"

"I mean, I was like one of those fire worm things the dwarves fought. I melted the rock, turned it into lava and swam down into the mountain. Then I used the molten rock to form the dragons. I worked for days, maybe even weeks—I'm not sure. I couldn't stop. I just kept making them, molding their bodies and wings. Then I added gold to form their hearts and breathed life into them with my fire."

"Wow," Zollin said, unsure what else to say. "That's amazing."

"I know. When I was done there was a huge cavern deep in the mountain. It was incredible. Afterwards, I named each dragon.

A little over half of them left to go on their own. The others stayed with me."

"That is incredible," Zollin said. "I wish I could have seen it."

Brianna smiled and nodded. She understood how he felt. For months she had seen him doing the most incredible magic, but she couldn't feel what he felt or understand how he did those things. Her magic was different than Zollin's, but she understood what he meant and she was actually happy that he could relate to how others felt around him.

"So, what are you going to do now?" he asked.

"I'm not sure. I came to help."

"Well, I won't turn you away. I need all the help I can get. I really have no idea what I'm getting myself into."

"Do you think Mansel will trust me?"

"I don't know," Zollin said. "He's not the same guy we knew. He's seen and done some horrible things. I think he really wants to find a quiet place to heal his wounded soul with Nycoll."

"What is she like?"

"I don't know really," Zollin said. "When we found her, she had tied herself to one of the pilings under the dock." He pointed toward the path that led to the shore. "She was hiding from the army, which for some reason doesn't seem to care if certain groups pillage, rape, and burn their own villages."

"And the army is from Falxis?"

"Half of it; the other half is from Osla. We heard rumors that King Zorlan had the Oslan generals killed and took control of their troops. Anyway, Nycoll had been in the water for almost two days. The seawater had caused the rope she used to help her stay hidden through the night become impossible to untie. Even Mansel couldn't get it loose. I had to use magic. Needless to say, she was in shock, and dehydrated. Other than that, she seems fine. She's shy, a little older than Mansel, and a widow. He said her husband was a fisherman who was lost at sea. She seems sad to me, but she was happy to see Mansel."

"Will he go with us to Osla, now that he's found her?"

"I think so. I guess they both will. We still have a long way to go though. And with armies fighting in Osla, I'm not sure what we're going to find."

"What armies?" Brianna said. "Didn't you say the Oslan army was with King Zorlan?"

"Yes, but the witch has brought the army from Ortis with her."

"This is confusing," Brianna said.

"It is, and dangerous too. Are you sure you want to get mixed up in it?"

"I want to be with you," she said. "I can take care of myself, and my pride will make their own decisions. But we can help you, Zollin. I really hope you see that."

"I do," he said, moving closer to Brianna. "I was just surprised, that's all."

Just then the ground shook as Ferno landed roughly, not far behind them. The big, green dragon stomped forward several paces, then gently laid a deer carcass on the ground.

"Oh, great, supper's here," Brianna said, smiling.

"That whole deer is for us?" Zollin asked.

Ferno shook its head and flames flew from its nostrils, causing Brianna to laugh. "No," she said. "We'll take what we need, and the dragons will take the rest. Did you find more meat than this?" she asked the dragon.

The beast looked deeply into Brianna's eyes and she smiled.

"Good, it's past time you fed well. We'll stay here at least until sunrise, then we'll decide what to do."

Zollin dropped to one knee and used his knife to remove one of the deer's back legs. Then he stood up and backed slowly away from the dragon. "Thank you," he said.

Ferno growled, but there was less menace to the dragon's response than before. It picked up the rest of the deer and flew into the darkness. Zollin let his magic flow out and found that the other dragons were feeding nearby. They had found a herd of deer and were enjoying their meal.

"They are amazing," Zollin said.

"Yes, they are. Each one is different," Brianna explained. "They're intelligent too, but young. And you may have noticed they're a little protective."

"Yes, I picked up on that," Zollin said, laughing.

They cleaned the venison meat and then Brianna cooked it. She could heat the meat almost instantly, making sure that it was well cooked all the way through. They took the food back to where Mansel was resting with Nycoll. Zollin built a small fire and they divided the food, setting aside a portion for Mansel and Nycoll to eat when they woke up. Zollin felt his eyes growing heavy as he ate, and afterward they both slept soundly, with one of the dragons standing watch over the camp.

The next morning dawned bright and clear. Zollin woke up eager to see the dragons again. Nycoll wasn't ready to see the dragons up close, so she stayed with Mansel and they hung back while Zollin and Brianna met with the pride in the clearing where Nycoll's cottage had stood.

Zollin was amazed at the dragons. They were proud, but also curious. He felt their rough scales and leathery wings. They sniffed his clothing and nudged him with their tails. Then Brianna talked to them, while Zollin waited.

"Zollin is the wizard I told you about," she explained. "He is going to fight a very powerful evil wizard. The same wizard that has enslaved Bartoom. There are armies that are going to fight each other. It will not be a safe journey, but I am going with him. Zollin is my mate, the first member of my pride. You must decide if you will go with us. I'll let Zollin explain what we're doing."

"I'm not sure what we're going to find," he said. "Offendorl is the master of a group of wizards who call themselves the Torr. They've controlled magic in the Five Kingdoms for centuries, but they aren't good. I have to stop Offendorl and any more like him. I could use your help, if you're willing."

Brianna waited for a moment, letting the dragons send their mental response to her. Then she laughed.

"What is it?" Zollin asked.

"They want to see you do some magic," she said.

"Are you kidding? I'm not a traveling performer, you know."

"Come on, they're curious. I've told them about you, but they've never seen a wizard do magic before. Show them what you can do."

Zollin sighed. He wasn't angry, just a little embarrassed. He was proud of his magic and what he was able to do, but being put on the spot was new. He'd performed tricks in Brighton's Gate on the night when Quinn decided they should tell everyone who Zollin really was. At first the townspeople had been entertained, but when trouble showed up at the small mountain village, they had blamed Zollin.

He decided to levitate the rocks around what had once been Nycoll's well. The soldiers had knocked down the walls of stone, and what was left was an untidy pile. Zollin let his magic flow into the rocks, then he lifted them simply by thinking the command. He raised his arms, holding his hands out toward the rocks; it wasn't necessary, but it seemed more theatrical. The rocks spun and bobbed, then followed each other like children playing follow the leader. Zollin sent them soaring into the air, then diving back down to earth. The dragons watched the rocks, their mouths open slightly and their tongues licking the air.

Then Zollin settled the rocks back on the ground in a neat stack, leaving only one to float in the air. It shimmered almost like mirage, then seemed to melt before their very eyes. The dragons bobbed their heads, growling happily. Then the liquid rock reformed, only this time it took the shape of a woman, with high cheekbones and long, flowing hair tied back neatly with a simple ribbon.

Zollin let the stone bust float down on top of the pile of stones. Tig was especially curious and began nosing closer and closer to Zollin, who suddenly sent a ball of fire straight into the dragon's face. The other dragons didn't exactly laugh, but they roared in a chuckling sort of way. Tig staggered back surprised, but not hurt by the fire. Zollin knew enough about dragons to know that simple flame didn't hurt them. He then sent a billow of fire skyward and the dragons turned their heads up and joined him.

"They love it," Brianna said.

Zollin smiled, then transformed his fire into molten energy. The dragons could feel the heat and power of the blast. Then Zollin changed it to electrical power, which snapped and popped like a sustained bolt of lightning, twitching and cracking through the air so brightly that it was hard to look straight at.

The dragons recoiled instantly, instinctively knowing that electrical energy could harm them. Their growls of approval turned menacing and they lowered their heads while lifting their wings, which made them appear even larger, and also made them ready to take flight. They had all moved back quickly, but then, before Zollin realized his display of power was having an adverse effect on the beasts, Ferno charged forward, trying to get between Zollin and Brianna.

The sudden movement caught Zollin's eye and he saw the thick, green tail swinging toward him. He brought up a shield just before the tail struck. Zollin was knocked backward, flying through the air for several yards before crashing onto his back. The shield kept him from being crushed by the massive blow, but it stunned him. He lay on his back, blinking slowly as Brianna and Mansel rushed to him.

"No, Ferno," she screamed. "Zollin!"

"What the bloody hell?!" Mansel shouted back.

The dragons held their ground, all but Ferno looking frightened, which would have been humorous in other circumstances.

"Zollin, are you okay?" Brianna said, as she dropped to her knees beside him.

"That beast could have killed him," Mansel said angrily. "They're dangerous."

"Of course they are," Brianna said angrily. "They're not puppies."

"I'm okay," Zollin said. He was shocked by the blow, but not physically harmed. He was also drained from his magical display. Performing magic was similar to lifting a heavy object, draining the user's strength the longer it was sustained.

"Ferno was just trying to protect me," Brianna explained. "The lightning scared them."

"I should have known," Zollin said. "I used lightning to drive the black dragon away from Orrock."

"I don't think spending time with these creatures is a good idea," Mansel said.

"They aren't creatures, they're dragons. Young dragons at that," Brianna said. "They may have a lot to learn, but don't speak of them as if they are vile or evil by nature."

"Well aren't they?" Mansel said. "I've seen one kill hundreds of men."

"That was one dragon. You've seen people kill each other, but you don't judge them all by the actions of one person."

"That's a bit different," Mansel said, helping Zollin sit up.

"How? Dragons are intelligent beings. They make choices just like you and me. Some make bad choices, but that doesn't mean all of them are bad."

"Well, they're dangerous," Mansel said. "That's all I'm saying. It's not safe to be around them, you should know that."

"I've been around them for weeks. I've never been hurt. They were just trying to protect me. They're fiercely loyal and I love that about them."

"Well, I'm just trying to protect Zollin and Nycoll."

"Don't fight," Zollin said. "I'm okay. It's my fault really. I wasn't thinking about how the dragons might react to the magic."

Brianna returned to her pride, calming the nervous dragons. Mansel returned to Nycoll, who had watched the entire episode with awe. She was amazed at Zollin's power and more than a little afraid of him. The dragons simply terrified her; they were beautiful and terrible at the same time.

Zollin found some food and settled down to rest. He knew that if the dragons decided to help him he would need a plan. They were both an asset and a liability. They brought a great amount of strength to Zollin's efforts, but there was no way he could coordinate with the dragons and stay hidden. He had planned to make his way to the Grand City quietly and map out his options for facing Offendorl once he was there. Now, if the dragons joined him, he would have to change his plans.

It was only a few minutes before Brianna approached Zollin, the dragons following behind her. She sat down and took Zollin's hand.

"We want to help," she said. "Do you have a plan?"

"I was just thinking about that," Zollin said. "I really don't know what to expect."

"Well, we can help with that," Brianna said. "We can travel fast and scope out the situation."

"You mean split up?"

"For a short while. I don't think it would be too dangerous for you to ride on Ferno or Selix, since you can levitate, but they couldn't carry you all the way. It would exhaust them and then they wouldn't be able to help you."

"I understand," Zollin said. "But if we split up, how will you find me again?"

"The dragons can sense your magic. I can't," she explained, "but they are almost drawn to you. I guess that's how Bartoom found your ship at sea."

"Yes, that would explain a lot, although I've got my defenses up. They shouldn't be able to sense me at all."

"What can I say," she teased, "they're amazing."

"Well, okay, I accept your help, gratefully," he said, looking up at the dragons. "I take it you've been flying by night to avoid detection?"

"For the most part," Brianna said. "We flew in the daytime only when we were following Bartoom, but we were so high that I doubt anyone spotted us—or if they did, they probably just thought we were big birds."

"Okay, so we wait until nightfall, then you scout ahead. We're still a long way from Osla and there's no way for us to get around the army. I had just planned to follow along behind and see how that shakes out. Wouldn't it be great if they all just kill each other and we can go home?"

"We should be so lucky," Brianna said.

"I know. With my luck, we'll be fortunate to get home at all."

Chapter 18

Offendorl let his anger propel him. He had left the main road several days back and ridden to a small village called Castlebury—although there was no castle anymore. The village was nestled next to the ruins of an ancient fortress, which had built on a small hill overlooking the Euradies River, one of three major rivers in an otherwise arid part of the kingdom. The huge stone towers had fallen centuries ago, but thick walls still stood, outlining where the castle had been.

Offendorl entered the town at dusk. His carriage rumbled to a stop and he climbed slowly out, stretching his aching muscles. There were children playing in the street, and the small inn, which served mainly as a tavern and cafe for the residents, was bright and noisy. Offendorl stepped inside and made no attempt at civility.

"Do you know who I am?" he asked.

The townsfolk—farmers mostly, who had rarely if ever left the village—stared blankly back at him.

"I am the Master of the Torr," he said softly. Then he flicked his hand the way one might shoo a fly, and an empty table went crashing into the empty fireplace, the wood breaking apart and piling up on the cold stone hearth.

"I require unwavering obedience," he said as fire roared to life in the fireplace.

The townsfolk, who had been frozen since Offendorl entered, flinched at the fire. They huddled together, not speaking as he stared at them. Finally one man found the courage to speak.

"We don't want any trouble," he said. "We're a peaceful village."

"You are now a subservient village," Offendorl said. "I require food and your best wine. Everyone else must return to their homes immediately. No one is to leave the village. Do as you're told and you shall live. You have no other choice."

"King Belphan shall hear of this," said a skinny little girl. Her mother was trying to force her to sit back down.

"No he won't," Offendorl said kindly, smiling almost benevolently. "You're a brave little girl, but I'm afraid the king is dead."

"No he isn't," the girl shouted angrily as her mother pulled her back down onto the bench where her family was sitting.

"You say the king's dead?" a man nearby asked.

"That's right."

"And how do you know that he's dead?" someone else asked.

"Because I killed him," Offendorl said menacingly.

There was a collective intake of breath. Offendorl wasn't surprised. He doubted if Belphan had ever even heard of Castlebury, much less cared about its inhabitants, but many people idolized their king, even if he was a cruel and careless ruler.

"No," screamed the little girl, who had pulled away from her mother.

"Cute girl," Offendorl said, "but sadly lacking in manners."

He waved his hand again and the girl went rigid, falling over onto her side. She screamed a high, piercing wail that brought the men of the town to their feet. Many of the women were weeping. The girl's back began to arch and she was crying out for it to stop, but she couldn't control herself.

"Stop it!" screamed her father, who was a small man, but livid with rage. "Stop hurting my little girl or I'll kill you."

"Unwavering obedience," Offendorl shouted over the voices in the inn.

There was a pop, like the sound of damp wood burning, then the little girl died, her back broken.

"No!" screamed the girl's mother.

"Bastard!" shouted the girl's father, who rushed forward with a small knife in his hand. Offendorl didn't move, but the man went flying into the thick ceiling beams so hard his skull was smashed. Another man drew a thick Hax knife, which was more tool than weapon, but still a deadly instrument. He tried to ease closer to Offendorl, but the elder wizard lashed out with a stream of fire that engulfed the man and severely burned several others around him. The man on fire flailed about for a few seconds, screaming uncontrollably before finally collapsing. The smell of burning flesh was sickening and several people vomited.

Offendorl tilted his head and looked at the villagers questioningly.

"Do we have an understanding?" he asked.

The men nodded.

"Good. Return to your homes," Offendorl said. "But the women stay. I'll need them to look after my needs. I assure you no harm will come to them if they do as they are told."

"They aren't staying here with a monster like you," said a young man who was shielding his young wife with his own body.

"Don't worry, their virtue is safe—although you won't be able to enjoy it," Offendorl said.

"Aaaarrrrggggghhhh!" the young man screamed as he grabbed his groin and doubled over in pain.

"Stop!" shouted his young wife. "Please, he didn't mean it."

"He may not have, but I do," Offendorl said. "I will maim the people you love, and kill anyone who does not obey me fully. I am the master of the Torr, Wizard of the Five Kingdoms. Do not try me. I have no patience for your futile attempts at resistance." His voice had turned cold and dangerous. His face wrinkled with undisguised contempt for the villagers. "I have no empathy for your weak, pathetic lives. Do as I say, remain silent, and perhaps you may live. I shall not be denied. Do you understand?"

The villagers all nodded. Some kissed their wives, although most of the villagers had come alone and there were less than a dozen women in the entire group. The young man who had spoken out was carried out of the inn, still crying about the pain in his groin, which was beginning to swell.

"Clean," Offendorl ordered the women. "And you," he pointed to the young woman. "Bring me pillows for my seat."

Everyone got busy, except for the woman whose daughter Offendorl had killed. She was kneeling over her daughter's body, sobbing uncontrollably. Offendorl reached out with his magic and punctured the woman's heart. It was a small effort, but the woman collapsed on top of her daughter, killed instantly.

The inn now smelled of burned flesh, vomit, and offal. Offendorl stepped outside. The night was muggy and uncomfortable. Other parts of Osla were relatively dry and cooled dramatically once the sun set, but along the Euradies basin the air seemed saturated and held the day's intense heat long after dark. There were mosquitos as well—swarms of them near the river.

Offendorl walked slowly toward the ruins of the castle on the hill. He was sweating by the time he reached the summit, but he felt more at home among the ruins than in the small village. It had been ages since he'd exerted his power onto people in such a direct way. He'd had very little contact with most non-magic-users. Only kings and their most trusted advisors ever bothered him in the tower. Now his rage had been unleashed on the people of the village, and he savored the feeling of power and strength. Subduing the village had been child's play for a wizard of his power, but it still felt good to feel powerful again.

His magical strength had been slow to return and it was taking a dreadful toll on his body. His eyes were sunken and his skin had begun to wrinkle in earnest. Offendorl was not a vain man when it came to his appearance, but he had resisted the signs of aging as he renewed his physical body. Now, however, he was beginning to look as ancient as he felt.

He let his magic flow, pulling the small, thin crown from the velvet bag he kept tied to his thick, leather belt and placing it on his head. He reached out and made contact with Bartoom. The black dragon was close, although it had flown out to sea and was now making its way down the coast. Offendorl had ordered it to fly south almost a week ago, but the dragon had been attacked. The elder wizard was shocked to learn of so many dragons, and of the girl who flew with them. He seemed to remember stories about humans who rode dragons and were impervious to fire, but he couldn't be sure. His vast knowledge was eroding like a riverbank in a heavy storm. The toll on his body had affected his mind as well, and he found small details slipping his mind more and more often.

He needed time to rest and to return to his home in the tower of the Torr, where his vast library was kept. Once he had his books around him again, he was sure he could restore not only his physical health, but his memory as well. Still, the missing bits of information hurt him—he knew that. Knowledge was the key to his power, and a pride of dragons was a threat he could not contain. He had thought of trying to woo the dragons, the way he had Bartoom, using his magic to coax the beast to come to him. But he knew he would need to learn each dragon's name to control them, and not even the great wizards or kings of old had dominated entire prides.

Offendorl knew there were major fights coming. He would have to help Bartoom kill the other dragons, or at least drive them away. Once that was done, he would turn his attention to the Torr and cast the sorceress Gwendolyn down. He would make the upstart witch's sister his plaything. Andomina was Gwendolyn's weakness, and Offendorl knew he could exploit it.

Once everything in the tower had been set right, Offendorl would turn his attention back to Zollin. He knew the young wizard was coming south. Bartoom had fought the boy at sea and then seen him again not far from Cape Sumbar. But Zollin would have to wait—as dangerous a threat as he was—until Offendorl had regained his advantage. He would not make the same mistake he had made in Orrock, underestimating Zollin's growing power and facing him on the open field of battle. No, he would have to make a special plan for Zollin, ensuring that the odds were all in favor of the master.

Offendorl smiled at the thought of seeing Zollin kneeling before him, pledging his magic, his loyalty, and his life to the Torr. He vowed silently to himself to make that thought a reality. Then he ordered Bartoom to come to Castlebury. Finally he turned and walked slowly down the hill. His display of magic had weakened Offendorl, and he would have preferred to rest immediately. But the mess inside the inn was simply too great to endure, and besides, he needed to avoid any appearance of weakness to the people around him. Still, his legs were trembling slightly when he returned to the inn. It was nothing a good meal and a good night's sleep wouldn't cure, but it left him wondering if he was up to the challenges ahead. He needed loyal servants who would see to his every need.

He opened the door to the inn hoping he might find what he was looking for. The bodies had been carried outside and the floors scrubbed. The small room didn't smell good, but it did smell better. A large wooden chair had been brought in and set up near the fireplace, which still had the embers of the fire he'd started in it. The chair was covered with a thick quilt, and there were pillows arranged for his comfort.

"Wine," he said harshly to the young woman, who seemed to be the only one of the women who didn't cower at his every word. The others were all acting busier than they really were and looking for any excuse they could find to go into the kitchens. The inn only had a few small rooms in back. The innkeeper and his family occupied some of them. The others were for the occasional guest, but Offendorl knew that he could sleep just as well in the chair that had been prepared for him.

The young woman brought wine and poured it into a pewter cup. Offendorl frowned, but didn't complain. He would send the women for better tableware tomorrow, he determined. For now, the plain metal cup would do. The wine wasn't good, but it was strong enough that Offendorl felt his strength returning with each sip.

"Heat water for a bath," he instructed the woman. "And send for my meal." To another of the women he barked more orders. "I want pallets against the wall for all of you," Offendorl told her. "You'll sleep here in case I need anything in the night."

The woman nodded and hurried away, while another brought out a full rack of lamb, with boiled potatoes and summer greens smothered in rich gravy. Another woman brought bread and cheese, while a third arrived with fruit.

"This will suffice," Offendorl said. "Clean the kitchens and prepare for tomorrow."

The women left without a word. He could hear them moving about in the kitchens but he couldn't hear them talking, which he was grateful for. He missed the silence of the Torr. He hated to be disturbed by idle chatter, which was one of the reasons he had the tongues removed from his servants. Also, it kept them from repeating anything they might hear in his presence. It was a prudent practice, although he knew that many people found it repugnant. They could die with their high morals, he thought, while he lived through the centuries with the power to do as he pleased.

Chapter 19

Prince Wilam was exactly where he'd always wanted to be—at the head of an army. As a young boy he'd learned sword craft from the finest swordsmen in Yelsia. He had been tutored in tactics by his father's generals and given squads to lead, then centuries, and finally his own legion. He'd fought in some minor skirmishes with Shirtac raiders, but he'd never led an army to war. It had always been his dream, since he was little and could read the histories of the great conflicts of the Five Kingdoms. His father had sent him to Osla as the ambassador to the high court of the Five Kingdoms to learn how to deal with political maneuvering. Now he was back in Osla, not as a king or at the court, which had been razed by the troops he now led. Instead, he was the commander of Gwendolyn's army, and although his mind was still entranced by the witch, he was very aware of how fortunate he was.

The army he led was not as grand as the one he'd dreamed of as a boy. There were only two centuries of cavalry, and the rest were foot soldiers, but they were anxious for a fight. It seemed that Gwendolyn's spell brought most men to the precipice of violence. The prince himself had killed on other occasions, including King Oveer and two his closest generals. He doubted that the troops he now led would even care that their sovereign ruler was dead—they would probably be glad there was one less person to vie for Gwendolyn's affection.

Prince Wilam had spent days leading the army along the northern road that led from the Grand City into Falxis. The terrain was flat for the most part, with short, stunted looking trees. He could see for miles in every direction and had scouts out looking for any signs of the invading army. He had hoped to find a hilltop from which to direct the fighting, but hills of any kind seemed few and far between, as did water and fresh supplies. Prince Wilam had finally decided his best bet was to camp his men next to a good supply of water and food.

He put his engineers to work building him a tower. The army tore down barns and even a few homes to salvage enough wood for the project. It was a simple wooden structure, with a staircase that wrapped around the heavy timber beams. It was sturdy and three times the height of a man. Prince Wilam positioned the best archers he had at the tower with him. He had four legions of troops and four generals, three of them newly promoted. The plain where Wilam expected the battle to take place was a wide, grassy field that he hoped would keep the dust to a minimum. His greatest fear was that he would lose sight of the battle by the dust of thousands of feet tramping hard upon the dry ground.

"Sir," came a shout from one of the lookouts posted on the tower. "A scout is returning."

"Good," Wilam said, rising from his canvas camp chair and climbing quickly down to meet the scout.

There was a lot activity around the base of the tower. The army was encamped almost half a mile to the rear of the battle plain, but Wilam kept his troops ready for action. They arrived at the battle site each morning at dawn, drilling through the day so that they would be ready to follow his orders in battle. The prince envisioned a battle where he had strict control of his troops' movements and formations. The chain of command was well prepared and he had devised three separate battle plans, as well as a system of flag signals so that he could order the units around the field of battle.

His generals were nearby, each coming to attention when he drew near.

"A scout is returning," he told them. "Hopefully we'll have news of the invaders."

The generals nodded. They were men accustomed to taking orders, and while they longed to return to Gwendolyn—as each man in her army did—they could see that Prince Wilam was competent, unlike King Oveer. Following Prince Wilam's orders was not always easy, but the orders always made sense and the prince himself was not afraid of getting his hands dirty. He worked tirelessly, from demonstrating the proper sword technique to a lowly foot soldier to ensuring that there was food and provisions ready. His tent was illuminated late into the night, where the generals found him planning and testing every conceivable outcome to the battle. He had earned their respect quickly, even if they still saw him as a rival for the witch's affection.

The rider came galloping into the camp and only slowed once he neared the tower. Then he flung himself off his horse and came to a rigid salute.

"Report," Wilam barked.

"Sir, there are enemy troops half a day from here."

"How many?" Wilam asked.

"I couldn't tell exactly," the scout said. "There was a lot of dust and no real vantage point, but if I had to guess I'd say a force equal to our own."

"I don't want guesses," Wilam shouted. "I want facts. I want numbers of troops, of cavalry. I want to know if they have siege engines or trebuchets. I want to know how they are being supplied and if they are tired. I want to know everything."

"Yes, sir," said the scout sheepishly.

"Get a new mount, I'll send for the rest of our scouts," Wilam said. "You said they were traveling together, correct? Just one main body?"

"Yes, one formation, if you can call it that. There didn't seem to be any real order to their ranks, sir."

"Alright. Are they marching south on the main road?"

"Yes, sir."

"Good, that's very good. Get your horse and get back out there," Prince Wilam said. "I want regular reports. I'm sending other scouts to help you."

The scout nodded and hurried away. Wilam turned to his generals.

"Well, if they're half a day out, that means they'll be in sight by sundown. I want our troops ready. Let's get every man into position and then make sure they have food, enough for tonight and tomorrow. We aren't leaving the field and I'll be damned if I'm going to be out maneuvered."

"Aye, sir," the generals said before moving away to carry out their orders.

Prince Wilam went to his command tent, which was merely an awning with a table full of maps and wooden pieces carved to resemble troops. He used the wooden pieces to demonstrate the maneuvers he planned. He gathered the maps and hurried back up the tower platform. There was enough room on the square-shaped platform for twenty archers. They had large quivers of arrows hanging from the guardrail that ran around the edges of the platform. Wilam had a small pedestal on the center of the platform where he could see over the archers. There was a sturdy roof over the top of the tower so that volleys of arrows could not rain down on Wilam or the archers. It was where he planned to stay until the battle was over.

Adrenaline was pumping through his veins now and he had to fight the urge to go down and join his men on the front lines of battle. He knew that strategy was best made from a position of cool detachment. He couldn't send men into harm's way if he was worried about them. Nor could he make good decisions if he was too emotionally tied to the outcome of the battle. He had to rise above his baser instincts and lead.

He neatly rolled every map and made sure they were all easy to reach. Then he waited. The scouts returned in ones and twos. He had men spread out in every direction from the camp to ensure they weren't taken unaware. None reported any signs of the enemy, so he sent them to help scout the large force that was moving toward them on the main road toward the Grand City. Prince Wilam had guessed that the invading army would take the easiest and most direct route to Osla's capital. Whoever held the Grand City ruled Osla, and the invaders would obviously want to hold what was arguably the most important city in the Five Kingdoms.

They hadn't spread out or divided their forces yet either. It would make sense to come at the capital from different directions, but they were almost a full week's march from the Grand City and probably weren't expecting resistance. The most obvious approach to defending Osla was to take refuge inside the city walls. Even if those walls were breached at one point, the defenders could fall back to the next set of walls, since the city had been built over the centuries in carefully planned parcels with massive walls around each new addition. There were good wells within the city, but food would be an issue—especially when you factored in the number of troops that Wilam commanded. He had left two full legions to defend the city, while he marched with four. There were large storehouses full of grain, but fruit, vegetables, and livestock were brought in from outside the city on a daily basis. Prince Wilam didn't like the idea of sustaining an army on bread and water, which is exactly what a siege would force him to do. The invaders would grow strong while the defenders grew weak. It would still be an incredibly difficult feat to breach the Grand City's walls, but not impossible.

Wilam also knew that in a confined space with fear and hunger rampant, the tempers of his men would break easily and they would fall to fighting each other. He had seen it among Queen Gwendolyn's army. It was better to keep the men busy, even with false promises of the queen's favor, than to let them sit idle day after day.

So, Prince Wilam had proposed a plan to catch the invaders off guard. He proposed to march out and meet them on the field of battle. He could pick the ground and meet the opposing army with fresh troops who were eager for battle. King Zorlan's forces would be tired, more eager to pillage and burn than to fight. And hopefully they would be surprised as well. All the intangibles would be in Wilam's favor, and he calculated that it was enough of an edge to drive the invaders back into Falxis at the very least, although he hoped that he could wipe out King Zorlan's forces completely. Then, nothing would stop Prince Wilam from taking Ortis and Falxis for Gwendolyn. He could hand over Yelsia to his queen without war once his father was dead. Then, only Baskla, the smallest of the Five Kingdoms, would remain. Wilam respected King Ricard, but he doubted if Baskla would even resist the might of the other four kingdoms unified against him.

The afternoon seemed to crawl by so slowly that Wilam was forced to sit and wait just to keep from giving the false impression that he was nervous. He wasn't worried—just anxious to see his plans come to fruition. He had considered every variable and he was prepared for anything that King Zorlan might try. He had divided his small cavalry so that there was a century of horsemen on either flank. A century was a rather small number of light horses, but Wilam knew the cavalry could outmaneuver any force sent to attack from the rear.

All he had to do now as wait. The archers waited at their posts and the soldiers lounged across the field of battle as they waited. Servants worked tirelessly to ensure that every man had plenty of food and water as the sun began to set. Finally, as the sky turned red and a steward set about preparing a table for Wilam's own supper, he saw the dust cloud in the distance. The troops themselves were hard to see, but Wilam saw the evidence he had been waiting for. They would meet in battle shortly after dawn the next day. His destiny awaited.

"Sir, your supper is ready," the steward said.

Wilam sat and ate with gusto. There was a steady stream of scouts comingto give reports. The enemy had spread out and made camp. There were even reports of skirmishes among the scouts. Exact numbers were sketchy, but the enemy was reported to number around 4,000 with a full legion of cavalry. The horse breeders in Falxis were renowned among the Five Kingdoms for producing excellent horses, but they were not warriors. Falxis alone among the Five Kingdoms had no enemies. Yelsia, Baskla, and Ortis were forced to guard their borders from violent neighbors, and Osla dealt with pirates and raiders on a regular basis, but Falxis was surrounded and protected by the other kingdoms. The closest other nations were the small, indigenous tribes of Tooga Island, but they were not seafaring people and did not cross the ocean to raid the shores of Falxis.

In Wilam's mind, Falxis' years of peace and prosperity had made them soft. King Zorlan was marching to war, but Wilam doubted the weak-willed king was really prepared for it. He had been driven from Yelsia, and now he would be driven from Osla.

The night came with a thousand stars in the heavens and thousands of small fires in the camps below Wilam and across the plain. He knew sleep was not an option, and so he waited until late into the night and then sent for General Trevis.

"You sent for me, sir?" said Trevis. The man had not been sleeping, but his eyes were sunken and his face lined with fatigue.

"Yes," said Wilam. "I'm making a slight adjustment to our plan. Pick the best leader you have in your legion and send him with three centuries to the east. I want them to circle around the enemy, just out of sight. Tell them to watch for a flaming arrow, which will be their signal to harass the enemy. I don't want them to fully engage. I want them to attack and withdraw, over and over. Have them hit any weak spots they see, but tell them not to worry about causing serious harm."

"Are you certain, sir?"

"Don't question my orders, General," Wilam said angrily. "Do as I say or I'll have you removed."

"Aye, sir, I'll do it now."

"See that you do. I want those centuries moving quietly, and I want them out of sight before dawn. Is that understood?"

"Yes, sir."

"Good," Wilam said, dismissing the man with a wave of his hand.

As the night came to a close, Wilam felt a knot of nervous tension in his stomach. He knew he needed to relax, but he didn't see how that would happen. He no longer cared about any woman but Gwendolyn, and she was far away in the Grand City. He hoped that soon he would be marching back to her victorious, but just the thought of seeing his queen again filled Prince Wilam with nervous energy. He couldn't sleep and he didn't want to dull his senses with strong drink, so he forced himself to sit in his command tower and wait for dawn.

He rose to his feet as the sun came up and his troops prepared themselves for battle. He could see them strapping on armor and checking their weapons. As much as Wilam felt anxious for the battle to begin, he also knew that it was better to let the enemy come to fight on the ground he had chosen. His men had been drilling on that ground long enough to know it well. It was one more advantage they had over King Zorlan's forces.

A slow hour passed, then another with no sign of the invaders doing anything. Scouts reported the enemy forces preparing for battle, but there was no sense of urgency. Wilam finally could wait no longer.

"Saddle my horse," he bellowed. "Send for the generals."

There was flurry of activity around the tower. When Wilam descended he found his horse saddled and ready, his generals mounted and waiting on him. He climbed into the saddle and rode away without a word, the generals following behind.

Wilam rode through the ranks, eyeing his troops critically, and was pleased to find them ready for battle. He turned when he reached the front lines and began shouting. “Men, our enemy waits out there,” he said, pointing with his sword in the direction of the invading army. “They are slow to action because they are afraid. We have every advantage on this field of battle and we will make them pay with their life’s blood for engaging us. We fight for the Queen of the Sea. We fight for our Lady Gwendolyn. We will show her our valor and bring her glory, and then we shall reap our rewards.”

The soldiers shouted. Wilam had no doubt that each man envisioned his reward in Lady Gwendolyn’s bed, but if it motivated them, he saw no harm in it. He would harness that desire and use it to give his queen the Five Kingdoms, then he knew she could no longer deny him.

Prince Wilam turned his horse and rode out across the plain, followed by his generals. He could hear the cheering of his men and it gave him a sense of pride and excitement. When they came within sight of the invading army they stopped and waited. General Trevis raised Lady Gwendolyn’s flag, which had been designed by a tailor while they were still in Lodenhime. It was outline of a woman in gold on a background of sea green.

They waited several moments, no one talking, just watching their enemy. Finally, one of the generals spoke.

"What is taking them so long? Surely they were ready for battle?"

"They are afraid," General Trevis said.

"If they fear to engage us, why invade Osla?" the first man asked again.

"They aren't afraid," Prince Wilam said. "It's a tactic. By making us wait they try our nerves and, at least in their own minds, elevate themselves. Don't underestimate your opponent, gentlemen. Prepare for every possibility, even if you feel certain you know what the enemy will do. If you are prepared for everything they might do, then nothing they actually do will daunt you."

"I don't like waiting," said another general. "We've lost the element of surprise. We should attack. They're obviously using this time to prepare their troops."

"That's exactly what they want us to do," Prince Wilam said. "By attacking them, we forfeit all our advantages."

"But they're unprepared," the general said. "We could crush them if we attack."

"Are you certain of that? Are you sure it's not a tactic to lure us into engaging them? We cannot know, but we do know the ground we have selected and the maneuvers we have drilled these last several days. You don't throw that all away because you're nervous, general."

The chastised general fell silent and they continued waiting. It was almost half an hour before King Zorlan appeared with a much larger retinue of men. They rode horses that seemed to prance rather than walk, lifting their feet high with each step and bobbing their heads. They all wore brightly polished armor and weapons. One held the flag of Falxis, another the flag of Osla. They spread out in a line facing Prince Wilam and his generals.

"Prince Wilam," King Zorlan said in a haughty voice. "I am surprised to see you here. I heard you fled north after you were convicted of harboring a wizard and spying on your fellow ambassadors in the Grand City."

"Turn your army back to Falxis," Prince Wilam said menacingly, "and perhaps the Queen of the Sea will let you live."

"Ah, you are referring to the witch from Lodenhime?" Zorlan said. "As I recall, Lodenhime is my sovereign possession, which makes her my possession too."

"The queen belongs to no one, especially not a pompous fool like you."

"Well, that's to be determined. For now, I request that you march your army back to Ortis, or that King Oveer does. Where is the good king? I prefer to converse with equals."

"A worm is superior to you, Zorlan," Wilam sneered. "Do not bother us with questions or demands. Surrender or be destroyed. You have no rights here."

"On the contrary. I am leading the Oslan troops home. It is you, my young upstart, who has no rights. You are invaders and usurpers. You have broken faith with your fellows and I must insist that you stand trial for your crimes."

"I'm glad you've shown your hand, Zorlan. You always were a pompous windbag. We shall await you on the field of battle. Then you shall know our quality. We value actions, not words."

Prince Wilam didn't wait for a reply. He turned his horse and rode away. The generals hesitated only for a moment, watching King Zorlan's men to ensure they wouldn't be attacked from the rear. Then they too turned and followed Prince Wilam.

"What did that accomplish?" General Trevis asked when the generals had come even with Prince Wilam again.

"Nothing of merit," Wilam said. "But I was anxious to find out who exactly we were facing. I did not see King Belphan or any of his generals, so the rumors must be true."

"King Belphan was killed, you mean?" asked one of the generals.

"Yes, and his generals too, or so it would seem. The good King Zorlan has some gumption then, but he seems like the same fawning imbecile I took him for in Falxis. He is weak willed, but greedy for more power. I don't think he expected to face an army led by warriors. He'll be even more hesitant now, fearful and probably second-guessing every decision he makes. I want scouts out beyond the flanks of our forces. I wouldn't put it past the coward to try and go around us without fighting."

"And if he does?" Trevis asked.

"Then we'll be forced to destroy him."

Chapter 20

Eustice finally arrived late the following day. Zollin had begun to worry about the mute servant, but he came riding merrily into the camp they had constructed near the broken down well and burned cottage. Nycoll had gotten more comfortable with Zollin and Brianna after the dragons had gone hunting. The great beasts slept out in the bright sunshine during the days and roamed through the countryside at night hunting.

No one else came by, and Nycoll, unaccustomed to visitors, was slow to join the group. But by the time Eustice arrived she was sitting with the others, adding an occasional comment and even laughing at Mansel's jokes. Brianna had tried to bond with Nycoll, who was only ten years older than Brianna—although she seemed much older than that—but Nycoll kept her distance. It was obvious to Zollin that Nycoll couldn't journey far with them. They would have to find a safe place to leave her while they continued on. He wasn't looking forward to bringing the subject up with Mansel, but he knew he would have to do it sooner or later.

Once Eustice arrived with the spare horses and provisions, they made plans to break camp the next morning. That night, Brianna said her goodbyes and took her pride back into the sky. Her task was to scout the situation to the south and report back. The others slept through the night and then set out at dawn. There was now one horse for each of them and two packhorses, although their supplies were dwindling quickly. The sun was bright and there was a pleasant breeze blowing in off the ocean, making the ride pleasurable for everyone except Nycoll. She had spent the last decade of her life in the little cottage, and although Mansel had left a horse with her when he had been pursuing Prince Wilam, the horse had been lame and was traded in the local village not long after Mansel had left.

They rode for an hour, then stopped to stretch their legs. Zollin offered to help Nycoll, but she refused. He guessed that by the end of the day she would be sore enough to allow him to help, but he didn't want to force her to do anything. She was a cautious person, and Zollin understood why. She had experienced heart-wrenching loss, and he respected the pain she felt, as well as the boundaries she had erected to protect herself.

"Thanks for offering to help," Mansel said quietly to Zollin as they walked their horses for bit. They were far enough ahead of Eustice and Nycoll, who seemed to like the eunuch almost as much as she liked Mansel. "She'll come around eventually."

"I'm not worried about it," Zollin said. "But you know she isn't strong enough to stay with us."

"She's stronger than you think," Mansel said defensively. "She's lived alone in that cottage for years, fending for herself. You don't know her like I do."

"I agree, and I'm not trying to say anything about her character. I just don't think it's right for us to drag her into a war, not if we can help it."

Mansel thought about what Zollin was saying for a minute. Part of him was angry that anyone would suggest that Nycoll wasn't strong enough to do something, but part of him agreed with Zollin wholeheartedly. The last thing he wanted was to drag her into a dangerous situation where she might be hurt. On the other hand, he was loath to leave her behind. They had found her in the nick of time. A few more hours in the water and she might have died. It was a wonder she hadn't drowned when the tide rose.

"Tell me what you're thinking," Mansel said.

"I'm not going to do anything you and Nycoll don't agree with," he explained. "But I was hoping we might find a place to leave her. You could stay with her too," Zollin added quickly. "Or Eustice. I'm not trying to get rid of her, even if it seems that way. I only want to protect her. There's really no need for you to stay with me. Between my magic and Brianna's pride, there isn't much you can do."

"Never underestimate the value of good steel and someone who knows how to use it," Mansel said. "Your father taught me that."

"It's good advice," Zollin said. "You tell me what you want to do."

Mansel thought for a few minutes before speaking. "I guess you're right," he finally admitted. "I just don't like the thought of leaving her behind."

"So, stay with her."

"I don't like the thought of leaving you behind either," Mansel said, smiling.

"Let me ask you a serious question then. Are you coming along because you feel you owe me something? Because you really don't. Killing Kelvich wasn't your fault. You weren't acting on your own mental powers."

"I know, but that doesn't make the responsibility any easier to bear. I took a man's life, a man who had never harmed us and who had helped us a great deal. That's something I don't think I'll ever be free of."

"He wouldn't want you to suffer," Zollin said. "You didn't know him like I did. He wasn't proud of a lot of things he had done in his lifetime either. He knew what it was to feel remorse. I don't think he would want you to live with guilt over his death."

"But I do, Zollin. I want to help you, and I want to stay with Nycoll. Hell, I even want to bust some heads just because I like to, but the honest truth is, I feel like I have to do something to redeem myself."

"You don't. I forgive you. I'm sure Kelvich would too."

"But I can't forgive myself," he said quietly.

Zollin didn't respond at once. He knew self-forgiveness was difficult. He had struggled personally with the death of his mother, even though he was just an infant and his father had told him many times it wasn't his fault. Still, the guilt plagued him all through his childhood, every time he missed her, or every time he saw the pain of loneliness in his father's eyes.

"Well, I've got your back, whatever you decide to do," Zollin finally said.

"I appreciate that," Mansel said, looking Zollin in the eyes as he spoke. "Your family has been better to me than I deserve. Better than my own family ever was."

"You will always have a friend in me," Zollin said. "And I know my father loves you like a son."

Mansel smiled. "I wish Quinn were here now," he said. "I could use a good pep talk."

"Well, I'm not Quinn, but I think you know what you need to do. You just need to give yourself permission to do it."

They rode through the day, and made camp at sunset. The small villages along the coast were leery of anyone they didn't know after the army's foul treatment. Their winter stores had all been taken. The men who weren't drafted into service or killed outright were busy fishing or rebuilding homes—many of which had been burned to the ground. No one had food to sell or time to bother with strangers, so Zollin and Mansel chose a secluded spot surrounded by tall sea dunes. Zollin made a fire and then saw to the horses while Eustice prepared supper. Mansel looked after Nycoll who never complained, but was obviously very saddle sore. She still refused to let Zollin heal her, so after he had seen to the horses he began transmuting some of the stones he found around their campsite to gold. It was long, tedious work, but it kept him busy and gave Mansel and Nycoll some privacy.

The next day, he gave the gold to Mansel.

"I didn't think she'd accept it from me," Zollin said, handing over a small bag full of plain gold coins.

"What's this for?" Mansel asked.

"You'll need it, or she will once we find a quiet inn where she can stay. That should be enough to keep her housed and fed for a year. Or, if you prefer, it will help the two of you make a new start together."

"You didn't have to do that," Mansel said. "I can work, you know. I'm a pretty good carpenter."

"Yes you are, but I hate to think of you selling your sword for tools," Zollin said smiling.

"I'd rather cut off my own hand," Mansel joked.

"Well, then use it for whatever you need. I'll feel better knowing that you have it."

"What about you?"

"I can always make more," Zollin said.

They had to stop more frequently because of Nycoll's pain. She was bruised all along the underside of her upper thighs and bottom. Even walking was painful, and finally around noon on their second day she relented and agreed to let Zollin help. He let his magic flow into her body, sweeping away the blood and antibodies that were making the bruises so painful. He also used some of the remaining Zipple Weed to boost her stamina.

The next three days passed quickly. They had left the trail of the army and were following the coast south. The army was traveling southeast, making straight for the Grand City. Zollin hoped they could reach a village that hadn't been razed by the army where they might find a safe place for Nycoll. She seemed less intimidated by Zollin since he'd healed her, but she was still a melancholy woman, not given to idle talk or laughter. She seemed to come alive when Mansel paid her attention, but she faded into the background when the group was all together.

Staying along the coast also allowed Brianna an easier way to find them once she had information to report. Zollin couldn't keep himself from worrying about her. Her powers were amazing and her pride would do all in their power to protect her, he knew, but she had gone toward the Grand City and the Torr, the one place he would have liked to keep her from. He still had no idea what to expect from Offendorl and the Torr. He didn't know if there were other wizards there, or if the place was empty. It made sense to assume that Offendorl was there—he had fled south and Brianna had followed the big black dragon—which she claimed he was able to control—almost to Osla. All the evidence suggested Offendorl was going back to the Tower, which meant he would be more dangerous than before.

And Zollin wasn't sure what to expect from the witch that had cast a spell on Mansel and his father. They both assumed that Prince Wilam was still with her, and now she too had an army, if the rumors were true. Just surviving this crazy quest was probably more than Zollin could hope for.

The next day they came to a sizable village. There was a good-sized harbor, although Zollin doubted that large trading vessels used the port. There were over a dozen fishing boats, and the market was busy when they arrived. They decided to stay, rest a little, and reprovision. They ate boiled seafood with spicy cornbread that was fried. There was also fresh fruit, cheese, steamed vegetables, and ale. They settled into a two-story inn that overlooked the ocean. Zollin made sure that Nycoll had a room with large windows that faced the sea.

She retreated to the room while Zollin and Mansel shopped for more supplies.

"Should I be buying enough for you?" Zollin asked as he haggled with the smoked fish vendor.

Mansel looked down. "I don't know," he said.

"I think you should stay," Zollin said. "Give her some time to decide what she wants. You said she would never leave her cottage, but it's gone now. So maybe you go north together. Find a new place to live, or maybe go back to Tranaugh Shire, introduce her to your parents."

"I don't want to scare her away," Mansel joked. "Besides, I wouldn't feel right leaving you when you're still in danger."

"It's okay, Mansel, really."

Zollin bought fish, but just enough for himself and Eustice. When he made his order, Mansel didn't object. They bought more bread, cheese, fruit, and vegetables. There was no beef or mutton in the village, not even pork—only fish. Once they had enough supplies they looked in on the horses and then returned to the inn. There was a bard at the inn that night, and they ate a hearty supper of thick, spicy stew. Zollin drank wine and watched as Mansel showed incredible self-control with the ale. They listened as the bard sang songs of battle and of love. Zollin even dropped a gold coin into the bard's upturned hat. Then they turned in for the night.

The next morning, Zollin sent Eustice to prepare their horses. They were taking three, and leaving Mansel with the rest.

They saw their friend at breakfast, looking haggard. It was obvious he hadn't slept.

"Is Nycoll okay?" Zollin asked.

"She's fine," Mansel said.

"Well, you look terrible and you didn't even drink too much," Zollin joked.

"I'm staying," Mansel said, his voice distressed. "I'm sorry."

"Don't be sorry," Zollin said. "You're doing the right thing. What are your plans?"

"We don't have any, at least not yet. I told her I was staying and she's happy, but we haven't talked about what we're going to do next."

"Well, if you leave here, let the innkeeper know where you're headed. If things work out, I'll be back this way."

"If you need me, for anything at all—" Mansel began.

"I know," Zollin said, smiling. "Stop feeling guilty. I'm happy for you, and so is Eustice." The mute servant gave Mansel a big smile and thumbs up gesture.

"See? Now, go take care of Nycoll. You deserve some happiness."

Mansel saw them out after they had eaten.

Zollin felt a hollowness as he climbed into his saddle. He had spent years as a young boy resenting Mansel. When Quinn had taken the big warrior on as an apprentice Zollin had been humiliated. When Mansel had outperformed Zollin at every task, he had felt worthless. And Mansel, the youngest of a large family, had done nothing to make Zollin feel any better. In fact, he had taunted Zollin, always making sure Quinn's son knew that Mansel was the better carpenter.

But when Zollin had been forced to flee their small village, Mansel had come too, abandoning his own family to take the sword in Zollin's defense. Mansel may have come for Quinn, but he'd become an outstanding swordsman, saving Zollin's life on more than one occasion. He'd fought the Skellmarians in Brighton's Gate, stood with Zollin against the King's Army in the Great Valley, fought with Zollin in Orrock to first save Brianna and then later to help save the kingdom. In the midst of all the fighting and struggle, Mansel had been there for Zollin.

Now, as he looked back and saw his friend waving from the yard in front of the inn, he realized their lives were diverging, going in opposite directions. Zollin had never thought about how leaving Mansel would feel, but there was an emptiness as he rode away without his friend. He knew Mansel was doing the right thing, but somehow, going on without him felt wrong at the same time. Zollin looked back one last time, but Mansel had gone back inside and Zollin wondered if he would ever see the big warrior again.

Chapter 21

Brianna and her pride had just taken flight. They were being cautious, waiting until the sun was fully down before taking to the skies and then finding a place to take cover an hour or so before dawn. They had nearly caught up with the army on their first night, and now they could see King Zorlan's force spread out below them. The fires from the camp winked and glistened in the darkness. Brianna and the dragons could see the men moving around or curled next to their fires. It was a warm night and very few of the soldiers had bothered setting up tents, preferring to sleep out in the open.

They saw Prince Wilam's army across the valley. Brianna didn't know much about war or battle. She had heard stories, of course—mostly songs by traveling bards—but she was able to count the numbers of men far below. It didn't seem as if they had met in battle, since she saw no wounded or slain, or large areas where healers seemed to be working. She had gotten as much information as possible and was about to return to Zollin when an image flashed into her mind.

Brianna couldn't hear the magical voice calling to her pride, but the dragons did. They were almost like eager puppies, anxious to run to whoever would give them attention. Brianna thought of Zollin and pushed the thought out toward her pride.

Selix, on whom Brianna was riding, seemed to be the least affected by the magical voice, but the others seemed convinced they should seek it out. They sent her images of a kindly, older wizard calling out to them. Brianna had no idea how they came up with the images—Zollin was the only wizard they had ever seen, and yet they all sent back mental pictures of a kindly looking man with a long beard and a pointy hat.

She sent them images of dragons in chains, and of Bartoom. They sent back images of dragons fighting and killing the slave masters. She sighed, wishing they could understand the danger, but the truth was she couldn't be sure what the danger was. All she knew was that Bartoom had heard a voice too, right before Offendorl had enslaved the massive, black dragon. Still, the dragons were insistent, and so she allowed them to go. She wasn't their master, only a member of the pride. In most cases they followed her lead, but she refused to force them to do her bidding. She had seen the pain and loathing in Bartoom's eyes. The big, black dragon had no choice but to obey, and that fact filled the beast with hate. She would not be the source of such anguish for any dragon.

They flew south, rising high into the air where it was difficult to breathe once the sun came up. Brianna lay across Selix's back and neck through the day. The air was cold and she was forced to hop from one dragon to the next so that they could warm themselves with fire as they flew. Brianna had no spare clothes, so she couldn't let the flames wash over her and warm her like the others. By evening she was exhausted and aching with cold, but they were near the source of the magical voice.

The other dragons had sent her mental images of castle ruins on a hill, which they spotted just as the sun set. Brianna was leery, but she was too tired to resist. The pride was tired too. They had been flying for nearly 24 hours without rest or food. The smaller dragons were affected most. They didn't eat as much as the larger dragons, so they needed to feed more often. They were circling the hill, which was near a wide river and a small village. Brianna was surprised to see that no one was moving about in the village. There were animals, but no signs of the villagers at all.

"Danger," Brianna shouted, pushing the emotion out to the pride, who would be hard pressed to hear her words in mid-flight. "Beware."

She sent them mental images of people moving around in a village, but she wasn't sure they understood. They were searching for the source of the voice in their heads, which was calling for them to land in the castle ruins. The twins, Tig and Torc, landed first, stretching their wings and letting their heads droop a little.

There were cattle tied up in the center of the ruins. Cows, sheep, goats, and pigs, all crying out in terror at the approaching dragons. Images of eating the cattle popped into Brianna's head. Ferno joined the twins, but Selix and Gyia were more cautious, even when the others began to feast on the defenseless animals. It only took a moment to recognize the trap, but for the three dragons in the castle ruins it was too late.

* * *

Offendorl had devised a simple yet devious plan. He had spent a full day stacking the huge slabs of stone back onto the sections of castle walls. The effort had been stupendous, but he was beginning to feel his strength returning. After nearly a month of desperation, he was growing strong again. The women at the inn were terrified of him, all except for the young woman whose husband's manhood Offendorl had ruined. She alone seemed happy to take care of the wizard's every need. She made sure food and wine was always available and kept the other women working hard.

The inn had become a fortified palace, and Offendorl was the king. He spent most of his time in the large chair, which was covered with blankets and quilts. There were finely embroidered cushions as well as animal skins. The village had been searched, and Offendorl was now served all his meals on fine dishes and crystal goblets. Offendorl didn't need gold or jewels, but he insisted that the women sew new garments from the best linen and silk in the village.

Then, Offendorl called to the other dragons. It was a simple technique, not unlike the way Brianna spoke to her pride, but Offendorl amplified his wishes, sweetening them with magic that made them almost irresistible to the dragons. They were drawn to magic and thrived whenever they were near it. So Offendorl had called, starting before dawn, sending images of himself as a kind wizard who only wanted to help them. He kept the crown he used to control Bartoom close at hand, and the women fed him throughout the day to keep his strength up. He knew he would need all his magical prowess if he were to defeat the pride of dragons.

Then, as the last light of day faded, the dragons arrived. Offendorl hurried to the large window of the inn and watched as the dragons circled the castle ruins. He waited as first the two smallest dragons landed, and then he enticed them to eat. A third dragon, a great green brute, landed next, but the other two seemed hesitant. Offendorl decided that two dragons were no match for Bartoom and his own power. He reached out with magic and pulled the loose stone slabs down. From the four corners of the castle ruins the heavy stones fell. They were large stones, easily several tons each. The dragons feasting on the cattle had no warning before the stones fell. Ferno launched itself up, trying to fly out of the trap, but the stones battered the hulking green dragon back down, knocking it senseless. Fortunately, the green dragon deflected most of the stones, saving the smaller dragons' lives. One managed to escape without injury, but the other's wing was broken. There were savage roars of anger that made the women in the inn cower, covering their ears, and several even began to cry. Offendorl laughed at their fear and misery, then placed the golden crown on his head and ordered Bartoom to attack.

* * *

Brianna watched in horror as the castle walls fell. Dust rose in a thick cloud but she didn't wait for it to clear. Instead, she dove off of Selix's back, rushing toward the hill like a cliff diver, disappearing into the dust cloud before she flipped and slowed her descent. The sound of rocks and stones sliding and bouncing filled her head with a cacophony of noise as she landed. Torc raced past her, roaring in fury, while Tig limped to her side. The small blue dragon's left leg was gashed and its wing was broken, the leathery skin in tatters with shattered bone gouging through the flesh at an unnatural angle.

Brianna placed both of her hands on the injured dragon, sending magical fire into its body to begin the healing process. She was looking over at Ferno, who was still breathing but who was also covered in a mountain of broken stones. Then, only seconds after she had landed, fire lit the sky. Selix and Gyia were spewing fire, illuminating the massive form of Bartoom as the beast dove past the larger dragons, blowing through their fiery breath the way a child would splash through a fountain. Then it swooped, its talons outstretched, fire flooding from its open maw, and snatched Torc right out of the air. The smaller dragon was defenseless, held fast by Bartoom's massive claws.

"No!" Brianna screamed, but Bartoom was already climbing back into the sky.

Bartoom reached down with its long neck, sinking its teeth into Torc's neck and then ripping. Brianna felt the life of the small dragon extinguish, the way a candle flame is snuffed between fingers. She felt her own heart break with grief as Bartoom dropped the body of the small dragon.

Selix and Gyia attacked from opposite sides, even as Tig roared in fury, billowing orange flame and black smoke into the sky. Bartoom swung its massive black tail at Gyia but then turned its full attention to Selix. The two dragons met in mid-air, their talons clawing at one another while their tails lashed and their jaws snapped. Bartoom was slightly larger and much stronger. The big black dragon's scales were harder as well, making Selix work harder to inflict damage, but Bartoom's wing was not fully healed and it struggled to get a dominant position.

Selix and Gyia were working together, so Selix didn't try to injure Bartoom—merely distract it. Gyia had flown wide of Bartoom's initial attack, easily dodging the black dragon's tail, but now it dove back into the fray. The purple dragon hissed as it dropped heavily on Bartoom's back. Talons ripped across scales that weren't quite as strong as those on the rest of Bartoom's body. It was the exact spot that Zollin had hit the dragon with his electrical magic blast. At the same time, Gyia's jaws snapped shut on Bartoom's injured wing.

Bartoom arched its back and roared in pain. Selix flew back, letting the two entwined dragons fall past, then dove back down, intending to strike again, but a bolt of lightning shot down behind the golden dragon. Only Selix's dive had saved it from being killed by the lightning bolt that Offendorl had conjured, but Selix was close enough to feel the shock as the bolt skimmed its tail. Then the clap of thunder startled everyone.

The villagers, watching through shuttered windows, trembled. Brianna ducked her head and felt the shock of fear from all the dragons run through her mind. Lightning was the one thing that dragons feared, but there had been no foul weather in the area, only puffy clouds gliding silently on the wind.

"Flee!" she shouted, pushing the mental thought out with force.

Bartoom crashed to the earth at the base of the hill, but the force of the impact shook the ground and collapsed another wall. Gyia had released the black dragon, who was bleeding, its wounded wing now in tatters, although the bone wasn't broken. Selix had flown wide of the battle to avoid the lightning, but Gyia, close to the ground, was climbing slowly back into the air, an easy target.

Brianna pushed a thought toward Gyia and the purple dragon obeyed instantly, diving back toward Bartoom. Lightning struck nearby, but Offendorl couldn't risk hitting Bartoom, giving Gyia the time it needed to gain speed and altitude. Brianna had healed Tig's broken wing, but not the dragon's wounded leg. Still, she sent it flying, low, away from the battle. Then she ran to the pile of stones covering Ferno. She could sense the dragon beneath the rubble. It was alive, but only barely—so many of its bones were shattered that it was only a matter of time before the beast's heart gave out. Brianna jumped high into the air, her body exploding into flame, her clothes incinerating instantly, and she dove into the pile of rocks, which melted like candle wax before her. The mountain of stones covering Ferno glimmered, then glowed with heat before streaming away from the dragon like a lava flow.

Brianna poured healing fire into the dragon. It wasn't a technical process, unlike Zollin's magical healing, which was precise and driven by his knowledge of anatomy. Brianna's magic was more a force of will. She was like a small star—the heat from her healing powers even melted the ground beneath them. The castle's foundation had been built from huge stones, expertly laid on the bedrock of the hill, but the stones melted into a pool of molten rock.

Offendorl was trying desperately to hit Gyia with lightning, the sky crackling with electricity and thunder claps making the ground shudder. The elder wizard didn't see Selix returning to the fight. The golden dragon roared as it breathed fire onto the inn where it sensed the magic of Offendorl. The fire tore through the small structure's roof and poured into building, setting it ablaze instantly. Offendorl had just enough time to surround himself and the young woman who had served him so faithfully since he'd arrived at her village and humiliated her husband. Fire raged around them and she dropped the wine she had been holding for him and clung to his ancient body, but the heat and flames were held at bay by the shield spell.

"Flee!" Brianna ordered again, sending the mental order out to Gyia and Selix.

Bartoom was roaring in pain and Ferno was just coming to when Selix sent Brianna the mental image of Offendorl escaping from the inn. The lightning that had been pursing Gyia had ceased, but Brianna knew it was only a matter of time before another of her pride was killed. Selix circled in the air, golden scales glimmering brightly in the light from the fire that was consuming the village inn. Offendorl was holding one hand up, palm out toward Selix, who dove toward the wizard, swaying from side to side to avoid being an easy target for the elder wizard's magic. In his other hand he clutched the golden crown to his side.

Lightning struck again—this time it was wide of Selix, but sent the dragon careening away from Offendorl. The lighting hit another of the buildings in the village, which exploded under the force and set several other buildings ablaze.

Brianna swam up out of the pool of molten rock, followed closely by Ferno. The green dragon took to the air while Brianna ran to the edge of the hill and jumped off. The hill wasn't extremely steep, but it gave Brianna enough air to rise up on a wave of heat from behind her, and then dive down toward Offendorl. She was like a fiery comet, streaking through the air almost too fast to keep up with, her body covered in flames.

The Master of the Torr turned just in time, throwing up a magical barrier that Brianna crashed into. She felt searing pain as her shoulder was knocked out of socket, but Offendorl and the woman were sent sprawling on the ground from the force of the impact. Brianna rolled to her feet, holding her injured arm to her body and blinking away the tears that blurred her vision. She was just about to send a gout of fire at Offendorl when Bartoom crawled between them. Brianna hesitated as the dragon roared at her.

"No!" she screamed. "Move aside."

Bartoom stood resolute as an image flashed into Brianna's mind of Selix diving for her. She jumped into the air and felt Selix's tail wrap around her as the great golden dragon swooped upward. Brianna watched as Offendorl put the golden crown on his head and then pointed at her. Bartoom, wounded and in pain, flapped its good wing and slowly clawed its way into the air.

She guessed the crown had to do with how Offendorl enslaved the black dragon, but she had no more time to ponder the situation, as the lightning began to slash down at them.

Her shoulder was aching and her vision grew blurry as Selix zigged and zagged through the night sky. They soon outpaced the wizard's reach, and as Brianna looked up just before she passed out from pain and fatigue, she saw Bartoom lumbering after them.

Chapter 22

It was well past noon before King Zorlan ordered his troops forward. Prince Wilam's patience was wearing thin and his men had long before grown restless. Trumpets braying across the field of battle alerted them all to the invading army's approach. They could see the foot soldiers moving forward, with the cavalry taking a position to the rear. The horse soldiers were armed for battle, but stayed in reserve. Wilam guessed that King Zorlan expected his line to break, creating an opening that his cavalry could exploit.

Scouts reported positions as the army moved closer. So far, none of King Zorlan's forces had made a move that Prince Wilam wasn't expecting. He had a full legion of foot soldiers held in reserve, and the rest spread across the field, forming a shield wall that was four men deep. They had been lounging in the sun, using their shields to keep from baking in the heat. Now they were on their feet and Wilam knew that when he gave the order they would lock their shields together, using short swords to hack beneath the shields, the men behind using their weapons to reach over the shoulders of their comrades to slash and stab. It was an age-old tactic that was ruthlessly efficient against the Skellmarians, and, Wilam had learned, the Norsik, who attacked Ortis regularly through the Wilderlands. But if Zorlan's forces were well disciplined, two shield walls could fight for hours and accomplish very little.

The thought crossed Prince Wilam's mind that perhaps Zorlan wasn't hesitant. Perhaps he was just allowing his troops time to rest so that they would be ready for a long battle, while his troops languished through a restless night and then waited through a large part of the day in the blistering heat of the sun. It was a wily strategy, but Wilam had a few tricks up his sleeve as well.

"Loose the fire arrows," he ordered.

The archers on the platform with Wilam lit arrows that had been soaked in oil. The oil made the arrows burn and produced black smoke. The archers had to lean out over the guardrail in order to shoot the arrows high up into the air. The awning over the platform extended several feet beyond the platform to give it the maximum protection from falling projectiles. Six arrows arced through the sky, leaving a trail of greasy, black smoke behind them.

The invading soldiers faltered in their march when they saw the fire arrows. They expected the battlefield to be soaked with oil, creating a barrier of flame between the two armies, but the arrows fell harmlessly into the open field. Prince Wilam was left to wait once more. The invading army was moving slowly, conserving their energy, and King Zorlan's cavalry had not yet moved into position.

It was hard for the prince to stay calm, but he managed it. He wanted nothing more than to be in the middle of the shield wall, fighting shoulder to shoulder with men he trusted, but he couldn't fight on the front lines and direct the army. He waited, watching the mounted cavalry far across the plain. Suddenly a large group of horsemen turned their horses and rode back into their camp. Prince Wilam could only hope it was to stop the troops who were harrying the supply train and reserve troops. He doubted that King Zorlan could lead effectively while being attacked from the front and the rear.

"Archers," Wilam said.

An aide beside him began waving colored flags to signal the appropriate group. Wilam had 200 longbow men. They were not marksmen in the traditional sense—instead they were trained to fire at specific distances. By firing large volleys they could rain down death on an enemy while staying out of reach at the same time.

"Two hundred yards," Wilam ordered. "Fire away."

The aide waved more flags, and Wilam watched as a volley of arrows whistled into the air. Marching troops used shields to keep the arrows from falling on them, but unless they stopped and knelt down, they would be at least partially exposed. The arrows were costly, and firing volleys of 200 arrows at once used up great numbers of them in a short amount of time. Still, it caused the invading troops to huddle together, their officers barking at them to maintain their ranks and pace. The invaders inevitably slowed, and they were forced to carry their heavy shields over their heads. As the arrows rained down a few men were wounded. The casualties were negligible but the Ortisan soldiers cheered anyway.

Prince Wilam saw that the cavalry troops returned to their position, but he knew his men would keep moving, keep hitting the enemy in different locations before retreating again. He hoped it would keep King Zorlan and his generals occupied.

"One hundred yards," he ordered the aide, who signaled the command.

When the latest volley of arrows went up, a horn blew and the invaders charged. They screamed their battle cry as they dashed forward. The volley of arrows caught a few, but most flew over the heads of the invaders. They were no longer in straight, even rows. It was another tactic intended to save the invaders from the threat of the arrows and also give them a chance at using the force of their charge to break Wilam's shield wall.

As a commander on the field, Wilam had always welcomed the test of his shield wall. He trained his men relentlessly and knew without a doubt what they could withstand. Now, leading an army of foreigners, he stood at the rail of his platform, leaning forward eagerly to see how his troops would hold up.

The clash of the two armies was like thunder at first, the crack of shield against shield, then swords against shields, and finally the cries of rage, fear, and pain. The sounds rolled across the plain and made Wilam's blood run hot. For a brief moment he had no regard for anything else, not even his queen. But then his line staggered back and the shield wall became a mass all its own, straining and heaving as the two armies pushed against each other.

Wilam frowned. He didn't have the resources to sway the conflict—success now rested on the soldiers who were fighting on the ground. For several minutes the line swayed, like water sloshing in a bucket, first one way, then another, but soon it was obvious the two forces were deadlocked. It would take hours, perhaps days for the foot soldiers to gain an advantage. And then King Zorlan did something Wilam had expected, but couldn't adequately counter. The Falxisan king sent his cavalry to both ends of the Ortisan lines. Wilam had already positioned his own mounted troops on either end of the battle line, but his cavalry were outnumbered four to one.

Wilam had hoped that his small force attacking King Zorlan's forces from the rear would force the invaders to keep a larger number of troops in reserve, but it hadn't worked. Either Zorlan had more nerve than Wilam had thought, or the invading king had anticipated Wilam's tactics. By dividing his forces, Wilam was now at a disadvantage, with no foreseeable way to counter the invader's tactics.

"Sir, the enemy cavalry are moving to attack," Wilam's aide said.

"I see that, fool. Don't speak unless you are ordered to do so."

"Yes, sir," said the aide, rigidly.

"Order one century of archers to each flank. I want them moving at a run!"

The aide didn't answer—he just turned and waved his flags again. Wilam was tense as he watched the archers move. He knew the bowmen stood no chance once the cavalry reached them—they would be cut down like winter wheat before a farmer's scythe—but if they could get to the edge of the battle in time, they could fire at the enemy's horses.

"Order them to fire at will once they reach the edge of the line," Wilam said, his voice loud.

It took almost a full minute for the bowmen to get into position and fire. By that time, the enemy cavalry were at full gallop. The archers fired sporadically, many missing their targets. It took a direct hit to bring down the warhorses; the others would carry their riders until they dropped dead. Wilam saw a few of the riders stumble and fall, but most continued through the fray. The Ortisan officers leading the cavalry on the right side of the line moved forward and engaged the enemy. They were outnumbered and their chances for success were slim, but they spared the archers from the brunt of the enemy's attack and allowed the bowmen time to pull back and offer support from a position of safety.

The officer on the left end of the shield wall was not so wise. He ordered his force to wheel, turning away from the action, which spared his cavalry from the brunt of the invaders' charge but left the archers exposed. The officer must have expected the enemy to follow his mounted troops away from the battle, but instead they cut down the archers and turned to flank the line of foot soldiers. The cavalry tried to re-engage, but the damage was done. The shield wall broke on the left side of the line—men were cut down or deserted their comrades in order to retreat. Wilam cursed as he watched his line falter and break. It moved down the line of soldiers from left to right, like a wave, until there was only a jumbled mass of humanity.

"Sound the retreat," Wilam said bitterly.

The aide waved his flags and trumpets blew. It was a sickening sound to Wilam. His plans had been thwarted, and now his hopes for winning Gwendolyn's affections were lost. His only hope would be to retreat to the Grand City and take cover behind the city's massive walls.

He didn't wait to see the final outcome, but climbed down from his platform and mounted his horse. Men were beginning to run past him, terror on their faces. He despised them. They should have stayed and fought for their queen, he thought. They should have given their lives, to the last man, but instead they had deserted the field of battle, and many would not fall back to their camp but would instead flee. His force, defeated in battle, would be reduced further by their cowardice, and King Zorlan's army would now be bolstered by success on the battlefield.

"Fall back," he shouted. "Fall back to the camp."

It was almost dark by the time they began their retreat in earnest. They had lost over half their force, including all but a handful of the archers and cavalry. They abandoned their supplies, carrying only their weapons as they marched through the night. The camp, Wilam hoped, would be enough of a distraction to the invaders to buy them some time to distance themselves. The invaders would loot the camp and celebrate their victory while Prince Wilam limped home.

His troops marched at a slow, dogged pace. Their feet seemed to drag along the path.

His generals had survived, and they rode beside him now. No one spoke, and Wilam was sure they were planning how to report his defeat to Gwendolyn in hopes of stealing her favor.

Despair washed over him, and he felt like a little child. There had been times when his father had called him to account for a misdeed. King Felix of Yelsia was a stern man who brooked no failure, especially in his firstborn son. Disappointing his father had happened infrequently, but it had happened. Now he felt the same sense of dread. Clouds rolled across the sky until it was so dark out that torches had to be made and lit.

Wilam guessed correctly that their progress was too slow. They would have to march through the day, his men moving slower and slower. If it rained, it would only make things worse. They had very little food and water, and each stop to rest would bring their enemy closer. They were four days from the Grand City, perhaps five at the pace they were moving. Prince Wilam estimated that they would be caught late on the third day, or early on the fourth. Despite his gut-wrenching failure, he began to plan how to save as many of his troops as possible.

* * *

Offendorl was sore. His back and legs ached, but the young woman's hands kneaded his ancient flesh. Her hands were warm and she rubbed lineament and oils into his skin. Normally, Offendorl did not rely on physical healing methods, but now the elder wizard was conserving his strength. The battle had drained him, and he'd been forced to take shelter in a small cottage after the fire burned most of the village. The townsfolk were either dead or gone, having deserted the village in the midst of the fires. Offendorl didn't blame them. He was surprised, however, that the young woman had stayed with him. He had cast no spells on her and wasn't sure exactly why the woman had taken to him so strongly. His only guess was that she was attracted to power. He understood that, and would reward her loyalty.

He hadn't destroyed the other dragons the way he had hoped, but he felt he had at least bought enough time to deal with Gwendolyn. Bartoom was in bad shape, but Offendorl wasn't the type to care overmuch about the people or dragons around him. He had called the massive black beast back to the village when it became obvious that Bartoom could not match the speed of the other dragons in its wounded state.

Offendorl hadn't known about the girl. Of course she had created the dragons. He'd read of her kind, but he had not expected her to be with the pride. Her ability to heal the dragons was unique. Gold was the only other thing he knew of that could heal a wounded dragon, if the beast did not heal naturally. They were strong creatures, without many weaknesses, but once their almost impenetrable hide was rent, they were as vulnerable as any other creature.

Offendorl needed Bartoom healthy when he faced Gwendolyn. He had gathered as much gold as he could find for the dragon, but the village was poor and most of the homes were piles of smoldering rubble now. Still, it would have to be enough. The elder wizard forced the black dragon to heal its wing first. The wounds in its back were serious, but the beast could fly and breathe fire with a wounded back. The dragon was worthless to Offendorl if it couldn't fly. At least the wing had not been broken, like the little blue dragon that had been caught in the trap he'd set in the ruins of the ancient castle. The woman had healed that dragon rather quickly, and her ability to control fire was unheard of. Even Offendorl himself couldn't endure heat to that extreme. The entire top of the hill had been melted and now resembled a lake of obsidian, like a black, glassy pond.

He would have to make his next moves carefully. Returning to the Grand City undetected would be difficult. The woman would be of service there, he thought to himself as he calculated his plans. He would have to refrain from using magic—even the smallest spell could be detected if Gwendolyn was being careful. He had to assume that she was, even though the arrogance of taking over the tower of Torr gave him doubts. Perhaps she thinks I'm dead, he pondered. Why else would she act so brazenly?

It didn't matter what her reasons were. He had to assume she was at the peak of her power. She also had access to his library. It was the largest collection of ancient books and scrolls ever collected. Each volume was filled with information that a wizard—or in her case, a sorceress—could use. But he would get it back. He would make her pay in pain and blood. Her penalty would be slow and agonizing. And Offendorl would start with the witch's sister.

"Tell me your name," he ordered the woman who was massaging him. Although she had seen to his every need, he had not bothered to learn her name. If she was going to help him in the Grand City, he would need to rely on her even more.

"Havina," she said, caressing his skin affectionately.

"Good child, you shall be of service to me in the Grand City."

"As you wish, master," she said in a coy voice.

"Don't play games with me. I do not care for your safety or lust for your body. Is that clear? You will do as I say or be cast aside."

He knew that being replaced or sent away was more threatening to the power hungry girl even than death. Her face revealed her fear and confirmed his suspicions. She would do whatever he wanted, as long as he was the most powerful person in her acquaintance. She would be useful against Gwendolyn, although he might be better served to discard her before he faced the young wizard Zollin again.

"Now, find my carriage and a horse. It's time to move on from this place."

Chapter 23

Brianna's heart ached almost as much the searing pain in her dislocated shoulder. She and Selix had reached the coast just south of Brimington Bay at dawn. They found the other dragons waiting. Tig and Torc had not been twins in the conventional sense, but she had made them together, breathing the same breath of fire into their stone bodies so that they shared a bond even closer than the other dragons of the pride. Tig's grief over the loss was staggering. The dragons wailed, almost like abandoned kittens, not quite roaring but making more noise than was prudent, given how close they were to one of the largest cities in Osla. They were nestled in an area of sandy dunes not far from the shore. The dragons nuzzled one another, and especially Tig. Brianna sat on the crest of the dune, watching for signs that someone or something might approach to investigate the heart-rending cries of her pride.

Brianna had never felt such grief as she felt over the loss of the small, blue dragon. She had created Torc, had watched the dragon grow in wisdom and friendship. She could not get the image of Bartoom tearing the smaller dragon's head off out of her mind. She felt sick and afraid at the same time. When they had fought Bartoom before, she had been nervous for the safety of her pride, but now she felt terrified they would all be killed. She had to fight the urge to lead them back north. She wanted to take them and hide in the Highlands, to keep them far from danger, but she knew that they could only hide from that danger for so long. If they ran now, Offendorl would only grow stronger. The threat he posed would become greater and their fates would be sealed.

Zollin was her only hope now. Zollin had to defeat the evil wizard, she thought. He had to win or they would all be killed—or worse, enslaved. Brianna had been hurtling at breakneck speed when she had smashed into the elder wizard's magical defenses, but she had noticed the young woman clinging to him. The wizard was an ancient looking man, powerful in magic, but his body seemed as fragile as a dried reed. Still, he had taken her blow with less injury than she had. The pain in her dislocated shoulder was so intense she was sweating. She knew that soon they would have to find Zollin, or she would have to go into a town alone to look for a healer. Leaving her pride undefended simply wasn't an option at the moment, which meant she would have to endure the pain and let the dragons carry her to Zollin.

The day passed slowly, the sun rising high as the dragons finally gave in to grief and exhaustion. Brianna was exhausted too, but she was in too much pain to sleep. She tried lying down on the edge of the sandy hill, but she simply couldn't get comfortable. Her head was swimming by the time the sun began to set. She roused the dragons and sent them mental images of Zollin.

Selix was full of concern, but Brianna knew that all the dragons were tired—partly from the battle and partly from shock. Still, they had to move. She doubted that Bartoom could follow them—the big black dragon's wing was shredded and it had not been healed from their last encounter. That was a clue that led

Brianna to believe the wizard who controlled Bartoom did not have the power to heal the dragon.

Selix had some minor scratches and bruises. Ferno and Tig were healed of their major injuries, but both were still in shock from the damage done to their bodies in the trap. Tig's right leg was hurt, but the small dragon refused to have Brianna heal it. The small blue dragon acted almost as if the injury was a badge of honor. Gyia alone had been unharmed, but the graceful purple dragon had been chased by lightning and the terror of that was enough to shock the normally calm and strategic-minded dragon into irrational fear.

"We must go," she said through clenched teeth. "He can heal my shoulder."

Selix agreed, nuzzling Brianna on her uninjured side, but Ferno looked almost shamefaced. Brianna saw an image in her mind of the dragon unable to carry her. She nodded at the muscular, green dragon.

"I know. We'll stop and rest when we need to. But we can't stay here."

She felt their fear and was helpless to reassure them. She knew Zollin was their only hope, but she wasn't sure that they would survive that battle she knew was coming. She would have to explain to them the best she could, and then give them the opportunity to stay and fight, or to return to the mountains.

Selix wrapped her in its long, golden tail, trying to move her gently, but causing Brianna to wail in pain just the same. Ferno roared suddenly, filling Brianna's mind with images of anger and hatred. The fierce green dragon had not seen Torc ripped apart by Bartoom, but the others had, and the mental images they shared when they spoke of it were graphic in nature. The big dragon was angry now, anxious to finish the fight or die trying.

"In time," she assured Ferno. "Soon we will see the wizard destroyed and make Bartoom answer for the death of our brother. But now we must regroup. We cannot be swayed by the magic of the elder wizard again. We must join Zollin and fight with him," she said, her voice fading as spots began to appear in her vision.

She swayed on the dragon's back, but Selix used its long tail to steady her, then it took to the air, the other dragons following. The sky turned dark as the big, golden dragon sailed along. It stayed only high enough to be sure no tree or hill impeded their path. Brianna was naked, having burned through her clothes in her efforts to save Ferno, so the dragon let its fiery breath wash over Brianna as often as it could. There were many settlements along the coast, but whenever there was an area that looked sparsely populated, the dragons breathed fire onto Brianna, who was now between consciousness and sleep. She trembled with chills brought on by her injury more than the cold night air.

Selix was forced to stop twice in the night to rest. Ferno, weak from the injuries it had sustained, still took up a guard position. Tig, in shock from injuries and grief, dropped unceremoniously onto the ground whenever they landed and went promptly to sleep. When dawn broke, the dragons could feel Zollin ahead of them, but they still had several hours to travel. There were clouds in the sky, so the dragons flew into the clouds, doing their best to remain undetected, but of course it was a futile effort. It was almost noon by the time they came within sight of Zollin and Eustice, but the wizard was in a small town, and although Selix wanted to take Brianna straight to Zollin, Gyia convinced them to wait in a tall grove of palm trees not far from the settlement.

* * *

Zollin had just purchased a basket of fruit and was looking forward to eating some of the cool, sweet items. The daily heat was growing more intense the further south they traveled, despite the cool breeze from the ocean. He thanked the vender and joined Eustice, who had just strapped a small keg of ale to the back of their packhorse. The ale made Zollin think of Mansel.

He had left his friend the day before, but it felt longer to Zollin. He missed Mansel, and Kelvich, and of course Brianna—he even missed his father.

"We can go soon, I just need to see if I can get any information about what is happening in the Grand City," Zollin told Eustice. "Mansel always said that taverns were the best places to hear the local gossip. How about we get a cool drink and see what we can learn?"

Eustice, as silent as ever, smiled and flashed Zollin a thumbs up. They led the horses to a tavern that seemed busy. Inside, there were fishermen and merchants. Girls younger than Brianna served as tavern maids, fetching drinks or food. Zollin sat at a table in the shady tavern. Unlike the inns Zollin was used to, most of the buildings in Osla had no walls—just an elevated floor and a sturdy roof. He supposed that it never got cold enough to need protection from the weather. It gave the area a decidedly foreign feel, as did the towering palm trees.

"Can I get you something?" one of the young maidens asked.

"What do you have that is cool and refreshing?"

"We have spiced coconut milk," the girl said. "It's very good."

"We'll have two pints of it then," Zollin said. "And maybe a little information," he added as he slid two silver marks across the table. It was enough money for the two men to drink on for the rest of the day. The girl glanced around before snatching the coins up and tucking them into the neck of her shirt.

"I'll be right back," she said, then pranced off toward the kitchens.

"They like their girls young in this town," Zollin said to Eustice. "It's hard to believe that girl is old enough to be out of essentials school."

Eustice shrugged his shoulders, gesturing that he didn't know.

"I don't guess you got a chance to go to school, did you?" Zollin asked. "How old were you when you went to the Torr?"

Eustice held up eight fingers.

"Eight years old? What about your parents?"

Eustice shrugged his shoulders again. Then the barmaid returned, followed by a gruff-looking man who was carrying his own drink.

"These are the strangers, Papa," she said, setting down wooden mugs in front of Zollin and Eustice. She flashed them a smile and then hurried away.

"I hear you gentlemen are looking for information," the gruff looking man said. "I'm Ornak, owner of this establishment."

"Zollin," the young wizard said, "and this is Eustice. We saw an army marching into Osla a while back. Any news about what's going on?"

"Lots of rumors," Ornak said. "Word is King Belphan was killed up north. Although that's just rumors, mind you. I've also heard that King Zorlan from Falxis is leading that army, although King Oveer from Ortis beat him to the Grand City."

"You think they're trying to take over Osla?" Zollin asked.

"I'm sure there is something going on. First King Belphan takes the army north. Now armies are marching into Osla. It's all shady from my perspective. I mean, what happened to the treaty between the kingdoms?" Ornak said before taking a long drink then wiping his mouth with the back of his hand. "The latest word we got just this morning was that King Zorlan's forces routed Oveer's troops."

"You don't seem bothered by this rumor," Zollin said.

"Well, I don't know all the details, but from what I've heard, King Falxis was marching with the Oslan troops. That makes 'em more on our side, I suppose."

"I guess so," Zollin said. "But from the way they burned and pillaged their way through Falxis, I'm not sure I'd want them turned loose anywhere near me."

"Soldiers are all the same," Ornak said. "Been that way forever, I suppose. To the victor goes the spoils—that's the old saying, anyway. I'm just grateful we're out of their way."

"Well, you've given us a lot to talk about on the road," Zollin said, sliding another silver mark toward the man."

"No hurry, is there?" Ornak said. "You can have all you want to eat and drink."

"We've had our fill for today. Delicious drink though," Zollin said, draining the last of his spiced coconut milk.

"Come back and visit us on your way back up the coast," Ornak said, taking them to be traders. "We're always open and you're always welcome here."

"Thank you," Zollin said.

He and Eustice left the tavern and climbed into their saddles. Zollin had enjoyed the drinks, but he was eager to get on the road again. He wanted to find Brianna and see if what the tavern owner had told him was true. If King Oveer had failed to stop the invading army, there was nothing that would stop them from laying siege to the Grand City. Zollin was just wondering if that would help him or hurt him in his quest to stop Offendorl and the Torr when he heard a familiar growl.

The horses, suddenly nervous, started backing away from the grove of palm trees ahead.

"It's okay," Zollin said, trying to calm his horse and Eustice, who suddenly looked worried. "I think it's Brianna."

He handed the reins of his horse over to Eustice and told him to wait. He then walked slowly toward the grove of trees.

There were large bushy plants growing around the base of the trees, which were tall and skinny. The sound of the ocean waves lapping against the shore obscured all other sound. Zollin let his magic flow into the trees and was rewarded to find the dragons. He also felt Brianna's pain and he bolted forward.

"How bad is she?" he said in a loud voice as he pushed his way past the shrubs. The light inside the grove of trees was mottled and Zollin was suddenly aware of the strong, musky scent of the dragons.

A low growl was the only reply, but he saw Brianna lying on the sand, her body covered with palm fronds. Her skin was pale and she was trembling. Zollin hurried over, ignoring the massive heads of the dragons as they followed her. He noticed in the back of his mind that there were only four dragons with Brianna, and that the smallest one seemed to be sleeping. He assumed the fifth was on watch somewhere, perhaps even high overhead, but those concerns were far from his mind as he knelt beside Brianna.

Zollin started to remove the palm fronds that covered her, but Selix, the great golden dragon, hissed a warning, lowering its massive head in front of Zollin and baring its teeth. Zollin let the branches go, holding up his hands.

"I only want to help her," he said. "Thank you for bringing her to me."

He was careful not to touch anything but her hand as he let his magic flood into her and immediately noticed the shoulder that was out of its socket. It was the same shoulder she had injured before in Felson when she had been accosted in the streets. He nudged it gently with his magic. In most cases, popping the shoulder back into place was a strenuous and painful ordeal, but because he sensed exactly what needed to be done to move the shoulder back into its socket, he could do it with a minimum of pain or discomfort. The shoulder slipped back into place easily enough, but the muscles and tissues around it were swollen. Zollin took his time removing the fluid from the tissues until everything seemed normal. Brianna's bones seemed lighter and Zollin took his time inspecting her body. It had changed since she had found her powers. There was less fat and more muscle tissue, although it wasn't dense like he expected. There was space between the fibers, almost like a loosely woven garment.

Her bones were different too. More porous and even flexible, but incredibly strong at the same time. He couldn't find anything else wrong with her, but she was still sleeping. He guessed she probably needed time to sleep and recover, but he needed to make sure she was alright.

He shook her softly and watched as her eyes fluttered open.

"Zollin," she said. "I'm glad to see you."

"Me too," he said, grinning despite his concern. "Are you okay? What happened?"

"Bartoom and the wizard attacked us," she said, her face growing red and tears streaking from her eyes. "He lured the dragons to him and then tried to kill them. Torc was killed before we escaped."

The dragons around them growled and moaned. It was a frightening yet incredibly sad sound. Zollin looked up and saw the three big dragons looking at him. Smoke was coming from Ferno's mouth.

"I'm so sorry," he said, first to the dragons and then to Brianna. "I'm sorry. I got you into this mess. I should have been with you."

"No, it isn't your fault," Brianna said. "I knew…we all knew it was risky going to the wizard, but we thought we might learn some useful information. Everything just went bad so quickly."

"At least you're all right now," Zollin said. "And you're safe." He looked up. "You're all safe. I won't let this happen again. I swear I'll stop Offendorl, if it's the last thing I do."

Then suddenly an image appeared in Zollin's mind. He saw the hulking green dragon battling with him, side by side. It was so vivid and clear he knew it wasn't just a thought.

"What is it, Zollin?" Brianna asked.

"I'm not sure," Zollin said, taking a deep breath and then looking up at Ferno. "Did you just do that?"

The dragon nodded and the image flashed into his mind again. "Okay," Zollin said. "We'll do it together."

Chapter 24

King Zorlan had pushed the pursuit and Prince Wilam had been fighting a rear action retreat for almost two days. His men were exhausted, but there was simply no time to rest. If they stopped, they were attacked. First, archers had begun to pick off the stragglers. Then, as night fell on the third day of their retreat, Zorlan's cavalry charged, catching the rear of Wilam's column completely off guard. He lost a third of his force, which was barely over half of what he'd started with. They now had around 1,300 men, and more were lost every hour. They could see the enemy troops to their rear, content to push Wilam's retreating force.

The young prince directed the rear action himself. The rear of the column was mostly the wounded soldiers who still had the strength to keep moving but were slower than their companions and naturally fell to the rear. Wilam moved the few archers he had remaining to the sides of the rear column. He rode his horse, and when the enemy moved forward he blew a war horn that signaled the archers to fan out to either side. They dropped to one knee and fired their arrows before turning and jogging backward again.

Usually the volley of arrows was enough to stop whatever force tried to close the distance between the two armies. They weren't set on destroying Wilam's troops, at least not yet. In fact, Wilam doubted that King Zorlan's main force was even within a day's march of his troops. But, the Falxisan king had been smart enough to send a band of cavalry and archers to harass their retreat. If they survived the retreat, they would be worn out and exhausted for days. Wilam, his whole body aching and his stomach twisting in knots, rode silently, half turned in his saddle so he could keep a watch on the pursing force.

The Oslan countryside was arid and dusty. There were few farms and fewer villages along the road, most spaced a full day's walk apart. Food was plentiful throughout Osla because of trade, but most of the land was unfit for farming. Silk production and diamond mining were the chief industries, but those were found south of the Grand City. In the almost barren plains leading to the capital there was no respite from the sun's heat or the dust that seemed to fill the air, invading Prince Wilam's nose and mouth. His eyes burned from the dust, and as the day wore on he had trouble even seeing the enemy behind them.

Then, when the young commander thought things couldn't get worse, a strong wind began to blow from the north. It should have been a good sign—having the wind at their backs—but the wind blew the dust tramped up by the troops pursuing them into Wilam's face. It billowed out like a dirty, brown fog that obstructed his view. The wind blew for three hours before arrows fell from the pursing force. They struck with no warning, landing all around the rear of the retreating column. Two hit Wilam's horse and he was thrown when the animal reared in pain. He fell hard on the unforgiving ground, his head whipping back and hitting so hard he was knocked unconscious.

When he opened his eyes again, it was dark. He was in a tent, the wind making the canvas structure flutter loudly. Nearby was a man Wilam took for a healer. He wasn't in armor or a uniform of any type. Of course, that could have been because he was sleeping, but the man slept in a camp chair, slumped over uncomfortably, and Wilam could feel the bandage wrapped around his aching head. He tried to remember what had happened, but the last few moments before he lost consciousness were lost.

His mouth was so dry his tongue felt twice its normal size. His eyes seemed full of grit, and as he raised his hands to rub his eyes, his arms felt heavy.

He groaned and the healer woke up. The man uncovered a lamp, casting light all around the tent and hurting Wilam's eyes further. He squinted in the sudden light.

"You're awake," the man said in surprise. "That's good."

"Water," Prince Wilam said, his voice croaking.

"Yes, of course. Here you are."

The man slid his hand gently behind Wilam's neck and lifted the prince's head slightly before dribbling water from a long handled dipper into his mouth. Wilam felt like a helpless child, but the water was cool and sweet. He slurped at it greedily. After several moments, he lay back. He felt better after his drink, and truth be told he wanted more, but he was too tired. His gritty eyes burned with fatigue.

"How long was I out?" he asked.

"Just a few hours," the man said. "We've been waiting for you to wake up. Stay awake, the king will want to question you."

"Question me about what?" Wilam asked, and then as if a dam had burst in his mind, the memories came flooding back. The healer didn't bother to answer, but hurried from the tent. Wilam lay in shock as he realized what he had done. He remembered going to Lodenhime with Mansel and Quinn. They had been returning to Yelsia, but the witch had cast her spell. He remembered building her army, remembered killing her steward in the Castle on the Sea. He recalled sacking the Grand City and killing innocent people who were trying desperately to flee their homes. He recalled his confrontation with King Oveer and how he'd slain the sovereign ruler of another kingdom.

Tears welled in his eyes as he remembered what he had done. Shame, as bitter as bile in his mouth, settled in his heart. He wished for death and felt around him for a weapon or instrument with to end his life, but there was nothing but blankets and bandages.

Then the tent opened again and three men entered. One was the healer who had given Wilam the water, the next was a man the prince didn't recognize, and the third was King Zorlan. He no longer looked as pampered and disinterested as he had in the Grand City when he had arrived for the Council of Kings. Now he looked stern and focused. It was a look Wilam had seen often enough from his father—a look he had tried to imitate many times.

"See, he's awake," the healer said.

"Good," King Zorlan said. "Prince Wilam. My how the tables have turned. Wouldn't you agree?"

Wilam just stared silently at the king. He didn't know if he should tell them what he knew or not. His loyalty was divided. His first duty was to Yelsia and his people, although the witch's spell had made him somehow forget that duty. Before him was one of the kings who had invaded Wilam's homeland, causing untold damage to Wilam's people and their homes. For that alone Wilam wanted to resist aiding King Zorlan in any way. On the other hand, he knew that Gwendolyn was dangerous. He didn't want to see the Grand City destroyed in a useless war, but he didn't see how that could be avoided. The men left in the city had specific orders and there was no way to break the witch's spell. Wilam had no idea how he'd managed to break her influence now.

"How noble," said King Zorlan. "You don't want to talk. That's just what I expected. Unlike our brothers, I knew you would be a good king—perhaps not wise, but noble at least. You have that stubborn character that most kings have, the kind that won't allow you to change. And you shouldn't feel bad that I defeated your army in battle. Our cavalry are unstoppable."

"It wasn't my army," Wilam said, his throat still so dry his voice was a ragged whisper. "The witch had us all under some type of spell."

"How convenient for you," said King Zorlan. "And quite political too. Passing the blame is a crucial part of good leadership. Tell me more about this witch of yours?"

"You can't get close to her," Wilam said. "You have to surround the city and cut off their supplies. It's the only way to beat her."

"You see, that's your problem. You rely too much on traditional tactics. That's how I knew how to beat you on the field of battle. I could see your plan the moment my scouts reported your position. Perhaps in Yelsia you could have found a place to make a stand, but out here, in the wide-open plains, your tactics were antiquated. Flanking you was a little too easy, and after my troops had been given plenty of time to rest, pursuing you immediately was not difficult either. Now you advise me to lay siege to the city, but you see you've already given me the information I needed. This witch of yours is the key, can't you see that? We don't need to lay siege to the city. No, that would take months and put thousands of lives at risk. What we need is a little more information about this witch, so that we can kill her. Then, her spell will be broken. I'll send King Oveer back home with a slap on the wrist and Osla will be absorbed into Falxis."

"I knew that was your plan," Wilam said in disgust. "You have no honor. You are breaking the treaty—"

"No, King Oveer and King Belphan broke the treaty when they pushed for war on Yelsia. I just knew how to turn those events to my advantage."

"You were driven out of Yelsia."

"True, our wizard deserted us when yours bested him in battle. That was a sight to behold too. There hasn't been anything like it in centuries. Still, the old man had enough strength left to kill Belphan. I saw the opportunity to improve my fortunes and I took it. There's nothing in the treaty about that."

"King Oveer is dead too," Wilam sneered. "I guess that means fate is handing you another kingdom."

"Perhaps ..." King Zorlan said. "Oveer is dead, are you sure?"

"I killed him," Wilam said.

"Oh, you are a nasty boy, aren't you?"

"I wasn't in my right mind."

"Of course you were. Oveer was a pompous, power hungry fool. A bully of a king, always looking for ways to get more than his share. You did the Five Kingdoms a favor. How did you do it?"

Wilam looked away. He was ashamed of what he'd done. He agreed that King Oveer had been a pompous, power hungry fool, but that didn't make what Wilam had done any less dishonorable. He had murdered men because of some misguided passion for a woman he couldn't even remember. He could visualize Gwendolyn, at least everything but her face. In his mind she seemed to be in a silhouette, her face an indistinct blur.

"Come now, Prince Wilam, don't fret. Your secrets are safe with me. In fact, if you help me defeat the witch and take Osla, I'll help you defeat King Ricard. You shall be king of the northern kingdoms and I shall rule the south. What do you say? Let's work together."

"No," Wilam said in a whisper. His body was beginning to shake. Fatigue was overcoming his strength and he wanted to die.

"Don't be unreasonable. You could be my right hand. Together we can return peace to the Five Kingdoms."

"Don't you mean the 'Two Kingdoms?'"

"Soon enough. Don't you see that united we will be much stronger and more prosperous?"

"I can see that you will be more prosperous."

"I did not start this asinine war," King Zorlan said angrily. "I was content with my kingdom, but Belphan and Oveer insisted. You were not there to defend Yelsia—what were we to think? But now the die is cast and it cannot be taken back. Osla and Ortis are without a king. It is my duty to rule them."

"Your duty? What about Belphan's sons?"

"They are children," Zorlan argued. "And sickly ones, from what I hear. I doubt they will live long enough to fill their father's role as king of Osla. And if they do, they will need guidance."

"And you are the person to give it to them, I'm sure, as long as they pay you tribute?"

"Your insolence is beginning to wear on my nerves. I think perhaps it is time that Ebain took a turn with you. Getting stubborn people to see reason is his specialty, although I dare say you won't enjoy it as much as talking with me. I shall return in the morning to see if you are not more willing to cooperate."

King Zorlan stood up and walked briskly from the tent. The other man that had come in with the king opened a pouch and pulled out a long metal device that tapered to a point.

"I cannot watch this," said the healer, hurrying from the tent.

Ebain didn't speak, but rather laid his instrument to the side and removed a set of leather manacles. Wilam tried to resist when Ebain bound his hands and feet, but he simply had no strength. He struggled, but Ebain subdued him easily. Wilam was panting by the time Ebain had him bound hand and foot, and his vision began to blur. He wanted to be left in peace, to close his eyes and never wake up again, but he knew that wasn't going to happen.

Ebain returned to his metal device. He handled it lovingly, as if it were the dearest thing in the world to him—a prized piece of art rather than a torture device.

"I won't bother asking questions," Ebain said, his voice almost monotone and completely without emotion. "The king will come back in the morning. If you answer his questions then, the pain will stop. For now, that is all you need to know."

Wilam's heart was racing. He struggled futilely against his bonds, but Ebain merely watched and waited. Terror of what was about to happen felt like a giant weight had been dropped onto Wilam's chest. He struggled to breathe and sweat began to pour off of him. Then, moving quickly, Ebain dropped onto Wilam's stomach. There was a large spike and heavy mallet in his hands. Wilam's vision narrowed and then he passed out.

Ebain seemed unconcerned. He merely lifted Wilam's hands over his head and drove the spike into the ground through the links in the leather manacles. Then he returned to his long, metal device. At first glance the tool seemed like nothing more than a highly polished spike, or some type of villainous piece of art, but on closer inspection its deadly nature became clearer. The tip was pointed and smooth for several inches, then two small blades protruded slightly. They were thin and delicate looking, but honed finer than a razor blade. Beyond that, the instrument became serrated with tiny teeth-like edges that grew taller and further apart. Ebain could skin, gut, and dismember a body with the instrument.

He started by driving another stake through the leather manacles binding Prince Wilam's feet. Then he sat back on his heels and stroked the prince's foot. Wilam was completely unconscious. They had removed most of his clothing shortly after they found his body on the side of the road. His troops, if they had seen him fall, had either believed he was dead or didn't care enough to rescue him. They had moved on, leaving the bodies of dead or dying soldiers in the road. Prince Wilam was found not far from his wounded horse, which lay in the dirt too exhausted to move.

Ebain placed the point of the device just under the edge of Wilam's big toe. He waited for just a moment, his hands holding the foot steady and the torture device ready, his eyes never leaving Wilam's face. Then he pushed the device down. Blood welled up around the toenail and Wilam squirmed, but didn't wake up. Then Ebain gave the instrument a sharp thrust. The toenail was ripped from the nail bed with a wet pop, and Wilam screamed. His eyes opened so widely that Ebain could see whites all around the irises.

Ebain watched for a moment, letting Wilam struggle against his bonds again. He watched the prince's face as it grew red. He ignored the blood running down Wilam's foot. It was a minor injury and he knew it would clot on its own soon enough. As Prince Wilam's cries began to die down, turning from screams of pain to whimpers, Ebain took hold of the other foot.

"No!" Wilam shouted. "Let go of me you bastard!"

Ebain moved with efficient precision. He drove his torture spike under the toenail on Wilam's other big toe. Then he proceeded with the smaller toes, his hands working like a musician's, seemingly with a mind of their own. Ebain was practiced in the art of pain, never looking down to make sure he was doing things correctly. The toenails were driven from their nail beds slowly, with a wrenching, prying action that increased Wilam's discomfort.

Sleep was no longer an option. Wilam's heart was racing, sweat poured from his scalp, face, and underarms. His voice, already hoarse from dehydration, was soon lost from his uncontrollable screaming. For the next six hours, all Wilam knew was pain. Ebain used his instrument and hands to pull each toe from its socket before slowly sawing through the Achilles tendon of each foot. Then, Ebain moved on to Wilam's knees. He started by tying thick straps around each thigh to constrict the blood flow to Wilam's lower legs.

"Please, stop," Wilam said, his voice a ragged whisper. "I'll give you anything."

Ebain ignored the prince's pleas. Instead, he stabbed his device under Wilam's right kneecap. The pain was so intense Wilam passed out. Ebain dumped cool water in Wilam's face, rousing him before he returned to twisting and sawing Wilam's knee with the long metal instrument. What seemed like random actions were actually practiced movements that grated against bones and severed ligaments. There was only one incision point, so bleeding from the wound was minor—although Wilam's knee swelled to almost twice its normal size, the skin turning purple.

Wilam's screams sounded more like whispered exhalations. Tears streaked from his eyes. His skin was white with bright red splotches. Somehow the pain grew more intense. The hours dragged on. Ebain crippled first one knee, then the other. Wilam's wrists and ankles were rubbed raw by the rough, leather manacles until they bled freely. Wilam strained so hard against his bonds that he pulled several muscles in his back, which spasmed and added to his pain. Bile rose in his throat and he vomited, but laying flat on his back he was forced to spit and spew the bile from his mouth. Inevitably some made its way down his windpipe, the stomach acid searing and burning the delicate lining of his lungs and causing him to cough and sputter.

The night seemed to never end, but eventually it did. Ebain's last act was to use his instrument to pry Wilam's left hip from its socket. Wilam passed out again, and this time it took more than water to rouse him. The healer was brought in and used thick, greasy salves to stop the bleeding. His feet were swollen and unrecognizable. His knees were gross mockeries of normal joints. And his left hip protruded at an impossible angle.

The healer used a mixture of potent smelling herbs to rouse Wilam. His eyes fluttered open and gazed around weakly.

"It seems you haven't enjoyed our accommodations," King Zorlan said. He was standing over Wilam and gazing down at the crippled prince. "I'm afraid you'll need to start talking or the pain will start again. Ebain has only just begun, really. Soon he'll work on your manhood. It's a vile art, torture, but necessary nonetheless. And they say you really haven't felt pain until Ebain breaks each of your ribs, one by one, so that every breath you take is sheer agony. I don't want that for you, no, no. You are of noble blood, after all—even if Yelsia is a backward land of lesser people. You could still be king of the stooges, after all. I'll send you back to Yelsia once I've slain your father and taken control of your kingdom. You can be a puppet king, a permanent example to everyone who sees you that I am a master both cruel and compassionate. What do you say?"

Wilam's mind had receded inward. It heard what King Zorlan was saying, but it had created a buffer around itself to protect it from the pain.

"I want to know about Gwendolyn," King Zorlan said. "Tell me where she stays and how many men protect her. Tell me what I want to know and I'll send Ebain away."

"The tower," Wilam whispered, not really thinking about what he was saying. In fact, all Wilam could think about was the pain. He spoke instinctively, answering the questions with no conscious effort. "The tower of the Torr."

"Excellent," King Zorlan said. "And how many men guard her?"

"A dozen at the entrance to the tower," Wilam said.

"Only a dozen? Come now, Prince Wilam. I know there are more than that."

"The tower is filled with magic users. Most are insane. Mute servants, and no one allowed in but me. Gwendolyn and her sister are on the top floors, but there's no stairs. They levitate to the upper floors."

"Damn, I was hoping the rumors about her magical powers were over exaggerated. I don't suppose that old fool Offendorl is with her?"

"No, she fears him."

"Is that so? She isn't in league with him then? That's interesting. I had thought they were systematically weakening the kingdoms in order to attempt a coup. But perhaps there is dissension in the ranks of the Torr as well. What of the other soldiers?"

"Guarding the city walls."

"And only a dozen guard the tower?"

"Yes, we never needed more. Although there are townspeople usually gathered in the streets around the tower, hoping for a glance of Gwendolyn. They aren't trained soldiers but will be violent."

"Excellent," King Zorlan said. He straightened and looked at the healer. "Give him something to help him sleep. You'll need to stay here with him—there's really no need to bring him along. I'll send for you once we take the city.

"Ebain," King Zorlan went on, "you've done well once again. You have my thanks."

"It was my honor, my liege," Ebain said in his cold monotone.

"Now, we must be off. I've a kingdom to capture and a destiny to fulfill." Zorlan swept out of the tent while the healer mixed a drink with strong medicinal herbs. He unbuckled the manacles on Wilam's arms.

"If you hurt me. I'll leave you here," the healer said. "I only want to help. I'm not the one who tortured you."

Wilam nodded but didn't speak. His arms were completely numb and ached terribly as he moved them back down to his sides. He couldn't have hurt the healer if he wanted to. Yet, even as the healer saw to his needs, first propping him on dry pillows, then coaxing the herbal mixture down his raw throat, Wilam's mind focused on one thing—vengeance. He knew he would never be able to walk normally again, but somehow, someway, he would kill Ebain—if it was the last thing he did.

Chapter 25

Eustice had brought Brianna blankets from their supplies and she was resting comfortably. Wilam sat with her, as did the dragons. Eustice returned to the village and bought clothes for Brianna, although there were no warm clothes to be had in the seaside town. He made do with what he could get, then bought a small herd of sheep and pigs. Zollin had to help drive the pigs to the clearing, but the dragons ate and rested. As night fell, Brianna awakened. In the center of the grove of palm trees was a small spring. She washed and dressed herself, then she spent time healing Tig and Ferno. Their remaining injuries had been minor, but she knew they would rest better without them.

That night they lounged around a small fire, sleeping and talking. The next morning they had a plan. Eustice continued toward the Grand City on horseback, but Zollin and Brianna mounted the dragons. Zollin was easily twice Brianna's weight, but Ferno seemed convinced he could carry the wizard. They took to the air and Zollin was both amazed and terrified. Ferno's back was broad, and unlike Selix there were no bones or spines to hold onto. Zollin had to lean close to the dragon and trust the great green beast completely. Of course, he knew that if he fell, he could levitate to slow his decent—but it was a small comfort as they hurtled through the sky at what seemed like breakneck speed.

The townspeople had suspected something when Eustice bought most of the animals the people in the small village could spare. Several had gone out to see what was going on and had caught glimpses of the dragons. Ferno's green scales could possibly have been camouflaged, but not Tig's dark blue or Gyia's rich purple, and especially not Selix's bright gold. The largest dragon was a wonder to behold—the dragon's scales reflected light almost like the precious metal they resembled. The scales were bright, almost glossy, and while the dragon had a fearsome appearance, it was obvious to Zollin that Selix's nature was maternal. Brianna had created the dragon, but Selix acted as if Brianna were its offspring. It was very protective, and Zollin thought it was sweet. Seeing them together made his heart ache for the mother he had never known.

Ferno was the opposite. The muscular dragon wasn't quite as tall or long in the tail as Selix, but it was easily twice as wide. Gyia was shaped almost like a flying snake, with a long, thin body, but Ferno resembled a massive bull. Its chest and back were broad, the front legs thick with muscle. Ferno's rear was narrow, but still muscular, and the hind legs were slightly smaller and shorter than the front. The green dragon's neck was as big around as the trunk of a full-grown oak tree. Its head was broad and flat on top, the skull obviously thick where the two spiral horns sprouted. The wide mouth was full of sharp, serrated teeth. Ferno's wings weren't as long as Selix or Gyia's, but they were broader.

Zollin could feel the powerful muscles in the dragon's back moving the wings. He could also tell that having the extra weight on Ferno's back made the green dragon struggle a little as it flew, but there was no way around it. They were flying high in the air, the cold stinging Zollin's skin and making his eyes water. He lay across Ferno's back on his stomach, tucking his arms in close to his chest. He would have to take a better hold if the dragon dove or turned sharply, but as they glided through the air, he was as comfortable and secure as he could get.

He didn't lay his face directly on the rough scales. Instead, he tilted his head to one side, peering over the dragon's shoulder. He could see the countryside far below. He was used to lush green landscapes. Yelsia was a kingdom of rolling hills and thick forests full of wild game and, as of late, even wilder magical creatures. But Osla was different. There was grass, but it was almost bleached white from the sun, and the soil was a tan color, more like sand than dirt. The grass grew sporadically, as did the trees, which were either stunted and short or towering palm trees, naked from the ground up until almost the very top, where their fronds spread out like green fingers.

From their height, everything seemed minuscule. They passed a few small communities, but no towns of any size or population—and even the communities seemed very far apart. Zollin guessed that most of the inhabitants of Osla lived in the southern portion of the kingdom, or along the coasts.

They flew all day to reach the battle plain where Prince Wilam's force had been routed. They saw carrion birds before they arrived and smelled the stench of decaying bodies. Even the dragons were repulsed by the odor. They landed far enough away that the smell was tolerable, and Zollin went alone to find out what had happened.

The corpses were bloated and ripped to pieces by the flocks of vultures and crows, but the armor and uniforms told the tale. Zollin saw quickly that the Ortisan soldiers outnumbered the Falxisan and Oslan uniforms by a great margin. The bodies were spread across the field. He spent an hour moving them into one large pile. The birds screamed in protest, but they didn't come near Zollin. Sweat poured from his brow as he levitated the bodies, even though the sun was setting and the day was finally cooling. Zollin didn't mind the heat—after being in the cold air on Ferno's back most of the day, the heat was welcome.

When he had all the bodies collected together, he returned to the pride of dragons.

"It seems the Ortisan force was defeated," he said. "The force from Falxis has continued on toward the Grand City."

"So we follow them?" Brianna asked.

"I think so," Zollin said. "We can hang back and keep watch. Like I said, maybe they'll do the work for us—but I have a feeling that King Zorlan will not like what he finds in the capital."

"Well, let's move further away from here, the smell is making me sick."

The dragons seemed to agree, but Zollin had other plans.

"You go on ahead. Ferno and I are going to burn the bodies."

"I don't want us to split up," Brianna said. We'll help. It will make the task faster than just the two of you alone."

Zollin took his time drinking from the canteen he carried. He drank almost the entire contents of water before stopping and taking his place on Ferno's back. The dragons flew up and then made pass after pass at the mound of bodies. The corpses burned, but it was slow and the smell was awful. Finally, Selix landed and Brianna burned the bodies. She sent waves of heat so powerful that even the bones ignited. When their grisly job was over, they flew away in the darkness, leaving a heap of gray ash in the middle of the battlefield.

They flew for a few more hours. Zollin couldn't see in the darkness like Brianna and her pride, so he let his magic flow down. The dragons seemed excited whenever he used magic—Tig, Gyia, and Selix took turns swooping down beneath Ferno, like children splashing through a fountain. The effort was taxing on Zollin, who was already tired from moving the bodies. They found a small settlement and landed nearby. In the darkness, the dragons were safe, so Zollin and Brianna went to the small inn.

There were lights on in the building, but it was quiet inside. Zollin knocked before pushing the door open. The interior was stuffy, and although he could smell the familiar scent of stale ale and pipe smoke, there was no hint of food being cooked.

"Hello," he said tentatively.

"Oy! We've got guests," came a gruff voice. Then a man with a lantern in hand appeared. "I'm sorry, but we've not got food or drinks. I can offer you a place to sleep for the night, but we've no food to spare. The godforsaken soldiers drank all our spirits and left us destitute."

"I'm sorry," Zollin said. "We were hoping for a warm meal, but we have rations. Perhaps a bit of news would be worth your time."

"You looking for news or bringing it?" the man asked.

"Looking for it," Zollin said. He pulled two gold coins from a pouch tucked inside his belt. "This won't make up for what the armies took, but it could get you restocked—although you'll probably have to make a trip to the coast."

"That's not a problem," the man said, holding out his hand for the coins. "And I won't begrudge your charity either. Hainsforth is a small settlement, but I'll share your wealth with my neighbors. Thank you."

"What did you hear from the armies?" Brianna asked.

"They're making for the Grand City," the innkeeper said. His wife brought out cups of water for them to drink.

"I'm sorry its naught but water," she said.

"It's fine," Zollin assured her.

"We may have some bread left," the innkeeper's wife said. She was a short, plump woman with a pretty face.

"No," Brianna said. "We have rations. In fact, if you'd like you can use that to fix supper for all of us."

Zollin laid the pack on the table between them.

"Oh, we couldn't do that," the innkeeper said.

"Yes, you could," Brianna said. "We insist. Besides, we need to know as much as we can about the armies and what is happening in the Grand City."

"Who are you folks?" the innkeeper asked. "I didn't catch your names."

"I'm Zollin and this is Brianna. We're from Yelsia."

"You're a long way from home then. What brings you south?"

"The same thing that brought the armies," Zollin said. "I'm a wizard, and I'm trying to…" He let the thought trail off. He didn't want to say that he was hunting another wizard. At the same time he didn't want to lie and say he was there to help when he really wasn't. He didn't know what the king of Falxis was up to, or how things would turn out between the southern kingdoms. He hadn't really thought much about it. His focus was on Offendorl, and then he would look into the witch Mansel had warned him about.

"To kill the witch, I hope," the innkeeper said. "She came through first, several weeks ago. Had an army all her own, but several of the men from Hainsforth went with her. I just happened to be in the brewhouse when she passed by. I never saw her, but several of the womenfolk hereabout said that when their men saw her they just dropped what they were doing and started following her."

"That's horrible," Brianna said. "What about their wives and families?"

"Abandoned 'em, that's what they did. One look is all it takes, they say, although that's just rumors. We don't really know what happened, but none of the women seem to be affected by her spells. Anyway, they passed. Then a week or so ago, they came back and they drank us dry. I brew my own ale and usually sell extra kegs in the Grand City every other month or so. They ate, drank, fought, and then left without even an offer to pay us. They were gone nearly a week before they came running back along the road, their tails between their legs this time, and an even bigger army following. That army was from Falxis, but there was plenty of Oslans in their ranks. They took what we had left. We managed to hide a little, but until you showed up we didn't know what we were going to do."

"Did the second army, the one from Falxis—did they stop?" Zollin asked.

"Nope. Just marched straight through. I was expecting worse, especially with several of the women nearby without their menfolk. But the army didn't seem interested in looting or raping. Their officers were driving 'em hard, from what I saw."

"They're pursing the Ortisans," Zollin said. "King Zorlan wants to wipe them out before they can reach the Grand City."

"I can't say I understand what's happening," the innkeeper said. "I've never seen anything like it before."

"None of us have," Brianna said.

"It's a shame," Zollin said. "I think the fault lies with the Torr. The master wizard there sent armies to Yelsia to capture me."

"And now you're here," the man said.

"Yes, we broke the siege they laid in Orrock. But I didn't stop the Torr wizard."

"And what about the witch?"

"I don't know," Zollin said. "I've heard rumors. It seems that she bewitches men and they'll do anything she tells them to."

"And you're going to stop her?" the innkeeper's wife asked. "That's what you're here for, isn't it?"

"I guess," Zollin said, scratching his head and looking at Brianna. "We just don't know enough to have a plan or to say exactly what we'll do."

"I could make a fine stew with these ingredients," the innkeeper's wife said. "But I'll only use enough for the two of you. Angus and I can't take your food."

"Sure you can," Zollin said.

"We insist, really," Brianna added. "You've both been a big help to us."

"Well…" the innkeeper's wife hesitated.

"Go on, Hydee, you've not had nothing but stale bread for two days," her husband told her.

She nodded and gathered the food she needed.

"How far are we from the Grand City?" Zollin asked Angus.

"You're three days' riding, four walking—unless you're carrying a heavy load."

"And the armies passed by here, when?"

"The second passed two days ago. I imagine they've caught up to the first by now."

Zollin sat back, deep in thought, as Brianna chatted with the innkeeper. Four days' ride on horseback was less than a day's flight on the back of a dragon. Still, they would need to move slowly. Zollin didn't want to give away his position, or even that he was approaching the city.

He wondered if Offendorl could sense the dragons approaching. He hoped not. He really wanted to sneak into the city and confront Offendorl—perhaps catch the elder wizard off guard. But it sounded like just getting into the city was going to be a difficult task. Of course, they could fly over the walls, but the last thing Zollin wanted was for armies to be used against him or the dragons. He wasn't sure if Brianna's pride were as thick-skinned as the big black dragon she called Bartoom, but he didn't relish the idea of being shot at by hundreds of arrows or spears.

They needed a vantage point to watch the city, to draw out their enemies and meet them on open ground. Zollin didn't like the armies that were burning villages and invading sovereign kingdoms, but he didn't want to see anyone else get killed because of him.

It took Hydee an hour to prepare the stew, but when she returned the smoked fish and vegetables were tender and flavorful. Zollin ate three bowls full, and felt like he could eat more—his body seemed to long for the nourishment. He checked his magical containment, but it seemed intact and strong. He guessed he was just tired and hungry from a long day. Angus showed them to a small room with only one bed.

Once he was gone Zollin looked at Brianna. "I guess I should have asked for separate rooms," he said, smiling awkwardly. "Sorry."

"Don't be silly, Zollin. I want to be with you. But I want to wait until we're properly wed to, well…" She hesitated, her face blushing. "You know what I'm saying. Nothing's changed since we were in the mountains. Not for me anyway."

"Not for me either. I want to marry you," Zollin said. "In fact, I think about it all the time."

"So let's get a few hours' sleep. I don't want the people here to see the dragons."

"Me either."

They lay down together. Brianna rested her head on Zollin's shoulder and he wrapped his arms around her. The room was stuffy, but they were both tired and fell asleep quickly. Zollin woke up at dawn, his body stiff from lying still so long. He luxuriated in Brianna's warmth, smelling her hair for a few moments before waking her.

"Time to go," he whispered.

She stood up and stretched. Then they left the inn quietly. The sun was casting the sky in a bright pink when they reached the pride. Zollin knew the big beasts were surely hungry and exhausted, but the dragons took to the air without complaint.

It was an hour before they saw the lone tent. Zollin's curiosity got the best of him and the pride landed within sight of the conspicuous structure. There were no forests to hide in, not even a hill to land behind. Distance was their only defense. They were well over a mile from the road and the tent, which was set up a short ways off the road. The sides of the tent had been rolled up so that the breeze could pass through—what little breeze was to be had in the hot, arid countryside.

Zollin let his magic flow toward the tent. He was sure whoever was inside had seen them, but they hadn't fled. Zollin sensed the healer first—the man seemed settled into a nest of cushions, nursing a bottle of wine. Then Zollin touched Prince Wilam with his magic and recoiled instantly. Zollin couldn't read a person's mind, but if he let his magical senses flow and opened them fully to the environment, he could get a sense of what was happening or the way a person might be feeling. Just touching the crippled prince sent a shock of horror and agonizing pain through Zollin.

"Zollin, are you all right?" Brianna asked. Behind her Ferno rumbled angrily. The big green dragon was ready to launch itself toward the tent.

"They've tortured someone," Zollin said, his voice shaking a little. "We have to help."

Zollin didn't wait for the dragons or Brianna. He levitated through the air. A mile seemed like a long way, but he moved the full distance without even thinking about it. He knew he needed to help, to stop the pain no matter who was in the tent. He came down just outside the small structure, causing the healer to scramble to his feet.

"Who, who, who?" he stammered."

"I'm here to help," Zollin said. "Who are you?"

"Zorn. I'm a healer. I'm helping this man."

"Who is he?" Zollin asked.

"I don't know who you are," Zorn said, obviously torn between fear and awe. He'd seen Zollin drop from the sky right in front of his tent, but he was beginning to think he'd drunk more wine than he realized.

"I'm a wizard. I can help him," Zollin said. "Who is he? Why was he tortured?"

"He's a prince, I believe. From the north. King Zorlan had him questioned. I had no part in that. I'm just trying to help."

"You've done enough," Zollin said. "Are you from Falxis?"

"Yes."

"Good, get moving north. Right now. Don't stop. Just go. I'll know if you leave the main road and I'll kill you. Don't stop, you understand?"

"I, I, I understand," the healer said. He started gathering his things. The tent and cushions had been carried on a wagon, but that wagon had gone on with King Zorlan when he moved after his troops. The healer had no horse, so he packed his medicines and started to take the wine.

"Leave that," Zollin said. "I'll need it."

The healer didn't argue. He took a canteen of water and some of the food rations. Then he hurried away. If he saw the dragons, he made no sound, just kept his head down and walked as quickly as he could.

"Who is that?" Brianna asked. She had come into the tent after Zollin's conversation. "My god, what did they do to him?"

"The tortured him for information," Zollin said. "And if I'm right, he's our future king."

"You mean?" Brianna said, the shock evident in her voice. "You mean this is Prince Wilam?"

"I think so," Zollin said, "but there's only one way to find out for sure. Tell the pride to keep watch—we're going to be busy for a while." Then he knelt beside Wilam and let his magic flow into the prince's ruined body.

Chapter 26

Offendorl and Havina entered the Grand City through the southern gate. Normally the Grand City was full of people. Usually there were merchants and vendors selling every type of good from all across the Five Kingdoms. The streets were often crowded, the inns busy, the marketplace a cacophony of haggling voices. Now the city seemed almost deserted. Except for the men on the tall stone walls, there was no one to be seen.

"It seems deserted," Havina said in a quiet voice.

Offendorl was thankful that his young companion did not often speak, and when she did it was usually a comment that needed no reply. She drove the small covered carriage with as much skill as a teamster and brought them quickly to the city from the small village of Castlebury, which was little more than ashes and memories now. Offendorl had not wanted to draw attention to the fact that Havina was a woman. He suspected that most of the women in the Grand City had fled or been forced into menial tasks. There would be no women visiting the city, so Offendorl dressed her in men's clothing. She had submitted meekly, even allowing him to cut her hair without complaint. He had added a wide brimmed hat—which was common in Osla—to shade her face, which was still fresh and young. She was not a beautiful girl in the classic sense—her nose was a little too wide, her lips thin, and her eyebrows pronounced. But she was completely feminine, a quality not completely lost on Offendorl, which he found surprising. He offered her a rare reply to her comment.

"It is as I suspected it would be," he said. "Turn here."

They wound their way through the city, trying to look like visitors searching for a place to stay. Offendorl knew exactly where he wanted to go, of course, but he didn't want to draw unwarranted attention. They could see the tower before they reached the city, and drew closer to it with every step their horse took. They settled on an inn near the tower. The innkeeper was there, but he was glassy eyed and completely neglecting his guests. The men gathered at the establishment drank ale and ate because the innkeeper's wife continued to work, but there was no payment, and the morale in the inn was sour.

"Whom do I speak to about a room?" Offendorl asked.

No one responded.

Offendorl was undeterred. The inn had no stable, so Havina was seeing to their horse at a nearby livery stable. Meanwhile, Offendorl went from room to room until he found one unoccupied and with a semblance of cleanliness. The small beds were made and there was no trash or personal belonging scattered about. He went to the window and was pleased to find that he had an excellent view of the front entrance to the tower. There were soldiers on guard there, but only a dozen. As he sat watching them, Havina returned. She had seen to the horse and carriage, and now she seemed intent on providing for Offendorl's other needs.

He had given her coin as they traveled so she could buy food and wine for him. She went down to the kitchens and returned with a bottle of wine and the promise of a midday meal soon. After she poured his drink, she sat on the small bed, quietly watching the Master of the Torr. He sipped his wine and watched the tower. He was reasonably sure that as long as he did no magic, Gwendolyn would not know he was there.

He'd been watching for an hour or more when a frantic looking soldier came running to the Torr. The soldiers guarding the tower must have recognized him because they didn't question him or hinder his entrance to the tower.

"Something is amiss," Offendorl said. "Go and see what you can learn around the city."

"Yes, my lord," Havina said.

She put the wide brimmed hat back on, pulling it down low so that it covered her eyebrows. She left the inn and walked through the streets with her gaze low, allowing the hat to hide her face. She wandered aimlessly. The news of the army's return was being talked about all over, and after discovering that only a small fraction of the original force had returned, she reported her findings.

"So, Gwendolyn has suffered a loss on the battlefield," Offendorl said, speaking his thoughts out loud. "Of course, she did not go herself, no. That would never do. She won't leave the tower until she has defeated me, not even to fend off entire armies. Are they locking down the city?"

"I believe so, my lord."

"Yes, that makes sense. We can use the distraction to strike at Gwendolyn. Let us wait and see what will happen."

Offendorl never left the small seat by the window. The afternoon was hot and very little air stirred in the inn. Sweat dripped down the elder wizard's forehead and he wiped it away with a silk handkerchief. The wine did nothing to cool him, but he drank it anyway. He longed to be back in his tower, high above the stench of the city and the sweltering heat. Waiting, now that he was so close, was incredibly difficult, but he forced himself to wait. The time would come soon. If an army encamped around the city, Gwendolyn would be forced to deal with it, and when she did she would be exposed and vulnerable.

Night came and went, but Offendorl did not move. Soldiers jogged through the streets. Men were called from all across the city, even those who weren't soldiers. Every man was needed on the walls. The inn was abandoned by everyone except Offendorl, Havina, and the innkeeper's forgotten wife, who hid in the kitchens.

Offendorl watched as men ran to the tower and reported the enemy's movements. Offendorl couldn't hear the reports, but he could guess what was happening. Any competent military commander would surround the city and choke off its vital supplies. The walls could be defended by her men, but if the besieging army was of any size, Gwendolyn would have to drive them away. Offendorl hoped that with her attention on the army he could catch her unaware.

"It is time to finish this," Offendorl said to Havina. "Come, sit here," he said, rising from the chair he had occupied for so long. "You shall have an unrestricted view of what is to come."

Havina, trembling with fear and anticipation, sat in the small, wooden chair.

"You have been loyal and I shall not forget," he told her as he stretched his stiff muscles. Then he took a long drink of wine and placed the golden crown on his head.

"Now," he said out loud for Havina's sake. "Attack the tower."

Offendorl removed the crown. He could see the question in the woman's eyes. He decided to share his knowledge with the woman. After all, she was not a magic user, he reasoned. "The crown is inscribed with the name of the dragon," he told her. "It gives me complete mastery over the beast."

She smiled. The thought of his mastery over the huge, fire-breathing dragon made her pulse race. Offendorl smiled in return. He was ancient, his body kept alive by magical rejuvenation, and the passions of men had long since died for him—or so he thought. He had surrounded himself with men for centuries. He had no need for women, and in most cases did not trust other men around them. But now Havina, barely a woman, was awakening a part of the elder wizard he had not anticipated. He had strong feelings for her. Partly lust, partly simple appreciation for her service, but mostly he found himself hoping to receive her affection.

"When this is over, I shall make you my queen," he said. "If that would please you."

"It would, more than anything else," she said, her voice seductive and low, practically purring.

"Good, wait for me here," he said. Then he turned and swept from the room.

For days he had been anxious to do battle with Gwendolyn, to sweep her from her lofty perch and cast her down at his feet. But he had not expected the battle to be easy, and so a tiny pinprick of fear had stabbed at the back of his consciousness for days. He had resolutely ignored it, but the feeling refused to go away. Now it seemed that hope for Havina's affections had driven the fear completely away, and Offendorl found a new spring in his step.

Perhaps what Havina craved wasn't Offendorl the man. He understood that she was drawn to his power, not his physical form, but still he felt more alive than he had in decades. His body tingled with anticipation of returning to his full power in the Torr and seeing her look of hungry passion as she sat at his feet. He was ready, he decided. He only needed to wait until Bartoom arrived, then he would begin his attack.

* * *

The Grand City was always an imposing sight. Its high walls and lofty buildings spoke of untold wealth and prestige. King Zorlan had coveted the city since he had seen it for the first time as a boy. Now it sat before him and his army, a glistening jewel just waiting for Zorlan to pick it up. He imagined himself on the throne, ruler of two, perhaps even three kingdoms. The thought filled him with such a sense of excitement that he practically shook with anticipation.

King Zorlan had sent his assassins into the city a full day before the army arrived. The information that he had tortured from

Prince Wilam was invaluable. After discussing his plans with his generals, they had agreed to lay siege to the city. It was a diversion, meant to cause panic in the Grand City and at the same time lull the witch into a sense of security. If she was focused on the army outside the walls, she would not be watching for the assassins already inside.

"Your orders, my lord?" asked one of Zorlan's generals.

"See to it that men are posted around the city," he said. "I want to know if anything changes inside those walls."

"Aye, my lord."

"And see to it that everyone has rations. We shall celebrate our victory soon. There's no need to keep the men waiting."

"I shall make it so, my liege."

The general bowed and hurried away.

"Ale," Zorlan bellowed. He was watching the northern gate of the city. A large canvas awning had been erected and he was sitting on a raised platform under it. He preferred wine, but in the stifling heat he couldn't bring himself to drink wine. The ale was cooler and more refreshing. A cup was brought and King Zorlan took it without a word of thanks or even a nod of appreciation.

He couldn't believe his good fortune. Osla was the wealthiest of all the kingdoms, and now it was practically undefended. For years Zorlan had dreamed of expanding his empire, but breaking three centuries of peace between the Five Kingdoms was not a matter to take lightly. When King Oveer and King Belphan had pressured him to join their quest, he had pretended to be uncertain. It was not a difficult act to play, since he feared the other kings and their wizard. But now war had begun, and as luck would have it, Zorlan had come out on top. He'd seen King Belphan struck down by the master of the Torr, but the wizard had not been seen or heard from since. And now fully half of King Oveer's army was destroyed. Even if the rumor of Oveer's death wasn't true, Zorlan was still in a position to dominate a third kingdom and expand his power.

But if the rumor were true … he thought to himself, unable to hide the smile that thought brought to his face. If it were true, he would rule three of the Five Kingdoms. And, once he had a firm grasp on the southern kingdoms, he would turn his attention north.

He had been mocked and easily dismissed in the high court. He had been a pawn during every Council of Kings. The other rulers had seen him as weak, fearful, and indecisive. But now he had risen to the top. His true quality was revealing itself and his good fortune had given the King of Falxis confidence.

"Sound the horns," he commanded.

"What for, my lord?" asked the general, who was watching the activity of the army as they spread out around the city.

The mobilization of nearly four legions of troops around the largest walled city in the Five Kingdoms would take time, but those orders had been delivered, and other than attack or retreat, the war horns were rarely used.

"I want to strike fear into the hearts of the men on those walls. I want to announce their doom. Now sound the horns!" Zorlan said irritably.

Dust from the troops spreading out around the city was rising into the air. The horns sounded their deep, braying notes. The sound rolled out and echoed off the city walls. King Zorlan could see the soldiers on the walls running back and forth as they prepared for what they assumed would be an imminent attack. He smiled once again, knowing that he planned no action until the following day. Then he would ride out with his generals and request a parley with this queen of theirs. Prince Wilam had said that she was sequestered in the tower of the Torr, but Zorlan would draw her out and give his assassins the opportunity to strike.

It was a genius plan, he thought; simple, yet sophisticated. And once the witch was dead, he would offer the soldiers in the city a chance to return home in peace as long as they pledged their loyalty to him. It was simple choice, really—if they stayed, they would starve or die by the sword. His offer would allow them to return to homes and family. And if King Oveer lived, he would swear fealty to Zorlan or die. Either way, the whole of three kingdoms would soon be his alone.

"Sire," said one of the generals who was sheltering under King Zorlan's tent. "What is that?"

Zorlan looked up, and for the first the time in weeks fear erupted in his heart. He had seen the black dragon in Yelsia—the beast was unmistakable.

"The Torr," he hissed. "That is the wizard's dragon."

Chapter 27

Zollin had healed broken bones, stab wounds, and even burns, but he had never encountered the total destruction of a man's legs like Prince Wilam's. It was as if whoever had tortured him knew where every bundle of nerves lay so that they caused the maximum amount of pain without risking his life. It took hours to repair the damage. The swelling was so intense Zollin was forced to reopen wounds to let the blood drain.

It was fully dark by the time Zollin finished, and Prince Wilam was still unconscious. The tortured prince was pale, his skin glistening with a sheen of sweat. Brianna had spent the day beside Zollin, offering him wine when he took breaks. She had prepared a simple meal for them when he finished, and had unbuckled the prince's leg manacles. The bruising and swelling was gone. Zollin didn't have Wilam's toenails to replace, so the prince's feet would be tender until the nails regrew. Brianna gave Zollin his supper and then began bathing the prince with a cool, wet cloth.

"Will he be okay?" she asked.

"Physically yes," Zollin said. "Although I can't imagine what that kind of torture would do to a man. He may be completely insane—I don't know. We'll have to wait and see."

"How are you?"

"Tired, but okay," he said, smiling up at her. "Did the dragons feed?"

"No, they're waiting until tonight. I didn't want them to be spotted in the air."

"That's a good idea," Zollin said. "I don't want to give away our position too soon, but I'm curious as to what is happening in the Grand City. Have the dragons been called by Offendorl again?"

"No," Brianna said. "I wish I had hurt him more when I had the chance."

"He's dangerous. I know you can take care of yourself, but I don't want you anywhere near him."

"Well, I can send one of the dragons to check on the Grand City after they return from hunting. They slept all afternoon, they'll be fine."

"Dragons are amazing creatures," Zollin said. "I can't believe you made them."

"I'm one of them," Brianna said. "I don't know how, but I feel a connection to them."

"I'm not surprised. You don't just have amazing abilities—your anatomy has changed."

"My what?" she asked teasingly.

"You know what I mean."

"Are you saying you don't find me attractive anymore?" she said, moving closer.

"No, not at all," Zollin said with a smile. "If anything, I think you're more beautiful than ever. I wouldn't change a thing about you."

"Maybe I should give you two some privacy," said a weak, scratchy voice.

"Oh, you're awake?" Brianna said in surprise.

"Yes, but I wasn't sure who you were," Prince Wilam said. "I was eavesdropping, I'm afraid. What's all this talk of dragons?"

"My name is Zollin. I'm a wizard from Yelsia."

"Yes, I suspected you might be. You did something to me?"

"I healed your wounds," Zollin explained. "We found you earlier today."

"Were you looking for me?"

"To be honest, we're not even sure who you are."

"I'm Prince Wilam of Yelsia, although I don't deserve that title, not anymore."

"Are you referring to your actions under the influence of the witch?" Zollin asked. "We've had some experience with that. You can't blame yourself for what you did while you were under her spell."

"I am the crown prince of Yelsia—I should be held to a higher standard."

"Be that as it may," Zollin said, "we still have to stop Gwendolyn. Why don't you reserve judgment until she can no longer use her power to bewitch others?"

"You're right," Wilam said. "I must stop her. Although I'll admit I'm not sure how I can do that. I don't think any man can withstand her charms."

"Perhaps no man can," Brianna said, "but maybe a woman could."

Zollin laughed, but Prince Wilam seemed unconvinced. His face was pinched with worry and shame. He struggled to sit up. His body was healed and there were no lasting effects from the torture, but it was difficult for his mind to accept his new reality. And his strength was drained—both from the long fighting retreat he'd led and the night of agonizing torture he had endured.

"Do you think I might walk a little?" he asked. "My mind is still convinced that my legs are ruined."

"Physically, you're fine," Zollin said. "I don't see any reason you can't go for a walk."

"I'll take him," Brianna said. "You need your rest."

Zollin agreed and sat back, resuming the meal he had yet to finish. Prince Wilam rose slowly. Brianna stood beside him and steadied him as he stood. He was lightheaded and dizzy at first, but that soon passed. They walked out from under the shelter of the tent. The night was finally cooling down and insects sang in the trampled fields around them. They walked slowly, Wilam stretching his legs as they went.

"I am thankful for all you have done," he told Brianna. "I doubt I would have ever walked again after King Zorlan's torturer ruined my legs."

"Zollin has a gift for healing," she said. "He healed your father from the poison that had made him so sick."

"That's right," Prince Wilam said. "Quinn is Zollin's father, isn't he?"

"Yes, that's right."

"I didn't make that connection right away. It's hard to believe that dragons and wizards no longer surprise me. The world is changing."

"Yes, it is. Hopefully for the better."

"Well." The prince thought about Brianna's hope. "I would like to think so too, but war in the Five Kingdoms is troubling. Were you in Yelsia when King Belphan and King Zorlan invaded?"

"No, actually I wasn't. But Zollin was there—he helped save Orrock."

"It seems we owe your friend a great debt."

Brianna just smiled.

"May I ask why you've come to Osla?" Wilam said.

"Zollin could explain things better than me," she said.

"Well, I'd very much like to learn more," Wilam said. "Shall we head back now?"

Brianna nodded but didn't speak. The pride was returning and Selix sent her a mental image of Prince Wilam walking with her.

"Are you okay for another surprise?" she asked.

Wilam looked at Brianna with concern, not sure what was about to happen.

"Just keep in mind that they won't hurt you," she said.

Then, before he could ask the inevitable "who" question, the dragons dropped down around them. Selix and Gyia looked curiously at the prince, while Ferno glowered menacingly. Of the four dragons, only Tig seemed uninterested. The smaller blue dragon went behind the tent to a patch of grass, curled up, and promptly went to sleep.

"This is my pride," Brianna said.

"Oh, my god," said Prince Wilam.

He had heard of the dragon in the north, terrifying villages and demanding gold. He had thought it a rumor cooked up by King Belphan or King Oveer in order to invade Yelsia. Even after he met Quinn, who gave an eye-witness account of the dragon, he had trouble believing it. It wasn't until he had fallen under Gwendolyn's spell that he realized the rumors of magic and dragons were true. Still, nothing could have prepared him to see Brianna's pride up close.

"This is Selix," Brianna said. "This is Gyia and Ferno. Over there is Tig."

"Magnificent," Wilam said. "They are yours?"

"Well, I don't control them. I'm part of the pride."

"Part of the pride?"

"Yes, I'm what the dwarves call a Fire Spirit. I can control fire and I create dragons."

"You create dragons?" he asked, incredulously.

"Yes," Brianna said, laughing at the look of consternation on Wilam's face. "It's difficult to explain. Perhaps it would be easier to show you."

She ignited one hand and orange flames danced to life.

"I can't believe it," he said. "Is it burning you?"

"No, I feel the warmth, but fire doesn't harm me."

"Do the dragons breath fire? Like in the stories?"

"Yes," Brianna said, as Ferno growled deep in its throat and flames licked out of its mouth and around its broad head.

"Unbelievable."

"Just wait until you see what Zollin can do," Brianna said.

"Where did you both come from?" Wilam asked.

"Tranaugh Shire," she said. "It's a small village— "

He cut her off.

"Southwest of Peddingar Forest. Yes, I know of Tranaugh Shire. I have not been there personally, but I have spent hours studying the map of our kingdom. I had no idea there were wizards there."

"There aren't," Brianna said. "Zollin didn't even know he was a wizard until a year ago."

Brianna told their story—how Zollin discovered his magic and how the wizards from the Torr had come to take him away. The dragons had not heard the story either and they gathered around Brianna as she told it, her hand burning all the while. Wilam sat on the ground, entranced by the story, and didn't even notice when Gyia settled in around him, the purple dragon's long body coiling in the shape of a horseshoe.

Brianna told how they had stayed in Brighton's Gate through the winter and foiled the Skellmarian invasion. She described facing Bartoom the great black dragon for the first time, and how she was captured by Branock, a wizard of the Torr, and taken to Orrock. She explained how Zollin and Mansel had come to rescue her, but that she had escaped on her own, and how Zollin had defeated Branock in a wizard battle in front of the castle. Then she told Wilam how Zollin had saved King Felix from the poison Wilam's younger brother Prince Simmeron had been feeding their father.

She went on to tell how she and Zollin had gone in pursuit of the black dragon Bartoom, and how they had nearly died in the mountains. She told him about the dwarves that led them through caves and passages deep under the mountains, and how they had given her a beautiful ruby that turned out to be a firestone that unlocked her powers. Then, after leaving the caves, she explained how she had come to realize that she could no longer hunt the dragon, and how she had come to save Bartoom. She even told Wilam and the dragons how she had tried in vain to convince Bartoom to stay with her even though Offendorl was calling to the beast. Ferno growled again, and this time Selix joined the green dragon. It was obvious none of the dragons was fond of Bartoom.

Then she told how she had created the dragons. The pride moved in close when she spoke about their creation, and even Brianna spoke reverently. Prince Wilam was entranced, and none of them noticed that Zollin had come quietly in the dark to hear the tale. He stood back from the group a little ways, not wanting to interrupt the story.

Brianna then told how the pride had flown south and learned of the invasion that Zollin had helped push back. She said they had all agreed to fly south and find him, but they found Bartoom first, and although Brianna tried to reason with the great black dragon, they had ended up fighting instead. She explained how they had found Zollin, Mansel, and Nycoll. Then she told of their second battle with Bartoom and how they had lost Torc.

All at once, Tig, who everyone assumed was asleep, howled almost like a wolf. The blue dragon's long, lonely wail made the night seem dark and melancholy.

"Then we came here," Brianna said, once Tig had settled back down. "We saw the battlefield and burned the bodies left there. And the next day we found you."

"I was foolish," Wilam said. "I led the army that was defeated. I completely underestimated King Zorlan. I thought we would rout his troops easily, but I was wrong."

"We all make mistakes," Brianna said, noticing Zollin standing near Ferno for the first time. "There was a time when I lost trust in Zollin. It was foolish, but I pushed him away. I'm glad he didn't lose faith in me."

"Never," Zollin said.

"And now you are going to fight Gwendolyn?" Wilam asked.

"Yes, Zollin said. "And Offendorl."

"And the dragon he has enslaved," Brianna added.

"Offendorl led the invasion of Yelsia," Zollin said. "He was the driving force behind King Belphan and King Zorlan's invasion. He found a way to control Bartoom and used the dragon against your father's forces."

"You were there?" Wilam asked.

"Yes, for part of the battle. The invaders pillaged their way north from Lorye to the Tillamook valley. Your father met them there and had trebuchets built, which stalled their invasion. Then the dragon came by and torched your father's camp. The army pulled back into the city. I arrived there shortly before they did with Commander Hausey."

"But isn't he in the light horse legion at Felson?"

"He was, but they had been sent to deal with the dragon and were almost completely wiped out. When word came of the invasion, the light horse legion—what was left of them—were called to the capital. Hausey and I had worked together trying to drive off the dragon."

Brianna glanced at Zollin, silently thanking him for not saying they had been trying to kill the beast. She was sure her pride understood the need to destroy Bartoom now, but she didn't want anything to color their perception of Zollin. He was not a wanton killer, although he was not afraid to use deadly force when necessary.

Zollin told Wilam and the dragons the rest of the story. How they had driven off the army after it laid siege to Orrock, and how he knew that until Offendorl was dealt with no one in the Five Kingdoms would be safe. He told about their journey south and how they had fought the kraken and Bartoom in the open sea. He explained what they had learned in Lixon Bay about King Zorlan and the force he was taking south into Osla.

"Do you think he killed the Oslan generals?" Wilam asked.

"I think he had them killed. It makes sense. He obviously wants Osla under his control."

"Not just Osla—he wants all of the Five Kingdoms," Wilam explained.

"That's madness," Brianna said.

"Perhaps, but the truth is, he's close to achieving it. King Oveer is dead. I pushed him out the window of the tower in the Grand City," Wilam said, hanging his head in shame. "The witch's spell creates such jealousy that men will kill over her. I have done it more than once."

"You can't be held responsible," Zollin said.

"No," Wilam argued. "I must be held responsible. We must all be held responsible and do all we can to bring peace to the Five Kingdoms once more."

"We're trying to do that," Zollin said. "We won't let King Zorlan or anyone else usurp the sovereignty of any kingdom."

"Then I will go with you," Wilam said. "I'll fight with you—it's the least I can do."

"No," Zollin said. "It would be better if you return home. Yelsia and Baska must be prepared to stand together if I fail."

"I won't," Wilam said stubbornly. "This is my fight. I will see it through."

"But our people need you," Brianna said soothingly. "Can't you see we need you to lead our people into the future?"

"I cannot," Wilam said in anguish. "How can I lead our kingdom when I am nothing more than a lowly murderer? I shall fight with you and die on the field of battle. My death shall redeem the shame I have brought on my family and on our kingdom."

"You would really throw your life away when we need you most?" Zollin said.

"You don't need me," Wilam said, his voice so harsh it sounded as if he were spitting the words.

"We need you more than ever," Brianna said.

"She's right," Zollin agreed. "You've made mistakes. Some were your fault and others weren't, but that's not really what's important now. What is important is that you learn from them. Osla fell because its king didn't care about the people or what was right. And if King Zorlan marches north with the armies of three kingdoms, we will be hard pressed to stop him.

We will need a bold leader who knows the cost of war. We will need someone who won't take King Zorlan—or any other threat—lightly. We need someone who will care more about the people of our kingdom than their own pride. We need someone like you."

"I am none of the things you described. I'm stubborn and slow to learn. You don't know me."

"Perhaps not," Brianna said. "But we know who you could be. This is your second chance—not many people get more than one."

"Think about it," Zollin urged. "You are not the man you were before. And now you can become the man we need—but not if you stay with us. Our goal is to stop Offendorl and Gwendolyn, no matter what it costs. We can do that. But Yelsia needs you, now more than ever."

"I will think on it," Wilam said.

"We should sleep on it," Brianna said. "We could all use some rest."

They went back to the tent and settled in for a few hours of sleep before dawn woke them. The dragons took positions on each side of the tent. Zollin and Brianna slept well, but Prince Wilam couldn't get their argument out of his head. His desire to find King Zorlan and his torturer was like a fire in his belly, undeniable and seemingly insatiable. But the wisdom Brianna and Zollin had shared was sound as well. He was needed, even if he wasn't worthy. He did consider his second chance to be miraculous, and although he owed King Zorlan for the pain Wilam had suffered at the Falxisan king's hand, he also owed his life to Zollin for healing him. In fact, the more he thought of it, his family and the kingdom of Yelsia owed Zollin more than they could ever repay. He tossed and turned through the night, trying to reconcile his desires.

The next morning he went for a walk once more. He was lost deep in thought and didn't notice Gyia walking quietly behind him. The purple dragon's long body moved as gracefully on the ground as it did in the air. It was only when Wilam turned back toward the tent that he noticed the dragon behind him.

"You are a beautiful creature," he said, trying to appear braver than he felt. The truth was, Gyia was both beautiful and terrifying. The dragon was a sight to behold, with its long, serpentine body and thin, aristocratic head. The sunlight seemed to sink into the rich purple scales, and although Gyia's pointed teeth were always visible, the dragon seemed benevolent somehow.

A thought entered Wilam's mind, clear and easily understandable. It was a mental image of Wilam as king, with a crown on his head, standing on the tower of a large castle.

Wilam was surprised by the thought, and somehow comforted by it as well. The thought appeared again in his mind, but this time Gyia was there with Wilam.

"Are you somehow putting thoughts in my head?" he asked the dragon.

"Yessss," Gyia hissed.

"Can you read my mind?" he asked, horrified for a moment, but Gyia shook its head. "So, you think I should return to Yelsia too, eh?"

An image of Wilam riding through the air on Gyia entered his mind. He looked surprised.

"You want to take me?"

Gyia nodded. An image of the night before came into Wilam's mind. He saw himself surrounded by Gyia's purple body, the firelight flickering on his face as he listened. And at the same time as the mental image came, he was flooded with a feeling of peace and the sense that what he was considering was the right thing to do.

"I guess I'd be a fool to argue with a dragon," he said. "But what about your pride—don't they need you?"

The feeling of peace came over him again. "All right, I suppose we should go and tell the others." They walked back to the tent, where Brianna and Zollin were gathering their things together.

"I've made my decision," Wilam asked. "I shall return to Yelsia, as you have so wisely counseled. I want to thank you for your help."

"It was our honor," said Zollin. "Here, I've packed enough rations to last a week or so. There's water in the canteen and some wine in the pack as well."

"Thank you, that is most kind," Wilam said.

"Until we meet again, your highness," Zollin said, holding out his hand to the prince.

"May it be soon and often," Wilam replied, grasping Zollin's forearm. "You shall always be welcome in Yelsia."

"We plan to return once this is over," Zollin said. "Wish us luck."

"What?" Brianna blurted in surprise, but she wasn't talking to Zollin or Wilam. They both looked at her with concern.

"Are you sure?"

The other dragons were crowding in close to Gyia.

"Of course you are free to go, but we will miss you," Brianna said. "Still, I think it is an admirable choice." She turned to Wilam. "Look after Gyia. Don't let anyone mistreat my sister."

"Never," Wilam said. "Gyia is wise, and I will trust her with my life."

"They aren't male or female," Zollin said softly, with a teasing nod.

"Oh, I didn't realize that," Wilam said. "I have a lot to learn."

"Gyia will be a good instructor," Brianna said. "In the air, trust your dragon. Gyia will need to rest several times a day, and hunt as well, but that shouldn't be a problem."

"The army followed the road and pillaged along the way, so many of the villages were left with nothing or burned down. You might travel to the coast and then turn north. You should be able to get whatever you need along the way by stopping at the coastal towns. Here," Zollin handed the prince his pouch of silver marks and gold crowns. "That should be enough to get you home."

"I can never repay you for your kindness," Wilam said.

"Just get home safe. And be prepared in case we fail."

"I shall, you can count on me," Wilam said.

Gyia's tail coiled around the prince and lifted him onto the dragon's back. There were small ridges on the purple dragon's shoulders where the front legs joined the long, smooth body. Wilam slung the pack over his shoulder and took hold of the ridges, one in each hand. His legs wrapped three quarters of the way around Gyia's body, and he looked secure.

"Stay close to Gyia's body for warmth," Brianna said to Wilam. And then to Gyia she said, "And don't forget your passenger and roast him when you get cold."

"Yes," Wilam said. "Please don't roast me."

They all laughed, even the dragons, which caused smoke to puff from their noses. Tig was the last to say goodbye, nuzzling Gyia affectionately one last time. Then Gyia jumped into the air. The purple dragon's wings flapped in mighty waves that lifted Gyia and Prince Wilam high into the air. Then they were gone, flying north toward safety and home, while Zollin and Brianna turned south.

"Well, it's time to get moving," Zollin said.

He levitated onto Ferno's back. Brianna jumped high in the air, flipping and twirling before landing gracefully on Selix's back.

"Show off," Zollin said.

Tig roared, then took to the sky.

"He's scouting ahead," Brianna said.

"Well then, let's go."

Ferno and Selix took to the air smoothly, but Zollin had a feeling that nothing in their future would be as smooth and easy as their flight had begun.

Chapter 28

Nothing filled Offendorl with more glee than seeing Bartoom wreak havoc. The dragon looked like a large bird at first, so high in the sky that it seemed like an indistinct blob. Then it dove, like a streak of black lightning.

Offendorl was in the street across from the tower of the Torr, lingering in the shadows. It had taken the dragon an hour to arrive, but once the beast was in sight of the city, it moved with purpose. Offendorl watched as men along the walls pointed at the dragon, although he was sure none of them knew what it was. The soldiers guarding the tower were oblivious to the danger. Offendorl held his breath as the dragon dove, then, at the last instant, he realized his mistake.

The dragon blew its fiery breath onto the tower, whose windows were wide open to catch the breeze. The fire would, Offendorl realized too late, destroy his library. His hands fumbled with the heavy gold circlet, jamming it on his head.

"Not the tower," he said out loud, almost shouting. "Attack the soldiers on the walls!"

The dragon abruptly ceased its raging attack on the tower and swooped away. The soldiers in front of the tower were now pointing up at the black smoke that was flooding out of the top floors of the tower. Offendorl cursed as he stalked toward them.

Half of their number ran inside before he reached the courtyard that surrounded the base of the tower.

"Halt!" shouted one of the soldiers.

Offendorl flapped a hand, as if he were shooing a pesky fly. The soldiers were knocked senseless by a wave of magical energy. Offendorl glanced up at the inn window to see if Havina was watching. She was leaning out of the window and he forced himself not to acknowledge her. He was acting like a child, he and berated himself mentally. He forced thoughts of the young woman out of his mind. Just climbing the many flights of stairs to reach the upper floors to reach Gwendolyn would undoubtedly be difficult enough, and there was no telling what manner of surprises the witch would have for him along the way.

* * *

"Great gods in heaven," King Zorlan said. He couldn't believe his eyes. First, King Belphan had been killed in Yelsia, giving him the opportunity to assassinate the Oslan generals and take control of his rival's army. Then, he discovered that King Oveer had been killed, and Zorlan had destroyed the greater part of the Ortisan army with ease. Now, with his forces surrounding the Grand City, the black dragon had appeared and was raining down fire on his enemies.

King Zorlan had been afraid that the dragon would attack his men, but instead it was roasting the men on the city walls. Zorlan watched as it swooped down, snapping up one man in its jaws and swatting four more off the high walls with its tail.

"Prepare to attack the main gate," Zorlan shouted.

"Sir?" his general said in surprise.

"Do as I say or I'll use your head as a piss pot, general," Zorlan said angrily. "Do not question my orders ever again. Order the attack. I want the men to form up here, right in front of my tent."

"Yes, my lord," the general said, hurrying off and shouting orders to the troops.

Zorlan had planned to wait several days before calling his troops into action, but they could rest when the city was his. Opportunities like the one before him now only came once in a lifetime. Zorlan had never been a religious man, but he couldn't help but feel that some divine being was smiling down at him, making his ascent to power almost too easy.

His troops began to take formation in front of him. They lined up in rows, the first carrying oversized wooden shields and the second row carrying scaling ladders. Their goal would be to get on top of the gatehouse and fight their way down so that they could open the gates. The soldiers on the walls were occupied completely with the dragon. Archers were firing arrows at the beast, but the arrows just bounced harmlessly off the dragon's glossy, black scales. It was chaos on the walls and Zorlan knew it was the time to strike.

"Send the first unit," he bellowed. "And bring me my horse!"

* * *

Offendorl had ascended two flights of stairs when he felt his body grow stiff. From a small doorway came a glassy eyed man with tangled, greasy hair and a ragged beard that was matted with drool.

Offendorl had several warlocks in the tower. Most were completely insane, and although he could not control their powers like a sorcerer, their proximity seemed to boost his own magical prowess. Now that power was being used against him. Gwendolyn was a sorceress and she would turn every magic user in the tower against him.

Suddenly, without any sort of indication from the drooling warlock, Offendorl felt as if he were in the grip of a giant, invisible fist. He had to strain with his own magic to push back against the warlock's power. He knew the warlock was completely under Gwendolyn's control, like a puppet whose invisible strings only she could pull. But Offendorl also knew the fears of the warlocks in the tower, knew their weaknesses. Fire erupted from the elder wizard's hands, billowing out in orange clouds.

The warlock screamed in fright, now turning his considerable strength to fighting off Gwendolyn's control. Offendorl knew that the warlock feared fire, so he used it to frighten more than harm the man. The warlock shrank back into his cell, the magical grip loosening on Offendorl. The elder wizard felt his magic burning inside him. It was hot, but not too difficult to handle yet. Unfortunately, he had a long way to climb before he faced Gwendolyn and her warlock sister Andomina. But he knew their weakness too, and he would defeat them, of that he was certain.

* * *

The soldiers jogged forward. Occasionally an arrow would streak down from the walls, but none penetrated the oversized shields that the first rank of soldiers carried. The second rank stayed close to the first and the big warriors lifted the shields so that only their legs were exposed, while the shields protected their vital organs and the men behind them. The open plain should have been a killing ground, easily defended by the soldiers on the walls, but the terror of the great black dragon was overwhelming.

When the soldiers reached the gatehouse, they leaned their ladders against the tall structure. The gatehouse was made from massive stone blocks that were smooth on the outside. The gates themselves were wooden, made from heavy oak timber imported from Yelsia, bound together with thick iron plates and hung on massive hinges. Normally the gates never closed—the Grand City was a constant hive of activity with people coming and going at all hours—but now the gates were closed. It was up to the soldiers to scale the ladders, fight through any resistance, and unlock the massive gates so that the invaders could gain entry to the city.

King Zorlan knew that, under normal circumstances, if his forces managed to breach the outer walls, the defenders would fall back to the next series of walls within the city. The Grand City was almost like a patchwork quilt, with each new section of the city surrounded by more walls. If the Grand City had been well defended, it would have taken a much larger army months to fight through the city to the elegant castle at its center. But Zorlan wasn't facing a well-defended city, and his goal wasn't to reach the castle. In time, he would ascend the Oslan throne, but for now, while the dragon attacked the defenders, Zorlan only wanted a foothold on the city. It would make his offer to the Ortisans seem more generous.

King Zorlan watched his troops from the saddle of the black horse he rode on. Unlike the massive destriers of the north, Falxisan horses were slender, faster, and more graceful. They were trained for endurance and speed, not to carry heavily armored knights. Still, Zorlan's mount was tall and muscular, completely black, and spirited. But the dragon was making the horse nervous and it stomped the dust, wanting to turn and run, causing Zorlan to focus more on controlling the beast than observing the battle before him.

"My lord, more dragons," a general said in alarm.

Zorlan looked up in surprise as three dragons streaked toward the gatehouse.

* * *

Offendorl was nearly impaled by a soldier on the fourth landing. The man had hidden behind a thick wooden support beam and lashed out at Offendorl just as the elder wizard passed. Luckily for Offendorl, he had a magical shield in place that stopped the steel tip of the spear, but the powerful thrust knocked the ancient wizard off balance. Two more soldiers rushed forward and a fourth fired an arrow from a bow. The arrow glanced off Offendorl's invisible shield and ricocheted into the first soldier, who screamed as he clutched his belly and toppled down the stairs.

The other soldiers were unfazed by their comrade's demise. Their queen had ordered them to kill, and the jealous rage that simmered just beneath their control had blossomed into full-blown blood lust. With a thought, Offendorl knocked the two soldiers rushing toward him together with such force their skulls were smashed. The soldiers dropped dead at Offendorl's feet.

He paused for a moment to catch his breath. He knew that staying calm and retaining as much strength as possible was paramount in his plan to defeat Gwendolyn. It was tempting to rush to the top of the tower to confront her, but he needed to slow down. The sorceress wasn't going anywhere, and the smoke that was beginning to fill the air in the tower made it evident that the dragon's work had done its job. Offendorl had to stop himself from falling into despair over the loss of his precious books. His only hope where that was concerned was that Gwendolyn might possibly save at least a portion of his library.

The soldier with the bow had slipped away, almost certainly hoping to catch Offendorl on the floors above. Most of the warlocks in the tower were below him now. In fact, most were kept in the dungeon-like cells below ground. Only the less dangerous warlocks were allowed to occupy the upper floors. And soon Offendorl would be among the alchemists, who would pose no real threat. They spent their days tinkering in workshops, trying to perfect methods of transmuting simple objects such as lead or brass into gold, silver, or steel that was both stronger and lighter than that made by blacksmiths in their smoking furnaces. They documented their progress, but their work was never shared outside the Torr. Of course, Offendorl could transmute almost any substance, but the alchemists studied not only for the outcome, but also the process. Offendorl's power came from knowing how things worked, so he had filled the tower with magic users who could increase his knowledge.

It pained the elder wizard to know that their research could be lost too, if Gwendolyn didn't get the fires under control. At the next floor, he found two men waiting for him. They stood blocking the path to the stairs, their eyes closed and a massive magical shield protecting them.

"So," Offendorl said out loud. "Gwendolyn has changed her tactics. I know you can hear me, witch." He spat the last word with as much contempt as he could muster. "I will pull this tower down from beneath you if I must, but you shall not take my place."

One of the warlocks spoke, his voice deep, but the words came from Gwendolyn high above.

"Don't test me, master," the warlock said. "I have become even more powerful than you. But I must admit, the dragon is a nice touch."

"You won't think so when you are roasting in the flames of the beast's fiery breath."

"Oh, I think you'll be surprised at what I'm thinking. You'll find out once you get here, but I doubt even you will be able to get past my defenses easily."

"You underestimate my power at your peril," Offendorl warned.

"And you have underestimated mine for the last time, old man!" the warlock shouted, the rage in his voice carried through from Gwendolyn's hatred of her master.

There was a deafening crack, then a huge segment of the ceiling above Offendorl fell. The floors in the tower were made with paving stones, several inches thick and supported by a wooden subfloor that was reinforced by massive wooden beams. The warlocks retreated up the stairs as the ceiling dropped onto the elder wizard. Stones, heavy timber, stacks of lead and gold, and furniture all rained down. The weight dropped on Offendorl before he could react.

His magical shield protected him from being harmed, but he was buried in the heavy rubble.

Dust filled the air above the rubble, and then, before Offendorl could cast off the debris that covered him, the floor he was on collapsed. Floor after floor fell, the rubble and debris growing while the elder wizard tumbled downward, completely out of control. When the destruction was over, the lower floors of the tower were gone; only the stone staircase spiraling up the thick stone walls of the tower was still in place. And Offendorl was nowhere to be seen.

Chapter 29

Tig had scouted far ahead of the pride. The small blue dragon flew high and fast, racing above the clouds and basking in the bright sunlight. One of the things the little dragon loved was the feeling of the sunlight on its back, and also reflecting off the clouds below to shine on its stomach at the same time. But the clouds were few and far between now, and although Tig would have loved to forget everything else but the feel of sunlight on its scales, it knew that it had a job to complete.

Tig saw the army surround the great city. It took several moments of awe-filled wonder, gazing down at the Grand City, before it felt that it had seen enough. The small dragon had seen large towns and small villages. The dragon understood the need for shelter and sometimes missed the security of the lair high in the northern highlands that it had shared with the pride. So, houses and buildings made sense to the dragon—but it had never seen anything like the massive capital of Osla. It was like a giant hive of mismatched buildings and walls. The sheer number of humans was staggering.

Tig took in the sight, then turned back and raced toward Brianna and the pride. They were half an hour from the city when Tig returned, sharing mental images of the city from memory. For Brianna, it was almost as if she had seen what Tig had seen.

They had landed to rest and allow Brianna to share Tig's report. Zollin could communicate with Ferno, but only Brianna could communicate with all the dragons—at least until they began vocalizing words. Speaking was difficult for dragons, and Brianna didn't push her pride to use words. Ferno was the first to try, saying simple words or phrases, usually to emphasize the mental communication the dragons relied on.

"The city is besieged," Brianna told Zollin, the dragons crowding close to the two humans. "It looks as though King Zorlan has surrounded the city, but there are soldiers on the walls. None of Zorlan's troops are engaging."

"Well, that may give us some time," Zollin said.

"What exactly is our plan?"

"I'm not sure. I mean, we need to stop Offendorl, that's our highest priority. As long as he lives we will never have peace. But we also need to deal with the witch. We may be the only ones who can."

"Okay, so if the witch is in the tower of the Torr, perhaps we should just fly there directly."

"And just let King Zorlan conquer Osla?" Zollin asked.

"Is that really our responsibility? I mean, we have enough on our plate with two wizards and a dragon, don't you think?"

"Yes, I guess you're right. But if we could find a way to thwart King Zorlan's plans, it would go a long way to restoring peace to the Five Kingdoms."

"Well, we still have no idea where Offendorl is. So, if we can stop Zorlan, we will, but let's stay focused on the goal at hand."

"Okay, so we're flying to the Torr. I think you and the dragons should stay in the air while I go in. I have no idea what I'm going to find there and I'd rather you cover my back."

"But what if the witch casts her spell on you?"

"I think I can deflect any magic she uses on me," Zollin explained.

"But what if her spell isn't like the others?" Brianna argued. "What if just seeing her forces you into her service, like Prince Wilam said?"

"Okay, you go in with me. I'll protect you with my magic and watch your back. Ferno and Selix will have to remain outside though. They're too big to be of help inside the tower."

Ferno growled menacingly but didn't object outright.

"Tig wants to help," Brianna said. "I think Tig might even fit through the windows."

"That's a good idea. We'll make that call when we get there," Zollin said to Tig. "For now, let's get a little closer. I want to see exactly what we're dealing with, and it doesn't seem like we're in a hurry.

They took flight again and circled the city from so far away that it was just an indistinct blur to Zollin. The dragons and Brianna could see much farther. And it was only moments before they spotted Bartoom approaching the Grand City.

Ferno began sharing mental images with Zollin of the city and the massive black dragon. Ferno's body shook with rage at the sight of the black dragon, but Zollin did his best to calm the beast he was riding on. He made a few quick decisions and shared his thoughts with Ferno, who passed the makeshift plan to the others. They moved slowly at first, watching to see what Bartoom would do.

Zollin was sure the black dragon's presence indicated that Offendorl was in the city. When they saw Bartoom attacking the soldiers on the city walls, Zollin deduced that Offendorl wasn't in charge. He decided that Gwendolyn must still be in control, and Zollin figured that his best approach would be on the ground but inside the city walls. He could levitate himself quickly around the city if he needed to, but the pride would have to deal with Bartoom and that meant that Zollin would need to confront Offendorl as quickly as possible.

Then, Tig noticed the soldiers moving out to attack the main gate. Zollin could not see the soldiers on the ground yet, but the city was becoming clearer. He told Ferno to drop him and Brianna on top of the massive gatehouse. The dragons sped up, racing across the open ground. Zollin's eyes stung from the wind, but he forced them to stay open. He could see the scaling ladders going up and the troops with their big shields slowly ascending. Then he jumped off Ferno's back. Falling through the air was terrifying and he quickly controlled his fall with the magic that was churning excitedly inside him.

Brianna flipped and tumbled through the air just above Zollin. When they landed on the gatehouse, that section of the city walls was nearly deserted. The soldiers had either been killed or fled in fear. Zollin used his magic to break the scaling ladders. The soldiers fell hard and were carried back from the wall by their comrades. Zollin didn't have time to concern himself with the second wave of soldiers King Zorlan sent to attack the gate—he and Brianna were watching as Selix soared high into the air while Tig shot forward and ripped at Bartoom's wing with the smaller dragon's needle-like talons. Zollin was waiting for Offendorl to reveal himself, but nothing happened. Bartoom was just turning to confront Tig, who had already raced away, when Ferno crashed into Bartoom.

Zollin could feel the rage pouring off of Ferno, but the bulky green dragon didn't fully engage in the fight. Both dragons were snapping at one another with their razor sharp teeth, but only Bartoom was flapping its wings and scratching with its talons. Ferno just held the bigger, black dragon, using its own weight to drag Bartoom down. They fell, and the descent took several tense seconds as Zollin and Brianna looked on. They were terrified for the green dragon, but Zollin used his magic to flip Bartoom onto the bottom just before they crashed.

Three stone buildings were destroyed, and when the dust cleared Zollin could see the two dragons fighting for their lives. Ferno was strong, but the green dragon's scales weren't as hardened as Bartoom's. Fire and smoke billowed as the dragons fought. More buildings were knocked down, the entire area was littered with rubble, and anything combustible was burning.

Brianna sent an idea to Selix, who dove immediately. Bartoom's back was still vulnerable from the dragon battle at Castlebury. Selix raced down, flaring its golden wings at the last second and extending talons like an eagle diving for salmon. Selix's talons sank into Bartoom's back and then ripped free, sending blood cascading through the air. Bartoom's roar of pain and rage shook the entire city. Soldiers stood dumbfounded, watching the battle between the dragons.

"Now's our chance," Zollin said to Brianna. "Let's get to the tower."

He flung Brianna high into the air with his magic before levitating himself toward the massive stone tower. Brianna flipped and bounced along, almost as if she were dancing through the air. Zollin saw Tig racing toward them too.

They were almost to the tower and Zollin had to ascend higher in order to land on the top of the tower, which was by far the tallest structure Zollin had ever seen. He had no doubt powerful magic was employed to create such a structure. He could see King Belphan's opulent palace not far away. It was a stunningly crafted castle, but it paled in comparison to the tower of the Torr. Then Zollin noticed the dust and debris billowing from the bottom of the tower and he realized that a magical battle was already taking place.

The top of the tower was flat, with small stone crenellations circling the top. The tower sloped ever so slightly as it rose, the top floors only half the circumference of the bottom floors. Still, the top of the tower was large, and Zollin, Brianna, and Tig all landed easily on top. Zollin took a moment to catch his breath, letting his magic flow down into the tower to give him an idea of what was happening inside. He felt Gwendolyn, who was hunched over a book in the top floor. Most of the room seemed seared with fire—there were books all around but most of them were blackened and curling. Beside Gwendolyn, sitting on the floor and grasping her sister's leg, was Andomina.

Zollin could tell immediately that Andomina was a warlock. He could feel childlike emotions, mostly fear, pouring from her, but she reminded him of his old staff that had once been a thick branch of a tree that was split by lightning. The staff had been full of magical power that almost reached out to mingle with his own power. Once Zollin had learned to tap into his own reservoir of magic, it had made the magic of his staff seem weak. But Andomina was brimming with magic—a dark, seductive power that filled Zollin with longing.

"They're just below us," he said. "And they know we're here."

Zollin felt Gwendolyn call to him. She knew his name, and the call made him burn with passion for her. Even with Brianna right in front of him and his magical shields surrounding him, he wanted to run to her.

"You have to go," Zollin said. "She's trying to seduce me."

"Not for long," Brianna said angrily.

Tig snarled and they both ran and jumped off the roof. Brianna somersaulted in the air, but Tig pulled a tight loop, twisting through the air and shooting into the tower with a strong flap of its wings. Zollin felt the desire to join Gwendolyn vanish as fire flashed out the opposite window. He used his magic to learn what was happening below him.

Gwendolyn had not been expecting an attack, and had only managed to shield herself from Tig's fiery blast. Andomina was burning alive. The usually silent warlock screamed, her wail freezing her sister for a moment before Gwendolyn brushed the fire away with magic. The damage to her sister's body was not life threatening; most of the burns were only skin deep, but her hair was burned away, as was the filmy dress her sister made her wear. Worst of all was the damage to Andomina's lungs. Tig's flames had seared the delicate lining of Andomina's lungs, making it difficult for her to breathe.

The blast of superheated air had also caused the humidity in the tower to form into drops of water that clung to the stone ceiling. Gwendolyn lashed out at the blue dragon with a blast of freezing air. Normally the cold didn't bother the dragons, but Gwendolyn froze the moisture in the air and hit the dragon with tiny shards of ice. Tig's scales were strong enough to deflect the ice, but the dragon's wings were pierced with hundreds of tiny holes. The blast forced Tig to dive out the far window at the same time as Brianna landed lightly just inside the other.

Brianna was stunned by what she saw. Andomina was writhing next to her sister, but Gwendolyn looked calm. She was watching Brianna with a sense of surprise mixed with fear and anger.

"You are dragon-kind?" she said, half asking, half stating the fact.

"And you are a witch."

Gwendolyn smiled. It was a sickly sweet look that reminded Brianna of rancid meat. "You should join me," Gwendolyn said. "Together we can rule the Five Kingdoms."

"I'm not here to join you," Brianna said, fire erupting from her hands.

"Surely you don't think you can defeat me?" Gwendolyn said. "I hold the Torr—not even Offendorl can stop me."

"Maybe not, but I know one person who can."

Zollin was on top of the tower, monitoring what was happening. His first instinct was to run to Brianna's aid, but he didn't. He could feel Andomina's magic fading. The poor mute warlock was struggling to breathe—the pain in her body from the burns was overwhelming. Then Zollin saw Tig, struggling to fly. The blue dragon's wings were in tatters. He reached out with his magic and pulled the dragon up onto the roof. Tig growled, but there was no malice in it.

Zollin then looked out at where Ferno and Selix were still battling Bartoom. All three dragons were on the ground now, their heads lowered and the haunches up, like dogs. Ferno was clearly the strongest of the group, but the green dragon was favoring one leg where Bartoom had sunk razor sharp teeth into the thick muscle, and there was blood dripping from several long gashes in

Ferno's stomach. Bartoom's scales were almost impenetrable except along its back between the massive wings, and Bartoom was as deadly with its long, thick tail as it was with its gnashing teeth and razor sharp talons. Selix was forced back by Bartoom's tail.

Zollin sent the green dragon a mental image. It showed Ferno and Selix dropping as low as they could get onto the ground. Zollin was several hundred yards from the battling dragons, but he let his power build into a crackling ball of white-hot magical energy. Tig hissed and backed away from Zollin, but the young wizard didn't notice. He sent the ball of power streaking toward Bartoom, who had just reared on its hind legs, preparing to lunge at Ferno.

Bartoom saw the ball of magic, but even though the massive beast jumped, flapping its wings and rising into the air, Zollin magically maneuvered the spell straight into Bartoom's chest. The magic snapped and sizzled, weakening the dragon's scales.

Selix shot into the air after the black dragon, but Ferno stayed on the ground, watching the golden dragon attack. Bartoom hadn't been hurt physically by the magic and must have thought its scales had saved it from the attack. But Selix closed with the massive black dragon, ripping with thick talons at Bartoom's chest. The black beast was shocked to feel the pain as the talons tore through Bartoom's scales and shredded the flesh beneath.

Bartoom was torn between the order it had received from Offendorl to attack the city walls and its own desire to survive. It chose the latter, pulling away from Selix and turning to escape. But Ferno had been expecting Bartoom to flee. The green dragon flew up and sank its teeth into Bartoom's tail. Once again the black dragon was dragged out of the air and crashed into a tall stone building that crumbled beneath Bartoom's weight. Ferno's teeth didn't penetrate the hardened scales on Bartoom's tail, but the green dragon held on, keeping the black dragon from flying to safety. Selix swooped in once more, extending talons like a bird of prey, catching Bartoom's neck in its hind feet and pinning the black beast's head to the ground.

Bartoom was defeated, but not destroyed—the dragons would not kill their own kind. Zollin found that realization noble, but he had no time to focus on it. Brianna was in danger.

Chapter 30

Offendorl lay in darkness. His magical power was weak, like hearing a voice from far away. He strained to feel the familiar heat, but it was like glowing embers that produced no warmth. He remembered falling, and how the world seemed to crash around him. Now, he could feel the sharp angles of wood and stone beneath him, and the weight of debris that covered him. He lay still for a moment, letting his senses return. First had been touch, and then smell. He could smell the dust and freshly rent wood. Finally his hearing returned, first with a harsh ring deep in his ears. Then, as the ringing faded, he heard something else.

It was the frantic sound of someone digging through the debris. Offendorl felt fear at first, as he remembered that Gwendolyn had turned her warlocks against him. But then he realized that Gwendolyn would have moved the debris with magic. The sound, coming nearer and nearer to Offendorl, was the frantic work of a non-magical person. He could hear grunts of effort as the person moved the debris, piece by piece.

Then, last of all, sight returned to the elder wizard. Light appeared in the darkness, tiny shafts poked down into the jumbled mess around Offendorl. He moaned and tried to move. The weight on top of him shifted a little, and the sounds grew closer.

"You're alive?" a voice said.

It was Havina, and Offendorl felt relief flooding through him. She had come to his rescue. He knew he only needed time to regain his strength. Gwendolyn wasn't stronger than he was—she had only tricked him. His magical shield had protected the elder wizard, but now he needed time to regroup. Hatred for the sorceress was like ashes in Offendorl's mouth. He hated the thought that she had gotten the better of him, even for an instant. He would make her suffer in ways that no one had ever suffered, he swore to himself.

"Here," he said. "I am here, Havina."

She continued digging, and soon he could see her. She stood over him, staring down, the sun shining into the tower through a high window so brightly that she was just a silhouette, a living shadow above him. She reached down and he raised his arm, but she didn't take his hand to pull him up. Instead, she began feeling his body. At first he thought perhaps she checking to see if he was injured, but then her hand groped inside the pouch at his hip and pulled free the gold circlet with Bartoom's name inscribed.

"What are you doing?" he asked in total surprise.

But Havina didn't answer—she turned and ran from the tower. Only then did Offendorl realize that he had fallen prey to the young woman's true intentions. Her loyalty was to power, and although he knew he wasn't defeated, it made sense that Havina would believe that he was. So she had cast him aside and taken the golden crown. He wasn't sure how she would be able to use the circlet to control Bartoom. She had no magical power, but his studies revealed that non-magical kings had controlled dragons in ages past, so he guessed it was possible.

For a moment a tenderness he had not expected rose up inside him. Havina had left him, but he couldn't blame her for that. It was, after all, that same lust for power that had driven her to take care of his every need and follow him to the Grand City. Then anger erupted inside Offendorl, first at himself for being so emotionally tied to the young woman. He had cast off such mortal concerns long ago—and for good reason, the elder wizard remembered. Then, his anger turned to Havina. The young woman had gotten the upper hand, but not for long, he vowed. Once he had settled his business with Gwendolyn and Zollin, he would make it his life's work to track her down and show her the meaning of true power. The anger stirred the weak magic inside him, prompting him to find a way to get back on his feet.

He pushed his anger for Havina aside. Gwendolyn would not hesitate to slay him in his weakened state. He rose slowly, realizing that the pile of debris was heaped up around him and very unstable. The last thing he needed was to fall and break a bone on the wreckage around him. He summoned his power, but it was like trying to hold water in his hands that kept seeping through his fingers. He tried to levitate himself clear of the wreckage, but he was only able to lift himself a few feet and then pain shot through his chest. He felt like a stone had crashed onto him and was squeezing the life out of him. He struggled to breathe and then dropped to his knees as his vision began to fade.

He thought perhaps it was the dust from the debris that was hindering his breathing, and so he crawled outside. The wreckage cut his hands and knees, but the pain was minor compared to the weight on his chest. He gasped, trying desperately to fill his lungs, but the effort was futile. His ears began to ring again, and then he felt the world tilt and he fell to the ground unconscious.

* * *

"Send in the next wave," King Zorlan ordered. He had been appalled when Zollin and the girl appeared. Zorlan remembered the wizard from Orrock. He recognized the young man's lanky frame even from a distance. He was not surprised when Zollin swept his first wave of soldiers from the gatehouse, but the king was undeterred.

"Tell them to wait until the wizard moves on from the gatehouse, then attack," he instructed.

"Aye, my lord," said the general, who passed on the order.

King Zorlan watched as the second wave of shield barriers and ladder carriers hurried forward. The appearance of more dragons and the wizard from Yelsia was disturbing. He wasn't sure what was happening, but Zollin's attack on his men seemed almost like an afterthought. The dragons were fighting each other, and then, to King Zorlan's relief, Zollin and his companion flew up toward the tower.

The king almost danced with glee. The wizard was here to face the witch, not his invasion force. It was almost too good to be true. Once the Yelsian wizard had dealt with the witch, there would be no stopping King Zorlan from expanding his empire. Falxis would incorporate the kingdoms of Ortis and Osla. He was the only king left in the three kingdoms. The wizard would not be able to stop Zorlan's rise to power.

He watched with satisfaction as his troops moved to the gatehouse unchallenged. They raised scaling ladders and ascended to the top of the gatehouse easily. Then they disappeared on the far side. The Grand City wasn't built in exact circles, so Zorlan wouldn't be able to circle around and open the southern gate without fighting through the troops that were still stationed on the city's outer walls. Still, by taking a strong position in the city, the Ortisan troops would be forced to fight, retreat, or surrender.

"Send a full legion forward," King Zorlan commanded. "I want commanders with me. We will take position on top of the guardhouse. Move out!"

Around him the army began to move. Troops that had been spread out around the city were now returning to King Zorlan's position. He knew it would take hours to get his troops back together and prepared to make a major push into the city, but he had at least three centuries of soldiers to hold the gatehouse. It was more than enough to give them a foothold on the city.

"Sire, are you sure the gatehouse is the safest place for you?" said one of Zorlan's generals.

"You don't win wars by being safe, general," Zorlan said. "The gatehouse will give us a view of the city's walls. We need to be able to see what the enemy is doing. It will also stand as a symbol of our impending victory. When we hold the gates to the city, nothing can stop us."

"But sire, there are dragons."

"Yes, I am aware of that, but the beasts seem content to battle each other." They were almost forced to shout over the horrific roars of the dragons. It was impossible to forget the mythic beasts were at war with each other somewhere inside the Grand City.

They rode forward and watched as the troops strained to open the massive wooden gates. Zorlan guessed that oxen or teams of horses were used to swing the gigantic structures when they were opened or closed. His men were straining to swing open just one of the massive doors. It creaked on iron hinges as it opened. Troops in front of the small group of officers hurried forward to help.

Zorlan savored the moment as he rode through the city gate. Victory, he decided, was the sweetest thing he'd ever tasted. He climbed down from his horse and handed the reins to a soldier who stood nearby. Just inside the city gate was a large open area, wider than the broad street that led into the city. There were houses and shops nearby, but the area around the gate had been cleared so that soldiers could hold their ground and repulse any invaders who made it through the gate.

"Send scouts through this section of the city," King Zorlan ordered. "I don't want any surprises."

"As you wish, my lord," said one of the generals smartly.

Zorlan turned and found the entrance to the gatehouse. Inside was a spiral staircase that led up to the top of the city gates and gave access to the city walls. Zorlan took the steps quickly, despite his bulky frame. Zorlan was not excessively fat, but he had lived a sedentary life for many years, with servants always at the ready to do his bidding. Marching to war had helped trim a bit of the fat from the king's frame, but he was still panting by the time he reached the top of the gatehouse.

Zorlan looked out across the city. He could see the dragons battling. The troops on the walls seemed frozen, neither moving to attack his men on the gatehouse nor retreating. Smoke and dust rose from the tower of the Torr, although he could not make out what was happening there. He decided he would deal with the wizard—or witch—once he had secured the city. He looked down and saw his men pouring into the open area around the gate.

"I want men on either side of this gatehouse," Zorlan ordered. "We must strike while the iron is hot. We may not get a better chance to take the city than we have right now."

Men ran to fulfill his orders. Soon, King Zorlan had armed troops making a shield wall that stretched across the city wall. He decided it was time to sweep the Ortisans from their lofty perches.

"We shall move forward," he ordered. "I want reserve troops holding this position and more reinforcements joining us on the wall as quickly as possible."

"Aye, my lord," said an officer.

Zorlan drew his sword. It was brightly polished and more ornamental than useful. The sword was long and heavy, but the hilt was only long enough for one hand to hold the ornate weapon. Zorlan could hold it and lift it above his head, but fighting with the sword was impractical. The heavy weapon would be swatted from his hand easily. The hilt was full of gemstones and the crosspiece was made of gold, which any forged blade would cut through easily. There was gold filigree decorating the blade, but it still felt good to Zorlan to hold it in his hand.

He raised the sword and called to his troops.

"Move forward," he shouted.

The sound of their boots marching along the stone wall brought a smile to Zorlan's face.

He wished that he could have been on his horse, but the truth was he was more than a little afraid of being knocked off the wall and falling to his death. He stayed away from the crenellated edge of the wall, and well back from the troops that were now marching toward a group of soldiers several hundred feet along the wall from the gatehouse. He was confident that he could win the day, but he wasn't the kind of man to take chances unnecessarily.

The Ortisan troop formed their own shield wall, but they looked uncertain as Zorlan's forces came near. The king was just about to order his men to attack when a sound like thunder made them all turn and stare at the tower of the Torr.

Chapter 31

Brianna sent fire raging toward the witch, but Gwendolyn was ready for her. As Zollin looked on from the rooftop above, using his magic to sense what was happening below, he saw Brianna's raging fire roll back, as if she were in an invisible bubble that was slowly shrinking back. Terror for Brianna's safety almost caused Zollin to panic, but then Brianna's heat increased exponentially and she dropped through the stone floor. Gwendolyn rushed over toward where Brianna had been, but Zollin was no longer hesitant to act.

His magic was churning inside him like his own personal tornado. He felt the power rushing into the ancient stones of the tower and then he tore them away. It felt like he was ripping a head of lettuce in two, the massive stone blocks giving only the slightest resistance to his overwhelming magical power. The sound of the stones breaking was like thunder. Tig roared behind Zollin, who stood near one edge of the tower's roof while the other half was ripped apart, the demolished stones and wooden supports falling and crashing down around the base of the massive tower, with hundreds of books and scrolls tumbling after them.

Gwendolyn looked up in surprise, and then her expression changed. She went from a woman in shock to a woman in desperate need. Zollin felt his desire for her explode—all thoughts of Brianna were utterly banished. All Zollin could think about was saving Gwendolyn and making her his. Then Tig swooped in. The blue dragon was small compared to the other dragons, but Tig was still as large as a full-grown horse. The blue dragon spread its ruined wings wide to slow its descent, extending the needle-like talons on all four feet while spewing fire from its mouth. Gwendolyn blocked the fire, but the force of Tig's weight crashed down on her and the floor, weakened by Brianna's fiery escape, collapsed beneath them.

When Gwendolyn fell, her spell was broken. Zollin felt shame coloring his cheeks as he realized just how close he had come to being seduced by the witch's beguiling spell. But he didn't have time for self-pity—he knew he had to help Brianna and Tig. He started with Andomina, who was still shrieking in pain from Tig's first fiery attack. She had crawled as far from the fighting as she could and was now perched on a little shelf next to the wall that was still intact. He levitated her out of the tower. It reminded Zollin of trying to lift fish from a stream when he had first learned to use his magical power. Andomina was in full-blown panic, kicking and writhing in an effort to escape the magical hand that lifted her into the air, oblivious to the certain death that would result if she managed to break free.

Zollin set her down gently on top of the royal castle, which wasn't far from the tower and was the tallest building in the Grand City apart from the tower of the Torr. Then he turned his attention back to the battle going on below him. Tig was like a rabid dog, biting and tearing with teeth and talons, using the long tail to swipe at the witch, and all the while billowing flames. Brianna was leaping and flipping through the air, sending balls of fire flying around the room. Gwendolyn was trying desperately to hold both back, but the sorceress was overwhelmed. She was moving toward one of the windows as Zollin peered down from the ruined top floor. He could feel the heat from the battle radiating up from the collapsed floor and he decided not to rush into a situation he wasn't sure how to help in.

"She's going to escape!" he shouted, but Tig's roaring was too loud for Zollin's voice to be heard.

Gwendolyn dove through the open window. Zollin turned and rushed to the edge of the demolished roof to see what happened to the witch, but then she rose up into the air in front of him.

"Zollin," she said, her voice as smooth as honey.

He felt himself drawn to her again and tried to look away, but he couldn't.

"Come with me," she purred. "I am not the enemy."

"No," he said between clenched teeth, although he was saying it more in response to his own passionate urges than to Gwendolyn's offer.

Fire billowed out of the window below her, but Gwendolyn moved deftly out of range. "Hurry, Zollin, there isn't much time," she said. "Come with me."

"No Zollin!" Brianna shouted from below.

Tig roared and Zollin could feel his desires being stretched. His entire body was tense, like a harp string just before it snaps. Zollin felt his reason slipping away. And then a face rose up in his mind. Zollin wasn't sure if it was from his own memory or if Ferno had been trying to communicate with him, but he saw Brianna's face clearly. She was laughing and smiling, her beauty heart-wrenching. Then the world began to grow dark around him and he knew he had to fight. He focused all his mental and magical energy on standing his ground. Around him books began to fly off the shelves that were still intact. Rocks and bits of stone—the rubble from where Zollin had destroyed the roof of the tower—swirled around him.

"No!" Zollin shouted as he heaved back on his reason and awareness. It reminded him of working with Quinn, struggling under the heavy weight of a thick beam of timber. So many times as a child with his father he had been shamed by his lack of physical strength, but this time things were different—this time he was strong enough.

The swirling mass of debris went bolting toward Gwendolyn, battering her through the air. Zollin was sure she had a bubble of protection around her, but the force of the flying debris knocked her back from where she hovered, trying to seduce him with her power. He watched as she went flying, end over end. Unfortunately, she soon regained control and moved toward her injured sister.

"Zollin?" Brianna called from below. "Are you okay?"

"Yes," he shouted back. "I'm fine, but Gwendolyn got away."

"Okay, I'm seeing to Tig's wings."

Zollin didn't answer. He was watching Gwendolyn. The sorceress had not fled as he had expected her to do. Nor had she seemed interested in healing her sister, who lay moaning on the broad, flat roof of the castle. Gwendolyn began to walk in circles, chanting. Zollin couldn't hear what she was saying, but he could sense something happening. It was old magic, dark magic.

He could feel it stirring. Dark clouds began to form in the sky above the castle and spread over the city.

"What's happening?" Brianna asked as she hurried up beside Zollin.

Tig, with fully healed wings, soared out of the tower, circling it several times before coming to a graceful landing on the small section of roofing that was still intact.

"I have no idea," Zollin said, "but it can't be good."

* * *

Offendorl opened his eyes. His vision was blurry and his mouth tasted like vomit. He was lying in the dirt, staring up without really seeing the roof of the tower. He rolled over, his chest still aching, but the awful weight was gone. His breath came in ragged wheezing gasps, but he could move. He rolled over, then waited while his head seemed to spin a little. He let his magic, which felt weak and small, search his body for what had happened. One of the thick arteries leading to his heart had split open and blood was flooding out with every beat of his heart. He healed the artery and siphoned the blood in his chest cavity back into his circulatory system. It was tedious work and required all his mental attention. Finally he opened his eyes again and struggled onto his hands and knees.

Flames shot from the upper window of the tower, but Offendorl was oblivious to the magical battle happening above. The ringing in his ears drowned out all other sounds. He crawled forward and used the side of the massive tower to pull himself up to a standing position.

Once again he was forced to wait while the world spun and tilted around him. He used the tiny bit of magic he still controlled to inspect his body. He could feel his heart beating, but it was so weak it was like trying to bail water from a sinking ship just by using your hands. His blood was still moving, but slowly. He allowed his magic to strengthen the dying muscle and immediately he felt better. He could sense that the heart was working more efficiently. His lungs weren't working well either and his body was crying out for more oxygen, but he knew he would have to wait for his magical strength to return before trying to heal anything else. He stumbled forward, his legs feeling both heavy and weak.

Offendorl had just managed to stagger out of the courtyard of the Torr when the roof came falling down. The rending of the ancient stone had been deafening, but the falling debris shook the ground and made the elder wizard double over in fear. He covered his gray head with both arms and staggered further from the chaos. His magical power was slowly returning, like the ocean tide coming in. He felt the magic flowing through him, and although he knew he needed rest and nourishment, he also knew there was none to be had in the Grand City at the moment.

He staggered away from the tower, ignoring the magical battle above, and returned to the inn where he'd stayed the night before. It was empty, as he had expected it to be. Havina was long gone with her new prize, and the innkeeper's wife had probably fled in fear. He found a pitcher of ale and sat heavily on one of the many benches in the common room. He drank and felt his strength growing, both physically and magically.

Then the room began to dim. At first Offendorl thought his sight was being affected by his heart again, but this time it was different. There was no pain in his chest and he could still see clearly—the room was just getting dark, as if it were twilight and no one had lit the lamps around the inn.

He stood and walked as quickly as he could to one of the windows. Black clouds were spreading across the sky. And then Offendorl felt the ancient summoning magic. He had felt it once before, as a young wizard who was just learning to control his power. It was during one of the many struggles for power between the wizards of that lost age. He didn't know what would happen, but he knew whoever was using the summoning spell had to be stopped. He tossed the wine aside and hurried outside. The sky was dark and it was becoming difficult to see, but Offendorl followed the sensation he felt. It was like being in a large pool of still water that had suddenly been disturbed.

The elder wizard of the Torr pushed away the thoughts of discouragement he felt. He had seen his precious books and scrolls among the debris that had fallen from the top of the tower. He knew that his home, his refuge from the world, had been destroyed.

There was so much to regain, it almost felt like he was lost forever. Discouragement rose up like a tidal wave. He felt as if he were staring at the end of his rule, the end of his unnaturally long life. But he refused to accept that fate. He would not die quietly, nor would he slink away to eek out a half life in hiding.

It was fully dark when he wearily climbed the broad steps that led to the royal castle. He wasn't sure what he could do. His magic was churning, but using it was like touching red-hot coals. Still, someone was working magic that was long since forgotten, and he could not allow it to happen. The Torr had been formed for just this purpose. The summoning magic sprang from the very heart of evil. It was not a power that was ever intended to be set loose on the world of men. He went to the massive wooden doors of the castle and pushed. The heavy doors resisted only for a moment, then they swung open and Offendorl lurched inside.

* * *

"Who is that?" Brianna asked, pointing down toward the narrow, winding streets below.

"I have no idea," Zollin said, glancing away from what Gwendolyn was doing on the roof for a moment. He knew he needed to do something to stop the sorceress but he wasn't sure how. Long ago he had learned to recognize magic in other objects and even people. His staff, filled with magical power after being hit with lightning in a storm, had radiated a strong, powerful magic. The willow tree in the forest near his home in Tranaugh Shire had been full of a wonderful, life-giving magic. The white alzerstone ring had seemed to emit a power that repulsed magic.

Now, he could feel the magic that Gwendolyn was working, and it sent a shiver of fear up his back. It was so dark it made him feel like he was gazing into a tomb.

"It's the wizard!" Brianna exclaimed. "The same one who attacked us."

"You mean Offendorl?"

"Yes, the wizard who has been controlling Bartoom,"

At the mention of the great, black dragon's name, Tig roared defiantly. "Where do you think he's going?" she asked.

"To the castle," Zollin said. "I don't know if he's going to help her or stop her, but that's where he's going."

"I've got a bad feeling about this," Brianna said.

"Me too," Zollin agreed. "I think you better take the dragons and get clear of the city."

"What about you?" she asked, the concern in her voice unmistakable.

"I have to try and stop them," Zollin said.

"Not by yourself," Brianna said.

"I don't know what she's doing," Zollin explained. "But it's magic like I've never felt before. It's ancient and it's evil."

Before he could explain further, the castle rooftop burst into flame. The fire formed a perfect circle just outside of the circuit that Gwendolyn had been walking around her sister. The light from the fire made it possible for Zollin to see what was happening, and his magical senses felt the bubble of magic that had formed around the ring of fire.

"Zollin, please," Brianna said. "I can't stand the thought of losing you."

"If I don't do something, we may all be lost."

"What do you mean?" Fear echoed in her voice.

"I don't know," Zollin said. "I can't explain it, Brianna. I just know that whatever she is doing is so bad that it terrifies me. Get your pride out of here."

"What about the soldiers?"

"Warn them if you can, but get away from the city. Go north and wait for me. I'll find you."

Brianna's lips brushed Zollin's check, then she ran for the far side of the gaping hole in the tower's roof. She jumped into the air, falling for only a moment before she went soaring up on a gust of wind. Tig roared, then followed Brianna. Zollin glanced over and saw Ferno, Selix, and the black dragon Bartoom taking to the air as well.

Zollin watched Brianna moving through the air, gliding like an eagle until Selix flew just beneath her. Then she settled gracefully on the golden dragon's back and they flew north. Zollin turned his gaze back to the roof of the castle and saw Gwendolyn healing her sister. The sight should have been reassuring, but there was dark intent that seemed to be pouring off the roof of the castle. Zollin shuddered in fear, then he levitated himself and went flying toward the witch.

Chapter 32

King Zorlan was exuberant. He had seen the tower of the Torr ravaged from within, and the Ortisan soldiers were falling before his shield wall. Very few of the men had the fortitude to fight, and those that did were usually wild eyed with blood lust. In most circumstances a berserk type rage would have made them formidable opponents, but against a well-disciplined shield wall, their wild attacks broke like ocean waves against a cliff.

King Zorlan and his band of soldiers were nearly a quarter of the way around the massive outer wall of the Grand City when the sky began to grow dark. At first the king merely thought that time had passed more quickly than he realized. Then, one of his aides pointed to dark clouds spreading across the sky from directly over the royal castle.

"What is that?" wondered one of Zorlan's officers out loud.

"Sorcery," Zorlan barked. "What else could it be? I want this position held. Is that understood?"

"Aye, my liege," said the officer.

"Hold this line until I return or send word. I'm going back to check on the progress along the other side of the gatehouse."

It took King Zorlan only minutes to see what was happening at the gatehouse. Long before he could travel back along the wall to where his soldiers had been ordered to muster, he could see them flooding back out of the main gate. At first he suspected that a well disciplined counter attack had been mounted by the Ortisan soldiers holding the city, but the soldiers fleeing didn't regroup outside the gate—they ran in terror from the city. Even as the light faded to the point that it was hard to see, King Zorlan recognized that his conquest was lost. Everyone was fleeing the city.

Panic rumbled up from the thick stone walls and began to invade King Zorlan's resolve. The darkness carried with it a feeling of terror that reminded Zorlan of being a child. He couldn't say what was frightening him, or why he suddenly felt the urge to flee the city. He tried to remain calm, but the feeling of panic grew. He guessed it was a natural reaction to seeing his forces flee the city, but no matter how hard he tried to rationalize his fear and put it away, the panic grew.

Then the king heard the flapping of great, leathery wings. He looked up and saw that even the dragons were fleeing the city.

"Sound the retreat!" he bellowed as he ran along the wall. The officers accompanying him were just as panicked and no one obeyed their orders. Some ran past the king, others stayed behind.

I'm going to die, King Zorlan thought. He had never felt such fear. Even in the days when the other kings bullied him and Offendorl had worked his sorcerous magic so close to Zorlan that the Falxisan king trembled with fright, he had not felt the fear of death that he felt now. He had watched Offendorl slay the Yelsian high counselor in a gruesome fashion that gave him nightmares for days. He had been caught up in the press of battle when the Yelsian heavy horse routed his army, which had been rendered defenseless by an overwhelming sense of panic on the battlefield. That fear had been different, though—it had been mental, like an idea that was hard to get out of one's head. Now the king felt a certainty in the deepest part of his being that he was going to die.

Resentment rose up like bile in his throat. Why did he have to pursue such grandiose ideas of glory, he thought. Why go south with an army when he could be safe in his castle in Luxing City? The thoughts were like bees stinging his brain, which had been laid bare and exposed by fear. He no longer cared about an empire, or ruling the Five Kingdoms. He only wanted to get off the infernal wall and out of the Grand City forever.

* * *

Havina ran through the streets with long strides that stretched the muscles in her legs and back, but the effort felt good. She carried the circlet of gold in her hand, although she knew she needed to hide it soon. She was far from the tower, moving south, away from the elder wizard. Just the thought of Offendorl made her skin crawl now. The ancient wizard had seemed invincible, his power unlimited. It had lit a fire deep inside her that she had not known existed. She wanted that power, and just being near Offendorl had given her a thrill. But whatever she had felt for him died when she had seen his ancient body covered in dust and grime in the tower. He was just a weak old man and she had no use for him. But, he had revealed how he controlled the great black dragon, and so she had gone to him and taken the circlet. She wasn't sure how she would use it, but she knew she needed to get out of the city if she was going to have a chance.

She ran and ran, grateful that she was wearing men's clothing, including thick boots. As a child she had loved to run barefoot through the sandy hills around Castlebury, but the streets of the Grand City were paved with cobblestones and there was trash littering the streets. The heavy boots protected her feet; the men's pants she wore didn't flutter or tangle up between her legs.

She saw the livery stable where she had left the horse that had pulled Offendorl's carriage and decided to duck inside. There were horses still in the stalls. She quickly saddled the nearest horse and climbed into the saddle. As she rode the horse out into the street, she was passed by several soldiers who ignored her, running past and making the horse sidestep nervously. She had noticed the waning light and now she saw the dark clouds spreading across the sky. She settled the circlet on her head and kicked the horse into action, racing for the southern gate as fast as the horse could carry her.

* * *

Zollin came down on the roof of the castle, his magic like a bonfire inside him. He knew the unnatural sense of fear that had come over him as he flew toward the castle was stirring his magic into a frenzy. His magical power responded to emotion much more than reason or even will. He could do anything he could envision in his mind, but it was emotion that gave his magic its might.

He moved slowly toward the ring of fire, which was dancing and whipping almost chest high. The first thing Zollin noticed about the fire was that it wasn't hot. In fact, the closer he got to the strange, dancing flames, the colder he felt. In almost every instance that he had been near magic, his own internal power had strived to connect with the outside magic. When he had used the staff he'd found in the woods outside of Tranaugh Shire, his magic had naturally connected to that of the staff. When he had battled with Branock and Offendorl, he had felt drawn to the other wizards. But the strange ring of fire was different. Zollin could actually feel his magic striving to move away from the foreign, dark power.

Nearby, a door opened and Offendorl stepped out onto the roof. Zollin already had his defenses up, but now his whole body tensed. He stood on his toes, ready to dash from harm's way, but Offendorl took no interest in him. The ancient wizard was pale, his gray strands of hair clinging to his skull and plastered with sweat. He was breathing in great ragged gasps, his eyes wide at the sight of Gwendolyn inside the ring of fire.

"So, we meet again, master," she said, ignoring Zollin completely.

"What are you doing?" Offendorl growled. His voice was ragged, almost hoarse, but still filled with a magical power.

"I am fulfilling my destiny," Gwendolyn said. "Surely you know it. I found it hidden in the books you refused to share with me, or anyone else. You have hoarded your power and secret knowledge too long. Now, your strength is broken and mine is just beginning."

Offendorl lashed out, casting a stream of crackling fire at Gwendolyn, but the witch just laughed as the fire bounced harmlessly off the invisible barrier created by the ring of fire.

Offendorl tried again, this time levitating a massive stone, his face grimacing in pain as his magic began to tear at his physical body from the strain. The stone flew through the air and Zollin moved backward, away from the ring of fire, raising his own shields to ensure that he wasn't hurt by the stone. The rock crashed into the invisible barrier and shattered, sending shards of rock flying in all directions except toward Gwendolyn.

Offendorl rocked unsteadily on his feet, and even though Zollin knew the elder wizard was evil and dangerous, he felt sorry for his ancient adversary. Gwendolyn just laughed, the flames around her and her warlock sister growing higher and becoming translucent.

"I want you to see," Gwendolyn laughed. "I want you to see it all, old man. And you," she said, turning to Zollin. "I want you see real power. You may have resisted me in the past, but no longer. I shall unleash a power the world has not seen since the dawn of time."

"Don't do it," Zollin said. "We'll give you the city. You can rule Osla."

Gwendolyn frowned. "Do you honestly think you can buy my obedience? Shall I bow and lick your boots because you want to give me what I already have? Osla is mine; the Five Kingdoms will cower in fear before me. I shall become the great queen of darkness, the immortal god of this world. Then I shall have your bones polished and hung on the walls of my throne room as a reminder to all who might oppose me."

Zollin wanted to run, but he couldn't turn away.

"We must stop her," Offendorl said, his voice sounding weak and strained.

"How?" Zollin asked.

"Break the barrier and her spell shall be broken."

"How do I break the barrier?"

But Offendorl didn't answer—he was struggling just to breathe. Zollin moved closer to the ring of fire. He knew the dark magic was strong, having just seen it resist Offendorl's attacks. Zollin reached his hand toward the dancing flames, even as his breath billowed in thick clouds of steam from the cold. Zollin remember lying helpless in the snow deep in the Northern Highlands. The cold then had seeped into his body, first burning and then hardening as if his body were freezing solid. The ring of fire seemed even colder, but he believed Offendorl. Gwendolyn was planning something terrible and she had to be stopped.

Zollin touched the dancing flame, the cold so terrible that he almost instinctively pulled back, but instead he pushed his hand through. The flames didn't resist, but he could feel his arm burning with frostbite. He jumped across the barrier.

"You dare enter the circle of power?" Gwendolyn hissed.

Andomina was healed, but her skin was wrinkled and warped from the fire that had burned her in the tower of the Torr. She lay flat on the rooftop, her naked, hideously disfigured body outlined by what looked like white powder.

"You must stop," Zollin said. "Your sister needs help. End this dark magic and I will heal her."

Gwendolyn laughed.

"My sweet sister, burned by your dragons," she said. "Now you care about her, about us?"

"I don't want to see you fall into darkness," Zollin said.

"I live in darkness, fool. I come from the darkness, and now I summon it forth." Gwendolyn raised a wicked looking dagger with a black blade and silver scrollwork.

Zollin acted without thinking, levitating the knife from Gwendolyn's hands. The witch fought back, sending an icy blast at Zollin that pushed him back toward the flames.

"Don't leave the circle," Offendorl shouted.

Zollin tried to push back with his own power, but he was too close to the flames—the icy cold seemed to sear his back and sap his own magical strength. He felt his feet sliding across the rooftop's gritty surface. He knew he couldn't push back hard enough to stop Gwendolyn from pushing him out of the circle, so he spun to the side. Gwendolyn followed his movement, but she was a fraction slower than Zollin, who kept moving. He ran, moving a little further from the ring of fire with each step. Then, when he felt his strength returning, he sent a wave of magic hurtling toward Gwendolyn.

The witch raised her defenses, but at the last minute Zollin altered the wave's course and pushed Andomina toward the ring of fire.

"Don't touch her!" Gwendolyn shouted, her voice cracking with fear.

"She's the one with power," Zollin taunted. "You're nothing but a controlling witch with no real power of your own."

Gwendolyn took hold of Andomina with a magical grip, but Zollin reacted again, this time sending an electrical blast at Gwendolyn. The magic found its mark, but Gwendolyn had a magical shield up to protect herself. The magical energy snapped and popped, but did no damage to Gwendolyn. The witch then turned her eyes back to Zollin and he felt the fight go out of him. Instead of fighting, he wanted to take Gwendolyn in arms. He wanted to protect her, to make her happy, to make her love him.

"Men are all the same," Gwendolyn said. "You may be stronger than I am, but your weaknesses are obvious and oh so pathetic."

"Fight her charms," Offendorl snarled from outside the circle.

"No, fight him," Gwendolyn said. "Leave the ring of fire and kill Offendorl. Then I'll give you what you want. What every man wants. Me."

Zollin felt the decision to obey Gwendolyn was wrong somehow, but he wanted to obey her. He wanted to do whatever she wanted. Fighting her was painful; he wanted to give in. He turned and ran outside the ring of fire.

Immediately the knife dropped to the ground. Gwendolyn summoned it magically, levitating it into her hand and plunging it down into Andomina's heart in one fluid motion.

As soon as he stepped out of the circle, Zollin knew that he had made the wrong decision. It was like a brand of shame burning into his shoulder, a mistake that he could never take back or undo.

Lightning began to shoot down from the black clouds overhead.

"Nooooo!" Offendorl shouted.

Zollin wasn't sure what was happening, but he could feel the dark magic surging.

Something bad was about to happen and there was nothing he could do to stop it.

Chapter 33

What happened next was seen by people all over the kingdom of Osla, and in parts of Falxis and Ortis. Light seemed to pour down from the sky above the darks clouds. The light was brighter than the sun, causing people to cover their eyes and look away from the sky. Then the light focused, and a fiery object was seen plunging toward the earth.

When the object broke through the smoke, Gwendolyn looked up, her sister's lifeblood staining her hands. Zollin had felt Andomina's magical power wink out, but the dark, sinister magic had only grown. The fiery object slowed as it descended.

"The destroyer," Offendorl said in awe.

The object seemed at first like a ball of flame, but then the flames pulled back and revealed a creature inside. The flames took the shape of great fiery wings. The creature was covered with black fur and had thick muscular legs and feet that resembled giant hooves. The feet touched down on the rooftop with a sound like thunder, the stone roof cracking under the iron-like hooves.

The creature's upper body was similar in shape to a man's, but was still covered in the short, black fur. Hulking muscles could be seen through the fur, and the creature's face was anything but human. The face was almost like an empty space that had been filled in with flames. Eyes were visible, set deep into the waving flames. Hair hung down in oily ropes that outlined the fiery face.

When the creature spoke, its voice was deep and carried to Zollin and Offendorl, who stood like statues watching what took place inside the ring of fire.

"You summoned me," the creature said. "I am the destroyer. My name is destruction. You have spilled the blood of the innocent to call me forth. You shall be cursed as the queen of death."

With that, the creature thrust one hand toward Gwendolyn. The movement happened fast and the hand seemed to plunge into her chest like a sword. The witch gasped in shock, pain, and surprise. Blood gushed from the wound, running down the front of Gwendolyn's silky dress so that it clung to her body in a gruesome mockery of sensuality.

Then Gwendolyn's face turned blood red. Her long hair fell from her head and the soft curves of her shoulders and hips thickened with muscles. Her fingers grew into pointed talons and her eyes began to shine with a wicked green light. Then she threw back her head and laughed.

"I give you an army to rule," the creature said.

Then it held up its other arm and the ground began to shake. Zollin knew in that moment that escape was not possible. His fear was so great his chest began to ache with it. The castle rocked and swayed like a tall pine tree in a storm. The creature pulled its hand from Gwendolyn's chest, leaving a ragged hole in her dress just below her breasts. Zollin saw the flesh take shape where a mortal wound should have been, and dark hair, almost as thick as the creature's own fur, covered the wound. Gwendolyn's shoulders were bare and no hair grew there, but the creamy white flesh was gone, replaced by the crimson that seemed to flow down from her face. Her neck thickened with veins, muscles, and tendons until it was much wider than before, the blood red skin pulled tight over the muscles and tendons so that they stood out. Zollin could almost see the blood pounding through the exposed veins.

Then the creature moved behind Gwendolyn, like a servant. The ground was still trembling and then it cracked, like the shell of a walnut. The crack tore the castle in two, causing Zollin to stumble back and then scramble away from the center of the rooftop where the split was. The roof tilted, but did not collapse. The buildings around the castle were not so lucky—they crumbled like ashen logs in a fireplace.

The air was filled with a horrible rending sound as the crack grew wider. Buildings fell, and then the city's walls—the great, massive stone walls, once considered impregnable—crumbled. The crack stretched wider and wider, and screams could occasionally be heard. The Grand City was now in shambles, but Zollin could not see beyond the light from Gwendolyn's ring of fire. The dark smoke-like clouds overhead had stretched as far as Zollin could see and grown so thick that the sunlight was completely blotted out.

Then, a new sound was heard. To Zollin it sounded like thousands of warhorses galloping across the field of battle. Smoke rose up from the crevice that had wrecked the city. The crack was still snaking its way east and west, opening up a gulf between the northern portion of Osla and the southern.

Offendorl was on the same side of the castle as Zollin, and both were clinging to the crenellated edge of the rooftop. Zollin felt completely lost in the darkness. A small part of him felt like a little boy again. There were nights after especially hard days with his father when he had lain in bed, the room in their small cottage completely dark, weeping for the mother he never knew. He had always felt out of place in Tranaugh Shire. He wasn't skilled with his hands like his father, and didn't make friends easily. He had felt invisible in the village, and utterly alone on those dark nights, almost without hope. He felt that same feeling now. He could see Offendorl in the dim light from the now distant ring of fire. He could see Gwendolyn, terrible and frightening as she gloried in the destruction around her, the nightmarish creature behind her impassive. Still, he felt completely alone.

Then Zollin thought of Brianna, her face clear in his mind. He felt both joy and sadness as he realized he would never see her again. He had loved and been loved by Brianna, and her memory was bittersweet. Then other faces appeared. His father's face, determined yet loving. Mansel's face, jovial and passionate. Kelvich, his late mentor, wise and also mischievous. Finally, Todrek's face appeared. His oldest and best friend who had died in Tranaugh Shire. Guilt once more pierced Zollin's heart as memories of his childhood friend flashed through his mind. Todrek had not wanted to follow Zollin from the village when the wizards and mercenaries from the Torr had attacked. Todrek had just married Brianna the night before. It had been the culmination of his friend's dreams to take a wife and settle into life as an adult in the village. Zollin still imagined his friend, fat and happy, with children playing at his feet. That was what Todrek had wanted, but a mercenary's blade had torn Todrek's throat to ribbons and Zollin had been unable to save his life.

Then, shattering Zollin's memories of the past, came the most hideous creatures he had ever seen. They rose on long oval wings like dragonflies. The wings buzzed with frenzied movement and the sound of thousands of the creatures rising from the rocky abyss was the rumble that Zollin thought sounded like galloping warhorses.

The creatures had bodies like horses, with short, thick legs and hooves, but from the chest up the creatures had the bodies of men. Shoulders and thickly muscled arms stretched out, with hands that were like claws. Their faces were oddly human, but their mouths were larger, and great, glistening fangs protruded from between their lips, reminding Zollin of the lions in the Northern Highlands. They also had long flowing hair that hung down past their shoulders to the middle of their backs. It was held in place by golden headbands. Their eyes had the same green glow as Gwendolyn's now had.

But the worst part of all were the tails, which rose up from the thick, muscular hindquarters of their horse rumps and curled up over their backs. The tails were smooth and jointed, like the body of a spider. And on the tip of the tail was a massive stinger.

The creatures came in waves, pouring out of the dark crevice and swarming over everything in the city. Zollin didn't think about what he was doing, but immediately began blasting the creatures with powerful bolts of magical energy. He didn't give much thought to his magic, and the spells certainly weren't sophisticated. He was fighting for his life and unleashing raw power that lit up the rooftop. Not far away, Offendorl was similarly engaged, sending streams of fire that burned the creatures up. Zollin's energy attacks made the creatures shake violently, then fall to the ground in smoking heaps, their bodies blackened wherever the magical energy touched them.

The creatures that rose up from the dark crevice in front of Zollin attacked, but those to either side moved past him as if he wasn't there. The bodies of the creatures began to pile up, their combined weight on the ruined rooftop making the building sway toward the crevice uncertainly.

"We have to get out of here!" Zollin shouted to Offendorl, but the elder wizard did not reply.

Zollin could smell the burning flesh of the bodies around him. But where his attacks seemed to stop the creatures cold, Offendorl's fire wounded more than killed. The creatures kept coming at the master of the Torr. Then the castle shifted again, and Zollin climbed up onto the crenellated edge of the roof. More of the vile creatures were coming toward him, but he had just enough time to glance over toward Offendorl. The elder wizard was like a maelstrom of living fire, but two of the closest creatures stabbed through the fire with their scorpion tails, their stingers piercing Offendorl's ancient body.

The elder wizard's scream sent chills down Zollin's back. He didn't hesitate anymore, but leaped from the edge of the rooftop that was leaning more and more toward the giant crack in the earth. He used his magic to see that he landed safely on the broken cobblestone street below. As soon as his feet touched down, he could feel the vibrations in the ground, but he didn't have time to ponder why the ground seemed to continue to shake. Two of the creatures had followed him down and were almost on top of him.

Zollin let his magic blaze up, a single crooked bolt of magic lancing out from each hand and striking the creatures, one in each chest. The magic killed the creatures, but didn't stop their momentum. Zollin was forced to swat them away with a powerful wave of magic that also hit the royal castle. The half of the massive structure that Zollin and Offendorl had been on collapsed, crumbling into the abyss with a crash so loud that it made Zollin's ears ring.

Dust flew up and hid Zollin from view for a few seconds, allowing him to catch his breath and try to calm his heart rate a little. His magical containment was glowing hot from the amount of power he was using. He knew that if that magical containment broke down, the drain on his physical body from using magic would soon overwhelm him. He needed to get out of the Grand City, or what was left of it, but he didn't know how. All around him the buildings were breaking down. If they hadn't fallen from the violent movement of the earth when the crevice appeared, the horse-like creatures seemed to relish knocking them to pieces as they passed by. Zollin looked up and could still see Gwendolyn and her destroyer demon in the translucent ring of fire. Two of the centaur-like creatures were holding up Offendorl before Gwendolyn by their tails. Offendorl was writhing in pain as he hung in the air. Zollin wasn't sure what the witch had in mind for the master of the Torr, and the thought went through his mind that perhaps the wicked elder wizard deserved it, but Zollin didn't want to give Gwendolyn the satisfaction. He reached out with his magic, but it was once again repulsed by the ring of fire. Then Gwendolyn looked down at Zollin, obviously alerted to his presence when his magic touched her magical boundary.

Zollin didn't wait to see what she would do—he simply turned and ran. He jumped over mounds of crushed stone, hurdling beams of timber that stuck out at odd angles like broken bones. Occasionally he supplemented his physical strength with magic, levitating himself over larger mounds of debris, but he tried to use as little magic as possible. He didn't want Gwendolyn tracking his movements through his magic and he wanted to save as much of his magical power as he could.

He could hear the whirring of wings behind him and he glanced back to discover a small horde of the creatures coming for him. He knew he couldn't outrun the creatures, so he ducked behind a small pile of fallen stones and shot energy back toward the creatures. One was hit—it spasmed in the air then fell dead in the street.

Zollin knew that blasting the creatures down one by one was not the best use of his magic, nor did it give him much hope of surviving the attack. There were at least a dozen more creatures rushing toward him. He let his magic flow out, and suddenly he realized that the tower of the Torr still stood. The mighty bastion of magical power had survived the earth-shaking crevice that had split the city in two and toppled most of the buildings in the Grand City. Zollin sent a spell flying up that smashed the already ruined roof of the tower. Then he threw up a magical shield around himself and covered his head with his hands as the debris began to fall around him.

The creatures were caught unawares by the falling stones and timber beams. Most were killed from the impact, but two survived, although both were wounded. Zollin had just enough time to look up and see the creatures struggling out of the rubble, blood pouring from wounds they had endured.

It was then that Zollin realized the creatures were real. Perhaps they were conjured by dark magic and controlled by the witch, but they were flesh and blood. They could be killed. Gwendolyn may have wreaked havoc on the Five Kingdoms, but Zollin realized in that moment that she could be stopped. But he had to find a way to get out of the city if he was going to lead the fight to destroy Gwendolyn and her destroyer demon.

Chapter 34

King Zorlan had almost made it back to the gatehouse when the lightning began. Fires erupted around the city as buildings were struck with the violent bolts of ragged, white energy. King Zorlan and his officers stopped running. Sweat was pouring off the overweight king, his face red from exertion and his chest heaving as he gasped for breath. The king had a sharp pain in his side and his legs felt like stone, but fear had kept him moving until the lightning started. Now, Zorlan felt naked and exposed. Only the roofs of a few buildings stood taller than the city's outer walls.

Then the fireball descended from the black clouds above. It was radiant and captured the king's attention, along with everyone else around the city. King Zorlan watched as it slowed, and his heart seemed to squirm in his chest like a restless puppy. He knew the display was magic, knew the fear that was making his heart race was magical, yet that knowledge did nothing to settle his nerves. He stood watching the distant rooftop of the royal castle as the light faded. Then the darkness set in so heavily that he could no longer see the wall beneath his feet.

"Light!" he bellowed. "Someone light a torch or lamp or something."

"Sire, we've no materials."

"I don't want excuses," Zorlan shouted. "Find a way to get me off this wall now!"

The darkness seemed to press down on King Zorlan. Then he heard the scream as one of the men around him fell from the wall. The scream chilled the king's blood. Around him the officers fumbled about blindly. Zorlan got down on his hands and knees, crawling forward, determined to find the gatehouse and escape the terror of the city. His hands were rubbed raw and his knees aching with pain, his trousers torn and soaked with blood, but Zorlan didn't stop. It was so dark he could only just make out the surface of the wall at arm's length.

Then there was a crack so loud it made Zorlan cover his head with his arms. The king began to sob uncontrollably. He just wanted off the wall, he thought over and over. Then the ground began to shake and the sounds of buildings crashing made him feel like death was about to squash him under its boot heel at any moment. When the dark crevice reached the outer walls, it sent a shockwave through the stone that tossed King Zorlan into the air. He crashed back down, landing on his left side and jarring his shoulder. The horrible rending sounds continued, but Zorlan was moving again, his pain forgotten as he scrambled on all fours toward the gatehouse.

Then the rumbling of thousands of wings filled the air. Despair filled the king's heart until he realized that he had reached the gatehouse. He searched frantically for the winding staircase that led down to the courtyard below. The sound of the thunderous wings grew more intense until King Zorlan was on the verge of panic. Finally he found the trapdoor and pulled it open. The stairwell was pitch-black, but the king didn't hesitate. He scrambled to his feet and then, using his hands to steady himself against each wall, he hurried down into the darkness. A few moments later he was outside again, but this time he was on the ground. He couldn't see, but he could hear the sound of something approaching and he didn't want to be in the city when it arrived.

He felt his way to the massive gates and slipped through. The wide plain was before him and he began to run again. His feet hurt with each step, his knees ached and his hips seemed to grind in their joints as if someone had poured sand into the sockets. Still he ran, sweat dripping into his eyes, which he rubbed frantically. There was light in the distance, and he could make out the shadows of his the tents and the wagons of his army. Torches were being lit and a sense of relief flooded through King Zorlan. He would be safe, he though. He could hear someone barking orders, getting men into position. When he came close enough to be seen by the soldiers, several started yelling.

"It's the king!"

"It's King Zorlan, sir."

"The king's returned."

"Silence!" roared the duty officer. He was an older man, his back as straight as a rod, his face a mask of cold fury. He marched toward Zorlan, who was bent over, his hands on his knees, gasping for breath.

"Sire?" the man said, the uncertainty in his voice evident.

"Yes," was all Zorlan managed to say.

"Orders, sire?" the man said, falling back on his training when the uncertainty of conversing with his king overwhelmed him.

"Name?"

"I'm Gentry, sire, Century Officer."

"I want a horse, Gentry," King Zorlan said. "Then I want a controlled retreat," he panted. "I want to get as far from this place as possible."

"Aye, my lord," the officer said. "You heard the man—sound the retreat. I want soldiers around the king at all times. First squad, move your lazy asses."

Soldiers surrounded the king, many with torches. A horse was led forward, but the animal was wild-eyed with fear. The sound of the thunderous approach was growing louder. There were screams coming from the darkness toward the city.

"We need to move, Captain."

"I'm not a captain, sire, just a squad leader. Our captain was killed" the gruff man said.

"You're the general of my army if you get me out of here alive," Zorlan promised.

"Aye, sir. Let's move men," Gentry shouted.

They had moved beyond the tents and rows of wagons and were heading toward the main north-south road when the creatures from the dark abyss struck. There were nearly three hundred troops behind Zorlan now, all armed and marching in formation at a quick pace. The back row was struck first, and was the furthest from the light of the torches that surrounded King Zorlan. When the soldiers began to scream, King Zorlan turned. What he saw filled him with terror.

The centaur-like creatures were stabbing the soldiers with their long tails, using their stingers almost like spears, then flying up and carrying the men away. Zorlan could see the wounded soldiers writhing in pain as they were carried off. The gruff squad leader shouted orders. Half of the soldiers broke and ran in sheer panic, but the others were more disciplined. They had been trained to respond to the horrors of war by banding together. Shields were lofted, and swords drawn. They formed a shield wall that curved around King Zorlan.

"Get off that horse, you dammed fool!" Gentry shouted, dragging Zorlan out of the saddle. The king fell hard and the horse bolted away. Fury contorted Zorlan's face, but the soldiers crowded in on him, their shields held high just as a wave of the creatures struck. Stingers punched through the wooden shields, vile venom dripping from their barbs. The men who were stung wailed in pain, many falling to the ground, but the shield wall held.

"Give 'em hell, men!" screamed Gentry.

Swords lashed out. The tail segments were impenetrable, but the joints were vulnerable. Tails were severed, causing the creatures to roar in pain. Their voices sounded more like wild beasts' than men's. The creatures' long pointed fingers were like daggers and they bit and tore any exposed flesh they could reach with their vicious fangs, but they had no defense. The soldiers on the front line struggled to hold back the powerful creatures with their shields while their comrades in the line behind them stabbed and hacked with swords, axes, and spears. The creatures were wounded and killed with each blow the soldiers made. They were like rabid cattle, striking without any concern for their own safety and without any sort of strategy or teamwork.

"Fighting retreat," the squad leader shouted.

King Zorlan was on his feet now. Someone had handed him a shield, which he struggled to put on his arm. There were creatures all around them now. Many of the torches had been dropped during the attack, but some were still being used like weapons. Fire seemed to be the only thing that the creatures feared. Then help came roaring out of the sky.

* * *

Tears streamed down Brianna face as she rode Selix through the gathering gloom. She looked back and saw Zollin moving toward the castle. Deep in her heart she feared it was the last time she would ever see him alive. Tig and Ferno took positions on either side of Selix. Bartoom followed them, although the big, black dragon's wounds made it move more slowly. They flew over the city walls and soon passed the camp of the soldiers.

Brianna sent a mental image of the pride landing and of her healing their wounds. They were circling around getting ready to land when Bartoom, who had been with them a moment before, suddenly veered in mid-flight, swooping back up into the sky and flying away south.

Brianna watched the black dragon flying away, but she no longer felt sorry for it. Bartoom was not a free dragon and they could no longer protect the ancient beast. She turned her attention to her pride. Ferno was hurt the worst. Bartoom had battered and clawed the hulking green dragon. Brianna, naked, but with her body covered in dancing flames, let her healing fire wash over the green dragon. It took several minutes to heal Ferno and the world seemed to crack while she was doing it. The massive noise was followed by a shaking and rumbling that made the ground ripple like waves in the ocean.

The dragons took flight, preferring to be in the air rather than on the ground, which no longer seemed stable. Brianna settled on Selix's back and began healing the golden dragon. She had just finished when the thunderous sounds of wings rolled across the plain. Brianna and her pride could see in the dark, their eyes zooming across the distance and seeing the sparks of light from the wizard battle on the rooftop. Then they could see the approaching hordes of creatures. The sheer amount of them was enough to make Brianna's heart almost stop. She couldn't believe Zollin was still in the city. Her hope for him was fading fast.

She ordered the pride to fly higher. They rose up to the dark, smoke-like clouds that were blotting out the setting sun. The creatures below seemed not to pay them any attention. They flew, but seemed to prefer to move just above the ground. Brianna watched as they attacked the soldiers who were running in panic away from the city. She saw the creatures spear the soldiers and turn to carry them back toward the city.

"Tig, find out where the creatures are taking those men," Brianna shouted. "Selix and Ferno, attack!"

The two big dragons dove, swooping toward the line of creatures. The dragons were higher in the air than the creatures, which still took no notice of them. They were like mindless monsters, with only one task fixed in their tiny brains. Ferno was the first to strike, spewing fire into the horde. Selix soon joined the green dragon. They lay down long blasts of fire, which incinerated the creature's delicate wings and burned them. Some of the creatures burst into flames, but most were merely wounded by the fire and able to continue on their destructive charge, running like horses.

Selix and Ferno wheeled in the sky and turned back for another pass, this time moving more slowly and concentrating their fiery attack. Ferno was in the lead and to Brianna's right. Ferno's pass wounded many, while Selix came in a little after the green dragon and destroyed those who escaped Ferno's first pass. It was an effective attack, but the sheer number of creatures made even the dozens killed by the dragons seem inconsequential.

Brianna was watching the battle, letting the dragons attack as they saw fit. She saw the swarming creatures pouring out of the city and watched for Tig to return. Then she saw the group of soldiers fighting the creatures and urged her pride to help.

Ferno made a scathing run that set many of the creatures on fire. The beasts bucked and dropped to the dirt in an effort to extinguish the fire that was burning them. Selix swooped in and landed behind the beasts that were too close to the soldiers to blast with fire. Selix billowed fire at the horde still approaching while also using its golden tail to swat the centaur-like creatures off the shield wall.

"Retreat," Brianna shouted, and the troops obeyed. They hurried backward, keeping their shields up. Then Brianna jumped from Selix's back, flipping through the air and landing behind the golden dragon.

Selix leapt into the air, and the hordes of creatures started to move toward Brianna. But when Brianna let the fire she controlled cover her body, the creatures tried to avoid her. She sent balls of flame flying at the nearest creatures and it was like she was a boulder in a stream. The waves of creatures broke around her, making her efforts almost futile. She ran and jumped as Ferno swooped low, raking the creatures with another fiery pass as Selix dove down and flicked Brianna up with its golden tail.

Brianna shot up higher and higher, holding her arms tight against her body and keeping her legs straight. She rose up through the smoke-like clouds and saw the sun setting and casting the sky in a crimson red color. Below her, the black clouds hovered supernaturally and she dove back through them. Selix was waiting just below the cloud cover and swooped under Brianna just as she slowed her descent. She landed gracefully on Selix's back and together they renewed their attack.

They had just made another attack when Tig returned. Brianna saw an image of a giant crack in the ground. It stretched out as far as she could see and swarms of the creatures were spilling out in either direction. Her heart sank a little. Then she saw the creatures returning to the dark abyss with humans impaled and writhing on their huge, scorpion tails. They carried the helpless but still living humans down into the dark crevice.

Brianna shuddered at the thought of what was happening to the people captured and carried away. The good news was that the centaur-like creatures could be killed, but there were so many that she simply couldn't fathom the amount of destruction that would result in their being turned loose on the Five Kingdoms.

Then another image appeared in Brianna's mind. It was of Zollin, leaping over a pile of rubble in the streets of the city, shooting his unmistakable magical energy into the creatures that pursued him as he dashed into the tower of the Torr.

"Zollin's alive!" she said out loud, her joy at the sight of her beloved almost making her head spin.

Before she could even think of what to do, Ferno was off. The hulking green dragon hurtled toward the city and Selix dove forward, once again covering the retreat of the soldiers.

Chapter 35

Zollin ran from one heap of rubble to another, always looking over his shoulder for the next wave of creatures that swooped down to attack him. The rubble had become his greatest asset in the fight. Whenever the creatures took notice of him and swarmed down, he pelted them with waves of the loose debris around him. Sending the piles of rubble flying up took less magical strength than blasting them outright. Zollin was tired, but he also felt strong. His magic seemed to be holding steady, and while the waves of debris didn't always take the hordes of awful creatures out of the fight, it seemed to give him the upper hand.

He was making his way to the one structure in the city that seemed to be enduring the unending nightmare. The tower of the Torr was not as tall and majestic as it had once been. In reality, it looked like a lone fang whose tip had been broken off, but it still stood stalwart above the wreckage of buildings all around it. Zollin lashed out with magical energy at the last two creatures still pursuing him, just before he rushed into the open doorway of the tower. It was pitch-black inside the building, but Zollin could make out the mound of rubble.

He kindled a small flame, illuminating the large interior of the room. Zollin saw the stairway leading up and the wreckage of the floors above him. It didn't take much imagination to realize that several floors had collapsed. He wondered briefly if perhaps the structure was not a safe place, but after running and fighting for so long, he was glad for the chance to stop and catch his breath. He moved slowly up the stone staircase, which rose in a circling spiral up the wall of the tower. The climb was taxing, but taking it slow allowed Zollin to rest along the way. If the creatures knew he was in the tower, they did nothing to pursue him.

After several minutes, Zollin finally came to the top of the structure. It was several floors below Offendorl's personal rooms. Two men huddled in a corner where part of the roof was still intact. Zollin could feel the magic radiating from the two men, but both looked out with vacant eyes. Zollin guessed they were warlocks, and it only took a slight magical probe—which caused both men to flinch—to prove his theory was correct. Their minds were drawn inward so deeply that Zollin doubted they had had any idea what was happening around them.

Zollin moved higher up onto the last floor, which was completely exposed. The only light he could see was the winking of the ring of fire on the rooftop of the royal palace, which seemed much farther way. Zollin could see a band of ragged blackness that he guessed was the crevice, and he thought he could see moving shadows far below, which he took for the creatures.

Zollin wasn't sure what to do now. He felt like he needed to strike a blow at Gwendolyn, but his magic had been unable to penetrate the powerful shield that encapsulated the ring of fire. Then an idea came to Zollin and he let his magic flow out. He was reminded of the night hunts he had gone on while spending the winter with Kelvich in the Great Valley. He would go out in the dead of night, letting his magic flow around him when he couldn't see to find the animals he was hunting. Now he let his magic stream forth from the broken tower to the castle on the far side of the crevice. He started at ground level, then let his magic move upward through the building, until he understood exactly what was holding the broken structure up. He knew he couldn't penetrate Gwendolyn's magical shield, but perhaps he could strike in a different way.

He heaved with magical effort, his power like a raging furnace inside him. Working magic at long distances was like holding a heavy weight with your arm extended. Every muscle in his body tensed with the effort, but finally the wall he was focused on collapsed. Zollin couldn't see what was happening, so he let his magic stay in the castle, sensing what his effort had produced.

There was a groan as the heavy upper floors of the building lost support, then a pop as a heavy timber beam cracked. Then another. Soon the castle was falling inward. Zollin opened his eyes in time to see the roof of the castle shake, then tilt. Then, as the castle started to fall, Zollin pulled. Sweat sprang up on his forehead and his breath grew labored, but he didn't give up. The castle was collapsing, but Zollin knew knocking the building down wasn't enough. He heaved in one last-ditch effort, his magic overflowing his self-constructed containment and leeching the strength from his body, but he didn't stop. The castle moved, the rooftop tilted again, and then the castle tumbled into the abyss.

Zollin sagged to his knees. He felt lightheaded. Hunger and thirst seemed overwhelming and he could hear his heart beating in his ears. Still, he had succeeded, although whether or not his efforts would make a difference only time would tell. The ring of fire was gone, but the abyss was still there.

Just when Zollin was starting to hope that perhaps he had succeeded, flaming wings appeared. A creature that Zollin could only describe as a demon was rising from the crevice and flying toward the tower. The demon was a small, horribly disfigured creature, with tiny legs that were twisted at odd angles. Its arms were long and bone thin, the chest seemed to arch inward, and the neck was angled toward one oversized shoulder. The demon's head was tall and egg shaped, with no hair. Its eyes were uneven, and one was larger than the other. The foul creature's mouth drooped open, revealing only a few blackened teeth. Its ears were large and pointed, and the nose was like a pig's snout. Light from the flaming wings illuminated the horrific creature and it took Zollin a moment to stop staring and prepare to face the new threat.

Zollin raised his defenses but the demon used Zollin's own tactics against him. A shudder ran through the tower, then it began to lean. Zollin knew he could levitate down to safety, but he was so tired he knew that levitating would take all his strength and leave him defenseless.

Zollin stepped up onto the jagged edge of the tower's broken wall as the building swayed beneath his feet. He worried briefly about the warlocks below him, but he knew he couldn't help them now. He jumped out into open space, away from the demon and away from the direction the tower was leaning. Time seemed to slow as Zollin fell. The tower was like one of the many tall pines he had harvested with his father. That moment just before the tree fell seemed to stretch out longer than normal. Then the tower was crumbling down and Zollin was falling. He used his magic to slow his descent, ignoring the burning sensation in his gut as he used his magic.

He fell hard onto the cobblestones below. His ankle twisted on impact and pain shot up his leg, but he didn't have time see to the injury. The demon was flying over him, directing a hoard of the centaur-like beasts to attack. They surrounded Zollin on three sides as the dust from the collapsed tower billowed over them. The creatures began to growl, and Zollin scrambled to his feet, placing his weight on his one good leg as much as possible.

When the dust cleared, the first of the creatures charged. The realization that the demon was controlling the centaur-like beasts flashed through Zollin's mind. He'd never seen them show any intelligence. They were like a hive of insects, swarming over everything in their path with no independent thoughts or actions. Now they were working together in a well-coordinated attack.

Zollin threw up an invisible shield that the first creature crashed into headfirst, the beast's face crumpling in anger as blood gushed from its nose. Zollin smiled. He was outnumbered and his chances of survival were slim, but he wasn't going down without a fight.

"Come and get me!" he snarled.

Two more beasts attacked, one from each side. Zollin extended both arms and let his magical energy burst forth. The creatures shook violently and then crashed to the ground in a smoking heap, but Zollin had no time to enjoy his handiwork. Four more creatures were rushing forward. Zollin erected another magical shield mentally, but he was unprepared for the force of the monsters' charge. They hit the barrier and were knocked backward, but so was Zollin. He landed painfully in a pile of rubble just as the rest of the beasts attacked. The first creature to arrive slammed its stinger down hard, intending to stab Zollin in the chest, but the young wizard rolled away from the attack. A second beast jumped like a lion, pouncing down on Zollin. The creature's talon like fingers sank deep into Zollin's hip.

Zollin's scream echoed through the abandoned city, and only one creature heard it that cared. Ferno was flying as fast as the big green dragon's wings would carry it. It had circled wide once it saw the tower of the Torr fall. Now it was flying in from behind the demon.

Zollin saw no more need to hold back his power. Electrical energy flashed out in all directions. The group of beasts sent to attack him were caught in the initial field and burned so badly by the magical power that there was nothing left but unidentifiable, smoking carcasses. But the beasts weren't the only things affected. The debris on the streets and the rubble of the torn down buildings were blown away. Huge timber beams were incinerated instantly, while large stone blocks were cast high into the air.

Zollin felt hollow inside. His magic thrummed, but instead of breaking through his containment field or straining his physical body, the magic seemed satisfied. It was almost like a powerful beast that had been let off its leash for the first time, and now it

purred happily within Zollin. The demon above the yo
looked angry as it beckoned more of the centaur creatur
Zollin.

Just then, Ferno struck. The big green dragon smash the demon's back with such force that Zollin heard bones The demon was sent flying over Zollin's head and the yo wizard levitated himself into the air. The effort was difficult, sin the pain in his hip had become a searing, burning sensation that ha hard to ignore and made it especially difficult to concentrate. Ferno had flown past Zollin too, the dragon partially stunned by the impact, but managing to stay in the air. The green dragon circled wide to turn back to where Zollin was, noticing that the demon lay in a heap of rubble and was not moving.

Zollin had come to rest on a pile of stone. His body suddenly felt more tired than he could ever remember. Blood flowed down his leg and he took a moment as the creatures moved toward him to stop the bleeding. The muscle and tendons were severed, making his leg useless, but with the bleeding stopped he knew he could heal the rest later. He couldn't put any weight on the leg though, and with his mobility gone, he knew he would have to rely on his magic to go anywhere.

The creatures were fast approaching, their arms reaching out for him and their stingers raised and ready to strike. Ferno flew down and landed behind Zollin, sending a mental image of the two of them fighting together. It brought a smile to Zollin's grimy face. Ferno climbed up the rock heap, the green dragon's body low to the ground, its teeth bared in a growl of fury.

…ked en masse, charging toward … right into the face of their charge. …rward momentum, but a dozens of the …ve. Zollin levitated the hurdling carcasses …t them crashing down on the far side of the …e he and Ferno fought. The beasts that still lived … the fiery attack, flying past Zollin and reforming … both.

…Get in the air," Zollin said.

Ferno obeyed instantly, jumping up and flapping the great …athery wings. Zollin hopped around, turning toward the crowd of monsters that were wheeling in mid-air to renew their attack. But the demon appeared above them, one furry arm hanging at an obscene angle. A patch of the gray skin on its dome-shaped head was gone, revealing the bloody skull underneath. The larger of its two eyes was swollen almost shut and blood ran down from the pointy ear on the right side of it's head, dripping onto the large, hairy shoulder where it trickled down the long, bony arm.

The demon rose up on flaming wings and then dove toward Zollin. The centaur creatures hesitated, blank looks in their glowing green eyes. Zollin raised an invisible magical shield, but the demon either saw the invisible barrier or had been expecting it. The grotesque creature slammed into the shield with its good shoulder, knocking Zollin backward. Zollin rolled down the pile of stones he had been perched on, the pain in his injured hip making him scream in agony. Still, he managed to keep the shield up, like a bubble of protection around his body that kept the sharp stones and protruding timber from ripping him to shreds.

The demon pounced on Zollin, raising its good arm, and Zollin knew it was about to strike him in a way that he could not recover from. Zollin put all his magical prowess into his shield. The demon drove its hand down, the fingers penetrating the magical barrier but stopping short of reaching Zollin. The demon's eye, spreading wide in furious anger, flashed with the same green light Zollin had seen in Gwendolyn's eyes. Zollin could feel his magic pushing against the dark magical energy of the demon that wasn't deterred by its initial failure. The vile creature merely pushed harder against the barrier. Zollin was reminded of when the black dragon Bartoom had managed to catch him in its lair and tried to crush him. His magic had held then, but now he wasn't sure. His body shook as he poured all his power into the magical barrier, the heat inside him roaring like a forest fire that was out of control.

Then Ferno arrived again, swooping down and snapping its razor sharp teeth into the demon's wounded shoulder. The teeth sank deep and the dragon's momentum carried it away, ripping the arm from the demon's body. There was a roar and then an explosion of fire. Zollin closed his eyes and held tight to his magical shield. Then the world went black.

Chapter 36

Zollin came to a moment later. He was lying defenseless in the rubble. His magical shield was gone, and so was the containment he normally kept around his magic at all times. He could feel the magic like a scorching summer wind, blowing through him like a desert storm. He rolled to his good knee, careful not bend or put any weight on his wounded hip. Fire was everywhere around him. Anything that could burn was burning, unless it had been protected by Zollin's magical shield. He could see the bodies of dozens of the centaur-like creatures, all smoking, their flesh burning. Black smoke rose all around Zollin, choking him and making him feel weak. He coughed and sputtered, then sank back down onto the rough ground where the air was cleaner. He lay back, gasping. He knew he couldn't stay there for long, but he needed time to catch his breath. His magic felt like it was eating him alive, so he rebuilt the containment around the magic, funneling it so that it was at its peak potency.

Then, he took a second to block the ravaged nerve ending in his leg. He didn't have the time to heal the wound correctly, so he just blocked the signals from the nerves so that the pain didn't rob him of his strength and concentration. Then he struggled back up, using his magic to lift his body into an upright position. His stomach felt like a tiny little knot and his mouth was so dry his tongue was stuck to the roof of his mouth. Still, he levitated himself out of the smoke. It was difficult to see much of what was happening—the light from the fires below Zollin made the Grand City seem even darker. Zollin heard a rumble, like the groan of a giant old man. The rumble was followed by the sounds of rock crunching and rolling down into the crevice.

Zollin strained to see what was happening. Then a huge, shadowy hand appeared out of the deep, black abyss. The hand crashed down into the rubble of the city and pulled up a giant.

Zollin felt despair rise up into his throat and he started to fall. Then a green shadow swooped below him and Zollin landed hard on Ferno's back. The dragon's scales were like gravel, but Zollin clung tight. They circled the giant as it climbed up from the great pit that the demon had formed. The giant had no eyes, and no hair on its head. Its shoulders were huge, easily the size of a large house. Its neck was so short and thick that it seemed like an extension of the great bulbous head.

"Ready to have more fun?" Zollin shouted.

Ferno roared in response. Zollin didn't know if the dragon was as tired as he was, but the green beast didn't hesitate. As they flew closer, the giant rose to its full height. Zollin had seen a giant deep in the Northern Highlands, but that giant was a dwarf compared to the great, sightless monstrosity before them. Even Ferno seemed small compared to the giant from the abyss.

Ferno swooped up, unleashing a pillar of fire at the giant, which did nothing to avoid the flames. The dragon's fiery breath spread across the giant's naked upper body, singing the thick wiry hair that covered its chest and shoulders, but didn't harm the otherworldly creature.

"Fly," Zollin said. "Get us higher."

Ferno obeyed, flapping the wide green wings. They rose in the air, the giant turning its head as if it could see them. Zollin's mind was racing. He had never fought anything so massive and he was sure the giant had been sent to kill him. It was extremely powerful, that much was clear, although whether it was acting on Gwendolyn's command or the creature who had come down from the sky was a complete mystery to Zollin. There had been no sign of the demon after the explosion, but somehow he doubted that he had seen the last of the flaming creature, or at least the last of its kind.

"Keep moving," Zollin told Ferno. "No matter what happens. If I fall, go back to Brianna."

Ferno growled, flames licking around the dragon's broad green head, but it didn't argue. Zollin closed his eyes and let his magic flow out toward the giant. The creature was repellent, like a strong odor. Zollin's magic didn't seem to want to go near it. He forced it closer even as his skin seemed to crawl and he felt goosebumps break out on his arms and neck. The giant was built like a man, but there was nothing human about it. Zollin could feel emotions but no intelligence; he could get no sense of the substance of the creature. It was so huge he had no idea how to fight it. Ferno circled close to the giant's head, billowing fire as Zollin unleashed magical energy. The giant roared, its mouth full of blackened teeth the size of large doors, and a blackened mark appeared on the giant's grayish skin where Zollin's magic had raked across its forehead. Zollin had trouble seeing it in the darkness, but Ferno sent mental images to Zollin that showed the mark. The dragon was hopeful that they had hurt the giant, but Zollin wasn't convinced.

He needed to find something that would stop the creature. He wasn't all that interested in harming the giant, but he needed to send it back to where it had come from. In his mind he remembered Brianna saying that she had created the dragons deep under the mountains. At first he rejected the idea, but he couldn't shake the feeling that Brianna was the only one who could stand against the giant. He hated himself for considering it and felt like a coward, but he could think of nothing else.

"We have to go to Brianna," Zollin said. "Take me to her."

Ferno banked sharply and flew out away from the city. Zollin glanced back and saw the giant following. His stomach felt like he was going to vomit. He couldn't believe what he was doing. He was a wizard. He could do practically anything he could imagine, but he knew instinctively that he couldn't stop the giant without killing it, and he wasn't even sure he could do that.

"Tell Brianna we're coming," Zollin said.

In the distance, Zollin could see Selix and Tig, both engaging the centaur-like creatures. The dragons' fiery breath had done more damage than Zollin would have thought possible. The ground beneath them was scorched and littered with the smoldering bodies of the centaur creatures. Shrubs were burning. There were very few trees across the wide plain, but the short grass burned and smoked. It made Zollin cough, but the ground fires didn't deter the monsters. Then Selix pulled up and flew to meet them. Zollin wished they could find a place to land, but the ground was covered in the creatures, like bees crawling over their hive. Still, he had to talk with Brianna, had to tell her what he was thinking.

"Clear a spot on the ground," Zollin said. "Then help me fend off those monsters."

Ferno spewed fire onto the ground. The flames hit the ground and spread in a big circle. The monsters that flew low to the ground swerved to avoid the flames. Zollin gathered his good leg under him as Ferno landed. Zollin then jumped to the ground, using magic to soften his landing and steady his balance so that he didn't end up putting weight on his wounded leg. Ferno didn't wait with Zollin but jumped back into the air, the downdraft from the dragon's wings stirring up the ash from the grass that had just been incinerated so that the ash floated around Zollin like snowflakes.

Zollin waited while the swarm started to return, then lashed out with magical energy, killing several of the beasts at once. Then Brianna landed lightly beside him, as if she had just stepped down off a ladder instead of leaping to the ground from over a hundred feet in the air.

"What is that thing?" she said, already staring at the giant lumbering slowly toward them.

"I don't know for sure," Zollin said. He couldn't see the giant anymore, but he could hear the huge beast's thunderous footsteps. "This may sound crazy, but I think you're the only one who can stop it."

"Why me?" Brianna asked.

"It's just a hunch," Zollin explained, "but it came from underground. I just thought maybe since you made the dragons underground that you could convince it to turn back."

The dragons were laying down rows of fire to keep the swarms of centaur monsters away from Zollin and Brianna.

Brianna looked at Zollin as if he had lost his mind. He started to tell her to forget the whole thing, but then she turned toward the lumbering creature, her face determined.

"Well then," she said, her voice harsh, "keep those other things off me for a while."

"Be careful," Zollin said.

The giant smashed through the city walls and the mighty crashes of the thick stone walls falling around its legs shook the ground. Brianna's face was full of awe as she watched the giant approaching. To Zollin it was just a vast shadow, but Brianna's eyes were much like those of her dragons. She could see in the dark almost as well as in the daylight, and even at a great distance she could make out the smallest details. Zollin was waiting for fear to cloud her features, but instead he saw compassion.

As the giant approached, its great tree-like legs stepping wide across the plain, the centaur creatures gave it a wide berth. It tilted its head down, as if it were looking down even though it had no eyes. Ferno and Tig circled the giant's head like large mosquitoes but the giant ignored them.

"What do I do?" Brianna asked.

"I'm not sure, maybe tell it who you are."

Brianna again looked at Zollin like he was insane. The young wizard just shrugged his shoulders. He was going on instinct. He wished more than ever that Kelvich were alive to tell him he was doing the right thing.

"My name is Brianna," she said in a loud voice. "I am a fire spirit. I am dragon-kind." The giant just groaned as it hunched over and raised a huge fist.

Zollin was standing behind Brianna, ready to throw up a magical shield to protect her. He felt ill, like he was hiding behind Brianna, or worse yet, sacrificing her to save himself. "No," Brianna said. "You don't want to do that. We don't want to hurt you. Go back where you came from."

The fist came hurtling down and Brianna jumped back, summersaulting in the air to avoid the blow. Zollin's magical shield protected him, but he was knocked off his feet. In the dark he saw bright spots flashing.

"We mean you no harm," Brianna shouted. She had landed on Selix's back and was soaring up toward the giant's head.

The giant raised its other fist, intent on swatting Brianna and Selix from the air. Brianna lashed out with heat so intense that it penetrated the giant's thick skin. Zollin saw the white-hot flame, almost as bright as a flash of lightning. Then the giant's gray skin curled back over it's huge knuckle bones as the fire penetrated. The giant roared in pain, but brought its upraised fist down once again.

Selix dove out of harm's way, but Brianna jumped from the golden dragon's back. She flew down near the giant's feet and turned her intense heat onto the ground. The soil looked for a moment like red-hot embers, then the ground under the giant transformed into lava. Zollin was forced to run back from the giant to avoid the blistering heat. The giant's legs sank down into the pool of red-hot lava, howling in fury and pain. It flapped its arms and struggled to get up, but Ferno came by and swatted the giant's head with its spiked tail. The lumbering giant lost its balance and fell back down.

The molten rock splashed up like candle wax, still too hot to touch, but thickening as the air cooled it. Brianna continued to blast the ground with heat so intense that even the dragons seemed uncomfortable. The giant sank back down into the lava, falling onto its hands and knees, then sinking down until only its chest and head were above the molten rock.

It bellowed in fury and pain.

"You left us no choice," Brianna said. "I'm sorry, but you shall be remembered."

Brianna then jumped high into the air, her body arched like a diver, then she dove head first into the lava. Zollin had to hold back a scream of despair, trusting that Brianna knew what she was doing. She had told him of heating the rock in the mountains and swimming in the lava, but seeing her disappear into the molten rock scared him more than the giant.

The lava began to bubble and Zollin knew that Brianna was heating the bedrock further down beneath the giant. He just hoped that she didn't get caught under the massive creature as it continued to sink.

In a matter of moments the lava was up to the giant's neck, its arms flailing in an effort to escape the molten rock. The centaur creatures seemed to have stopped coming out of the great crevice, and those that were still in the city were now going around the giant, spreading out to the east and west. Zollin lowered himself to the ground and the dragons came and landed near him. Zollin's leg was numb and he felt nauseous, but he didn't want to do anything until he made sure that Brianna was okay.

It took several minutes before the giant's head sank beneath the surface of the molten pool. Its arms at last went limp and it ceased struggling. Zollin expected Brianna to appear at any minute, but she didn't.

"Can you communicate with her?" Zollin asked Selix.

The golden dragon looked thoughtful for a moment, then shook its head. Zollin wanted to scream and curse, but he knew it was a waste of energy. He limped as close as he could get to the molten pool. The melting rock gave the area a soft, orange glow, but the darkness around Zollin seemed oppressive. He wanted to curl up in a ball and go to sleep. He wanted to close his eyes and forget everything, to make the pain of losing Brianna all over again disappear. Then she rose up out of the molten rock like a fiery goddess and Zollin understood why the dwarves called them fire spirits.

"Are you okay?" Zollin asked when Brianna came close, the worry making his voice hoarse.

"Yes, I think so," Brianna managed to say. She had no clothes on, but flames covered her body and her hair was smoking, although not a single strand was singed. Zollin thought she looked more beautiful than he had ever seen her.

"What happened?"

"The giant just sank down. It took a while, but it finally succumbed to the heat." Brianna closed her eyes. "How long was I gone?"

"About half an hour," Zollin said. He could see that she was exhausted. Her body was trembling and her eyes blinked slowly. "It's okay, you're safe now," he said, stepping close to her.

"No we aren't, Zollin," she said. "I saw what the witch is preparing. No one is safe. Maybe not ever again."

Chapter 37

The sky was beginning to clear over the ruins of the Grand City. Stars began to shine through the haze. The moon was just rising and the last of the swarming hordes were flying up out of the great crevice that now split the Five Kingdoms apart. The creatures moved on, destroying everything they touched.

Zollin mounted Ferno and Brianna mounted Selix. They took to the sky and began fighting the hordes of monsters. Tig was tasked with watching the crevice. Ferno, Selix, and Brianna were busy raining fire down on the mindless drones. Zollin had never felt so incredibly tired in his whole life. He held on to Ferno and let his magic flow into his wounded leg. The hipbone and thick femur were gouged, the tendons were torn, the muscle in his upper thigh was in ribbons. His magic was so hot it hurt him physically to use it, but he had no choice. The wound in his leg had to be dealt with, but the effort to heal himself was difficult to muster. He did as little as possible to heal the wound and then turned his attention back to the centaur-like creatures. They had spread out and were moving in roving bands. They destroyed anything they encountered, from the supplies of the army that had been set up around the Grand City to groves of palm trees. Nothing living was spared.

The dragons flew in formation, with Ferno diving toward the groups of monsters first, bathing the creatures in fire. Those that survived the initial attack were then hit by Selix and Brianna. The fire melted the creatures' insect-like wings and burned up their long, flowing hair. Their scorpion tails were rarely affected by the fire, but the human heads were very vulnerable. If the fire enveloped the beasts' heads, they died instantly. The rest of their bodies were then covered in horrible burns, making them easy prey if the dragons needed to make a second pass at the creatures. Occasionally some flew up in an attempt to ward off the dragons, but they feared fire and were quickly routed.

Zollin did very little through the night. Nausea twisted his stomach into a writhing, quivering mess. His head pounded, especially when Ferno swooped upward after a steep dive. By morning, it was all Zollin could do to hang onto the green dragon. He was grateful that Ferno had risked life and limb to save him. He was certain he wouldn't have made it out of the city alive without the green dragon, which seemed to have taken a liking to Zollin.

They fought until dawn, helping the remnant of soldiers surrounding King Zorlan escape north, but tens of thousands of the centaur-like creatures escaped into the countryside. When dawn came, Zollin and Brianna brought the dragons to the ground not far from the Grand City.

"What now?" Zollin asked.

"Rest," Brianna said. "We need to regroup."

Zollin tried to walk to where Brianna was sitting on the ground, her head propped on her hands, but his leg was stiff and weak. He limped forward.

"You're hurt?" she asked, seeing him moving awkwardly.

"It's nothing, I just need a little rest."

"You're limping," she insisted. "What happened?"

Ferno growled low in its throat.

"You were almost killed," she said, the green dragon having sent her a mental image of the centaur-like creatures swarming onto Zollin.

"One of the creatures clawed my leg is all. I healed it, I'm fine."

"You don't look fine. You're limping like an old man."

"Haven't you heard? All wizards are old men, with long gray beards and tall, pointy hats," he joked.

"I don't think now is the time for joking," Brianna said, her face pinched with concern.

"I think it's the perfect time. After what we've been through, we could use a good laugh. I wish Mansel were here. He always laughed at my jokes."

"You realize Mansel is in danger, don't you?" Brianna said. "There were thousands of those creatures released last night. We killed a lot, but we didn't even come close to stopping them all. Everyone we know is in danger, and they don't even know it's coming."

"What did you mean last night?" Zollin asked. "You said none of us are safe. What happened?"

"When I went underground I came into a huge cavern," Brianna explained. "The witch is building an army."

"Another one?"

"These beasts we've been fighting are just the beginning, Zollin."

"Are you sure?" he asked. "You went down miles from the crevice."

"That's what I'm trying to tell you, Zollin. Under the ground there are huge caverns."

"Like the dwarfish tunnels in the Northern Highlands?"

"Similar yes, but much larger. And there are creatures roaming through the tunnels and caverns."

"So, she's controlling the monsters below the earth?"

"Yes, I think she is, but she's using humans to create her army."

"Brianna, you're not making sense."

"Listen to me!" Brianna said, her voice rising in anger. "There's a whole world below our feet. And the horse creatures with scorpion tales aren't killing people—they're capturing them. I saw the witch sitting on a horrible looking throne made out of bones. The humans her creatures captured are being dropped into a pit and she's using magic of some kind to transform them into huge beasts!"

"Like the giant?" Zollin asked, dismay making his voice small.

"No, they aren't giants, but they are bigger than people, bigger than Mansel. Their faces are distorted and horrible looking. And they're vicious killers. Every once in a while she would send one of the humans into their pit without transforming it first. The others ripped them apart."

"And you're convinced she's building an army?"

"What else could she be doing?" Brianna asked.

"I don't know. None of this makes sense to me. She's using some sort of dark magic I've never encountered before. She sacrificed her sister to complete the spell. Some type of demon rose up out of the abyss and attacked me, but Ferno killed it, I think. Then that giant creature came out of the crevice. I'm not sure what to do now."

"Well, we can't fight thousands of her minions alone," Brianna said.

Just as she spoke, a group of the flying centaur beasts flew toward the city, each carrying a captured human.

"This is like a nightmare," Zollin said, yawning.

"She's unleashing horrible beasts below the earth, Zollin. These creatures are just the beginning. We can't fight her on our own."

"So what do we do?" Zollin asked.

"We have to find help," Brianna said, tears streaking down her dirty face. "We have to gather armies to fight her monsters."

Zollin wanted to argue. He wanted it all to be over, once and for all, but he knew it wasn't. He was surrounded by the bodies of the centaur-like creatures. Flies buzzed around their scorched carcasses and carrion birds circled in the sky above.

"At least the sun is shining," Zollin said. "That's a change. I didn't think last night would ever end."

But he could still see smoke rising from the crevice. He could see the walls of the Grand City, tumbled down in most places. The tower of the Torr was gone. The Torr was finished. Zollin had seen Offendorl being given to Gwendolyn, who no longer seemed to be human. He felt guilty that he hadn't been able to stop the cataclysmic events, but they had managed to stay alive through the night and they had managed to kill hundreds of the swarming monsters. It may have been a small victory, but he was happy to take it just the same.

Zollin was just about to suggest they find something to eat and get some rest when another of the flying creatures crossed the plain with a human hooked by its scorpion-like tail.

"We have to get some rest," he said. "I'm so hungry I feel sick."

"And we have to warn everyone we can," Brianna insisted. "We have to be ready when the witch is, or the Five Kingdoms will fall."

"Okay, so let's start with King Zorlan. We kept his troops alive through the night. Surely they'll help."

Brianna nodded and they flew north again. They could see bands of the roving monsters, but the centaur-like creatures became sluggish in the daylight. Some even landed and slept."

"It's good to know they get tired too," Zollin shouted.

Brianna just nodded, her face pinched with concern. Zollin worried about her. He knew something had happened when she dove into the molten rock to defeat the giant, but he had no idea what it was. They found King Zorlan's camp near a spring surrounded by tall palm trees. The dragons landed nearby and almost immediately lay down, sleeping while they had a chance.

Zollin wasn't surprised that they were tired. Flying through the night was one thing, but carrying someone on their backs and breathing fire for hours on end must have been exhausting.

Zollin and Brianna moved to the grove of trees. There were soldiers on watch, but most were already asleep. A tough looking man with a gruff voice met them at the tree line.

"We appreciate your help through the night, but I can't let you come any closer," the man said.

"But we need to speak to King Zorlan," Brianna tried to explain.

"He's resting just now. Perhaps in a few hours."

"Well, we could use some supplies," Zollin said. "Food, water, whatever you can spare."

"We can't spare anything. We're on emergency rations as it is."

"Are you hoarding the water too?" Zollin said angrily. "In case you didn't notice we were kind of busy all night fighting too."

"I'm sorry," the man said, although his eyes were hard, suggesting he wasn't sorry at all. "You'll have to find your own supplies."

Zollin threw his hands up. He was so tired the gesture made him pant. Brianna was more civil.

"Can we leave a message for King Zorlan?" she asked.

"I don't see why not," the man said, still watching Zollin and resting his hand on the hilt of his sword.

"Listen to me," Brianna snapped.

The soldier was surprised by her sudden burst of anger. "We aren't the enemy," she hissed. "Now listen well to this message and deliver it to your king as soon as he wakes. Are you listening?"

The man nodded.

"Good," Brianna said. "Tell him there are more creatures coming. Tell him we are going north, to warn Yelsia and Baskla. We have to make a stand. We'll meet him at the Walheta Mountains if he's willing to fight with us. Tell him to bring whatever soldiers he can muster to the mountains. Tell him to get his people moving north. Can you do that?"

"You're going north," the man repeated. "We need to gather our forces and move north as well. You'll be making a stand at the Walheta."

"That's right. And tell him there are more creatures coming. Worse than the monsters we fought last night."

"I'll tell him."

Brianna and Zollin walked away. Zollin was angry and tired, but the way Brianna spoke wasn't lost on him. She was making plans, strategic plans. He'd never known her to take charge in such a precise way, and while she was a fierce as Mansel in battle, he was surprised to hear her making battle plans.

"You want to tell me what has happened to you?" he asked when they neared the dragons.

"What do you mean?"

"I just mean, something is different about you. I can't say exactly what it is, but …" Zollin searched for the right way to express his thoughts. “You seem confident, more decisive somehow.”

“I don’t think now is the time to be indecisive,” Brianna said.

“How do you know that there are going to be more creatures coming up out of the crevice?”

“I just do.”

“You said you know what she has planned,” Zollin said. “How is that possible?”

“I don’t know, Zollin,” Brianna said, tears streaking down her face. “I don’t know how you work magic or how I make dragons, but it’s real, isn’t it? You’re a wizard. I’m dragon-kind. I don’t know what has happened to our world, but I do know that Gwendolyn isn’t defeated. And I’ve seen the creatures of the Darkened Realm.”

“What are you talking about?” Zollin asked.

“When I dove down into the ground, I just kept pushing and pushing. I melted everything around me, but I really didn’t go that far before the caverns below us opened up. It was sort of like a dream. You know when you have a nightmare and you can see things, but everything is dark and elusive? That’s what it was like, only there are real monsters in the Darkened Realm. The demon you fought, the giant I fought—they were just the beginning. I could see other demons in the Darkened Realm. It was rotting and grotesque. They do nothing but fight and maim each other, but they can’t die. And Gwendolyn was there. I don’t know how I knew it was her, but it had to be. She was surrounded by horrific creatures, Zollin, and she didn't look pleased."

Zollin was dumbfounded. He had seen Gwendolyn drive the knife into her sister's heart and couldn't imagine how incredibly cruel someone would have to be to sacrifice her own sibling just to get more power.

"Well," Zollin said, his throat so dry he had trouble getting the words out. "I guess now isn't the best time to pick a fight with King Zorlan's thugs. We better get moving if we're going to warn people."

"One of us should go north and warn King Felix. The other should warn the towns in Ortis and then muster the troops in Baskla," Brianna explained.

"I'll go to Baskla," Zollin said. "King Felix isn't too fond of me at the moment, but Prince Wilam should listen to you. I'm going into the mountains too, we'll need more help than just an army."

"What do you mean?"

"I think we need the magical people of the Five Kingdoms to pitch in and help us."

"The Dwarves?"

"Yes, the dwarves, the dragons, the mountain giants, the forest trolls. The magical people are drawn to me for a reason—maybe this it."

"So it's good-bye," she said sadly, "again."

"Not forever," Zollin said, taking Brianna in his arms. "I love you, Brianna. Maybe there will never come a day when the

Five Kingdoms know peace and we can settle into the life we've always dreamed of, but I won't stop fighting for that dream. And I'll never stop loving you, no matter what."

She smiled and rested her head against his shoulder, but their tender moment was short lived, as Tig came swooping down. The landing was sloppy, its big blue talons sliding into the soft turf and kicking up a cloud of dust.

Brianna's body tensed and then the other two dragons roared.

"What is it?" Zollin asked.

"The war," Brianna said, her voice tight with fear and tension. "It's starting."

Epilogue

When Offendorl came back to his senses, he was in the deepest depths of the Darkened Realm. All he knew was pain. Curved spikes protruded from his wrists, igniting a fire of pain that spread up both arms and made his shoulders spasm into thick, painful knots. The spikes were attached to thick chains that kept the ancient wizard's arms spread wide, with his feet barely touching the stone floor.

Thick mucus ran from the wounds that the two scorpion-tailed creatures had inflicted on Offendorl. The fluid was a mixture of blood, venom, and pus that smelled so foul it made the ancient wizard's stomach convulse. Sweat poured from his body, both from the unending pain and the intense heat of the dark cavern. Offendorl saw hideous creatures skittering over the stone walls and floor, but it was too dark to recognize what they were. Still, the wizard knew they weren't normal creatures. They were a twisted, evil version of animals from the realms of men.

Offendorl knew he should be dead, but he wasn't. His body had been rejuvenated by magic for centuries. He was ancient, but the magic he wielded had kept his muscles and organs functioning. But the wounds the scorpion-tailed creatures had inflicted on him should have ended his life. Something else was keeping Offendorl alive—something dark and powerful.

"You're awake at last," came a rasping voice that sounded oddly familiar to Offendorl.

The creature that had once been Gwendolyn stepped close enough to Offendorl for the elder wizard to see her face. Her skin was dark red and her body was now covered with a thick, scaly hide. She still had the features of a woman, but she had cast aside her silk dress and the reptilian scales now covered her nakedness.

"What are you doing?" Offendorl managed to say. His tongue was swollen and holding his head up was difficult.

"I'm doing what I was born to do," she hissed. "I've cast off my veil and embraced my true nature. I am the Queen of the Darkened Realm. My power has never been greater."

"You are foolish," Offendorl croaked.

Gwendolyn struck the ancient wizard in the side, snapping at least three ribs. Pain lanced his body and caused the wizard to gasp.

"Do not mock me!" Gwendolyn said. "I am the only thing keeping you alive."

"Let … me … die," Offendorl said.

"Oh, no, that would never do. You are a wizard of extraordinary power. I have plans for you. The venom of my horde will take effect soon. You shall become my greatest creation. Together, we shall crush the mortals above and establish my dominion over the realms of men."

"I won't," he said softly.

"You will," Gwendolyn said. "You have no choice."

She grabbed a handful of the ancient wizard's thin, gray hair, holding his head up and forcing him to look into her eyes. He could feel his body changing, feel bones snapping and re-growing, feel his skin stretching, feel muscles shredding and reforming. The transformation was nothing less than exquisite agony, but Offendorl's mind somehow rose above the pain. He became entranced by Gwendolyn, but not like before, when she had cast her spell of twisted love on the men of the Five Kingdoms. This spell was deeper, born of darkness; it had nothing to do with lust or desire, but it bound the defeated Master of the Torr to Gwendolyn more strongly than any bonds of steel.

"Soon you shall understand your place as my pet," Gwendolyn said. "And together we shall spread darkness across the Five Kingdoms and beyond. Nothing shall stop us now."

"As you wish, my queen," Offendorl said.

* * *

Havina rode the horse hard. Her body hurt, but she knew she needed to get as far away from the city as possible. The horse galloped until it could run no more. Then it began to trot, no matter how hard her heels dug into its sweat covered flanks. White foam dripped from the horse's mouth, but Havina kept the horse moving until finally it collapsed.

She fell hard, but she climbed back to her feet and kept moving. She put the gold circlet on her head, but nothing happened. She had expected to feel some sort of magical bond with the dragon, but she didn't.

"Dragon," she said out loud, feeling a little foolish, but there was no one around to hear her. "Dragon!"

Still she felt nothing. The ground shook beneath her feet and she waited, holding her breath in fear that the world would end, but it didn't. Soon the stars came out and a cool breeze blew across her feverish skin. She took the circlet off her head. It glinted, almost glowing in the starlight. Behind her the dark, unnatural clouds could still be seen, but she ignored them. She studied the crown, afraid that Offendorl had lied about it's power —but then she saw the name inscribed on the gold band.

Bartoom.

She put the crown back on her head and spoke in a loud clear voice.

"Bartoom," she said. "I am Havina, your new master. Come to me."

This time she felt a tingle in the back of her neck, just below her skull. Then, a dream-like image appeared in her mind. She saw the other dragons, one golden, one green, and a small blue one. They were in the air, high above the ground, but that is where the image came from. She heard a roar in her mind, then the image shifted and she realized that she was seeing what the dragon saw. It was turning, leaving the other dragons and coming to her.

It took all night to reach her destination. She had returned to the ruins at Castlebury. The big black dragon waited for her there. She climbed the hill, ignoring the burned ruins of her former home. When she reached the top, she saw Bartoom. The dragon was sitting proudly as the sun lit the sky pink in the east. She walked closer and the dragon lowered its long neck and growled at her, the scaly lips pulling back and revealing rows of razor sharp teeth.

Havina was both terrified and excited. The dragon obeyed her. It was more powerful than any creature she had dreamed of, and now it was hers.

"I want to fly," she said.

Bartoom growled again, but lowered its body. She climbed up onto the beast's back. Her hands were raw and bleeding by the time she settled, and once again she was glad that she was wearing the men's clothing that Offendorl insisted she wear. The dragon was so big that her hips ached a little because her legs were stretched so far apart. She could feel the heat rising off the dragon, and the way its ribs expanded with each breath.

Then Bartoom jumped into the air and Havina was flying. The air was cold, but the thrill of being so high in the air filled her with an exhilaration she had never experienced. She laughed for a long time, holding tight while the dragon rode on the air currents. Then she made a decision.

"Take us south," she said. "We need a new home."

* * *

They crawled up the jagged walls, their large hands gripping precarious nooks in the rock. Massive scimitars hung from their backs, which were covered with bony armor that was fused to their flesh. Their muscles bulged and their faces were swollen so that they no longer looked human. Their teeth were so large they protruded from between fat lips. They wore thick, metal helmets on their heads, and their eyes seemed small and beady in their oversized faces.

The bone-like armor was fused across their bodies so that they looked almost like hulking insects. They wore only thick belts and loincloths. Their feet were flat and large, their legs swollen with muscles. They grunted as they climbed. Their bodies ached from the exertion, but their only thought was to please their master. She was the queen of the Darkened Realm and she had given them only one task—to kill.

Author's Note

There is a lot I could say about the Five Kingdoms, but the most important thing is that the story isn't over. When I wrote Wizard Rising, I had no idea how the story would capture so many people's imaginations. I get emails daily from fans of the series wanting to express their gratitude for the Five Kingdoms books, and of course wanting to know when the next book will be available. I originally hoped that I could write five books about Zollin, Brianna, and their friends, but writing is a very organic process. When I write I usually feel more like I'm reading the story, or that someone else is dictating the story in my head and I'm just writing it down. Of course, I'm making all the decisions, but there are times when I'm completely surprised by an idea that occurs mid-sentence and changes the arc of the story completely. That happened when Gwendolyn became a witch at the end of *Hidden Fire*. I had only planned on her being a supporting character, but she took on a life of her own and wouldn't be denied.

I hope that you enjoyed Fierce Loyalty. I labored over this book, because everything in the Five Kingdoms has changed. The story has become bigger and darker than I ever imagined when I started writing about a young man who discovers, to his surprise, that he can work magic. I hope that you will stay with me for a few more books. I have lots in store for the characters we have come to love and the magical world of the Five Kingdoms. I want to say thank you so very much for buying my books and reading the stories I dream up. I'm looking forward to writing a lot more books and I hope you'll join me for those adventures as well.

Warmest Regards,
Toby Neighbors
April 4, 2013

Made in the USA
Middletown, DE
11 March 2016